Tall Chimneys

Allie Cresswell

ALLIE CRESSWELL

Contents

Acknowledgements

My grateful thanks to my beta-readers who have patiently read this book and pointed out all my spelling, grammatical and factual errors. I take full responsibility for any that stubbornly remain. They gave me helpful suggestions, encouragement and, in some cases, some pretty 'tough love', all of which has gone into making the book the best I can achieve. They are: Nikki Clark, Kath Middleton, Becca Dunlop, Sharon Turner, Jennifer Eds Peacock Smith, Terry Marchion, Catherine Clarke, Joanie Chevalier, Rosemary Noble, Patricia Feinberg Stoner and Angela Petch. Thank you to Abigail Gartland who let me bounce ideas off her and endured my endless deliberations about whether the Epilogue should be in or out. Thank you Sarah Reid, who so patiently and sensitively interpreted my ideas in her original artwork for the cover. Particular thanks to Kathryn Bax of One Stop Fiction for her invaluable advice and guidance. Thank you B. Fleetwood, encourager, cheer-leader and friend. Final thanks as always to Tim, who not only puts up with but actively encourages me to beaver away in the study despite the consequent irregularity of our domestic arrangements. I am so lucky to have you in my life. Dreams do come true.

Prologue

I have called Tall Chimneys home for as long as I can remember. But in fact this odd little gatehouse, standing sentinel at the top of the forested drive, feels more like home to me than Tall Chimneys ever did.

Tall Chimneys is a Jacobean house, added-to over the years, a wing thrown out here, stables, a gun room and an estate office built at the back, bathrooms squeezed in when proper plumbing became a priority. It stands amid a series of concentric circles. First, of gardens; the gravel walkways, lawns and tended shrubbery in front, the vegetable beds, soft fruit bushes, glasshouses and orchards behind. Then a middle girdle of coniferous and broad-leafed plantation thrown around the whole and rising up the sides of a bowl-like crater, like a lifted skirt. All this is rimmed by the escarpment of a natural depression in the broad-stretched moor.

The house's sunken situation was never a happy one. The air within the crater tends to stagnancy; the brisk moor air skims over the bowl without entering it. There is a strong propensity for damp; the lawn is often soggy, the cellar sometimes floods. The chimneys failed to draw for years until some ancestor had the idea of building them higher, making them reach like cathedral pillars into the vault of the sky, out of all proportion to the house.

In one respect only is the house well-placed; it is secluded. Our family annals suggest nocturnal visits of questionable political intriguers, secret stays by Catholic priests, even a visit by the Jacobite pretender, although history disputes this possibility. Its isolation in my lifetime has been both a blessing and a curse.

There is a kinship between Tall Chimneys and me; we are twin souls. I have placed my hands on its masonry in the midst of a storm and the tremors in its architecture have shaken my own foundations. I have felt the glow of warmth ooze from its ancient stones and seep like sustaining honey into my bones. I have burrowed into the darkest recess of its shelter and teetered perilously on its highest parapet without fear that it would let me fall. I have known love here, and abject sorrow, happiness, and dreadful despair. Tall Chimneys has soaked up my life, and poured out its own, leaving us both derelict.

We belong to a time which has passed, both designed for a life which is obsolete in these modern days, and although we have done our best to accommodate and adapt, our efforts have been outstripped by progress. We are calcifying, here, in this peculiar cauldron scooped from the prehistoric bog of ancient moor; we are petrified relics of an era long gone. And any little dramas we have enacted in our secret amphitheatre have been private and contained, and have caused no echo in the world at large.

I have tried to save Tall Chimneys, and if my feeble aid could have sustained its ailing stonework, I would have left nothing wanting. Almost nothing. But our ways seem destined to part, now. If one of us is to survive, the other must be allowed to fall.

1910 - 1929

I was born in 1910, the last of seven children, the youngest of four daughters, born when my parents had given up expecting (or, I suspect, wanting) any further additions to the family. I made odd what had been even before. A new baby caused a negligible stir; I was of scant interest to anyone. Nanny, who had been anticipating a retirement of darning and dozing by the fire in the nursery apartments in the east wing, grudgingly sent for the bassinet and other baby paraphernalia long-since consigned to an attic. My oldest brother was already at Cambridge, my oldest sister recently married and soon expecting a child of her own. One other boy and two girls were away at school leaving only Colin, aged six, to be my reluctant and sometimes rather spiteful playmate for two years until he, too, went away to boarding school.

My father was well into his fifties when I was born, my mother in her late forties. Having me, I have been told (again, by Colin, who likes to be cruel when he can) broke her health and more than partly explained her death a few years later. Personally I prefer to attribute her relatively early demise to the loss of my father and my oldest brother in the First World War, which began only four years after I made my arrival. I have only the very vaguest memories of either of them; my father tall, with grey eyes and wavy hair smelling of some unguent supposed to tame it into slick submission, my mother rather wispy, diaphanous in some garment which she cannot possibly have worn outside her bed- and dressing-rooms; I suppose I was taken to her in the mornings, before she changed out of her night clothes, and again in the evenings, while she dressed for dinner. I recall her always horizontal, on a day-bed or settee, listless and feeble.

With all the children but me at school and father at war, the house shrank into itself. Rooms were shrouded and closed up. Many of the male servants joined the local yeomanry and marched away to Flanders; a few housemaids, the cook, the house-keeper, a limping gardener and an ageing butler were all that remained of the household staff.

Those, and a sandy-haired stable lad.

He was older than me by about ten years - fourteen, perhaps, to my four - but he suited his speech and gait to mine; he was gentle and kind. He took my lonely hand one day and led me to the kitchen gardens. He introduced me to the wonders of the glass house where soft fruits could be picked and exotic flowers grew. He brought me to a hay-filled stable and placed a squirmy puppy into my arms. He led me through the woods to where a rivulet tumbled over mossy rocks, and we peeled off our shoes and stockings and put our feet into the icy water. His feet were grubby and calloused, mine pink and soft. He climbed a tree and brought me down a bird's egg, still warm, from the nest. But then he went away, to war, I supposed, and I was alone again.

I got used to being over-looked by everyone, the family and the servants both. Often meals did not arrive in the nursery for me. The governess supposedly overseeing my early years' education was desultory in her efforts and many days I sat alone in the school room while she pursued the local curate around the parish, trying to ensnare him. (She succeeded. They went as missionaries to Africa where they died of malaria, I believe.) I got used to exploring the lesser-used areas of the house, out-buildings and gardens on my own. I got into the habit of lurking in shadowy corners, listening in to conversations I was not supposed to hear. (That's how I found out about my governess and the curate.) I was nearly always on the look-out for food, haunting the larders, the pantry, the orchard and vegetable garden. That's how I first encountered Weeks, the gardener; he caught me gorging on strawberries in the kitchen garden, and took me home to his wife.

They lived here, in the gatehouse, an odd, hexagonal little building perched on the rim of the crater, the thick belt of woodland behind and below, open moorland and an impressive view to the front, where the drive meets the road to the village, a mile across the moor. It was small, just one up and one down in those days, with a lean-to kitchen at the back and a lavatory in a shed amongst the trees. But the gatehouse held a special appeal to my childish eyes, and still does - I am sitting in it as I write these memoirs. A fire burns in the grate, and the exposed stone walls are warm, the colour of honey. Its windows are small and crazed with leading but its exterior stonework is rather grand, with stone gables topped with ostentatious orbs and a crenelated parapet added, I suppose, to give a grand first impression. I didn't see the upper chamber until much later, but the living room was a wonder to me, a small child, like a scene from a fairy-tale; an old oak table and two chairs, a dresser with their crockery set upon it, a shelf with their three or four precious books, a rag rug before a tiny, shiny grate. The rug and crocks are long-gone, of course, but I am writing, now, on that same oak table and the dresser stands still in a shaft of sunlight from the milky, leaded window.

Weeks and his wife, childless, showed me more care and love than anyone at the big house. He would find me in the arboretum or loitering near the greenhouses, or, once, halfway to the village, along the windswept road across the moor, and take me to their cottage to be fed on warm bread and fresh cheese and sometimes cold cuts of pheasant and partridge about which, it was hinted, I should "keep mum". Mrs Weeks let me collect the eggs from their little flock, and taught me to sew and make pastry and bread. She showed me my letters, too, writing my name, Evelyn, with her finger in the soot of the hearth, tutting and sucking her teeth at my woeful lack of acquaintance with these things.

Anytime I could make my escape from the school room (which was often), my steps took me straight to their door, my lurking in gloomy shadows and dalliance in the grounds having lost their appeal. The days in the gatehouse passed in blissful happiness, exploring the further reaches of the garden they had hewn from the woodland while she stuck peas or weeded the onions, or basking by their fire while she stitched and he fiddled with his pipe in the late afternoon. Then, as evening came on, he would take me by the hand and lead me back to Tall Chimneys. Unconsciously I adopted the odd drag and hop of his game leg, the two of us making identical tracks through the leaf-mould of the secret woodland ways he showed me, past the fountains and through the parterre, delivering me with a sad eye to a side-door and leaving me there as he melted back into the night.

My father died early on in the war, my brother a year or two later. My mother's health broke down altogether in 1917 and I was sent away to live with Isobel, my oldest sister, who had a house by the sea on the south coast. She already had two little girls and, it was explained, I would be less inconvenient to her than to any other relative. This move surprised and angered me; I had been perfectly content at home. I didn't want to leave my friends at the gatehouse.

Isobel was an old-fashioned woman, even then, very strict; we girls were seen and not heard. She was a good woman but there was no nonsense about her, no softness, and she quashed a tendency to sentimentality in her girls. I frequently got into trouble for challenging her hard-line ideas and it was this - the threat and actuality of punishment - which eventually bent me to her will. I forced myself into her values as one might force a foot into a shoe that is too small. It hurt and I resented it, but the idea of being barefoot and vulnerable hurt more. It taught me two things about myself; I was not naturally 'good' and following my natural instincts would get me into hot water. Looking back now, I can see that my life has been defined by the tension of obeying rules I do not respect and finding that, when I have been wilful and fallen foul of society's mores it is myself that I automatically blame and punish, not them.

Being placed under Isobel's influence seriously curtailed my freedom but at least it meant I had the company of my nieces - a welcome addition - and my schooling was rigorously taken up again. The governess there informed me of my mother's death. I cried, but almost as a duty; death seemed such a very small step on from the listless, somnolent existence my mother appeared to me to have had in life. I lobbied to return - what disturbance could I create, now, I reasoned. But I was told Tall Chimneys was to become a hospital for wounded officers; no place for a child. This piqued my interest; I longed to see the wounded men and hear their stories. Colin, when he came to visit for his summer vacation in 1918, gave me lurid chapter and verse on the variously maimed and deranged soldiers sent there for treatment. If he'd hoped to shock or even sicken me, he failed; I was a self-assured, sensible girl even then, aged eight. Seeing he had botched his attempt to upset me, he got more personal, accusing me of being the cause of our mother's death.

'You were the last baby,' he said, spitefully. 'She was never the same after you were born.'

This news did distress me, but once Isobel had got to the bottom of my tears, she dismissed the accusation. 'Stuff and nonsense,' she said.

From my sister's I was sent to school, along with my niece Joan, to whom I had become very close. The school - like Isobel - was strict, run by Anglican nuns. Academically it was fairly good, but the whole school ethos was undergirded by the assumption that the women who emerged from it would be obedient and submissive, long-suffering adherents to the status quo. Once I came to terms with this school became a period which was not unhappy for me, but which has long since faded in my memory. I remember almost nothing about it except for a sponge cake occasionally served for dessert which oozed with syrup – it was delicious.

AFTER SCHOOL I returned to Tall Chimneys. I expected to experience a warm rush of home-coming, but ten years of absence had dulled the visceral associations of the house. Many of the staff I remembered had gone, including the Weeks. The gatehouse, now, was shut up and dilapidated, the woods reclaiming the Weeks' hard-won garden. My sister Isobel's house, I found, felt more like home - I had lived there since I was six and spent every vacation there. My nieces there felt more like siblings. I missed them, especially Joan. But returning to Isobel's permanently wasn't an option for me; they were going to India, her husband having been sent thither by Mr Baldwin as part of a parliamentary commission headed by Sir John Simon, to deal with the intractable Mr Gandhi.

[1] I wished I could go with them - I felt wretched to be left behind while they went out into a world of adventure and interest.

With the death of my father and oldest brother Tall Chimneys had devolved upon my middle brother George. He had served only at the tail-end of the war, escaped unscathed and married the daughter of a wealthy American businessman. They had spent most of the intervening years in London, part of a fast set who had flung themselves into a wild era of partying and reckless behaviour. According to Isobel they were dissipated and carefree, morally loose; no kind of guardians for a girl my age, but

---

[1] The Indian Statutory Commission was a group of seven British Members of Parliament of United Kingdom that had been dispatched to India in 1928 to study constitutional reform in Britain's most important colonial dependency. It was commonly referred to as the Simon Commission after its chairman, Sir John Simon. One of its members was Clement Attlee, who subsequently became the British Prime Minister and eventually oversaw the granting of independence to India and Pakistan in 1947. Some people in India were outraged and insulted that the Simon Commission, which was to determine the future of India, did not include a single Indian member. The outcome of the Simon Commission was the Government of India Act 1935.
Source: https://en.wikipedia.org/wiki/Simon_Commission

there was, she said, no help for it. Of my two other sisters, one was an invalid installed more or less permanently (and at great expense) in a Swiss sanatorium, the other single, in health and solvent, but wildly political, shockingly modern in views and behaviour, affiliated to the Bloomsbury group of which Isobel disapproved with a passion.

So, back to Tall Chimneys I went. I was admitted back into the household, as I had left it, with indifference, given some draughty rooms in the north wing and more or less left to my own devices. I was eighteen years old.

George and Rita were only rarely at Tall Chimneys. To their credit, though, using, I presume, funds from Rita's wealthy papa, they did initiate a programme of repairs and modernisation to the house; under their benefaction we had improved plumbing and electricity produced by a noisy generator installed in the cellar. We had a telephone but it was very unreliable, the wires strung across the moor and through the trees were very vulnerable. These up-grades, the house, lands and tenant farms were in the hands of George's agent, Sylvester Ratton, who oversaw their management in George's absence. Ratton was perhaps ten or twelve years my senior, a man of few personal charms but large ambition; I took an instant dislike to him. He had round, lashless eyes and a small, misshapen blob of a nose. Nothing escaped him, not the least suggestion of an extra bucket of coal in the servants' hall or the hint of a purloined hare in a ploughman's pot. He sniffed out and came down hard on any perceived misdeed, reducing housemaids to tears for the smallest misdemeanour and dressing down farm-workers in a voice which carried from the estate office, behind the stables, to the morning room without any tempering of volume or expletive colour. While parsimonious with others, he denied himself nothing, living, while George and his wife were in town, as de facto owner of the house, lording it over the servants and tenant farmers, occupying the second best suite of rooms and wolfing down the choicest of comestibles and the finest wines in the cellar.

The first evening of my residence we dined together, he at the head of the table, me at the foot – a ridiculous and anti-social arrangement which made conversation difficult and made extra work for the servants. It soon became clear that these things were entirely by Mr Ratton's design. He enjoyed sending the staff scurrying hither and thither, rejecting dishes and then changing his mind about them so they had to be brought in again. He spoke to me as though from a great height as well as a great distance, emphasising my extreme smallness and insignificance.

'You are lucky,' he stated, heavily, to me, 'that your brother and sister in law are prepared to accommodate you here. Many girls in your situation would have been placed elsewhere and expected to make their own way. Perhaps in the end you will think it might have been preferable.'

I told him in a quiet but prideful voice that I felt my good fortune. I would make the best of being allowed to return home.

'One wonders,' he mused, swilling wine around a heavily embellished goblet, 'why they did not accommodate you in town. Perhaps,' he gave a twisted, almost suggestive grin, 'they consider the tone there unsuitable. They do entertain some rather... outré guests.'

I made no reply to this observation.

'The house is sadly depleted since you were last here and George is here but rarely,' Ratton went on to observe. 'You will lack for company. You will be lonely. It is hardly suitable. Some might say it is hardly respectable. You ought to have a female companion.'

The idea of the smug, porky individual at the far end of the table posing any kind of threat to my maiden reputation was laughable, but I restrained myself from saying so. It was on the tip of my tongue to suggest that, if he felt the delicacy of my situation so keenly, he ought to move into the agent's quarters which I knew were provided for him above the estate office. 'I will use the time to improve myself,' I said instead. 'I shall enjoy the outdoors when the weather is fine. When it is not, the library is well-stocked.'

'Indeed.' He nodded. 'No doubt your education has left you lacking in real knowledge. Girls are taught accomplishments, merely. I cannot think your schooling will be much use to you here.'

I felt stung. This accusation was unfair; my schooling had been pretty thorough in arts and humanities although rather coy on the subject of science.

'While your brother is from home, I run the house very frugally,' he told me. 'I told Jones to serve dinner tonight to celebrate your arrival, but after this we will take it separately, in our rooms, unless there is company. You will not find it very convivial.'

I wanted to laugh at Ratton's idea of a celebratory meal; nothing could have been colder or less hospitable than the atmosphere at table. The prospect of dining alone, even in my rooms, which were dour enough, was a preferable prospect.

'Of course,' I agreed. 'I shall try to incommode your arrangements as little as possible.'

Clearly, having gained his object, Mr Ratton lapsed into silence.

We soon settled into a mutually exclusive routine; I took my breakfast in my rooms and my dinner also, as prescribed. I appropriated a small morning room in the east wing where I could not possibly be in Mr Ratton's way. Lunch was not served at Tall Chimneys unless there were guests. Mr Ratton and I took tea together in the library in the late afternoons as a gesture towards polite sociability, before each recalling some important errand or job of work which brought the encounter to a speedy close.

Almost in defiance of Mr Ratton's predictions of gloom and doom, I set out determined to make the best of my situation. I made acquaintance with the rector in the village, his wife and three daughters, walking there several times a week in search of company and sometimes receiving them for tea at Tall Chimneys. I volunteered to help Mrs Flowers, housekeeper, a harried woman given to an excess of nerves, initiating a programme of dusting and airing the unused rooms and protecting the house's more valuable artefacts from the carelessness of the builders who came and went. I persuaded one of the grooms to teach me to ride, which he was glad to do; the horses got hardly any exercise now George had bought a motor car to fetch him from the station. I wanted to learn to drive it but Ratton vetoed this plan. The rest of the time I read books from the library in an effort to improve my mind and wrote long letters to my niece Joan in India. Her letters were full of romance and glamour - balls at the Embassy, cards and cocktails at the Club, a thrilling elephant ride. Occasional letters from other school friends told the same story; dances and parties or interesting work in busy offices where they took shorthand and typed letters or operated the telephonic apparatus. Through them I heard about other classmates - qualified as teachers or nurses or working in laboratories. They all seemed to exist in a world which was running in parallel to mine, across a gulf I could not cross. All I could do was idle my days away in the silent rooms of Tall Chimneys and roam the grounds in much the same way as I had done as a child.

WHEN MY BROTHER did return to Tall Chimneys he brought with him large parties of socialites, many titled, from illustrious houses, also fashionable writers and artists, and rising men of industry. We often got little notice of these visits. Mrs Flowers and I were thrown into a frenzy of cleaning and bed-making to get the rooms ready and the cook needed much chivvying in sorting out menus and ordering supplies. Mr Ratton played no part in these proceedings, obviously, other than to indulge in lengthy converse and much sampling with Jones, the aged butler, on the subject of wine. Although stepping somewhat into the background for the duration of these house-parties, Mr Ratton did not disappear altogether as, perhaps, would have been proper. He appeared at dinner wearing a cheap, off-the-peg dinner suit, and presented himself for excursions and shooting parties as though one of the guests or, more accurately, one of the family. George allowed it without comment. I too, was included, but I kept myself at a distance from the heavy-drinking and hi-jinks which invariably characterised those affairs, retiring to my room as soon as I could, ignoring the leering innuendo with which I was often addressed and keeping the groping hands at bay. My early explorations in the house served me well; I was often able to evade the lecherous intentions of Viscounts and mining magnates by slipping down the little-known passageways of the house, losing them in linen rooms and the labyrinthine by-ways of the servants' corridors.

Apart from being tiresome in themselves, these assaults had another negative impact in that they changed Mr Ratton's attitude towards me. It seemed to dawn upon him that he might have missed an opportunity, with me. While never deigning to show me any attention while George was around, he became positively predatory at all other times. I would come across him lurking on my favourite walks or saddling up a horse just as I arrived at the stables for my ride, forcing us to walk or ride together. He lingered over tea, asking for more, sending for additional crumpets. He suggested we invite the rector and his family to dine for all the world as though we two were lord and lady of the manor. He invaded the sunny morning room I had adopted as my own, to read the newspapers, when he should have been out and about on estate business. I would not have cared if his conversation had been worth the having, or his person more attractive, but he made little attempt to be personable, only watched me, narrowly, through those lashless eyes, in a way I found unnerving and disgusting.

My walks took me further afield in an effort to avoid him and I had to use increasing ingenuity in the routes I took, rediscovering the shady groves and secret pathways Weeks had shown me all those years before. One day I found myself at the gatehouse and was swamped with nostalgia for the kindly couple who had looked after me there. I wondered where they had gone to and determined to make enquiries. In the meantime I walked round the odd little building. The windows were boarded up, the once neat garden swamped by invading bramble. Nobody used it now, and it occurred to me it could become, once more, a kind of refuge to me. Recklessly, I broke the flimsy lock of the kitchen lean-to, swept away the inveigling leaves and looping cobwebs and brought the Weeks' furniture back into service. I worked hard at it for most of the day, getting myself filthy in the process but happily occupied as I had not been for some time. As the afternoon drew on I surveyed my handiwork. The floor was clean of moss, the greenish slime scrubbed away from the sink in the lean-to. A dull shine reflected off the patina of the table. The window sills were empty of dead flies and desiccated butterflies. As long as no light shone through the chinks in the boarded windows, and I did not light the fire, I reasoned to myself that while the summer prevailed I could spend many happy hours there un-accosted by Mr Ratton, reading my books and writing letters to my heart's content.

And so I did. I augmented my comforts at the gatehouse by carrying provisions and further luxuries thither as I had need; fruit from the orchard and left-over pie from the pantry, a rug, a cushion, a blanket. I unearthed a little oil stove from an outhouse, found a battered old kettle and a chipped teapot, so I could make tea. I discovered a cracked ewer in a little-used guest room, and used it for bouquets of wild-flowers which I gathered on my meanderings. Smuggling these things up to the gatehouse without arousing suspicion became a sort of challenge. Mr Ratton and I were playing a clandestine game of cat and mouse, both pretending it was not so and yet each of us keenly aware the 'accidental' encounters and his sudden propensity to spend time indoors, likewise my ridiculous tendency to travel from one place to another via bizarre circuitous routes, my sudden yen to inspect a far-flung gazebo or to visit the ice house, were anything but unintentional. Before long I had moved my favourite books and writing materials up to the gatehouse. I stopped using the morning room altogether.

In pursuance of my determination to ask after the Weeks, I walked, one day, along the ribbon of roadway which crossed the moor at its narrowest point, and into the village. The place was little more than a gaggle of cottages, farms and utilitarian buildings which lined the road. At the near end the little grey church, a squat school house and the large, Georgian Rectory were Tall Chimneys' closest neighbours. Further along I passed an untidy farmyard where cows waited to be milked. Then, a public house, The Plough and Harrow, which I avoided, having the idea these places were disreputable. I sought out instead the little grocery store which provided villagers with tinned and dried provisions, tobacco, sweets and acted also as the Post Office. A delicious smell of freshly baked cake wafted from a room behind the counter when I opened the door. A woman hurried through the rear door at the sound of the shop bell, brushing flour from her apron as she did so. She was small and rather thin, with bony wrists and a head of red hair. She was friendly enough until I introduced myself, whereupon her demeanour soured.

'I'm enquiring about Mr and Mrs Weeks,' I explained. 'They lived in the gatehouse when I was a child. He was the gardener. I think she helped with the laundry. Have you any idea where they might have gone to?'

The woman sniffed. 'I don't remember them,' she said, 'my Kenneth might. He worked down there for a while, until he was dismissed. I don't suppose you remember him? He was the stable lad.'

'I do remember him, very kindly,' I exclaimed, although, to be truthful, until that moment I hadn't recalled the sandy-haired boy I had known so briefly. 'He was dismissed? I didn't know. I assumed he'd gone off to war.'

'He was dismissed for fraternising with the family,' she gave me a sharp look. 'Too nice for his own good, my Kenneth is. He did go to war, shortly after. What else was he to do? He was too young, of course.'

'I'm sorry,' I stammered. 'Did he..?'

'Come back? Yes.' She sniffed again. 'It ruined him, though.'

'I'm sorry,' I said again, more genuinely this time. I had seen wounded soldiers on station platforms going to and from school; broken pieces of humanity you couldn't help feeling sorry for but who, at the same time, had been rather frightening to a young girl.

'He does odd jobs,' the woman told me. 'Think of him, if you need anything done down there. Ratton won't give him a look-in, but if *you* were to ask. You owe him that much, at least.'

Whatever idea I had of the young ex-service man - Kenneth - scarred, amputated, disfigured, it was not realised in the man I caught sight of in the yard behind the shop as I passed on my way. He was whole, tall, wirily thin and generally rangy, with shirt sleeves rolled up to reveal freckled arms and that same cowlick of sandy hair falling into his eyes as he worked on some piece of machinery he had stripped down. He looked up as I passed, and I half raised my hand in greeting. I saw a glimmer of recognition light up his eyes for the briefest second before he turned his back and disappeared into the gloom of a tumble down workshop.

I walked to the end of the village and back again, encountering nobody else who could give me any information about the Weeks.

'Oh well,' I sighed to myself as I started the walk back across the moor towards Tall Chimneys, 'back to the game of cat and mouse.'

Mr Ratton was clearly both perplexed and infuriated by my absence that day and on others as I took refuge in the gatehouse. I know he watched me, followed me, as I loitered with a seeming lack of purpose in the gardens or chatted with the grounds men or the grooms, then, the moment his back was turned or his attention momentarily distracted, I would disappear, streaking through the stables and back into the house, through a side door and into the shrubbery on the other side of the building, then slipping through the lower branches of the plantation into the darkness of the wood. Or, from the kitchen garden, taking a route behind the greenhouses and through a narrow door in the wall kept hidden by a thick curtain of ivy, leaving Mr Ratton slack-jawed with amazement, as though he had just witnessed me disappear into thin air! Without a word ever being said on the subject, the servants became complicit in my evasions, denying having seen me all morning, claiming I had mentioned a trip to the village when they knew I was, in fact, crouched in the tack room with both hands over my mouth to stifle my giggles. I took care to use a variety of circuitous routes to and from the gatehouse, melting into the woodland at various points, emerging again at others, or arriving home down the drive as though from a visit to the village. Mr Ratton questioned me closely about how I had spent my day, standing proprietorially by the library fireplace with his cup balanced on the mantle and a dribble of butter down his chin while I sat at the table and arranged the tea things, and made vague responses to his enquiries.

I did not, however, forget my obligation to the Post Mistress' son, and requested that Ratton should find him work.

'He is a veteran,' I said, 'as well as a former employee here. We ought to find him something.'

'I know the lad,' Ratton sneered. 'A stuttering fool, reclusive and peculiar.'

'He seems good with his hands,' I persevered, 'even if he isn't very communicative. I'm sure my brother would want you to help him.'

Ratton humphed, and bit into another muffin. 'Where did you say you went today?' he asked, with his mouth full.

 **THESE SHENANIGANS WERE** curtailed pending another protracted visit by George, Rita and a posse of guests including a number of artistic types who cluttered up the hallway with their easels and bored me rigid each evening with lugubrious recitations of their over-worked verse.

I had a particularly hard time of it evading an emaciated, earnest young poet called Josiah Morely, who made no bones about his desire to 'break the holy hymen and enter the citadel of ecstasy,' and thereby 'release the inner bird, trapped and faint, to fly in rapturous crescendo.' I had several crumpled and ink-stained odes pressed into my hands or slipped under my door to that effect. Mr Ratton, inflamed by Morely's unambiguous language and intent, ratcheted up his own assaults, claiming me as his dinner companion and ensuring I took a seat next to him in the motorcades in which we travelled to various scenic waterfalls and panoramic view-points in the county in search of artistic inspiration. Both men were manageable, with cold, monosyllabic responses and withering looks, during the daytime, but as evening drew on, and their consumption of my brother's wines eroded their restraint, it became more difficult to handle them.

One evening Morely accosted me in the billiard room, pressing me up against the panelling with more strength than I had expected him to be able to muster, thrust his tongue into my mouth and his hand between my legs. In my struggle I knocked a marble bust from a plinth. Ratton was the first to arrive. He soon gathered what had taken place and while he took Morely to task, I slipped away and headed for my rooms. Unfortunately, Ratton gave chase, catching up with me on the landing of the north wing where my rooms were situated, a remote region of the house not used for guests because of its unappealing view over the stable block and kitchen gardens and a tendency to draughts in winter. It seemed unlikely help would come. I knew, by the dilated look in his eye and the lascivious pout of his full, rather womanish lips, what his intention was. He lunged at me without preamble and we tussled, briefly.

'Mr Ratton,' I protested, fending his fat little hands off my body and straining my neck in an effort to avoid his panting mouth, 'you will think better of this, if you calm yourself.'

'I'll bring you to heel, Miss Evelyn. This game has gone on long enough,' he said, hoarsely, snuffling into my neck. 'You'll be glad of it, when I've broken you. What Morely has begun, I will finish, and better than he could.' He was flushed and aroused, his pupils shrunk to pin-pricks, his tiny, doughy nose moist with rapid, shallow breathing. The smell of brandy on his breath was acrid. As Morely had done, he pressed me against the cold wall, his knee up hard between my legs, one hand firmly clamped onto one of my breasts while the other groped behind me for the handle of my door. If he managed to open it, and push me inside, I knew I was done for.

Help came from a tall, dishevelled man I had not seen before. He emerged from some room further along the landing where, I was later to discover, he had been ensconced for the duration of the visit painting a large and experimental canvas commissioned by my sister in law. He had been having trays of food sent to his rooms where he had worked feverishly day and night, taking no part in the entertainments and excursions organised for the other guests. His shirt was partially undone and smeared with paint, his hair unkempt, dark and unruly. He didn't look as though he had washed, let alone shaved, for days; a shadowed growth bristled on his chin and cheeks. His eyes were dull, clouded with fatigue or perhaps dazed by artistic frenzy which my scuffle with Ratton had disturbed. His feet were bare. He hoisted Ratton away from me and flung him without ceremony onto the landing, which was uncarpeted and probably rather dirty. Ratton scrambled to his feet and scurried off with his tail between his legs.

The man and I looked at each other. He nodded, and gave a distracted smile, then turned and strode away. Neither of us spoke a word.

Ratton was away for the next few days, looking after George's business interests further north. In his absence I tried to broach the subject of his behaviour with my sister in law Rita, but she dismissed me with a wave of the hand. 'A harmless upstart,' she declared. 'Any woman worth her salt can handle men like him.' The house party came to an end and everyone departed. For a few days I had the house to myself. Mrs Flowers and I supervised the housemaids as they stripped the beds and put things back to rights.

A cracked pane of glass in one of the rooms gave me the excuse I needed to send for Kenneth to fix it. 'While he is here,' I told Mrs Flowers, 'give him a list of other repairs you want done before the winter.'

'He's an odd young man,' she reported back to me, 'hardly speaks a word. Is he dumb?'

'Just shy, I think,' I said. 'Be patient with him.'

It was the end of the summer. September came in with squally showers. The housemaids had no end of trouble getting the linen dry. I returned to my cosy morning room, where I had the fire lit, and wrote a long letter to Joan describing all my adventures but fearing they would be plebeian indeed compared to hers.

Then Mr Ratton came back, and we were back to square one. My morning room was not my own, my walks intruded upon, my rides made burdensome by his company. He made no reference to what had occurred on the north wing landing but I knew from the way his eyes lingered on my person that he thought about it often, and more with frustration than with any shame or regret.

One afternoon, as we took tea in the library and rain like pebbles hurled itself against the window, precluding any escape outdoors, he began, uninvited, to tell me something of himself; the youngest of many, like me, of a respectable but somewhat impoverished family who had nothing to offer the youngest child. He had been well-educated but not at one of the illustrious schools, then forced to make his own way which, he flattered himself, he had done with some credit. '*You*,' he said, with some significant emphasis, '*you* must understand entirely my situation, sharing it as you do. Youngest children like us, even of good families, must be prepared to make their own way. I'm sure it has occurred to you, that before too long you'll have to look to your own resources?'

I looked at him at a loss. I had had no such thoughts.

'You cannot imagine remaining here indefinitely,' he observed. 'This spot is so very retired, so backwards, when out there, in the world, things are moving on at such a pace, especially for women.'

I felt his comment as a severe deprecation - it made me cringe with shame - but I made no response.

'Goodness, yes,' he mused aloud, 'one wonders what doors will *not* be open to them in future. They admitted a woman to the Bar a few years ago,[2] and now a woman is governor of the BBC[3]. Whoever thought such a thing? But even if you do not aspire so highly, there are jobs for women in offices, as nurses, even attached to the military although, naturally, not in a combative role. I met your brother in the military, as it happens,' he went on, helping himself to another buttered teacake. 'We were comrades in arms. I saved his life. Has he ever mentioned that to you?'

I shook my head.

'No? Well, there's a debt owed, let's leave it at that, and George is conscious of it. He has promised me advancement. I'm wasted here, in this god-forsaken county, as you are. George knows it. There are things abroad he wants me to set up for him. His father in law will help. America is a land of great opportunity for those with a nose for business and a respectable name.'

It occurred to me that Mr Ratton was announcing his imminent departure from Tall Chimneys. I could only rejoice, but I kept my jubilation to myself. 'It must be very gratifying to my brother,' I murmured, 'to have

---

[2] Ivy Williams was called to the Bar of England and Wales in 1922

[3] Ethel Snowden became the first woman governor of the BBC in 1927

people he can rely on, if he intends a new business venture. The Americas are a very exciting prospect, I'm sure.'

'Indeed yes,' Mr Ratton enthused. 'You see the situation exactly. A scion of an ancient English family, no matter how minor *here,* is counted as very splendid *there.* Anything English is bound to be successful. I'm assured we will be made most welcome, doors will open up to us on every side. We'll play the family card very heavily, meanwhile I'll attend to all the business. We cannot fail to achieve our aim.'

It gradually dawned on me he had ceased speaking of himself, singular, and was now speaking in the plural: what 'we' could expect; openings and introductions which would be made available to 'us.'

'Will George be an *active* participant, then, in the venture?' I enquired. Perhaps Tall Chimneys would be moth-balled if George and Rita were going to America. Where, I wondered, would that leave me?

Mr Ratton gave a strangled cough and, I thought, almost blushed, but it could have been the heat from the fire. '*That* will hardly be necessary,' he said, with a sort of lewd coyness I didn't understand. 'I'm sure I can manage all aspects of the matter very well without George's assistance.' He gave me a straight look, one eyebrow slightly raised. 'No,' he concluded. 'George won't accompany us, but he *is* in favour, if you are willing. I have that most certainly from his own lips. He is in favour. I have his backing and, not to put too fine a point on it, in this day and age, for people like us, well, we could both do a lot worse.'

Realisation came upon me like a bucket of ice cold water. His proposal (for such, I gathered, it was) appalled me. 'I am not willing,' I said, coldly.

He put his cup back on its saucer, not one whit deterred. 'We will see,' he said.

The weather continued inclement and even deteriorated; walking and riding were both out of the question. We were both trapped inside the house. I found Mr Ratton was frequently in my way apparently by accident, or actively sought me out. He behaved toward me with open familiarity, calling me by my first name or 'my dear', leaning cosily over me as I wrote or read, sniffing me, touching me, even kissing me, once, with wet, flaccid lips. I was denied the respite of taking dinner in my room; Mr Ratton commanded it should be served formally, in the dining room, Jones and a footman in attendance, and that I should dress and come down for it as I had done when the house guests had been with us. As then, cocktails would be served in the drawing room. He spoke constantly of 'our life' in America, leaving out books of American history and geography in the library and sending for American newspapers. My protestations and denials were ignored, or treated with indulgence, as though I were a child who would be brought to heel in due course either by persuasion or a good whipping, and, of the two, it was plain he would rather prefer the latter.

The house, as large and rambling as it was, became a prison for me. Mr Ratton became as adept as I was in negotiating its remoter passageways and disused rooms. There was no escape from him. He took an eerie kind of joy in stalking me; it was a game to him; he was the hunter and I was the prey. I sent off to London for some stout boots and a waterproof coat but they never arrived. Likewise a letter to George pleading for his intervention went un-answered. I suspected my letters had been intercepted. For my own safety I began to spend more time with Mrs Flowers; we commenced an inventory of linen which would be of no earthly purpose or use but made an excuse for us to be closeted together in her cosy parlour. I haunted the kitchens, refreshing my distant memory of Mrs Weeks' lessons in pastry and bread-making. I helped with the bottling of the season's fruits and the pickling of vegetables. I insisted on being inducted into the workings of the water pumping station and began to understand the way the ice house was used for the preservation of meats. If the servants were surprised at my sudden involvement in these tasks which would, ordinarily, have formed no part of a family member's duties or concern, they did not express it. Indeed, they rallied round me. They must have known, amongst themselves, how vulnerable I was to Mr Ratton's predation.

My friend the rector called, with his daughters. I served them tea. Mr Ratton, of course, was present, ensuring no private conversation could be had. The rector expressed concern: they had seen nothing of me, my visits had ceased, was I unwell? I shrugged and blamed the weather. Of course there was no reason at all why I could not have summoned the motorcar and been driven to the village, but I would not have been allowed to do so unaccompanied and the idea of being cooped in an even smaller space with Mr Ratton was insupportable. Mr Ratton talked gaily of a 'change of scene' likely to bring me back to health in the near future with an implication of intimacy which sickened me. The girls giggled, nervously. The rector gave a doubtful smile.

Kenneth was frequently at the house, these days, hammering reinforcement onto a hencoop, fixing a mangle or coaxing the generator which supplied our electricity into greater reliability. He was always dressed in clean overalls and his boots were well-polished - I saw his mother's hand at work there. He had a pleasant face - narrower than the one I remembered as a child, with a strong chin and wide-set, hazel eyes often curtained by the flop of his fringe. I always said hello when I encountered him but he would veer off into a workshop or duck into the pigsty, or suddenly discover the need of an important tool at the bottom of his box, and thus avoid the need to reply.

I understood, from what his mother had said, the war had had a severe impact on him. How could it not? He had been too young, and the horrors he must have witnessed were beyond my imagining. That terrible gulf of experience and suffering stood between us as it had not when we had played in former years. But, somehow, just knowing he was about the place, my old playmate, helped me feel less forlorn then as he had done so many years before.

At last the weather cleared and it was possible to go out. I told Mr Ratton I was going to spend the morning with Mrs Flowers and the cook supervising the organisation of preserves in the pantry and slipped out of the house as soon as he disappeared into the estate office, where a queue of tenants waited to see him. I ran across the lawns and past the fountain, entering the plantation and lumbering up the slope like an animal in fear of its life heading for its lair. The gatehouse represented my only refuge, safety, home.

To my absolute horror, someone was in residence. A saw-horse and a scanty pile of wet wood stood in the rear garden, the planks had been removed from the front windows, a wisp of smoke rose from the chimney. The kitchen door stood open, admitting an envelope of sunshine on the worn sandstone flags of the floor. I almost wept, standing there on the threshold which should have been mine, on the brink of sanctuary and yet denied admittance. My smothered wail of despair must have drawn attention to my presence. I heard the scrawp of a chair, the rattle of crockery on the table, footsteps.

My rescuer from the north wing landing stepped into view. He was cleaner, shaved, his hair had been cut. He wore shoes, now, but his shirt was the same, open at the neck and daubed with paint.

'Miss Talbot,' he exclaimed, taking in my distress at a glance. 'Let me help you.' He pulled me into the house and placed me on a chair. 'Tea? I've just made some.' He indicated the little tea pot which I had provided earlier in the year. 'There seems to be a knack to making it which I haven't quite got. Who could have supposed such a commonplace thing could be so difficult? Coffee I can manage quite well, after three years in Paris, you'd expect no less, but there isn't any here and anyway...' he wittered on in this vein, as much to give me an opportunity to collect myself as to impart any useful information, pouring tea from the pot, arranging and rearranging the pathetically inadequate crockery as though he could get it into some configuration which would make it more, or more satisfactory. I accepted the cup from him and took a sip, suppressing a shudder – it was much too strong – and he handed me a handkerchief (almost clean) with which I could mend my face.

'I'm John Cressing,' he said, holding out a belated hand.

'Evelyn Talbot,' I muttered.

'Ah yes, *that* much, I know,' he said, 'and I feel I must apologise at once. I'm intruding here. I saw at once the gatehouse was in use, not the derelict little bolt-hole George and Rita promised me at all.' He explained he had been offered the gatehouse by them as home and studio both, while he worked on a number of canvasses which were to form an installation at their new house in London. 'Of course they offered me room in the house, but I declined. That man... *insufferable.*'

I nodded, glumly. Insufferable indeed. Before I knew it I was pouring out my woes.

When I had finished John said 'I had no idea you were in permanent residence here. To think of you being subjected to that kind of treatment all the time George and Rita are away from the place! I wonder George sanctions it. Do you think he knows?'

'Mr Ratton says George has given his consent,' I replied, miserably.

'No wonder you've taken to using this place. Any asylum from that odious article.' He took my hand. It was a gesture of pure human sympathy, completely unweighted by the undertow of lascivious intent which characterised all of Mr Ratton's unwelcome, clammy caresses.

I fell, as though the floor had opened up to a bottomless chasm. I fell helplessly and entirely, in love.

THE NEXT PERIOD of my life was one of the happiest I can remember. With John's full agreement I visited the gatehouse every day. Having an ally, someone on my side, made all the difference. It gave me courage I had not had before. I made no secret of my destination to Mr Ratton, striding up there in plain view with a basket of provisions on my arm, telling him I was making sure my brother's tenant had everything he needed. Of course Mr Ratton imposed his company upon me at first, but John did not make him welcome. The bad blood between them on account of the business on the north wing landing remained very apparent. John treated Mr Ratton with stiff disapproval and a distant disdain, as though he were something unpleasant stepped on by mistake. He referred often and not very obliquely to 'certain caddish behaviour,' which made Mr Ratton cringe. He lost no opportunity of rubbing salt in the wound of Mr Ratton's situation at Tall Chimneys by calling George his 'very good friend' but, pointedly, only Mr Ratton's 'employer' or sometimes even 'benefactor.' The visits to the gatehouse soon became too uncomfortable for Mr Ratton, and he desisted from accompanying me there. He stood under the portico and watched me climb the drive each day, a chill, avaricious light in his eye.

Of course he took his revenge, accusing me roundly of neglecting what he called my 'duties' at the house. Failings in housekeeping were blamed on my absence and Mrs Flowers and the other staff used as scapegoats. He would strut around the kitchens tearing strips off them all until every one of them had been reduced to tears or, in Mrs Flowers' case, jibbering hysterics. He found some cause for complaint in Kenneth's maintenance of the water pumping system and dismissed him on the spot. I happened to be looking out of an upper window and saw the incident. Ratton stood in the centre of the yard and yelled at Kenneth, an assault so violent I felt sure they would come to blows. But Kenneth offered no resistance whatsoever, taking up, instead, a rigid stance with his arms clasped to his sides and his face set with stoical resignation, eyes semi-closed, brow furrowed, as though being repeatedly drenched in cold water. When

Ratton had exhausted himself - and got, as perhaps he had hoped, no reaction at all which could have excused him taking his fists or even a nearby horsewhip to the man - Kenneth simply gathered up his tool bag and his jacket and stalked away. What inner wounds - what hurt pride, what injured spirit - he might have suffered I could not imagine, but his stiff back and jutting chin showed immense dignity.

Ratton's cunning emotional blackmail saw me curtail my daily visits to the gatehouse until all the chores were done for the day. The staff was all compliance and helpfulness, as eager to avoid further recriminations as I was. Knowing the agent could not possibly find anything to complain of made me easier in my mind as I skipped up the drive to the gatehouse, although, to tell the truth, its draw on me was so powerful I am not sure a wailing chorus of distraught housemaids could have kept me away.

When I arrived, John would be on the look-out for me. 'You're late,' he would say. 'I thought something had happened.'

When at last I explained Mr Ratton's latest tactic he was furious. 'I'll put a stop to this,' he said.

A few days later Mr Ratton received a long letter from George. He received it in the morning room, where I was busy putting the final touches to the week's menu and grocery order. Mr Ratton grew almost puce as he read his letter, starting up from his chair and pacing backwards and forwards in front of the French windows muttering imprecations and apostrophic grunts of outrage. At last he screwed the pages up and hurled them into the fire, before storming out of the room leaving the door open. I'd like to tell you that reading someone else's mail is beneath me but it would be a lie. I lifted what remained of the pages from the grate and tried to make out their contents. Not much was legible, but I made out the phrases 'in debt to my friend Mr Cressing' and 'wounds me to have to remind you of your place' and 'by no mean press your suit if my sister...'

As unpleasant as the letter must have been to Mr Ratton's sense of self-importance, its message, at least partly, went home. Overt matrimonial references and all mention of any impending trips abroad were dropped from his conversation. They were not, however, dropped from his intention. His eyes continued to speak the words his mouth could not; they lingered on me with a possessive gaze. He brooded and sulked. His resentment against John redoubled although he was powerless to wreak any effective revenge.

Regardless of George's instructions, Mr Ratton maintained his façade of ownership and privilege at Tall Chimneys, unwilling to lose face in front of the servants and tenants. Indeed he increased his exacting requirements, coming down mercilessly on tenants who were behind-hand with their rents or lax with their building maintenance, holding sway over the household servants with an iron fist. Nobody dared challenge him. He began sending for the cocktail tray almost as soon as the tea things were cleared, and was often inebriated before dinner even started.

Drunkenness made him vile and on the days when I had been with John, Ratton treated me with particular cruelty. One evening: 'No dinner for Miss Evelyn this evening, Jones, she has been satiated already, at the gatehouse,' he commented lewdly. Jones looked as though he would protest on my behalf, but I shook my head at him. I sat and watched Mr Ratton gobble his way through four courses of dinner. Another night: 'Miss Evelyn will take her supper off the floor, like a dog; it is a position she is becoming accustomed to, I believe; she likes it on all fours.' Poor old Jones sent the footman from the room on some invented errand, and stood uncertainly with my plate.

'I will take no dinner this evening, thank you,' I said, rising to my feet. 'You will excuse me.'

'No,' he roared, 'I will not. You will remain.'

Dinner continued, Jones white-faced with tension and embarrassment. It was too easy for any staff member to find themselves subject to Mr Ratton's capricious will and I didn't blame Jones for keeping quiet. On the slightest pretext Ratton had been known to reject dishes, sometimes hurling them across the room. He might summon the cook to pour scorn on her culinary efforts, and thought nothing of sending poor old arthritic Jones back down the tortuous cellar steps for alternative vintages. We all heaved a sigh of relief when Mr Ratton finally drank himself into a stupor, or stumbled into the drawing room to sleep off his excesses and this, eventually, is how that evening's debacle concluded itself. I returned to my rooms drained, shaking with a mixture of nerves and anger. On that occasion, as before when I had been denied sustenance, I found a cosy supper laid for me in my chamber; nice things on toast, a flask of frothy hot chocolate. The staff and I often gave each other sympathetic looks and were on the look-out for one another against our common enemy, but no word was ever said.

My solution to these ordeals was simple: John began to join us for dinner, considerably improving that excruciating meal and enlivening the evenings in general. I would scurry through the gloaming to make tea in the library, enduring Mr Ratton's moody silences or barbed remarks, then hurry up to my room to while away the time until the dressing bell. John would arrive in the drawing room for cocktails wearing his least disreputable suit, his hair wet from a sluicing in the kitchen, smelling of autumn leaves and ripe apples, his nails still rimmed with paint pigments. The meal, at our end of the table anyway, would be lively. John spoke entertainingly about his life and experiences in Paris, studying art, about the great and the good on the London scene as well as the shocking and the beyond-the-pale. Mr Ratton sat at the head of the table throughout, frowning and gloomy, squat and dull as an old toad. His complaints about the food and wine were always smoothly contradicted by John, his orders gently but firmly countermanded until all Mr Ratton could do was choke down his dinner and wash it down with copious quantities of wine. John would decline to stay behind for port, such practices, he said, being totally out-moded, and follow me into the parlour where we would play card games or try duets on the piano. Mr Ratton could make no contribution to these amusements, our games being invariably two-handed and he being tone-deaf. Towards nine o'clock I would say goodnight. What transpired between the two gentlemen after my departure I do not know; whether John plied Mr Ratton with drink until he was insensible, or knocked him out with his fist, or merely threatened to do so is a mystery. But Mr Ratton did not, as I constantly feared, attempt to take advantage of my vulnerable situation there, alone with him in the house, by gaining admittance to my rooms in the night.

Occasionally I invited the rector's family to join us for dinner and the invitation was returned, including John but excluding Mr Ratton who, after all, was only my brother's agent who took liberties at Tall Chimneys he was not strictly entitled to. When the rector dined, he treated me as the lady of the house, the hostess, representing the family, and John as my guest. Mr Ratton was tolerated, his attempts to dominate proceedings gently but firmly quashed. Through the rector I became acquainted with other respectable families in the area. My social circle enlarged and my social life with it. I had occasion to call for the motor car to take me out to tea or dinner on several occasions, leaving Mr Ratton to his own, fulminating devices.

Some of the women I met were like me - occupying themselves with the running of their houses. They were very domesticated and I found I had much in common with them, swapping recipes and household tips. Others were much more social, going to Leeds or York on a regular basis to shop or meet friends for lunch. Several had houses in London or at least went there, for the season. They spoke of the Savoy and the Dorchester and gala dinners on Park Lane. I had nothing to add to these narratives and drank my tea in silence. A very few of them worked - one was a veterinary surgeon, another was a headmistress. I felt awed - and a little envious - of their accomplishments and success.

The weeks went by, September closed and October was upon us, and then almost over. Every day I went to the gatehouse when my work in the house was done, carrying provisions or John's linen which had been laundered at the house. Mr Ratton went about his business with a sore head and very bad grace; moody, sullen, resentful.

John and I were intimate. I do not mean sexually intimate, but we were close. When you consider my early years it is not surprising I responded to the first gesture of friendship I had received since Joan had put out a tentative hand, aged five. And given my precarious situation with Mr Ratton of course I grabbed hold of the assurance of John's protection. I had been starved of friendship since arriving at Tall Chimneys. I had been starved of care for my whole life; only Mr and Mrs Weeks had shown me any at all. Of course the gatehouse, with all its association of them, my idea of it as a refuge, also played its part; the gatehouse and John felt inextricably linked in my mind, both part and parcel of a sense of safety and home-coming. His smell, of manliness and paint pigments and turpentine, and some stuff he used to smooth his unco-operative hair, melded itself with the smell of the gatehouse; old wood, new bread, the resinous tang of the pines in the plantation, the smell of applewood burning in the grate and, in my fancy, the whiff of Mr Weeks' pipe. If I said we were at ease in one another's company it would be the truth but also a profound misrepresentation; there was, between us, a taut, singing wire of tension, not unpleasant, like violins tuning up before an explosion of music. I was critically aware of him as I had never been of any other person; my mind, my body, my senses somehow connected, in tune with his slightest movement or gesture, heightened so the least sigh, the smallest flicker of a frown, the crease at the corner of his eye which heralded a smile seemed to me like beacons across the moors; vivid, unambiguous signals I could neither ignore or misunderstand.

He would work in the upper chamber of the gatehouse, where the light was good. Meanwhile I would read downstairs, tend to the little necessaries of house-keeping for him, make tea, write my letters. My inner ear hummed to the sound of his footstep overhead, to the faint click as he put down and took up different brushes, to the silences as he stepped back to consider his next stroke. Then his foot on the stair as he descended for food or tea would stir a potent brew of expectation somewhere behind my ribcage, spreading, melting as it went until I was a flood of syrupy anticipation and breathless with a wanting I could not name. If I was flushed, then, as I served his tea, or if my hand shook as I passed the bread and butter, I am sure he noticed, but he made no comment. I was an open book to him, I suppose.

OCTOBER WAS A gentle month of golden sunshine and rosy sunsets. The leaves turned and fell, from a canopy above they became a rustling carpet under my feet as I travelled between the gatehouse and Tall Chimneys. Mornings saw the first rime of frost; I woke to find a fire lit in my dressing room grate. At night the sky was a wide yawn of stars; John named them for me, our breath rising in the chill air. Once November was with us there was a distinct change. Many nights the hollow of earth which held the house and gardens and its belt of woodland became a boiling cauldron of dense fog; no wind penetrated the crater to disturb it. Some days it lingered until after ten, a thin sunshine eventually penetrating its vaporous cloud, burning it away until all was bright and fresh once more. The days got shorter. Always, of course, in our peculiar depression, the sun was late to arrive and early to leave but once the equinox had passed this phenomenon became more marked than ever. I had to walk up the drive to the rim to find the sun which shone on the gatehouse while Tall Chimneys was still deep in shade.

One morning Mr Ratton appeared more agitated than usual, some item in the newspapers seeming to disturb him. We still received the American press, a week or so late, of course, and he stubbornly persisted in reading it along with the London news. After a while he left the room, taking the newspapers with him, and soon I heard the motor car start up and begin the climb up the drive towards the village.

I thought nothing of it, rejoicing only in Mr Ratton's absence. A party of guests was expected the following weekend and there was much to do; rooms to be aired, beds to be made, fuel for the fires brought in, much bustle and activity in the kitchens. Mrs Flowers and I worked hard all morning. I took a bite of lunch at one, something I did not normally do but as the servants were stopping for a break I had a plate of cold cuts sent up. Then, all being more or less in readiness, I wrapped a warm shawl around my shoulders and walked up to the gatehouse. The day was bright but there was scant warmth in the sun. The gardens, as I passed through them, looked skeletal, the summer's growth having been cut back. The earth was bare, the fountain, drained for the winter, dry and bleak.

When I arrived at the gatehouse John, too seemed agitated. As I entered he swept a letter off the table and stowed it in the drawer of Mrs Weeks' old dresser. I unpacked the food I had brought for him and he began to eat it while I chattered about the preparations for the house guests.

'Do *you* know who's coming?' I asked him. 'Is it the artistic cohort? Am I to expect a further onslaught from Josiah Morely?'

'Not if I can help it,' he smiled, but it was a somewhat troubled, distracted smile. He knocked the top off the bottle of cook's home-brewed beer. 'I have heard from George this morning,' he went on, 'but he doesn't mention the guest list.'

'Mr Ratton has gone out in the car,' I said. 'He seemed in a state about something. He must have gone to town. He's been gone a long time.'

'Had he received a letter also?'

'No.' I shook my head. 'He seemed upset about something in the newspapers.'

Normally, after eating, John would go back up to the upper room and recommence work, leaving me to tidy round, read or do some sewing. Today, however, he seemed reluctant to get back to work. He watched me re-arranging his crockery for a while, and laughed at my efforts to make a few fronds of greenery and some dried Allium heads look attractive in the ewer. Presently I settled by the fire with my book, but still he remained in the room with me, occasionally pacing, sometimes sitting and staring into the flames, but mainly with his eyes both fixed on me and also focussed on something far off.

Eventually I said 'I ought to go, and leave you in peace. I'm clearly a distraction, today.' I marked my place in my book and stood up.

'You *are* a distraction,' he agreed, 'but no more today than any other day. It's just that today, now, at last, when it's much too late and it can't possibly matter, I'm giving in to it.'

'What do you mean?' I stood before him, my book still in my hand. It came to me with a sickening rush that all these weeks, thinking we had been allies, believing our friendship to have been a mutually gratifying arrangement I had, instead, been a nuisance, a wearisome annoyance. 'I'm sorry,' I stuttered, taking all these things as read.

'Sorry? What for?' He rose to his feet, now, raking an agitated hand through his hair which was long, again, and ready for a cut. As he raised his arm I noticed a tear in the seam of his shirt. I made a mental note to repair it for him, next time it came to laundry.

'I thought I'd been helpful, in a small way,' I said, in a thin voice, 'taking care of the house for you so you could get on with the work.'

He laughed. 'Get on with the work?' he almost shouted.

I nodded.

Suddenly he grasped my hand and led me towards the stairs in the corner of the room. 'Come and see how the work progresses,' he said, sourly.

I had never been in the upper chamber before; as intimate and unchaperoned as we had been, John and I, in all the preceding weeks, *that* had seemed a familiarity too far. There was a fireplace, smaller than the one below, but no fire burned in it. Light poured in from windows on four of the six faces of the hexagon. In front of one of them, a rough table held paints, bottles of turpentine, other paraphernalia of John's work. Against the far wall was a divan, tumbled with bedding. At its foot a chair carried his spare clothing. Everywhere else canvasses were propped onto easels or leaning against the walls. Each one was daubed with some initial design, experimental sketches began strongly but then petered out, colour washes suggested background but no detail overlaid them.

I looked at them all, dismayed. 'I thought you'd been making good progress,' I cried. 'You said so, indeed.'

'Of course I said so,' he echoed, pacing around the room throwing despairing looks at all his false starts, picking up and throwing down paint brushes and tubes of pigment. 'I could hardly confess to the truth, could I?'

I looked at him blankly. This tortured man wasn't the John I knew, this sudden lack of concord between us felt like a stranger suddenly thrust into our midst, a cuckoo who would eat up all the trust between us. The silence stretched out. Outside, I could see, the thin sunshine of earlier had been eclipsed by cloud. The moor, under its grey mantle, looked dour and forbidding. The room was chilly, and I had left my shawl downstairs. I wrapped my arms around me.

'I see you're not going to ask,' he grumbled, almost to himself.

I didn't want to ask. To name it would make it real and I was afraid of what it might look like - too different, I feared, from all my girlish imaginings and romantic day-dreams. And yet, it appeared John wanted it named, needed it, indeed, to be revealed in order for him to move forward, as one needs a bad tooth to be drawn. Compassion for him eclipsed my selfishness. 'What *is* the truth?' I asked at last.

'The *truth* is,' he said, pacing with more and more energy round the room, his hands often in his hair, 'the truth is, while *you* are downstairs I can do nothing. I try and paint but I am listening to your footsteps on the flagstones. I have an idea in my head but the sound of your hands straightening furniture sends it right out again. I can see the scheme, right there,' he indicated a space about a foot in front of his face, 'it's as clear as day to me but then I hear you cough, or laugh, and all I can see is you. You fill my vision from one horizon to the other.' He came to a stop in front of me. '*You*,' he said again, fiercely, accusingly. 'You,' he repeated for a third time, his hands on my shoulders, then on my face, 'You,' he spoke again for the last time, his voice hoarse, his arms around me, his mouth in my hair, whispering into my ear. Then his mouth was on mine, and neither of us spoke any more.

**IT WAS VERY** late when I got back to Tall Chimneys, way past the usual hour for tea. There was a very odd atmosphere in the house, as though a great event had taken place but was now over. Things were not as they should be; the front door stood ajar, Jones was not in his usual place in the hall. No fires were lit, no lamps lighted, no curtains drawn against the on-coming night. The library was cold and dark, the tea tray absent. When I went searching for Mrs Flowers the servants' hall was deserted, the makings of dinner abandoned in the kitchen. The kitchen cat mewed plaintively next to her empty dish; I cut up some chicken for her and poured her some milk. I began to call out, and ran from room to room, but no voice answered mine. Mrs Flowers' little suite of rooms was empty, her wardrobe cleared of clothes, the patchwork quilt she had made herself gone from the bed. Round in the stable yard the horses were restless in their stables but had been left with hay and water. The motor car stood in the yard. This surprised me. I had not heard it pass the gatehouse but then, during the afternoon, my thoughts had been concentrated on the inside of that little cell. The four horsemen of the apocalypse could have passed by and I don't think I would have heard them.

Eventually my steps led me back to the library. I fumbled my way through the darkness, to find the lamp on the table by the sofa, imagining ghouls and monsters in the looming shadows of the book cases and cabinets. When I switched the light on I screamed and almost fell over a foot stool. Mr Ratton stood on the hearth rug before the cold grate. I don't know how long he had been there, patiently waiting, or why he had not answered my calls.

'There's no-one here,' I gasped, sinking down on the sofa. 'Where is everyone?'

'*You* are here, and so am I,' he corrected me, pedantically, 'although you are very tardy. The tea hour has been and gone. You were detained, I suppose, at the gatehouse.'

An uncomfortable feeling crept over me, he had been to the gatehouse, entered, even, stood and listened at the bottom of the stairs. In spite of myself a deep blush crept over me, my whole body felt flushed and hot, as it had done earlier, but with a different cause.

'Where is everyone?' I asked again.

'Gone,' he told me. 'I have dismissed all the staff.'

His words shook me. 'Dismissed them? Why? By whose authority?'

'By my own authority, of course, but with the agreement of your brother George. I have a telegram from him, if you care to read it.'

I would have liked to have read it, but Mr Ratton did not produce it.

'Why?' I said again, my voice little more than a whisper.

'There isn't any money to pay their wages,' he said, simply, as though it was as trivial as there being no lemon for the cocktails. 'George's father in law has been hit by the crash in Wall Street. He has been entirely wiped out. It is only his money that has kept Tall Chimneys going for the past few years; now it is gone. It is better for the staff that they know it, and find other situations, if they can.'

His information absolutely floored me. I felt I might faint. I thought, briefly, of the letter John had received that morning, informing him, perhaps, of something similar, that the commission for large canvasses could not now be paid for. John will have to leave, I thought, dully. That's what he had meant when he had said it was too late and couldn't matter. I felt wretched, used. Was he, this moment, I wondered, throwing his clothes into his bag? Perhaps he had already left, satiated, an irritant itch well and truly scratched, and was half way across the moor to the village to find conveyance to the railway station.

Mr Ratton waited patiently while these thoughts and their inevitable consequences unfolded. Whether he knew the exact train of my thoughts, or surmised their gist, or thought they ran upon different lines altogether I do not know, but he cannot have been ignorant of the distress they caused me. After a while he left the library and came back with my shawl, which I had abandoned somewhere during my search of the house, and a clean handkerchief, and a glass of brandy, which I gulped down.

'What is going to happen?' I enquired at last. Shock and perhaps the brandy had numbed me. None of it seemed real. My enquiry had a distanced, casual note as though I was mildly curious, but not really interested. We sat inside the pool of light from the single lamp. Beyond its halo the rest of the room, the whole house, seemed shadowed and insubstantial.

'To Tall Chimneys? Who knows? I suppose it will be abandoned, like so many of these obsolete properties. George can't afford to keep it up. Perhaps it will be sold, but my information is where America leads Britain is sure to follow; the next few years are going to see a slump in manufacturing and the mercantile sector; not many people, I think, will be able to afford to take on a property like this. In any case, the world that houses like this represent is over. It has been since the war, really. George has been living on borrowed time for years.'

I knew in my heart, while Mr Ratton was prone to exaggeration, to making theatrical but ill-founded pronouncements on subjects he knew little about, this time he was right.

'I meant, really, though,' I murmured, 'what will happen to *me*?' Once again, it felt as though the enquiry was offhand, a matter of casual interest relating to somebody else entirely.

'Ah,' Mr Ratton shifted himself in his armchair, making himself, I saw, more comfortable. He was looking forward to the next half an hour. 'Yes. It does all leave you in something of a predicament, doesn't it? Perhaps you are in *more* of a predicament than even I know?' He left his question hanging. His implication was all too clear. 'You can't stay here alone. How could you possibly manage a house this size by yourself? You couldn't cope. It would be too much, even if there were funds for the minimum up-keep, which there aren't.' He let this point find its mark. 'You can't go to George. My understanding is they will be going to America very soon, to see what can be recouped. My fear is nothing at all will be gained by it, but he seems determined. Your other siblings?'

I shook my head. Isobel was still in India, I didn't know the whereabouts of my other sisters and I presumed they would be as penurious as I. My brother Colin had some role in Westminster, an independent income, presumably, but my heart quailed at throwing myself on him. He had always been such a cruel, cold, callous boy. I had heard nothing from or of him for years.

'I don't think they'd be able to do anything to help me,' I mumbled. The brandy had made my lips flaccid and confused my thoughts.

'As I thought.' Mr Ratton placed his fingers in a steeple before him and rested his lower lip on them, as though giving serious thought to my quandary. 'It's a problem,' he said, at last.

Although I hated to raise the question of *his* plans in such close association with my own, I had no choice. 'What will *you* do?' I asked. My question came out slurred.

He seemed not to notice. He looked surprised I should even ask. 'Me? I've told you what my plans are. I shall travel. Now, more than ever, there will be opportunities for people like me. The middle classes will rise. Land, for example, will be available for next to no money. The slump won't last forever...' He talked on for some time, outlining possible opportunities, suggesting alternative destinations; the Far East, South America, Africa. His voice was low and soporific. My eyelids felt so heavy I could not keep them from drooping. The light from the lamp became a haze, and then only a distant pin-prick, then went out altogether.

When I woke up I was warmly wrapped in a thick travelling blanket and settled into the back seat of the motor car. I knew immediately I had been drugged – I had a bitter taste in my mouth, a ravening thirst and a dreadful headache – but my mind was surprisingly clear. From what I could tell I was physically unharmed. Beneath the blanket my limbs were not tied. I took stock of my situation quickly. The engine was running; the air was thick with exhaust fumes and also a dense wadding of fog which must have descended since my return from the gatehouse. We were still in the stable yard; I could hear the whinny and nicker of the horses in the stables and make out the dim light above the door to the estate office. From within I could hear someone – Mr Ratton, I supposed – opening and closing drawers, rifling through cupboards. The seat all around me was packed with boxes and loosely wrapped metallic artefacts; they clashed slightly as I shifted against them – the silver, I surmised, pictures, anything valuable which could be sold quickly without too many questions being asked. Mr Ratton was doing a flit, and planning on taking me with him.

Regardless of my fears about John earlier, and Mr Ratton's observation that I could not stay on alone at Tall Chimneys, I was determined not to be taken as a virtual hostage. I did have friends, even if John Cressing turned out not to be one of them; the rector and his family would give me refuge, or one of the other respectable families with whom I had struck up recent acquaintance. I had to get to them as quickly as I could, before Mr Ratton was able to drug or otherwise subdue me once more. I began to wriggle free of the blanket, trying not to disturb the haphazard arrangement of boxes and bundles in the seat which would alert him to my having regained consciousness. Once liberated, I re-arranged the blanket to make it look like I was still underneath it. My subterfuge would not stand close inspection but, in the dark and the fog, it might fool Mr Ratton for a few moments. I stepped out of the motor car onto the cobbles of the yard, glad he had left it there and not on the gravel on the front sweep. Then I ran, melting into the thick, vaporous air as quickly and quietly as I could. I took a route behind the stables and into the kitchen garden, behind the greenhouses and through the curtain of ivy which concealed the door into the plantation. Before I had even got that far I heard Ratton's roar of annoyance and frustration; he had already discovered my ruse.

I ploughed on up the slope, dodging the overhanging greenery, stepping almost as though by instinct over the roots and boulders which might trip me up or make me cry out. The fog was almost impenetrable; I called on some inner map of the topography which I had known so well since childhood to guide me. I could hear someone else – Ratton – in the woods. Not behind me, but pursuing a course which would intersect with mine in a little clearing a couple of hundred yards from the gatehouse. I altered my route, pushing through a little stand of alder trees, dropping back along a stream which ran down a ravine in order to loop behind my pursuer and come out of the plantation some way along the high stone wall which separated it from the moor. The moor, in this fog, was a dangerous place, full of treacherous bogs and pools of brackish water. Who knew if I would be able to cross it in safety, or find the winding ribbon of roadway which would lead me into the village? My clothes were shredded to ribbons, my boots, thankfully stout enough, were full of water from the stream in the ravine and beginning to rub. I struggled on, keeping panic at bay as best I could, stopping now and again to listen for Ratton who was making much more noise than I was, but was already at a distance from my new route. Presently I couldn't hear him at all, and allowed myself to relax a fraction; perhaps I had lost him; perhaps he had given up.

My desire to revert to my original route – to the gatehouse and thence onto the road – felt very strong; the draw of the place itself was so powerful as to be almost visceral, my idea of it as a safe haven further intensified now by the new associations it had taken on since the afternoon. John's voice, his hands, the smoothness of his shoulders and the tenderness of his fingers kept on re-appearing in my mind's eye, undermining my determination to evade Ratton and distracting me from the crisis at hand. How could he have betrayed me? I stopped for a moment and leant against the trunk of a tall Scotch pine which stood in a small clearing, and allowed sobs to wrack me until I had all but collapsed, thoroughly wretched, at its base.

It was a mistake, of course, to give in to such self-indulgent foolishness. I felt a hand on my shoulder and turned to find Ratton standing over me, his face puce with exertion but also exultant. 'You didn't think I'd been wasting all these weeks sitting at the house and pining for you, did you?' he panted. 'I've used the time well. I think I know these grounds as well as you do, now, lady.' He seized my arm and yanked me to my feet, pressing me back against the tree. Something other than anger and exercise was energising him. He had a look in his eye I recognised, now, with a bleak certainty. 'I can see I'll have to establish my possession once and for all,' he said, grimly. 'It isn't what I wanted, remember, but you leave me no choice.'

He thrust me hard against the tree with his whole body, pinioning me there so I was as helpless as a butterfly on a collector's board. Although not a tall man he was incredibly strong, and after all I had been through that day, I had no strength to resist him. He reached one hand under my skirts and began to fumble with my under-garments, the other pawed and kneaded at my breasts. He breathed in short gasps, licking his lips with a thick tongue. Every so often he forced my mouth open and stuffed his tongue inside, much deeper than was comfortable, thrusting it until I almost choked. The hand under my dress found its object; I shrank in revulsion as he probed and rummaged. He thrust a fat finger inside me, and then two. I was swollen and sore with a tenderness which had been precious but which now felt raw and painful. I would have cried out but he withdrew his hand from there and put his fingers into my mouth until I gagged. He gave a sort of moan, sucking his fingers in his turn and returned them to their work below. Meanwhile he began to struggle with the fastenings of his clothes. His mouth found mine again, wetness from his mouth sliding down my chin. He pushed closer, easing himself between my thighs; I could feel his stiffness nosing clumsily at me, like a blind dog. The bark of the tree behind me was like razors.

'Please God, no,' I cried.

He stopped and gave me an exultant smile. 'Oh yes,' he grunted, and steadied himself for his thrust, but at that moment the crash of low hanging branches across the clearing made his head turn sharply away. I leaned in and took his ear between my teeth, biting down so hard my incisors met through his flesh and his blood poured into my mouth. His scream was as high pitched as the Michaelmas pig's.

Footsteps thundering across the clearing, a roar of animal fury, and then John was hauling Ratton away from me. 'Run,' he shouted. 'Run home,' and I knew he meant to the gatehouse.

By the time John came back I was warm, and calm. There were no signs of his departure at the gatehouse; I had been entirely mistaken in my suspicions. The fire was still lit, the kettle still warm, his belongings where I had tidied them earlier that day. But he had been working; whatever impediment had prevented progress over the past few weeks had been cleared. A canvas on an easel bloomed with extravagant strokes of iridescent colour; exuberant swirls, splashes and whorls - clouds across the moor, sunshine on hills, light on water, tumbled covers on a divan – any and all of these things, very beautiful.

I ran into his arms. 'What's happened?' I asked, presently.

'He's gone, tail between his legs,' John replied.

'You didn't…?'

He gave a harsh laugh. 'I *wanted* to, but no. He's alive. He isn't very pretty, though.'

'He never was,' I murmured.

The next day John and I slept late, then walked down the drive to Tall Chimneys together. The house had been ransacked, paintings taken off walls, cabinets looted of valuable artefacts. The strong room off the butler's parlour had been plundered of silver and crystal. In the estate office the safe stood open, empty. The whole house had a forlorn, neglected appearance. We wandered through its rooms as though visitors from another time.

'What will you do?' John asked. 'Will you stay here, alone?'

I smiled up at him. 'Not quite alone, I hope.'

He returned my smile. 'No, but for propriety's sake, you must appear to be so. What passes to a blind eye in some sections of London society would certainly be frowned on here and you need the support of your neighbours; sometimes, you know, I will have to go to London or abroad. I'll need somebody to buy my work, if I'm to remain solvent.'

'Perhaps...' I began, wondering if I dare suggest we move there together, regularise our relationship, but John did not take up my train of thought.

I looked around the house. 'I ought to protect the property,' I said. 'Something will happen. Somebody will come. Ratton will not come back?'

John shook his head. 'No. He has gone off like a rat deserting a sinking ship, taking every piece of portable property he could cram into the motor car. That, too, he will sell, I expect, unless the police catch up with him.'

Together John and I closed Tall Chimneys down. We restored order to the rooms where we could, before throwing dust sheets over the furniture and closing the shutters. I mothballed the generator, reverting to the use of oil lamps. The pumping station too I closed down. These were luxuries I couldn't justify now; the expense of running and maintaining them beyond my means or capabilities. I contacted my new friends who agreed to house the horses for the time being. The rector urged me to move in with them until better arrangements could be made with my brother George, or another family member, but I declined. Then he suggested his oldest girl should come and be my companion; she was perfectly nice but rather a lumpen girl with little conversation and no practical resourcefulness. Gently, I declined this offer also. It felt wrong to accept their hospitality and kindness when I had crossed such a particular boundary of respectability. Not that I regretted it, but I would not add to my transgression by behaving as though it was not so.

Instead, I burrowed into Tall Chimneys, retreating - perhaps hiding - in its most sequestered accommodations. I removed my belongings to Mrs Flowers' rooms, a pleasant enough arrangement; her ground floor apartments comprised a bedroom and a small bathroom, a sitting room with a French door into a sheltered paved area adjacent to the kitchen garden. They were close to the kitchens where I kept the stove alight. The time I had spent with her and the cook paid dividends; I knew where the foodstuffs were stocked and could cook rudimentary meals. I was familiar with the workings of the laundry. I had everything I needed in that modest corner of the house to keep body and soul together. All through the winter I used the stores from the previous summer, some of which I had bottled myself. I tended the produce in the glasshouses, as Weeks had shown me so many years before, so we had tomatoes and cucumbers and melon with our Christmas dinner. I toured the house each day, ensuring it remained free of leaks and interloping animals. Each afternoon I walked up to the gatehouse where John would be waiting for me. He would work while I tidied the rooms for him. Then as the afternoon closed in we would walk together back to Tall Chimneys to eat whatever I had prepared at a small table in Mrs Flowers' sitting room, a merry fire burning in the grate, the thick curtains pulled tight against the weather. Then we would go to bed. Sometime during the night John would get up and dress, and walk back to the gatehouse.

One evening, as we sat in the semi darkness staring into the flames, John said 'I suppose you sometimes wonder about marriage.'

I held my breath. He was right. Marriage was in my thoughts almost all the time. Of course I expected we would marry - we must. It was both my heart's desire and necessary. The strict moral up-bringing I had received from Isobel and at school demanded no other outcome. Society expected it. I might, to coin a phrase, have slipped 'twix cup and lip, but this was a temporary lapse, private and safe within the isolated environment of Tall Chimneys.

Was he going to propose? His face was in shadow, so I could not read his expression, but when he spoke his words startled me more than I could express. 'George and his set would laugh. *They* think all that very outmoded and unnecessary, you know. They live very liberated, unfettered lives.'

Outmoded? Unnecessary? The notion they would consider my desire to be married boring and conventional unsettled me, but it did not negate it. Isobel had always considered George and his companions very louche.

But the remonstrance which had been on my lips faltered. I'd rather have died than become a fetter on John's liberty or creativity.

'But… I don't know,' John went on. 'I think there's something to be said for it, in some circumstances, if it were possible.'

'In some circumstances?' I stammered, hoping he would elucidate. But he only nodded and repeated 'If it were possible.'

The truth struck me like a fist in the jaw. There was an impediment.

'But it isn't?' I stammered.

He looked up then and gave me a sad, hopeless smile which articulated a complicity I was by no means party to. I wondered at the nature of the impediment; I supposed it to be financial - neither of us had prospects which were very promising, just then. But he only said 'In the future, it may become possible, but at present, it can't be done, even if we wanted it.' He turned his gaze back to the fire. In its ruby light, his brow was furrowed and troubled, so I didn't press him further.

The sense of having fallen down a moral cliff engulfed me, and I felt as though I was spread-eagled on a beach of ruin and disgrace. I swallowed a lump of panic. I didn't blame John - he had made no promises and our courtship had been unusual, unchaperoned, way beyond any boundaries of convention. I didn't blame myself, particularly. My liaison with John was one more figure in what was becoming a natural pattern for me. I had never had any control over my life; choice was not a luxury I had ever enjoyed. This was no different. Left to the machinations of Sylvester Ratton, subjected to his outrages, what else could I have done than fall for the man who had provided a bulwark of protection? Clearly there were circumstances which John was powerless to alter and if he was powerless, how much more was I? A small, carping voice - my sister Isobel's voice - chastised me for my gullibility; I had been taken advantage of, succumbed, when I should have resisted. But I didn't listen. I was in love with John and would pay the price, whatever it was.

Later John made love to me with additional, almost furious tenderness. His climax, when it came, seemed to be as much emotional as physical; I might say almost spiritual. The spasms which shook him came as sobs, inarticulate, guttural cries which were ecstatic and fervent; overwhelming, but in some way holy. Afterwards, but still elevated by the aftermath, he looked down into my face. 'We *are* married,' he cried, 'really, in every way that matters, aren't we?'

His words spoke what was written across my heart. 'Yes,' I responded, cupping his beautiful face between my hands. 'Yes, yes yes.'

We didn't discuss the topic again. It was clear to me it was an issue which lay uneasily with him and I didn't want to stir it unnecessarily. For myself, in my wilful blindness, I told myself no ceremony or piece of paper could make any difference to us. At Tall Chimneys I was as remote from the world as a savage on a desert island; I thought its standards were irrelevant.

1929 - 1936

I had been alone at Tall Chimneys about twelve weeks before I received news, not from my brother George but from my sister in law, Rita. Her letter, like the ones I occasionally received from Joan, seemed to come to me from a far galaxy - a region I would never access. She wrote from New York where, she said, she was staying with her mother. Her father was dead. I gathered, although she did not say it specifically, he had taken his own life, as so many bankrupt businessmen had done. George, she said, was doing his best to rescue what he could, but they were all-but ruined and all their property, virtually, would have to be sold. 'My mother will be reduced to penury,' she complained, 'assuming she survives the shock.' George himself, she confided, was unwell, sick with worry and struggling with some ailment. She confirmed she had heard nothing from Ratton. 'Enemies and friends alike have deserted us,' she grumbled, bitterly. She could offer me no comfort or hope that my situation at Tall Chimneys would be improved. 'There just isn't any money,' she wrote, 'and although our properties in England are safe from Papa's creditors here, there are no funds to keep them up. It is likely they will have to be sold or, at the very least, let, unless one of your siblings can do something. At the worst, Tall Chimneys will have to be demolished. Surely as a pile of rubble it will cost nothing to maintain? In the meantime, retrench; live as cheaply and quietly as you can. I thank God,' she concluded, bitterly, 'that George and I have no children. At least we are relieved of the worry of *their* future.'

Late in 1930 my sister Isobel returned home with her husband for a Round Table conference about the Indian question.[4] Joan accompanied them, and I had been both hoping and fearing that a meeting might be arranged. I longed to see them, those two, who had been mother and sister to me. But on arrival in London Joan wrote to tell me that her mother was so gravely ill she had not been expected to survive the journey. She had done so but the end was very near. It would be impossible for her to receive visitors, or for Joan to leave her bedside in order to see me. Joan, married now to someone on the Viceroy's staff, planned to return East 'in due course'. She informed me my invalid sister had passed away already. Of my last surviving sister she had no news but Colin, she wrote, was an influential supporter of the opposition, active in foreign affairs and a close confidant of Edward, Prince of Wales. With

---

[4]The three Round Table Conferences of 1930–32 were a series of conferences organized by the British Government to discuss constitutional reforms in India. They were conducted as per the recommendation by the report submitted by the Simon Commission in May 1930. Demands for swaraj, or self-rule, in India had been growing increasingly strong. By the 1930s, many British politicians believed that India needed to move towards dominion status.
Source: https://en.wikipedia.org/wiki/Round_Table_Conferences_(India)

these exalted connections it went without saying he had neither the desire nor the need to maintain any meaningful association with the family.

My life at Tall Chimneys seemed light years away from everything; the world at large felt like it had nothing to do with us and, because of my irregular relationship with John I did not court the world's attention. Elsewhere electricity had taken over from steam, the motorcar replaced horses. Women over twenty-one had the vote and were more and more independent. The old ways were disappearing, as Ratton had predicted. But we remained sequestered in our little hollow, shut in by trees and protected by miles of wild moor. The seasons had more impact on us than Mr MacDonald's government or Mr Hitler's plans to re-arm Germany. I toiled in the kitchen garden, the orchards and the greenhouses to provide food. Occasionally a lad from the village would bring some rabbits or other game; our own stocks of game birds had gone native - it was beyond me to husband them and what was the point, when no parties of gentlemen would be coming to shoot them dead? It occurred to me, as I handed over a few pennies for a brace of pheasant, I was probably buying my own birds back, but I didn't raise the issue with the lad. I nurtured a flock of hens and collected their eggs, reluctantly wringing the necks of the ones which stopped laying. From time to time I was invited to the Rectory to dine by that kind, Christian family. My friend the rector neither questioned, condoned nor condemned my relationship with John; he was all compassion and understanding, entirely non-judgmental, he demonstrated unconditional love. Oh! That all Christians could be so! My other contacts in the area dropped me, tactfully, from their acquaintance. Of course I could not return their hospitality and my relationship with John made me untouchable. I told myself I did not care. In any case, I was barely presentable. My clothes were threadbare and disreputable, my hair ungroomed, my hands calloused and the nails rimmed with soil.

I never went to the village, having the idea that, as discreet as John and I had been, everyone there would know our business. I gave up attending church, not sufficiently the hypocrite to sit through the rector's sermons or to speak the responses in the prayer book. Perhaps I misjudged the locals' loyalty to the Talbots - many of them, after all, had been employees on the estate or were tenants of our few remaining properties - they may not have condemned me utterly. But the moral climate at the time was somewhat dour and severe, right and wrong was understood in terms of black and white. I didn't want to risk an unpleasant scene.

John stayed on at the gatehouse, painting; it was a time of incredible inspiration and productivity for him. He helped me with maintenance around the house but despite our best efforts the cold and damp began to seep into the fabric of the building. Materials began to moulder; water ingress was an increasing problem; the books in the library became bloomed with grey fuzz.

John's work took him often to London. 'Come with me,' he would say. 'There are shops and restaurants. I can introduce you to the Mitfords or the Bloomsbury people.' But I would always decline these suggestions, shrinking from the public exposure of our private involvement.

'What would people say?' I would frown, blushing.

'They would slap me on the back and say "Well done, old man! What a catch!"'

'That's alright for you,' I retorted. 'But what would they say about *me*? It's different, for women. I'd better stay at home.'

The truth was I felt an ever-widening gulf between myself and others of my sex. They were grasping opportunities, working, learning, making their mark. They were breaking out of constricted indolence or enforced servitude in order to rise while I only languished, living my little life in a backwater. How could I take tea in Bloomsbury, where the talk was all of modern art and literature? How could I even meet the eye of the waitress in the Lyons Coffee House?

So John went alone and staged an exhibition there which was well-received, but which gained more critical than monetary acclaim. He took it to Paris also, where he met with old acquaintances and got some commissions which saw us through the next few months. Even though I understood conventions to be less rigid in France - our extra-marital relationship might have passed there with less comment - he did not ask me to accompany him. I wouldn't have done so, anyway; it would have been impossible. We could not have travelled together without attracting comment and to go separately would have been ridiculous and disingenuous.

The years went by. We were happy. Tall Chimneys was our haven, our bastion, our refuge.

 **IN DECEMBER OF** 1935 I heard from my sister in law my brother George had passed away 'after a long illness' which, I suspected was more than a little self-inflicted. I was sad, but as I had only met George on the few occasions that he had visited Tall Chimneys I felt in many ways he was a stranger to me. I had no recollection of him at all from childhood. 'George was always greedy,' my sister Isobel had always told me, 'an Epicure, he liked all the good things in life; food, drink, comforts of the flesh.' Isobel, too, by this time had been long in the grave, her daughter Joan, my life-long friend, had returned to India where she now had several children to occupy her; I did not hear from her very often. My sole surviving sister was a mystery to me and, with George's death, the estate devolved onto my youngest brother, Colin.

This was one of the two deeply disturbing consequences attendant on George's death - that Tall Chimneys and I myself would fall under Colin's control. It was alarming to me although I had no evidence the cruel little boy I remembered survived in the man. Now Mr Baldwin was back in power I understood Colin was deeply involved in matters of government, a close associate of Mr Chamberlain who stood poised to relieve Baldwin of leadership if he could. I comforted myself that, with any luck, matters of party and government would prevent Colin from interfering at Tall Chimneys.

On the other hand, it was obvious to me that unless Colin did interest himself, the outlook was dire indeed. I knew the death duties payable on George's decease would be enormous and could result in the sale or even the demolition of Tall Chimneys. Demolished houses incurred no tax and many of the old families were choosing that solution to the crippling duties levied by the government. Finding themselves with insufficient funds to keep up their properties, problems finding staff and realising that those old days of aristocratic living were simply untenable in the 1930s, more and more owners of stately homes were selling them off, leaving them to wrack and ruin or knocking them down. I wondered if Colin would follow suit. As successful as he seemed to be, it was surely unlikely he would have the funds to rescue Tall Chimneys and since, as far as I knew, he hadn't visited it since his boyhood, it appeared to me very doubtful he would exert himself for the sake of it.

In January 1936 news came of the death of the King.[5] The village went into mourning, but in truth the circumstances of the local people were so dire that the King's death could do little to dampen spirits already critically low. Here again, the active intervention of Colin was an absolute necessity. The village was small, perched on the edge of the moor, by-passed by the developing road network and without even a branch railway line, it was without any of the excitements of dance halls, shops and picture houses which the larger towns could offer, so it didn't attract new people or investment. Traditionally most inhabitants had worked in local agriculture or in service at the house itself, but work on the land was increasingly unrewarding and of course there was none to be had at 'the big house'. Many young people had left in search of brighter lights and work in mills and factories but unemployment in the towns and cities in 1936 was rife, poverty extreme, hardship almost unendurable. I regularly found itinerants at the door, asking for work, or food, or shelter. I did what I could for them, feeding them from my meagre stores, treating their illnesses from Mrs Flower's stock of herbal unguents and cordials, equipping them with clothing – old fashioned but serviceable – from the wardrobes of the rooms, and sending them on their way. When they discovered the situation at Tall Chimneys – not a monied stately home, just a crumbling shell of masonry, damp-infested rooms and a sole, struggling housekeeper (as they assumed I was) they left me in peace.

---

[5] A heavy smoker, in 1925 George V was diagnosed with chronic obstructive pulmonary disease. A few years later, he fell seriously ill with an inflammatory disease. He never fully recovered, and in his final year he was often administered oxygen. On the evening of January 15, 1936, it was apparent he was gravely ill, and the doctor was summoned. The king slipped in and out of consciousness for five days. After receiving an injection of morphine and cocaine by the royal physician, he died on January 20, 1936.
Source: http://www.biography.com/people/george-v-9308922#vast-changes-within-the-empire

Tall Chimneys still had a small number of tenant farms attached to it as well as some half dozen tied cottages in the village. I don't know what arrangements were in place for the payment of rents; certainly none of the tenants came to me offering payment but thankfully neither did they come complaining about their dilapidated farm-houses and draughty cottages. Perhaps they recognised in me a fellow sufferer of the times. Perhaps they felt I had negated any right I had to represent the Talbots. Whichever it was, the house, the land and the local community, all of which had been under the stewardship of our family for hundreds of years, were suffering terminal neglect. I was powerless. As much as I dreaded Colin's appearance on the scene, I could not deny it was sorely needed.

I received a letter from Colin in February, type-written on House of Commons stationery, announcing a visit with several 'influential' friends. He required the house to be made ready, he said, the cellar and larder to be stocked and below-stairs staff hired in preparation for a visit over Easter. As relieved as I was, I laughed aloud when I read his requirements, looking round the dilapidated rooms, sorting through the damp linen, surveying my diminished stocks in the larder. The window in the principal suite of rooms had been broken and a blackbird was building a nest in the armoire. A dripping tap in the bathroom had left a livid green trail of slime down the enamel of the tub, a soot-fall in the dining room fireplace and coated everything in greasy grey ash. Even without these issues, the absence of the pictures and silver, the sorry dishevelment of the rugs and tapestries and the thorough-going air of neglect about the place made it hardly suitable for a visit by anyone, let alone anyone 'influential.' I wrote back to Colin expressing willingness to undertake the preparations he required but listing the works which would be needed and the moneys required to complete them. I expected to encounter opposition but in fact he wrote back enclosing a generous banker's draft and instructing me to proceed without delay.

As welcome as this development was, it required me to engage with local people, something which I had been avoiding from a sense of personal unworthiness, shame, pride - a cocktail of hang-ups and insecurities attendant on my unorthodox relationship status. Very reluctantly, with extreme trepidation I took myself to the village and called in at the shop. I might not know much about the village but I did know this: I could do none of the things Colin required of me without the co-operation of Kenneth's mother.

She appeared to me exactly as she had done previously; the same fleshless frame, the same stiff apron, the same anachronistic aroma of sweet confectionery and indulgence.

'I have come to offer Kenneth employment,' I said, quickly, before she could harangue me with being the cause not once, but twice, of her son's dismissal, or with other crimes. 'There are to be wholesale improvements at the house and I want him to over-see them. No-one better, in my opinion.'

She looked at me narrowly. How much she knew of my historical ordeal with Ratton I did not know, but I almost hoped some details of it would have found their way to the ears of village gossips. Surely, I thought, that might ignite some spark of womanly sympathy? But then it was equally likely, I thought, she might brand me a harlot and chase me down the street with a tin of tar and a sack of feathers.

She put her hands on her scrawny hips. 'You want Kenneth to come down to the house?' she asked, in a tone which mixed exasperated incredulity with doleful resignation: she was amazed I'd had the temerity to ask, but knew with certainty - and against her better judgement - that he would oblige.

'Yes please,' I said, in a small voice. 'Indeed, we will need many people; gardeners, house maids, a cook. If you know of people in need of the work?'

'Ha!' it was a hard bark of laughter, cynical; everyone was in need of work in those straitened days, but I did not know if she would overcome her animosity to help me and them out. Still she looked at me with focussed intensity as though she was trying to read my soul. I trembled before her. Feeling, suddenly, tainted and unworthy.

'We've seen nothing of you for a long while,' she stated.

I nodded, and kept my eyes fixed on the pristine counter top. 'I haven't felt able to...' I trailed off, unsure as to how I could finish my sentence.

'Been managing, have you?'

'Barely - like everyone, I suppose. Keeping body and...' I almost choked on the next word, '*soul* together.'

Mrs Greene sniffed. 'You're young,' she said. 'Can't have been easy.'

Suddenly her demeanour relaxed and she placed her hands on the counter before her. 'I'll send Kenneth down,' she said. 'As for the rest, leave it to me.'

For weeks, all was hustle and activity. I hired every local man and woman Mrs Greene sent my way for repairs and cleaning, glad to give them employment and pay them good wages. Kenneth stripped down the generator which had provided us with sporadic supplies of electricity in former days and also the water pump which fed the plumbing - I had not used either for years. In addition to this he oversaw the outside works. Stone masons and carpenters repaired the roof and the windows. The chimneys were swept, the coal bunker stocked and the ancient furnace coaxed back into operation. An army of gardeners tamed the parterre and trimmed the hedges, the beds were dug over, trees pruned, gravel paths raked free of weeds. He directed these operations with quiet efficiency, a word of advice here, a request there, a muttered suggestion elsewhere, and, as often as not, grasping a rake or a spade to help the work along.

Indoors, Rose, a protégée of Mrs Greene's and daughter of the local butcher, proved her weight in gold in getting the house in order. Rose was a bright and chatty girl, not yet twenty. She was dimpled and delicious, with a cascade of dark, curly hair which no amount of pins could keep in check. She addressed me as 'ma'am' until I told her to call me Mrs Johns, a convenient fiction which worked for us both. She lived at home with her parents and a much younger brother, Bobby, a chubby toddler who she occasionally brought to work with her when her mother was indisposed. The physical resemblance between the two was impossible to misinterpret, not to mention the bond, which was more affectionate than you would expect for a young woman and a sibling. As proof positive this was in fact her own child, as he began to speak words which were comprehensible, he called her 'Mammy-rose'. Who was I to criticise? I told her she could bring him whenever she liked. He was no trouble, playing happily while we worked, and, indeed, it was a joy to see him running stoutly across the lawns or petting the new-hatched chicks in the poultry house. Whether it was because we were both women with 'a history' or simply because we were both young, we established an immediate accord.

I hired skilled carpenters to restore the beautiful Jacobean panelling in the hall and landings to its former glory. They replaced warped floorboards and rehung doors so that they stopped sticking and made windows and shutters operate without effort. An army of needlewomen mended rips in curtains and replaced faded soft furnishings. What a joy it was to see the house emerge from its doldrums and what a new lease of life I too experienced, overseeing and participating in its revival!

Then, when the workmen had departed, Rose and I opened the shutters of the rooms and pulled the coverings from the furniture with an almost ceremonial formality. With a team of women from the village, we set about the gargantuan task of cleaning and polishing. We hauled rugs outdoors for beating, shaking out years' worth of dust and debris, polished glassware and washed the delicate crystal droplets of the chandeliers until they glinted like diamonds.

Colin had instructed me to hire a number of below-stairs staff 'for the interim of our visit' so I employed a cook, Mrs Bittern, who came highly recommended by Mrs Greene from an establishment in York, a kitchen maid, two parlour maids (one of which was Rose), two gardeners and Kenneth as a general outside man. As for the above-stairs men - footmen, valets and a Butler - I did nothing. Colin had informed me these would be supplied from amongst his own, existing staff, people upon whose discretion and loyalty he could depend.

Mrs Bittern arrived and I immediately knew she would be trouble - a shrewish woman well past forty with a mean eye and a tone of voice which grated on the ear. She took one look round the kitchen before insisting that unless I provided a refrigerator, she would leave. To prove her point she sat down on one of the chairs without removing coat or hat, and folded her arms. I ordered a refrigerator, using the new telephone line Colin had dictated should be installed. The cook, the kitchen maid and one parlour maid took up residence in the old nursery apartments, the former servants' quarters in the attics being beyond the scope of Colin's improvements and utterly uninhabitable. I'd have thought these were rather more comfortable than anything they might have been used to, but it seemed not; I had strings of complaints: the windows rattled, the chimney smoked, the mattresses were lumpy.

I offered Kenneth the old agent's rooms above the estate office but he shook his head and muttered 'Stay at home, if it's all the same.'

Rose also preferred to remain at her parents'. 'Kenneth will see me home, won't you?' she said, brightly, 'and carry little Bobby?'

Kenneth blushed so furiously his freckles all-but disappeared.

'I think you had better not bring Bobby when the gentlemen are here,' I cautioned.

The two gardeners moved in above the estate office. I retained Mrs Flowers' rooms and maintained the fiction that I was a house-keeper. I did this for two reasons; I wished the servants to view me as experienced and competent so they would respect my authority, something they would not have done at all if they had known I was simply a daughter of the house making things up as I went along. Also, when Colin and his guests came, there would be no question of me playing hostess or participating in the entertainments. I dreaded a repeat of my experiences at George and Rita's house parties and shrank from any exposure which might embarrass Colin or put in jeopardy my tenure at Tall Chimneys. I explained as much to Colin in one of the frequent letters which now crossed between us, as I consulted him on various matters and kept him abreast of improvements.

'I have lived in seclusion for the past six or seven years,' I told him, 'perfectly content with my lot but out of step with modern thinking and behaviours, certainly with modern fashions. I am only as informed about politics and current affairs as diligent perusal of the newspapers and listening to the wireless can make me. In the august company you intend to bring to the house I would fear to transgress in opinion or ignorance. The last thing I would wish would be to embarrass you. Therefore I beg you will allow me to run things from a place of obscurity. I am sure your wife - if you have one - or another lady will be happy to act as hostess.' Colin's reply was reassuring. He had no wife, he informed me, the gathering would include only one principal lady who would bring her own entourage and need no entertainment. His guests would require no sport; their time would be occupied in political discussion and strategy. I was to ensure good food, adequate supplies of whisky and brandy, plentiful cigars and utmost discretion. It sounded dull indeed, and I was reassured.

Colin's letters were always matter-of-fact, typed - I suspected perhaps even composed - by a spinsterish secretary; they were without personality or style of any kind. A week or so before the visit was due to commence, I received a delivery which turned out to be clothing; two drear, mid-calf length skirts in quasi-military fabric and some dark blouses, rather mannish; they were very conservative, without trimming or frippery. It was out of the question that John had sent them to me - he was in Paris at the time, negotiating with an agent - their style didn't at all reflect his penchant for colour or flamboyance. I hadn't ordered anything from a catalogue. A short typewritten note arriving the following day identified Colin's secretary as the donor. 'Dear Miss Talbot,' the note ran, 'I hope the clothing is a suitable size; it will abet your desire to remain unnoticed. Do let me know if an alternative size is required. Yours truly, Giles Percy, Private Secretary to Mr Colin Talbot.' I smiled at the idea of Mr Percy (in my mind's eye, a replica of one of Jane Austen's curates, sexless and mealy) shopping for women's clothes; his choice was certainly extra-ordinary, suitable for the dour Matron of an institution. When I put them on the person who stood in the mirror looked like a stranger, very serious and severe, and old before my twenty five years. If my image of him had been vivid, so, too, I realised, was his idea of me; he must have formed it from my letter. The clothes made me look like a uniformed functionary by no means to be confused with a member of the family or a person of rank; I had been taken at my word.

I would have been depressed and disillusioned indeed if I had not received, by the same post, a letter from John. John was an excellent correspondent, writing colourful and entertaining letters which I read and re-read many times in my solitude. This one described a possible exhibition in Berlin with another, like-minded artist - a sculptor - he had met in a café. To this end, he told me, he intended extending his trip and had in fact travelled in company with his new associate to Germany. 'Everyone in France is very exercised about Mr Hitler,' he told me, 'either enthralled by the success and charisma of the man, or fearful of the mindless adoration and servitude he seems to kindle. There is no denying,' he went on, 'that the German economy is currently out-stripping every other European country. Their factories are all working round the clock, men are employed planting forests and building new roads. Wages are high; many families here have their own motor car. But it isn't all work. The Government here has set up an organisation called KdF[6] in pursuance of Mr Sleary's recommendation that 'the people must be amused' (you'll remember, from *Hard Times*, I am sure!). It makes sure there is plenty to occupy the workers' leisure time, with theatrical performances, concerts and sporting activities. My friend and I hope to cash in on a KdF sponsored art exhibition here next month. It's a promising prospect. They expect wealthy collectors and influential critics from east and west to converge here. We've taken lodgings on the top floor of a building on the Strasse Bendler. The light is pretty good and I've been working on a new set of canvasses. Jean is doing something very

---

[6] *Kraft durch Freude* (German for Strength through Joy, abbreviated KdF) was a large state-operated leisure organization in Nazi Germany.[1] It was a part of the German Labour Front (Deutsche Arbeitsfront, DAF), the national German labour organization at that time. Set up as a tool to promote the advantages of National Socialism to the people.

messy with papier mâché and plaster. In the evenings we eat pickled cabbage and snitzel and drink sickly Rhenish wine, and watch the world go by from a restaurant we've found close by. My darling, you can hardly imagine, from where you are in your sequestered hollow, what life out here in the modern world is like. One day I shall bring you, and you will be amazed.'

His words made him feel very far away from me, both geographically and emotionally. What would there be, I asked myself, after all his cosmopolitan adventuring, for him to come home to? Only me, old-fashioned and un-travelled and this remote, antiquated old house, the two of us marooned in a forgotten time and place as surely as if we were caught between the covers of a dusty old book.

 **THE MAIN GROUP** of guests was due to descend on Easter Saturday. On Holy Tuesday the advance party arrived; several male servants - footmen and a Butler - and two male secretaries including Mr Percy. He was nothing like the man I had imagined. In his mid-twenties, he was of medium height and well-made, with a shock of blond hair and a pleasant smile. He addressed me as Mrs Johns, at my suggestion - pandering to my desire to dissever the family association. He remained formal but beneath his stiffness I was sure I discerned a genial under-layer. He paid me the deference due to any ancient family factotum, visiting my little office often as a matter of politeness to discuss issues arising, but to all intents and purposes taking control of arrangements in the house. All Colin's men wore semi-military clothing akin to the garments I had been provided with, and I saw at once Mr Percy's plan to enable me to meld into the background; we were like a battalion of troops in which one is indistinguishable from another. Certainly they commenced operations with military discipline, doing a recce of the house and grounds, and then beginning a programme of unceremonious shifting and lifting, moving furniture from room to room, reordering the sleeping arrangements and bringing suites of rooms into play I had decided should be closed off. The secretaries commandeered the morning room in the east wing. The library was to become a meeting room, the sofas pushed back and two large desks dragged into the centre. A large folio of European maps appeared. The drawing room was declared too small and another room - a music room, much grander but never used in my lifetime - brought into use for relaxation and refreshment. The village women I had hired as maids and I scurried round for two days, making up fresh beds, fetching supernumerary chairs and bureaux from distant rooms, trying to add to the scanty comforts of some rooms with vases of flowers and draperies.

The secretaries took their meals above stairs, in a small sitting room. The Butler and the footmen joined the rest of the servants below, but were surly and uncommunicative, and scathing of our rustic amenities. Mrs

Bittern, with more mouths to feed than she had calculated for at this stage, had a fit of apoplexy and threatened to leave. It took all my powers of persuasion to change her mind.

Easter was late that year. Already the early spring bulbs had faded and the perennials were pushing through the soil. The air was soft and mild during the day but given to dampness in the evenings. The gardeners I had hired had been doing wonders with the neglected beds; the parterre was free of weeds for the first time in years, the old fountain un-choked and coaxed back into life. With their help the kitchen gardens looked like they would be the most productive ever; I had gradually reduced my field of operations down to three or four raised beds and a section in the glasshouse. Now everywhere had been weeded, compost and manure dug in, trees and bushes pruned, seeds sown. It felt like Tall Chimneys was experiencing a rebirth and the promised influx of company, although I had refused any social inclusion, regenerated my own spirits. I missed John, of course, and envied him his freedom to travel and experience life abroad which probably - despite his promises - I would never see as his accepted companion. The very public liaison between King Edward VIII and Mrs Simpson seemed to suggest that, very soon, such discretion might not be needed but for the time being ordinary men and women like John and I would not have dreamed of walking in their footsteps. In the meantime, however, the activity in the house, the easy rapport I had established with Mr Percy, even the anticipation of seeing Colin again all seemed to compensate. Tall Chimneys was my universe and I threw myself into it with enthusiasm, and tried not to think about the world outside at all.

On the evening of Maundy Thursday Mr Percy joined me as I perambulated on the lawn. He had finished dinner, and stepping through some French doors onto the terrace to smoke a cigar, spied me on my regular evening walk.

'May I join you?' he asked, falling into step beside me.

'Of course,' I answered. 'Is all in readiness?'

He nodded. 'Yes. Your brother and a couple of others will arrive tomorrow. The rest of the party on Saturday except for two, who will join us on Sunday for one night only.'

I said nothing. It was as I had been informed. The arrivals on Sunday were to have the two premier suites of rooms, adjoining each other off the east landing, the rooms I believed my parents had once occupied. They would bring their own servants who were to be accommodated close by. Their identities were shrouded in much mystery.

'You are not curious as to who will be visiting your home?' Mr Percy gave me a narrow look, although his words were casual, unweighted.

I wondered if it was a test. 'Of course,' I threw off. 'But the necessity for discretion has been emphasised so rigorously that I am determined not to wonder.'

He laughed. 'Very wise. And afterwards, not to talk.'

'I know my brother is a close confidant of Mr Chamberlain,' I offered. 'It is very gratifying, of course, and I am proud of his advancement and influence. But really, here,' I indicated the wall of trees around us, the high, pale sky, the ancient house, 'such things seem very remote, hardly part of the same world at all.'

'Indeed,' he agreed, 'your situation is very particular. Tall Chimneys is a throw-back, in many ways, frozen in a time which has long passed, and locked into a landscape which is almost other-worldly. You never go to London?'

I shook my head. 'Not for many years. My..' I checked myself, I had been on the cusp of saying 'my husband' ... 'my friends do, from time to time. They report it is a very busy place, now, full of hustle and bustle, motorcars, electric light.'

'And so it is. Also very cosmopolitan, full of immigrants, itinerants, the dispossessed. Order is breaking down. I think you had much better stay here, Mrs Johns.'

'I think I shall,' I agreed, 'although we have our share of the dispossessed here too. There is no work.'

'The state should never have allowed industry to get into private hands,' he commented. 'I hope that, soon, things will be rebalanced.'

We had arrived back at the terrace. It would have been natural for him to end his walk and go inside. He hesitated, however. He fiddled with the stub of his cigar and seemed to be struggling for an opening. It was the first time I had seen him at any kind of loss. 'I hope,' he said at last, 'that you will not be inconvenienced in any way by our party.'

'I don't suppose I shall be,' I assured him. 'It seems to me my work is done, now. Your people have everything in hand. The cook, perhaps, might need some...'

But he interrupted me. 'If you do find yourself... incommoded. You must come and let me know,' he said.

The next day my brother came. And with him, Sylvester Ratton.

COLIN WAS AS skinny and unprepossessing as he had been as a boy. A sharp nose and small, watery eyes at which he constantly dabbed with a monogrammed handkerchief, were his most arresting features. His hair was pale, and thin, scraped across the bony dome of his skull. He was smaller in stature than I had imagined; perhaps, in my memory, his cruel nature had given him more height than he had ever actually had. Like the others, he wore a military-style of dress, drab khaki with a wide belt. The belt was ridiculous, much too big for his skinny waist, the buckle kept creeping round to his side and he was forever yanking it back into place. All his clothes, in fact, though neat, looked as though they had been made for someone larger. The effect was of a little boy dressed in his father's apparel. I wanted to laugh, in spite of my nerves. He skipped nimbly up the steps of the main entrance to where I was waiting for him alongside the others of his staff. He shook hands with everyone genially, including me. No glimmer suggested he knew me as anything other than a housekeeper.

Mr Percy showed Colin into the rooms which had been prepared, murmuring already about matters of business, a sheaf of documents in his hands. The Butler and footmen dissolved and disappeared to their various duties, leaving me alone in the hall. Colin's party seemed to have arrived in a motorcade; several vehicles manoeuvred out on the gravel. The activity outside drew my attention. I stepped out under the portico. In addition to two motorcars there was a large van. It was reversing up to the doors. And there was Mr Ratton, exactly has he had been six years before except even more rotund, directing operations as he would have done then. He, too, wore the strange uniform; it made him look self-important and ridiculous but then, I remembered, I was wearing it, or a facsimile of it, myself. He caught sight of me and flashed what would have been a malevolent smile if his face, more doughy than formerly, as fat and bland as a half-baked bun, had had any flexibility of expression. I caught my breath, reliving, in that instant, all he had put me through before. It was as though a plug had been removed from my body and all my confidence allowed to pour through the hole.

I turned on my heel and followed Colin into the library.

'Colin,' I said, boldly, interrupting Mr Percy mid-flow, 'I need to speak with you.'

My brother flushed with annoyance but stood up from where he had been bending over some papers on the table.

'I am amazed at you,' he said, coldly, when Mr Percy had withdrawn. 'I thought you wanted to keep your distance. Considerable trouble has been gone to in order to maintain your façade of obscurity.'

'That was as much for your benefit as mine,' I said. 'I didn't want to embarrass you by claiming relationship, that was all. And Mr Percy knows full well who I am. But there is something you need to know about a member of your entourage. Mr Ratton. He is a thief.'

Colin gave a sort of snort. 'A thief?'

'Yes. When the news came through about George, he did a moonlight, taking all the valuables from the house. He would have abducted me, but was prevented. He behaved in an outrageous manner towards me.' I was shaking, but it was as though a geyser had opened up in me, filling up the space where, only moments before, my assurance had been, with anger and indignation. 'He drugged me. He molested me, Colin.' I collapsed into a chair, weeping. Colin looked on, coldly. I remembered, now, his cruelty as a child, his lack of compassion. By odd chance, following the rearrangement of the furniture in the room, he was standing on the exact spot which Ratton had occupied that night when I had found him waiting for me in the dark. The memory brought a shudder which almost convulsed me. Ratton, then, had been the author of my misery, and now Colin... I felt a terrible foreboding grip me.

Out in the hallway, beyond the double doors of the library, there was much bustle and activity.

'You ninny,' Colin spat out, at last. 'Ratton wasn't stealing those things, he was *saving* them.'

At his words the doors of the library flew open. Without a knock, without a nod, without a gesture of deference of any kind, Ratton strode into the room with a crate in his arms. 'Here we are,' he boomed, placing the box onto the desk, 'back where they belong.' He dusted his hands together as though he had accomplished a great feat of work, and, turning, appeared to notice me for the first time. 'Oh!' he cried, mock-startled, 'Miss Eve... Forgive me, Mrs *Johns,*' he spoke the name with derisive emphasis, 'I didn't know you were here.'

'Evelyn is just telling me, Sylvester,' Colin said, smoothly, 'about your heroics. She'd got quite the wrong impression. Seems she thought you were making off with the family silver!'

'Really?' Ratton guffawed. 'What a poor opinion she must have of me.'

'Indeed, I have,' I croaked, rising to my feet. For all I wished to present an image of wounded dignity and pride, I must have failed. Both men howled with laughter.

'Sylvester brought all the valuables straight to me in London,' Colin said, as though explaining something to an imbecile, or a child. 'As far as he knew the house was going to be closed up. Naturally he could not have left them here. I must say he's made himself very useful, since then. Now he's one of us. Quite on equal standing.'

'I never dreamed you'd stay on here,' Ratton put in, wandering over to the mantelpiece and taking up his old position with a self-possession which astounded me. 'Not when you had other more attractive options to pursue. How is Mr Cressing, by the way?'

'He is well,' I said, stiffly. 'In Berlin, just now.'

'Indeed?' This seemed to interest both men to an extra-ordinary degree. 'To what purpose?'

'On business,' I stammered. 'A possible exhibition...'

My explanation seemed to puncture the balloon of their curiosity. Colin turned away from me and began to rummage through the box Ratton had carried in. I glimpsed items of silver and crystal. 'I hope you can remember where all these things belong,' he muttered. 'Damned if I can.'

I nodded. 'Yes. I can restore them all to their rightful places,' I said, heavily.

'So you and Ratton are on the same page, after all,' Colin declared, losing interest in the trinkets in the box.

'There should be a lot more,' I remarked.

'There are. The van is full of them,' Ratton smirked. He lit a cigarette and threw the match onto the hearth. We both looked at it. Did he expect *me* to pick it up?

'And what about the money,' I re-joined. 'The money you took from the estate office safe?'

Ratton made a moue, narrowing his stony, reptilian eyes against the cigarette smoke. 'One had expenses,' he murmured, before going on 'In Berlin, you say. With Madame Cressing, I presume? I'm surprised. My information was she rarely leaves her villa in St Germain-en-Laye.'

I could not hide my surprise. I had had no idea John's mother was alive, let alone living in France. In spite of so wishing to appear mistress of myself, I stammered 'His mother?'

Colin and Ratton exchanged a mischievous look. 'Dear me, no, Evelyn,' Colin said, crossing the room and taking my arm. He began to steer me towards the door. 'His wife. Now you must excuse us, we have business to attend to.'

His words disarmed me entirely and I ran to my rooms and locked the door. In the house all was bustle and busyness; I could hear the occasional grunt and shout of men as they re-organised things, the shriek and scurry of women as they struggled to accommodate the changes and tidy up the mess. In my little enclave everything was still, my few belongings secure in their accustomed places but the same could not be said for my thoughts.

They jostled and jockeyed; ideas and solid rocks of fact which had stood immoveable for as long as I had known John were reconfiguring themselves and I, in my turn, twisted and tortuously recalibrated my feelings to take account of them.

John. Married?

This, then, was the impediment he had referred to all those years before. How stupid I had been not to guess it.

How unnecessarily secretive he had been not to mention it. A wife married in haste and repented of would not have disturbed me; I had been too far gone in love to care. I could have assuaged my conscience with images of a shrewish harridan, a mindless doll or an anaemic invalid, any of which would have been wholly unsuitable for a man of John's humour, intelligence or vigour. I would have told myself that I had saved him as he, in reality, had saved me.

But a wife not repented of but only substituted as need and opportunity had presented itself? What about that? An agreeable, competent, warm-blooded, wife? A compatible wife? A wife who welcomed him home warmly to their villa in St Germain-en-Laye, who regretted but graciously coped with the many mysterious weeks her husband had to spend in England? An advocate for his work, a companion for his travels? This would have been a circle very difficult to square by any moral parameters I could have summoned, and provided an object of consuming envy neither reason nor integrity could have supported. I was jealous now, I realised, mad with it; I wanted John all to myself. If she had materialised in the room I would have scratched her eyes out. I pictured her beautiful, of course, and sophisticated, worldly-wise and modern. She was *au fait* with current political and philosophical thought, a tour-de-force of informed and interesting opinion on any subject under the sun. She was up to the minute in fashion and yet coquettish in French lace and the kind of underwear designed to shock women and titillate men. She was athletic and inventive in bed... Before my eyes she slipped a frilled robe from a shapely shoulder and fluttered come-to-bed eyes at John, *my* John, who stepped towards her and ran his hands over the milky mounds of her balconied bosom… The thought of it made me retch, and I dashed into the little bathroom and lost my breakfast down the bowl of the earth closet.

I had more reason than ever to keep in the shadows, after that; my humiliation was wretched. I could barely look any of the servants in the eye, let alone Colin or Sylvester Ratton. How glad I was of Colin's Butler and footmen, who would supervise things upstairs, and of Mr Percy, with whom I could communicate anything of importance if necessary. I had no need to encounter Ratton or Colin at all, I told myself. They were the last people I wanted to have anything to do with apart, perhaps, from John, towards whom I nursed a bitter, burning antagonism.

After dinner on that Friday everyone retired early both upstairs and down, but I found Mr Ratton loitering in the kitchen after midnight. It was a shock to find him there. He was uncomfortably close to my little suite of rooms. I felt vulnerable and afraid, also stupid and embarrassed.

'Just refreshing my memory,' he said, helping himself to a leg of chicken from the refrigerator. In the meagre light from an oil lamp which we kept burning all night in the kitchen, his face was as pallid and greasy as the skin of the chicken in his hand, his ugly nobble of nose like a piece of revolting gristle.

'You'll have no business down here,' I said, stiffly, 'not now you're "quite on equal standing."'

'One never knows,' Ratton remarked. 'Do you occupy your old rooms in the north wing?'

I shook my head. 'Others entirely.'

'The place has gone to pot,' he observed. 'A shadow of its former self. I am embarrassed by the squalor.' Although ostensibly referring to Tall Chimneys I could not help thinking his comment masked an underlying observation about myself. Is that how I appeared to him? A shadow of my former self? Squalid? An embarrassment?

'I have done my best,' I said, bitterly. 'Alone, without income.'

'You have not been entirely alone,' he said. He sauntered from one end of the kitchen to the other, gnawing on the chicken, occasionally lifting the lids of dishes Mrs Bittern had left semi-prepared for breakfast, running his finger along the window ledge and inspecting it for dust. I remained rooted to the spot, unwilling to yield up possession of the room to him, less willing still to indicate to him the direction in which my rooms might lie. At last, with much sucking and slobbering, he finished the chicken and laid the bone on the table, a greasy imposition on that otherwise pristine, scrubbed surface. He smiled at me, showing shreds of chicken in his teeth, and licked his lips with deliberate and sickening intention. Then he gave me an odd, stiff little bow before leaving the room.

I could not sleep that night, hearing footsteps in the passageway outside my room, thinking the door handle was turning. At three or four a.m. I even considered throwing on some clothes and climbing up to the gatehouse, where I had always felt safe. But the idea of allowing him to intimidate me that far rankled. In any case I feared the gatehouse would be tainted for me, now, its haven in some way invaded and compromised by John's secret wife. I held fast until dawn glimmered through a chink in the thick curtains, and I heard the first blackbirds in the kitchen garden.

The following day I unpacked the boxes and restored Tall Chimneys' treasures to their rightful places, as far as I was able. Most of the silver went back into the strong room but some few pieces were allowed to adorn the dining room. Usually decisions of this kind, as well as overall responsibility for the household silver, should fall to the Butler, but as he was only temporarily in authority at Tall Chimneys I undertook the task myself. Colin, Ratton and Mr Percy spent the morning ensconced in the library, calling for a buffet luncheon at one. In the afternoon the telephone rang and we had news the rest of the party had arrived at the station - cars were sent to collect them. I went through the baize door and down the stairs as though down to my lair, intent on remaining there no matter what, for the duration of the house party.

Of course it was an impossible plan. My assistance was required at every juncture. Some of the gentlemen who arrived brought their own valets, who had to be accommodated. There was more bed-making to be done, towels to be distributed. Some gentlemen arrived without valets, declaring themselves quite able to manage, but then rang the bell every five minutes, and I was up and down the stairs repeatedly. The demand for hot water was inordinate – I had no notion men could demand so many baths. The furnace needed constant attention and in the end I sent for a lad from the village to tend it night and day. Then there was a rush and scuffle for the boot room and the press as valets tried to get their gentlemen's evening attire prepared.

Of course they talked, they let names drop and it was impossible not to know who we had under the roof, as much as I might try to distance myself from them. The guests of honour were Mr Oswald Mosley, leader of the British Union of Fascists and William Joyce, his right hand man. The novelist Henry Williamson, writer of Tarka the Otter, fresh from his recent visit to Germany also formed one of the party, and Neville Chamberlain, Colin's great advocate, Chancellor of the Exchequer. Several other men, minor satellites of Mosley's or governmental flunkeys made up the numbers. Chamberlain was already being tipped as the next Prime Minister; everyone agreed Baldwin had had his day. It seemed the Fascists hoped to convince Chamberlain to join them, stop the drive for rearmament and to seek to make stronger links between the British Government and those in Spain, Italy and Germany. To this end a number of foreign emissaries also formed part of the company, in particular three very austere German gentlemen, resplendent in military regalia, high boots and peculiar trousers very wide around the thigh and tight around the knee. There were two dark, shifty-looking Italians and a portly Spaniard who seemed to speak very little English - certainly, his valet spoke none - and, in any case, was suffering from a terrible cold for which his servant had to prepare a number of noxious-smelling remedies during the course of his stay.[7]

---

[7] There is no historical basis whatsoever that any meeting or informal conference such as the one I describe here ever took place. I am simply creating a link between Mr Chamberlain's efforts to pacify German aggression later in the

We sent tea up to the music room at four and then sat down to our own meal, a hurried affair under constant threat of interruption by the company above. The loud guffaw of male voices, the thick waft of cigar smoke, a cacophony of accents and the sound of someone playing the piano quite execrably emanated through the hallway and down to us in the servants' hall, drowning out most conversation. After tea they called for whisky. The heat and volume of the discussions above reached a climax only just equalled by the furore in the kitchen as Mrs Bittern prepared the various courses for dinner more hampered than helped by the well-meaning but perhaps misguided assistance of the village women. I had to soothe over one volatile outburst after another, smooth ruffled feathers, placate and mollify at every turn. At last the crisis passed and the dishes began to assemble themselves on the table; dressed salmon, roasted game, golden pies and glossy syllabubs in splendid array. In spite of the drama, they looked, to me, at any rate, really excellent, and my mouth watered even though I had eaten a few mouthfuls along with the rest earlier. The homely fare, plain stews and simple accompaniments I had served up for so many years seemed paltry, now, and unappealing. I suddenly wondered what John was eating, perhaps with his wife, what delicacies of German cuisine, rich sauces and fine wines they had had laid before them. Thoughts like these had distracted me throughout the day. I was beginning to doubt everything he had told me in his letter - the mysterious 'Jean', sculptor would be unlikely to make a third, wouldn't he? Unless it was a *ménage à trois* ... Really my opinion of John was such at that moment I would have put nothing past him, there was no excess of depravity or dishonesty of which I could not believe him capable.

The dressing bell rang at six thirty and the men all repaired to their rooms to bathe and change. I took the opportunity to visit the music room in order to ensure everything was in order, the tea things cleared, the fire well-stocked with fuel, and to supervise the lighting of the candles in the dining room. I busied myself around the rooms, plumping cushions,

---

decade and the Fascist movement led by Oswald Mosley which took Hitler's successes in Germany as its model.

drawing curtains, straightening chairs, the kinds of task which few men would notice had even been done, but I felt a kind of pride in my home, especially now it had been restored to an order as good as any I could ever remember. I felt vaguely uncomfortable about Colin's political leanings although, from what John had said, the situation in Germany under Chancellor Hitler was better than it had been for many years, industry booming, standards of living good, national pride at an all-time high. In comparison Britain was all depression and gloom. There was something about the Fascists which did not sit comfortably with me, but if Colin was going to keep Tall Chimneys up, use it, maintain and improve it, and would allow me to continue living there, I thought I might tolerate his political leanings. What impact could they have on me, here, I reasoned, so many miles from London? And if John - well, I hardly dared think about John; perhaps he did not intend to return. In that case, I considered, I would need my home here at Tall Chimneys more than ever, regardless of my brother's politics.

My thoughts were interrupted by a slight sound behind me. I turned, instantly defensive, expecting Sylvester Ratton to be lurking, but in fact it was Giles Percy, flushed and animated as I had not seen him before, his blond hair rather tousled, the collar of his usually immaculately pressed shirt askew. It was obvious to me he was tipsy. I found this rather appealing, a welcome change to the precise and very proficient automaton he usually presented.

'I thought you were all dressing for dinner,' I said, 'so I risked coming up, to make sure everything is in order.'

He grinned; a boyish, charming grin which utterly erased his habitual implacable façade. 'It's going awfully well,' he said. 'Everyone is very pleased.' His eyes, in the candlelight, shone. 'How are things down below?'

I smiled at his gaffe but it was a smile tinged with sadness. *Down below* was the old-fashioned euphemism used by nannies and nurses for a girl's private parts, according to polite thinking not a concept which should occupy a gentleman's mind let alone a phrase which should sully his mouth. Once, when I had suggested this to John - tangled in the sheets of the bed, the French windows open to the cooling breezes of a summer night, the moonlight a pale sliver across the carpet of the bedroom floor, the smell of sex on his breath - he had denied being a gentleman since my *down below* was almost constantly on his mind and as often as possible in his mouth. The memory of it pierced me, now.

'Below *stairs'* I corrected, gently. Giles' disarming manner, his gauche, slightly inebriated state lifted my melancholy. In this softer, more human iteration I found him powerfully attractive. I found myself wondering if *he* was married and then, rather shockingly, knowing I did not care.

Giles blushed, and stammered, 'Below stairs, indeed.'

I finished lighting the candles and blew out the taper. The wisp of smoke drifted in the air between us, connecting us in a miasmic haze. The fire in the grate crackled. High, high above us, at the top of the rigid column of decorative brick, on the chimney top, a rook cawed in the gloaming, using the smoke from the fire to fumigate its feathers. Its cry came down to us, disembodied and strange, as something raw and wild and almost dangerous. I placed the taper on the mantelpiece and took the three or four steps across the carpet which brought me to where Giles stood. I gave him a straight look. I could smell the whisky on his breath, see past the glassiness of his blue eyes to a deep, beckoning pool beyond, feel the heat which rose from the confines of his dinner clothes. Whether from our sudden closeness, or from his earlier blunder, or the abrupt realisation he was not quite sober and that it would not do, he stiffened quite perceptibly. The little window which had been opened up to me in his clipped, efficient, entirely proper demeanour was beginning to close.

'Indeed, yes,' I said, recklessly, into the taut silence between us. 'Everything is in eager readiness down below.'

I left him, stupid with shock, in the dining room.

From the raucous laughter which emanated down from the dining room and later the music room, we gathered the dinner had been a wild success. The Butler and footmen of Colin's staff served brandy with coffee and left a drinks trolley laden with decanters and bottles from which the guests were to help themselves and did so, it transpired, with great liberality. The men servants then retired below stairs bringing with them the unfinished wine from dinner, which they clearly considered a perk of the job; they brought glasses and distributed it among them. The staff from the village had already departed. The cook and the kitchen maid had gone to bed. I was the sole remaining member of the household staff still up and they kindly included me in their libations. I am ashamed to say I probably partook more liberally than I ought to have done; fatigue, relief and a sort of heady recklessness overtook me. With their jackets off and shirt studs removed, their shoe laces slackened, the men became almost unguarded, human, as they had not seemed before. They seemed genuinely excited by the prospect of the talks upstairs, that an agreement between the parties could be a new beginning for our country and a restoration of dignity and productivity for the working people. Mr Mosley, it transpired, was a powerful and persuasive speaker; one of the men had heard him at a rally in London and followed his cause ever since. 'We're in a struggle for our country,' he opined, pouring more wine into his glass, 'that's what Mr Mosley understands and what he's trying to get these governmental men to buy in to. Mr Hitler has done it and look at Germany! If we're not careful countries like Spain and Italy will overtake us. Us! The Britain my father and brothers died for! It's been going to the dogs for years, but this is our chance, now.'

The other men all nodded sagely.

'My husband says Germany is a country ahead of us in many ways,' I ventured.

'Indeed he is quite correct, Mrs Johns,' the loquacious man replied. 'It makes you wonder who really won the war, doesn't it? The Germans took the opportunity for a new beginning and look what a success they have made of it, whereas here, we've tried to go on as we always have done, old-fashioned and backwards-looking, keeping to traditions that are years out of date and should be consigned to the pyre. This house....'

One of the men coughed. 'It's a fine old place,' he murmured. Perhaps he had gathered my connection with the place was more than just occupational.

'It's a museum piece, alright,' the man conceded, with a sneer, 'but there will be no place for houses like this in the new order.'

'Why not?' I asked, in a small voice.

'Because they benefit a few people rather than many people.'

I thought about taking issue with him. Over the generations Tall Chimneys and my family's other properties had sustained and benefitted countless people through work and patronage. 'You're a Communist, then?'

'Not me,' he retorted, 'I'm a fascist and proud of it.'

'I'm not sure I really know the difference,' I admitted.

'You're not alone,' he smiled. 'Communism is about economics, fascism is about nationalism. Communism is about equality – everyone gets the same whether they earn or deserve it - but fascism is about merit. In a fascist country people like me can rise.' He sat back in his chair and drew on his cigarette. 'Yes,' he nodded, and repeated almost to himself, 'people like me can rise.' I thought about Sylvester Ratton, living proof that in Mr Mosley's regime small men could become powerful, and shuddered.

An hour or so later the men took themselves off to bed. Their talk had continued but I had played no part in it. I had continued to drink, though, my body and my head unaccustomed to the wine and yet steadily carrying on, as though seeking some oblivion which would not come. At the back of my mind was always the malevolent nearness of Ratton and, overshadowing even that, an image of John in the arms of somebody else.

At last the noises above stairs abated and I crept up to make sure doors were locked and fires had been left safe. I looked at it all aghast. The rooms were in disarray; glasses strewn everywhere, sticky rings on polished wood, furniture awry. Candles had been left to burn themselves down, their wax building yellowish stalagmites on the mantle-piece. There were casings of cigar ash on chair-arms, cushions on the floor, rugs askew. The unaccustomed evidences of masculinity seemed like an invasion, the wanton consumption of fuel and spirits, the careless treatment of furnishings like a kind of affront. Things had been moved around and disturbed to such a degree I felt personally molested, interfered with in a way that was outrageous. I banked down the fires and gathered the crystal together for the maids to carry down early in the morning, straightened rugs and restored soft furnishings but it all seemed unsatisfactory and ineffectual. I pulled back the curtains and opened the window sashes a little to admit fresh air to stir the fug but the staleness remained, stubborn and inert. I moved in a sort of jealous trance, outwardly calm and serene, like a hollow ghost, but inwardly seething with possessive fire. Regardless of the remedial influence brought about by Colin, the repairs and improvements, the literally life-saving consequences of him deciding to use the house, I didn't consider it to be his. It was mine and I wanted it back. But the rooms looked back at me with a sort of satiated smugness, as though they had enjoyed their mistreatment. 'This is what we were meant for,' they seemed to say. 'You know, we were never really yours.'

'Like John,' I thought, bitterly.

The cruelty of it was too much; everyone, it seemed, had turned their backs on me. I had no one and nothing. I was out of place, out of step, out of time. The loneliness was overwhelming.

I would like to be able to tell you that he came to my room in the night and took me by surprise. That I put up at least a token resistance. That I was seduced. But none of those things would be true. I took my candle and mounted the silent stairs. The shadow I cast on the new-painted walls was grotesque. In the hall the ancient long-case clock ticked with a sound like 'tut, tut, tut,' a head-shaking, finger-waving, sad remonstrance, but still I climbed to the landing and trod along the corridor to where I knew his room to be. I turned the handle and it yielded. I blew out my candle and stepped inside.

The room was dark and thick with the smell of inebriated male; a sour, chemical top-note of whisky overlaid a pungent vegetable baseline of cigar. Somewhere beneath and behind these was the smell of the man himself and his heat pervaded the room – it must have been him as no glimmer of fire remained in the grate. He must have opened the window before going to bed; the curtain billowed slightly in a breath of breeze, admitting also a sliver of moonlight by which I could make out the bed and his sleeping form. He was lying outside the covers in a semi-foetal positon, one arm thrown across the bed and the other sandwiched between his thighs. His blond hair looked like silk on the linen of the pillow. His shoulders, buttocks and thighs were well-formed and very pale, like alabaster, almost with a luminosity of their own. The heat in the room was almost suffocating; emanating not from him, I realised, but from me. I felt breathless and almost panicked by its intensity, as though I was literally melting and dissolving like the wax candles below. I began to pull off my clothes in a frenzy. But the more layers I pulled off the hotter I became, ignited by a burning fire which no amount of nakedness would ever extinguish. In the end, stripped entirely but still consumed by a passion so intense I felt like a human torch, I slipped onto the bed beside him.

His skin was cool, a balm I hungered for. He half woke as I pressed myself against him, turning in confusion as I rained kisses over the quenching coolness of his skin. I do not know if he would have remonstrated with me; whatever words were on his lips were swallowed by my eager mouth before he could utter them. My hands ranged over him – his chest, his navel, his buttocks, his groin. Whatever refusal his words might have uttered his body denied – he was erect in my hand and soon his own hands were as feverish as mine, assimilating my body with urgent caresses. We rolled across the bed, clutching and grasping at each other, kissing and biting with such ferocity it was hard to tell whether we were fighting or making love. Then I had him inside me. He was young, I suppose, and perhaps inexperienced. He came very quickly, too quickly. My arousal was not assuaged but he collapsed on top of me, panting and wet with perspiration. I moved underneath him, urging him on.

'Don't stop,' I whispered, 'we haven't finished.'

He groaned and it occurred to me with a dreadful, sickening awareness he was only half awake. 'Wha...?' he mumbled, lifting a hand and sweeping across his face. His eyes were closed, had remained closed throughout, I thought.

I pushed him over onto his back and sat astride him, but it was no good; he was semi-flaccid and already his breathing had returned to a stertorous snore. His head was twisted on the pillow. He wasn't looking at me, he probably didn't even know who I was or if I existed at all. I would be a boyish fantasy, half-remembered, just a wet-dream.

I climbed off the bed and got dressed. My passion, although not appeased, had shrivelled. I felt cold and sick and sober, and very ashamed.

I went down the servants' stairs and tiptoed along the service corridors back to my room. It was dawn. Across the silent moors and down through the still plantation I heard the bells ringing from the parish church. It was Easter Day, the day of forgiveness, new life, renewed hope. The sound increased my wretchedness. I wanted to crawl on my hands and knees to the church and confess to my friend the rector, beg forgiveness of the man on the cross. But I knew neither would shrive me. Only John could do that. I got undressed and climbed into bed without lighting the candle or looking at myself in the mirror.

THE FOLLOWING DAY the King[8] came to Tall Chimneys, with Mrs Simpson.

They arrived in a closed car; the weather had turned dreary with drizzle, it must have seemed to them they were coming to a sorry, sodden hole of a place. He climbed out with his hat pulled well down, she wore a scarf and dark glasses. She was taller than he was, very thin and not at all as attractive as I had expected. From my position in the hall, lined up with the other staff, and in my admittedly jaundiced mood, I failed to see what all the fuss was about.

Colin hurried down the steps with an umbrella and they were ushered inside, past us, and into the music room where the gentlemen waited.

My wretchedness from the night before persisted; even such an honour as this could not lift my mood. I was disgusted with myself and hung over to boot. I roamed aimlessly around the servants' halls and felt sorry for myself. I longed for the day to be over, for the morning to come when the guests would all depart leaving me alone at Tall Chimneys. I did my best to quell the excited gossip of the village women, who had guessed - correctly - the identity of our mysterious guests, and avoided at all costs seeing Giles. I had no idea what, if anything, he would recall from our encounter. As far as I was concerned, the less the better.

Of course my seclusion could not last. After luncheon the gentlemen went into the library to brief His Royal Highness on their discussions thus far, and Mrs Simpson went into a sitting room which had been expressly prepared for her. One of the secretaries was supposed to keep her company but he was soon summoned to the library and I was sent for. I tidied myself as much as I could and picked up a piece of sewing to

---

[8] It is well known that Edward VIII admired Hitler's economic, cultural and social reforms in Germany and it is suspected that he had Nazi leanings. Therefore it seemed likely to me that the imaginary conference I describe as taking place at Tall Chimneys would have included him as an invitee.

occupy my hands. At the door of the room I paused and took a few deep breaths. It came to me, in that short interval, we were very much in the same boat, Mrs Simpson and I. We were both at Tall Chimneys more or less incognito, connected far more intimately to our men than we ought to be, very much on the wrong side of every boundary you could name. As I entered the room, instead of awe and awkwardness what I actually felt for the poor, shivering woman I found, was pity.

She was huddled into a small armchair she had pushed as close as possible to the fire. She was poking ineffectually at it but it hardly emitted any heat - somebody had put damp logs on it and only a thick, acrid, yellowish smoke rose from the grate. Mrs Simpson wore a thin cardigan over a plain blouse. The scarf she had worn earlier was draped across her shoulders. I have no doubt the cardigan was cashmere and the blouse and scarf both silk, but they seemed to provide no warmth. Her face was pinched; a deep frown slashed her bony forehead which her starkly parted hair made very prominent in her face. I could see she wore a good deal of make-up but it did not disguise her discomfort. Bright red lipstick made her mouth seem very wide, and emphasised a blemish on the left side of her chin. Apart from the poker her hands were empty; she didn't seem to have any reading material with her, or anything at all to occupy the lonely hours she must have known she faced while the men talked.

I bobbed a curtsey - probably wrong - and went across to fire to mend it, taking the poker from her hand, which was ice cold.

'I've been sent to see if you need anything, ma'am,' I said. 'I can see immediately that you do.'

She gave me a wan smile and leant back in her chair as though exhausted. I soon had the fire burning better, and pulled the thick curtain across the window, to block out the draught. I lit the lamps and rang the bell. 'Bring tea,' I said, 'hot tea, and toast, and that thick mohair blanket from the settle in the hall.'

I took the liberty of tucking the blanket around her legs while she dozed, easing off her high heeled shoes and chafing her feet, which were frozen.

She allowed my ministrations without a murmur, and when the tea came I poured her a cup without asking and placed it on a table at her side. She roused herself enough to drink it, both hands cupping the fine porcelain, before lapsing back into sleep. Satisfied I had done everything I could to bring her ease, and with the fire now burning very brightly and the room altogether more cheerful and comfortable, I gingerly took another armchair and settled to my sewing.

Presently I looked up to find her eyes on me. 'What's your position here?' she asked.

I decided it was pointless to prevaricate. 'I hardly know,' I admitted, putting down my work. 'I am Colin Talbot's sister. I live here permanently but you wouldn't call me the lady of the house. Up until a few weeks ago I lived here alone, practically.'

'Ah! You're the reclusive sister.' Her American accent was pronounced; it would be clichéd to call it a drawl but it certainly had a languorous quality to it.

I felt a brief surge of anger. Her privacy had been protected at all costs, I fumed. Everything had been cloak-and-dagger to the extent I hadn't even known she was coming. My affairs, in contrast, it seemed, had been thoroughly discussed. 'I'm not a recluse,' I retorted. 'At least, not by choice. It seems to have been my fate, though. It's the part that has fallen to my lot, for good or ill. I can't deny, before the visit of these gentlemen, and yourself, Tall Chimneys has had no visitors since 1929.'

'Good God!' she ejaculated, and then, more musingly. 'What bliss.'

We sent for more tea. She smoked cigarettes. I told her what I could about the house - its history, as far as I knew it, about my brother George and the difficulties his death had caused. She seemed very interested to know how I had coped, all alone. 'I wasn't quite alone,' I mumbled, 'not all of the time, anyway.'

'I see,' she said, knowingly. 'Now I think about it, something was mentioned. I know Mr Cressing's work, in fact. I attended an exhibition of his, I believe.'

I said, wryly 'It seems you know all my secrets.'

'Don't you know, dear, there are no secrets,' she replied, bitterly.

We spoke of John for a while, and of the art scene in general. Mrs Simpson was surprisingly well informed. As I described John's work I was conscious of a pit of longing for him deep in my stomach. 'I wish he was here,' I blurted out at last.

'I'm sure you do,' she said, warmly.

From the library the hum of masculine voices had been growing louder as we talked. Subliminally I had heard the tread of feet along the corridor, the chink of glasses on a tray. 'The men have called for drinks,' I said. 'They must want whisky instead of tea. Perhaps the meeting has come to a close.'

'I'd like some whisky too,' Mrs Simpson said, stretching her feet out and groping with a silk-stockinged toe for her shoes. 'I ought to go and freshen up. Will you show me the way?'

I showed her up to her room where, I was pleased to see, a fire burned and the best towels had been laid ready. Her maid stood by to draw her a bath, evening clothes were laid across the bed and on the dressing table a case of jewels stood open.

'You won't join us for dinner, I am told,' she said to me as she paused on the threshold. I shook my head.

'That's a pity. Send the whisky, will you?'

As I came back down the stairs I was conscious of a sense of disappointment our afternoon's tête-à-tête had come to an end and that I could not indeed bathe and dress and go down to dine with Mrs Simpson and the men. Why should I be pushed into the shadows? Why had life left me marooned and increasingly out of step with its progress? I could not recall the last time I had spent so pleasant a time, or so long a time with another woman. The rector's daughters - all now married and moved away - and those well-to-do neighbours with whom I had briefly socialised were all my experience of such a thing. It had been comfortable and companionable. In spite of the disparity of our situations in life our circumstances had been surprisingly equal. I felt beneath the adverse publicity and manufactured scandal which attached itself to Mrs Simpson she was a woman like me, a woman who had found her soul-mate and would defy society's disapproval in order to keep him.

My longing for John was accompanied by a stab of guilt about Giles Percy, and, as though conjured up by it, there he was in actuality at the foot of the stairs as I arrived in the hall. His look on seeing me is hard to describe. He blushed, and a film of sweat broke out on his upper lip. I thought at first he would swivel on his heel and rush off to some excuse of an important task but he remained rooted. He opened his mouth to speak but no words came forth. His narrowed eyes spoke questions, doubts. A groove between his eyebrows denoted confusion. His head was tilted in such a way that one does when one has misheard something, or heard something that is just too impossible to believe.

He isn't sure, I thought to myself. He thinks something happened but he isn't quite sure. He thinks it might have been a dream.

I put on my very coolest manner. 'Good afternoon Mr Percy,' I said. 'How are the discussions going? I have spent the most pleasant afternoon with our lady guest.'

'Oh! Very well,' he stammered. 'That is to say, quite well, in the main, although, on one or two points... but no. That's all *in camera* as we say.'

'Everything at Tall Chimneys is *in camera*' I quipped, ambiguously.

Down the passageway I could see Colin emerging from the library flanking the King on one side, Mr Ratton flanking the other. The absurdity of this juxtaposition made me want to laugh out loud; Colin all scrawny with his ridiculous belt askew, Ratton - wobble-paunched and piggy-eyed, full of his own self-importance, and between them the King, suave and perfectly groomed, his hands clasped behind his back.

Percy's gaze followed mine and it reminded him of something he needed to tell me. 'They won't be staying, after all,' he murmured. 'After dinner, they'll discreetly withdraw.'

'Very well,' I nodded, and made quickly for the servants' door.

As Giles had predicted, the King and Mrs Simpson drove away after dinner, and I didn't see either of them again. I gathered a tone of discontent at the visit amongst the gentlemen left behind - it seemed things had not gone as well as Mosley and his cronies had hoped. Clearly the King had been hesitant about lending his voice to their cause. None of them stayed up late, and I was glad of it. I checked the fires and extinguished the lamps and took to my own bed as soon as I could, but sleep evaded me. I felt too tired to rest, strangely achy and uncomfortable. The image of the King and Mrs Simpson haunted me. I pictured them travelling through the night, the rain beading the windows of the car. I hoped she had a blanket, and was warm.

The next day, all was hustle and rush as the gentlemen packed up their papers and maps and departed. Cars drove them to the station to catch their trains. Only Colin, Ratton and the secretaries remained for luncheon, a scratch kind of meal, taken in haste.

I had the opportunity of a brief conversation with Colin before he too departed. I found him in the library staring out of the window at the soggy lawn and dripping trees beyond.

'Have things gone as you hoped?' I asked, gathering together the coffee cups which had been left on the table. I meant, really, whether he had been pleased with the way I had managed the house, but he misinterpreted my question.

'Very much so,' he said, busying himself with a sheaf of documents. 'Mosley is pleased. We will forge ahead with our plans. He has been invited to visit Mussolini.'

'I am glad for you,' I said. 'When do you think you'll be back here? Shall I keep the cook and the maids on? If the house is to be kept in readiness, I can't manage on my own.'

'About that,' Colin said, indicating I should take a seat. 'Surely you don't want to? Wouldn't you rather come to London, with us?'

I was stunned. 'I hadn't thought,' I stammered. 'To your London house, do you mean?'

'Ah, well temporarily, perhaps. But not long-term. Naturally you'd want to find your own way, wouldn't you?'

I laughed, incredulously, 'On what? I have no means!'

Colin made a show of rummaging for his handkerchief, and mopping his eyes. 'Women work, these days,' he said at last. 'In shops and offices and factories. You could find something.'

The idea appalled me, not because I was shy of work, or considered myself above menial or clerical tasks, but because it suddenly hit me that to go out into the world would be to leave behind, probably forever, Tall Chimneys and my enchanted life with John.

'What is to become of Tall Chimneys, then?' I asked, in a small voice. 'Do you intend to sell it? Or knock it down?'

'Hardly,' he sneered, 'not when I have spent a king's ransom on the repairs, and had all the silver brought back. I shall use it, from time to time, or allow my friends to do so.' He gave me a straight look.

'Do you mean Ratton?' I spat.

'It's possible, amongst others. I don't know why you have taken such a dislike to him. It's he, to tell the truth, who suggested you might prefer to come away.'

That settled it. Nothing on earth would persuade me to go to London with Colin. 'I told you,' I cried, 'he molested me. He almost raped me. He *would* have done if John...'

Colin made a moue of distaste. 'He remembers things differently. And, really, you're in no position to take the moral high ground, now, are you?'

His hypocrisy astounded me. 'Neither me nor Mrs Simpson,' I said, through gritted teeth, 'but if Ratton had attacked *her* I think you'd have something to say about it.'

'Now you're being ridiculous.'

I sighed. 'So you're going to keep Tall Chimneys on, then. You'll need a housekeeper.'

'Yes. But I'm offering you something else. Another opportunity. Don't you think you've been cloistered here too long? Wouldn't you like to step out into the world and see what's out there?'

I considered his proposition. I could go to London, find work and somewhere to live - Ratton would never have to know where. John could work there, as well as here, and he'd be closer to the hub of things. Now I knew our relationship could never be regularised, we could never be 'respectable', we might as well be disreputable in London as here at Tall Chimneys, and perhaps it would be easier, in the metropolis. That was, assuming John wished to carry on our relationship, or even came back from Europe at all. Without John, I didn't think I could face the Capital. There was a chance that, if I stayed in Yorkshire, I'd stay alone. But at Tall Chimneys I felt safe. I knew, whatever befell out in the world, I could survive and even thrive if Colin were prepared to keep the house. From what I read in the newspapers, London was an awful place, dirty and crowded. Politically I did not like the way things were going. There were even whispers of war; German troops had already occupied the Rhineland and Italy was fighting in Abyssinia; where would be next?

I looked around the library. Even with all its unhappy associations - I could picture Ratton, even now, standing proprietorially on the hearth - in its newly refurbished state, it felt like part of me. The sense of belonging extended throughout the house to its remotest room; the furniture felt like my bones, the curtains and draperies like my skin. Up the slope of the driveway, through the belt of woodland, I pictured the gatehouse, my last bastion, my place of peace. Tall Chimneys comprised all my memories. It was my world.

'No,' I said, firmly. 'Thank you, but no. I want to stay here, if you'll allow it.'

'Very well,' Colin said. 'Keep the gardener and a maid on, for now, but dismiss the rest. If we need to re-engage them, we will.'

Clearly, Colin had concluded our discussion, and done his duty, as he saw it, to his sister. He thrust the letters he had been holding into a folder and began patting his pockets, checking for his wallet and cigarette case. But there were some things I needed to get established. 'You'll fund their wages?' I asked, 'and the upkeep of the house?'

'Yes, yes.' He said, impatiently, making for the door. 'But not on any lavish scale. Be prudent.'

'Of course I will,' I said. 'And, Colin, just one more thing.'

He was already at the door. In the hallway, I could see Ratton loitering. The secretaries had assembled their boxes of documents and their portable type-writers on the steps. Giles Percy was loading things into the back of one of the motorcars.

'Yes?'

'About John. You have no objection...?'

'If you want to make a fool of yourself over him, go ahead,' he said, coldly. 'You could have done much better for yourself. You do know that, don't you?'

Ratton stepped forward just then and took the packet of papers from Colin's hand. They both looked at me, Colin with an icy reproach, Ratton will ill-disguised contempt.

'I'll be the judge of that,' I said.

I dismissed the two gardeners, Mrs Bittern and the kitchen maid that afternoon. They cleared out their belongings and left immediately; the kitchen maid didn't even finish washing the lunch dishes. I told Rose she could come to the house five days a week, and Kenneth likewise, but sent them both home early. I wanted Tall Chimneys to myself again.

The drizzle cleared towards the end of the afternoon and a watery sunshine warmed the vaporous air, giving it a brightness that was magical, like an aura; it touched everything and made it fresh and new. Everything shone, new-washed and lush with moisture; the lawn looked as though it had been strewn with diamonds. I wandered round my domain in a kind of dream. The gardens were burgeoning, neatly groomed as they had not been for many a year. The kitchen garden was already beginning to yield crops. The fountain splashed and, as I watched, a robin came and drank. He looked at me with a beady, conspiratorial eye.

Inside, everything was untidy with the haste of departure - furniture askew, cushions everywhere, beds unmade and damp towels in heaps. It was dirty with the kind of carelessness which only men can leave; clods of mud from unwiped boots, worms of cigarette ash, abandoned glasses. But I gloried in it. The house was sound once more, repaired, the neglect of years made good. The furnace was well-stocked, the generator purring like a cat on cream. Damp plaster had been replaced, paintwork refreshed, windows repaired. Better still, the house's treasures had been restored; cabinets shone with curios, benign ancestors smiled vaguely down from the walls. In the strong room, I knew, the silver glowed dully. Perhaps by accident, perhaps on purpose, a new radiogram had been left behind, a vast improvement on the old Marconi I had been using in the servants' hall. I felt more like a chatelaine than a skivvy, although, over the following days, there would be much work to be done.

As dusk fell I took myself into the kitchen and raided the refrigerator for left-overs. I took them to the dining room and helped myself to a glass of wine from a decanter on the sideboard. I dined in state; the curtains open onto the darkening night, a fire burning in the grate, the candles blazing. Music played from the radio. The house wrapped itself around me and I felt in some strange way as though I was not alone.

That night I took a bath in Mrs Simpson's bathroom, running the hot water until it almost slopped over the sides of the tub. I wallowed in it, drinking more wine, hearing the strains of the light programme floating through the house and up the stairs. When I got out, tiredness overtook me and I climbed into the bed which the King and Mrs Simpson were to have shared, and slept like the dead.

1936 - 1941

The spring and summer of 1936 stand out in my memory as a kind of arcadia. True to his word, Colin arranged regular payments into a bank account and I had a cheque book I could draw on for supplies of fuel and groceries and to pay the wages of Rose and Kenneth. I abandoned immediately the dour uniform with which I had been supplied by Giles Percy, and ordered myself some new clothes. Nothing flashy, but much more *à la mode* for the time. I ordered two calf-length skirts, figure-hugging over the hips and nipped in at the waist, and some brightly coloured blouses and long-line jackets and cardigans for warmth. I had some floral print day dresses, too, which were ideal for the unusually warm weather we had that year. I subscribed to some women's magazines; *Nash's* and *The Woman's Companion*, and from these I found I could stop wearing the dreadfully constricting underwear I had been struggling with and adopt newer and much more comfortable alternatives. The articles in the magazines brought me up to date with women's issues, politics and literature as well as fashion. I found out, for the first time, about the work of Marie Stopes, who had opened one of her clinics in Leeds, not thirty miles away.

When Rose saw the parcels being delivered she asked me why I had not simply gone into town to buy my clothes. I had never dreamed of such a thing!

'It's easy, there's a bus takes you all the way from the village,' she said.

The idea of it sounded like an expedition to the North Pole, to me.

I spent my mornings helping Rose around the house. I thoroughly enjoyed her bright, gossipy chatter as she filled me in on the news in the village and I found myself laughing often, and lapping up that species of close female friendship I hadn't enjoyed since my school days. I worked hard, although she did most of the really gruelling jobs. We closed off the north wing altogether and most of the bedrooms, keeping only a small number of the principal suites in readiness for guests, should they come. In the same way we made sure the library, dining room and drawing room were always clean, with fresh flowers in vases, but shrouded the rest. We aired all the rooms when the weather was clement, and, when it wasn't we lit fires to keep the chimneys clear. I seriously toyed with the idea of moving my things to what I thought of as Mrs Simpson's rooms but decided against it in case Colin or some of his cronies descended on us at the last minute; it would be embarrassing to have to move out in haste, and I didn't want to put myself in the position of having to play the role of hostess.

In the afternoons I put on some of John's old trousers and went out to help Kenneth in the gardens. I thoroughly enjoyed weeding the ornamental beds on my knees, sticking the peas and gathering in the produce. He mowed the lawns with a recalcitrant petrol mower he had stripped down and repaired, and clipped the hedges, laboriously, by hand. He didn't say much; nodding at a shrub and telling me its name, eyeing the sky and predicting 'rain later' or 'fair for the rest of the day.' His conversation tended to boil down to the essential verb and object ('ought to water the lettuces'; 'need to order onion setts'), obfuscating somewhat who, exactly, was to do the watering or ordering. But we rubbed along and got things done between us, developing an almost telepathic connection so I knew without him having to tell me when to step in to hold an awkward branch for pruning, what screw or nut he might need to fix an engine, and he seemed instinctively to know when I needed help, handling a grouchy cockerel, for instance, and would appear as if by magic in the poultry yard just at the right moment. Most of the time we worked very happily in companionable silence. When Rose joined us for a cup of tea in the middle of the afternoon she talked enough for all three of us.

The greenhouses and raised beds were so productive I regularly sent them both home with baskets of fruit and vegetables and eggs. Financially, things were as difficult as ever for working people. Kenneth's father had been killed in the war and he supplemented what his mother earned in the shop from the wages I paid him and what other money he could earn locally doing odd jobs. In return, Rose brought meat from her father's shop and Kenneth brought baked goods; Mrs Greene was the pre-eminent baker of the WI. A grocer's van began to call once a week, from which I bought some tinned and dry goods but I made it a habit to buy things from the local shop too.

With all my work and exercise I found I was ravenous at the end of the day. Sometimes, at night, I got up and feasted on food from the refrigerator, standing in the yellow light of its open door in my nightdress gobbling cheese and cold meat, or glugging milk straight from the pitcher in the pantry. I was sorry for it in the mornings, though, queasy and unsettled until mid-day.

As well as confectionery, Kenneth's mother sent me an invitation to attend one of the WI meetings. My standing in the community was very moot and I agonised over whether I should attend for quite a while. In days gone by none of the family would have dreamed of attending an event organised by or for the 'ordinary' village people other than, in a rather patronising way, to have shown their faces as a mark of special favour or approval. I feared the few older village inhabitants who were ex-employees at the house might resent or suspect my participation. Loyalty to the Talbots and the 'Big House' might remain strong enough to quash any criticism but then again it might make people feel entitled to voice it. That I would be the target of criticism, I had no doubt. To some in the village I would be the eccentric recluse who lived at Tall Chimneys, to others, undoubtedly, I would be the Jezebel who lived over the brush with the artist. I quailed at the thought of censure but I also thirsted for companionship.

I voiced my fears to Rose, who smiled, and told me that even the crustiest old die-hards had soft hearts and I should not worry - I'd win them over in the end. 'Those folks in the new houses won't even know who you are,' she said. 'You aren't as famous as you think.'

Rose and I agreed I could be introduced as an impoverished member of the Talbot family living by grace and favour at the house as housekeeper and guardian. As for the finger-waggers, I decided I would endure their vinegary looks and self-righteous sniffing, and hold my head high.

It was much more difficult than I had imagined. As I entered, the village hall was full and the meeting was in progress. At the creak of the door the Chairlady's spiel of notices and matters arising stammered to a halt. There was massed swivelling of heads, an audible gasp of surprise and a collected raising of eyebrows. The woman serving tea dropped the milk jug. I made much of removing my gloves and stowing them in my handbag, all the while scanning the rows of smartly hatted heads for Rose or Mrs Greene. The silence disintegrated into shocked exchanges of 'Well, did you ever?' and 'Of all the nerve!' I wanted the wooden floor to open up and swallow me whole.

Then I was yoo-hooed to a spare chair at the end of a row by Rose, introduced to her mother and welcomed very pointedly by Mrs Greene, which flabbergasted the tart contingent into silence. Then Miss Eccles, the school teacher, thundered the first chords of Jerusalem, and we all began to sing.

Membership of the WI opened up my circle of acquaintances to include Rose's mother, Patricia Coombes, whose husband ran the village pub, and Ann Widderington, wife of a local farmer. Rose's mother was an older, weightier replica of her daughter, all smiles and dimples and generous spirit. Patricia was a large, busty woman, landlady of the local pub. Although her husband held the licence and was nominally in charge, everyone knew it was really Patricia who ruled the roost. She was very loud, with blonde hair fading to ashy grey. Regular customers treated her with great respect and more than a little awe. But no one had a kinder heart. 'So you've decided to show yer face at last,' she cried, ''bout time too. You sit near me and try this cake. Baked it m'self. Doesn't touch Mrs Greene's but someone's got to eat it.' I liked her immediately in spite of the cake (which was soggy and under-baked) and for her part she seemed determined to take me under her wing. 'You call in to the pub any time,' she told me. 'You don't have to go through the bar. Come through the gate into the yard and hammer on the door. Don't worry about the dog - he's all noise but he's got no teeth, like those women yonder,' she indicated, with a nod of her head, a coven of ladies across the room deeply engaged in conversation which was punctuated by frequent sallies of withering looks in my direction.

I encountered Ann Widderington very briefly, the first time, after the meeting. Her bicycle chain had come off and she was trying to fix it by the side of the road. She was a tiny, wiry woman, nervous as a bird. Her small hands were oily and she had a smear of dirt across her face. Even in the pale moonlight I could see she was flushed and anxious. 'I'll have to leave it in the hedgerow,' she said as I came up to her. 'Jethro will be angry if I'm home late; he likes his cocoa promptly at nine.' With that she almost threw the bicycle into the ditch alongside the hedge, and scampered off down the narrow farm track which led to Clough Farm.

'People say he hits her,' Rose confided when I reported the strange incident to her. 'Jethro Widderington is known as a bully; my Dad remembers him from school - he was handy with his fists even then.'

'Poor woman,' I said, 'I wonder why she married him.'

'Oh, you know,' Rose threw me a cryptic look, 'the usual reason. Not everyone has a Mum and Dad as good as mine.'

I wanted to ask her about Bobby then. Who was his father? But, for all I knew she could have succumbed to an attack as easily as a seduction. Both were delicate areas, as I well knew, and so I did not trespass upon them.

Ann's bicycle gave me an idea, and I asked Kenneth to get me one and show me how to ride it, so I could cycle up to the village and back again, in the light summer evenings. Pedalling up the drive was very hard work, but free-wheeling down again was wonderful!

The bicycle widened still further my sphere of independence and society. Kenneth was assiduous in his tuition, showing me the unfrequented green lanes and farm tracks which cut across country and saved me from encountering both the traffic and the ambling herds and flocks on the roads. It was exhilarating to ride with the wind in my face, to see the fields and moors over the hedgerows. We might stop by a rushing stream to drink from cupped hands, or gather blackberries to take home. Kenneth's reserve relaxed a little. He spoke, still, in stilted sentences, and never wasted words, but those he spoke were always interesting and apposite. He knew a good deal about local wildlife, pointed out birds' nests and named wild flowers. When I talked, he listened, answering with a nod or a noise which came out as 'hmm' but which, depending on the facial expression which accompanied it, could mean approbation, agreement, denial or censure. Sometimes I even made him smile, and, at those moments, a kind of cloud which hovered around him like a hazy shield would lift, just briefly, and the boy I had known years before with a gap-toothed grin and a merry glint in his hazel eye would be visible.

I took advantage of one of these windows to remind him of our childhood association. 'You looked after me, when I was very small,' I commented one afternoon as we lazed on the periphery of a meadow in the shadow of a towering horse chestnut tree.

'Hmm,' he said. He was lying on his back with his hands behind his head.

'Do you remember?' I pressed.

He didn't reply for a moment. 'Course,' he said at last. 'Got the push for it.'

'From Ratton?'

He shook his head. 'Ratton wasn't there then. Your father. Said it wouldn't do.'

'I'm so sorry,' I said, sincerely. It seemed to me that Kenneth had had the short end of many straws.

'He was right. But you were lonely.'

'I was,' I agreed. 'When did you begin working at the house?'

'My father was coachman. Brought me when I was a nipper. Been going ever since.'

'Whether allowed or not?' I laughed.

He gave a rueful grin but then frowned, as though puzzling something out for himself before he spoke. 'That house,' he said at last, 'times gone, it belonged to the village as much as the Talbots. Everyone worked there, or were tenants, or supplied something.'

I knew exactly what he meant - Tall Chimneys didn't belong just to the Talbots and my role in maintaining it wasn't just for the sake of my family's traditions and history but also for the local community's. Their stake was as great as mine.

'It sustained the local economy,' I agreed, 'I wish those days would come back.'

'But they won't,' he sighed. He squinted at the sky. A thin cloud hazed the far horizon. 'Going to rain,' he said, getting up and holding out his hand to me. 'Better get back.'

When he was satisfied I would not get lost or fall off the bicycle, Kenneth agreed to my going out alone. It was ridiculous for a woman of my years - I was twenty six - to feel at once, so excited and so nervous about being independent, but I did. I had kept myself apart at Tall Chimneys in the early years because I had believed that was the traditional way of things - that strict demarcation, between landed gentry and the hoi-polloi. In the first part of the century no decent lady would have thought of going out unchaperoned and although times had moved on, I hadn't. I had been left behind by progress, marooned by time, like Tall Chimneys itself; we were both relics of history. Following the commencement of my liaison with John I had even hidden there, feeling the stigma of our adultery which, though I could justify it to myself, I knew would fail the strict test of prevailing morality. But now I found I was tolerated and even welcomed by most people in the village and my conversation with Kenneth had reminded me I had a responsibility to the local community. I took to cycling up there to use the post office and little shop, and to have tea with Patricia in the little parlour behind the bar.

Rose's mother asked me to tea also. 'Three or four of us get together on Wednesday afternoons for a knitting circle,' she said. 'It's half day closing. Why don't you come?'

'I can't knit!' I confessed.

'I'll teach you,' she laughed.

Rose came with me. Kenneth had agreed to keep his eye on Bobby for the afternoon. 'We don't go to the front door,' Rose warned me, as I made for the gate off the main street pavement. 'Nobody but the vicar and the bailiff ever uses those. We'll go round the back.'

I followed her past a neatly kept vegetable patch and a line full of drying washing and was welcomed into a warm kitchen where I was given tea and a slice of cherry pie, and handed a pair of knitting needles ready cast-on with coarse yarn.

'A dish cloth,' I was told, 'the ideal beginner's project.' I tussled with it as time passed, only half concentrating, enjoying the companionable chat of the women and finding I had fewer and fewer stitches and larger and larger holes as the afternoon progressed.

Emboldened by this experience of local society, one warm afternoon I ventured down to Clough Farm to visit Ann. The farm was tidy and well-maintained, the yard clear of the usual decrepit pieces of machinery and half tumble-down lean-tos which usually characterise them. The farmhouse was neat and recently white-washed. Tubs of geraniums stood either side of the front door but I knew better, now, than to knock on it, and found my way instead round to the kitchen door. Ann was suspicious at first, peering from behind the almost-closed door like a timid mouse. I made that first visit on the pretext of having heard her henhouse had been raided by a fox. I took her three pullets in a box balanced on my handlebars. She didn't even let me in the house on that occasion, but because I had been told at the WI that she was the best knitter in the group I went again, with a tangled attempt at a tea cosy, to ask her help. She invited me in that time - it transpired Jethro was away all day at market - and put me straight. Her kitchen was perfectly neat and clean, the dinner all made and keeping warm on the stove, the washing done and dried and ironed. She spoke in whispered tones, as though she might be overheard, and very quickly, as if time was short. At tea time three large lads strode in without taking off their muddy boots or washing their hands and sat themselves down at the table. She leapt up from her seat. 'Oh, you'll have to go,' she squeaked, flapping her apron and almost shooing me out, 'but do come again,' she mouthed, before closing the door.

Soon I was riding further afield, down lanes and up hills, making careful mental note of landmarks so I could find my way home again. One day I found myself in the little market town where the railway station was, and bought myself a cup of tea in café, feeling heady with daring. Afterwards I wheeled my bicycle along the pavements, looking into the shop windows where, I discovered, things I had needed in the past but had to do without, or improvise for myself, or send off for, were readily available. There was a women's outfitters which sold the kinds of personal requisites which all women need but which are never spoken of. A hardware store displayed all manner of useful things for cleaning and repairs. There was a library. Oh! Joy!

When I got home that afternoon it was like returning from an enchanted journey to a fantastical country, a place of dreams, which was odd, because, before this, Tall Chimneys had seemed to me to be the place which was remote and charmed, a secret hollow the world had not discovered.

I personally maintained the gatehouse at all times in readiness for John's return. Sometimes I went up there and made myself tea in the old pot, and lay on the divan as the sun moved across the windows, and thought about John, and how I missed him. I wrote to him regularly, telling him all my news but, consisting mainly of crops and cobwebs, as it did, it can't have been very interesting to him. I deliberated over whether to ask him about his wife but, in the end, decided not to. She, like the little market town, like the whole world, really, existed outside of the charmed cauldron of Tall Chimneys. In June I received a letter from him saying an exhibition was imminent and afterwards he intended staying on for the Berlin Olympics. The letter came to me as I sat on the terrace in the afternoon sunshine and altered one of my new skirts. Despite my busy regime I was putting on weight.

During the course of the summer Colin came back to Tall Chimneys about three times. He brought Ratton with him on each occasion, and usually two or three other gentlemen. They seemed to talk mainly politics and ate and drank more frugally than the party of men who had come at Easter. Once Ratton came without Colin. He brought with him a disreputable-looking lady, much painted and wearing clothes which even I could see were poor quality. She had a high-pitched, heavily-accented voice which set all the crystal tinkling discordantly, drank neat gin even with her meals and left black stains on her pillow - as well as on his - whether from hair dye or eye black, I do not know. I behaved like a dour housekeeper throughout their visit - po-faced and grudging.

By August it was obvious that my increasing waistline had nothing whatsoever to do with my ravenous appetite. I was pregnant. The knowledge of it came to me one evening as I dried myself after my bath. I stood in Mrs Simpson's bedroom - it had the deepest bathtub in the most opulent bathroom and was the one I habitually used - and looked at my body in the full length mirror. I had lit the lamps but left the curtains open. The light had a golden, gloaming quality to it, infinitely soft and full of blessing. Outside the open window I could hear the birds arguing about who would sleep where. My limbs were heavy with tiredness but it had been a splendid day; I had cycled up to the village and gone with some of the other women to Clough Farm where the harvest was being brought in. With labour being short this was a job the farmers did co-operatively, all hands to the pump. The women had occupied Ann's farmhouse kitchen and provided food for the workers. Afterwards we had gone out into the fields and watched the tractors and trailers at work.

Kenneth had been there, stripped to the waist, his bony back shockingly white against his tanned arms and neck. He was doing running repairs to one of the machines.

Nearby, two women were setting out jugs of lemonade on a trestle. Their chat was conducted at a louder volume than they had perhaps intended, to penetrate the din of the rattling engine. 'I hear his mother has set her heart on him marrying Rose,' one said, nodding towards Kenneth. He paused in his work and wiped his brow with his forearm. I knew he'd heard them although he could not have seen her gesture. 'Well, who else would have her?' the woman added.

'Or him?' her companion had chipped in. I seethed on behalf of my friends. What were they talking about? I thought Kenneth was quite handsome, not to mention finely honed, for a man of his years, and, as for Rose, regardless of her past, she was as beautiful as a pink peony.

'Anyone would be lucky to have either,' I retorted, loudly, getting up from my seat on the stubble and going to sit elsewhere.

When the work was done there had been beer and a good deal of flirting and giggling in the long grass at the edges of the fields. I had expected the romance and innuendo and furtive couplings to make me feel discontented but in fact I had felt strangely apart from it all.

Now, in the bedroom, I looked at my body properly; was I beyond such things? Too old for such shenanigans? My breasts were large and shapely, indeed, heavy and, now that I really looked, mapped with blue veins I did not recall seeing before. The nipples were darker and larger than I remembered. My belly swelled slightly beneath them. I prodded it, curiously; it was hard, without a trace of fat. As I caressed it I felt a tiny flutter in the pit of it, like a bird's wing settling for sleep, soft and very fragile. I had felt it before, and dismissed it, but now it felt like a sign, a signal from someone trapped underground. 'Here I am, here I am, here I am,' it seemed to say. It was like something in the back of memory which seeks to be recalled; a gesture half-seen, half-sensed, just out of eye-line; a snatched line of music which dogs you all the rest of the day as you try to bring it to consciousness. I watched my image frown as I tried to make sense of it and the line in my forehead brought Mrs Simpson powerfully to mind; hers had been almost permanently furrowed. She was to have slept in this room - how long ago? Four months? Five? And the night before she came I had gone to Giles Percy's room.

Past and present collided. Even in the evening light, with the lamps glowing, I watched with a kind of detached curiosity as the colour drained from my face. My eyes widened. One hand instinctively went up to my mouth, the other clapped itself onto my stomach. Shock and surprise, disbelief and certainty chased each other round my mind in ever decreasing circles. I felt over-taken and powerless and completely undone. What on earth had I done? What on earth *would* I do, now? A baby, and I unmarried and without any prospect of becoming so. A baby that was not even John's. But at the same time I was conscious of an overwhelming, ravening instinct to protect, a fierce sense of possessiveness; this was *my* baby. And this was the feeling which stayed with me, as I dressed and prepared supper, floating round the kitchen on a cloud of heady delirium; for the very first time, I would have something which was mine, and mine alone.

John came home in September. He walked into the kitchen as Kenneth was busy servicing the range, elbow deep in soot and grime. Rose was in the larder storing our bottled blackcurrants. John was tanned, much thinner than formerly, and his thick black hair had been cut short. As if to compensate, a bushy beard had sprouted from his chin and cheeks. His suit was crumpled from travel. He looked wild and oddly disreputable, but also vulnerable.

I gasped, and took a step backwards, momentarily alarmed - I didn't recognise him at first and took him for an itinerant. But then I saw his eyes - unchanged - and my apprehension turned immediately to relief. I don't think I had realised how deep the well of my loneliness had been during his absence, but it surged up, now, and threatened to overwhelm me. I must have made some sort of gesture - perhaps I held my arms out, I'm not sure - I know my eyes filled with tears. My face must have revealed the full story. Kenneth got to his feet with his face firmly averted and left the kitchen, leaving his tools scattered over the hearth. Rose likewise made herself scarce. John stepped across the flagstone floor of the kitchen and took me in his arms.

Much later, in bed, I nestled into the crook of his arm. Between us the swell of my stomach was perfectly accommodated in the curve of his side, as if someone had designed it to be so; we were a fit, as we always had been, as we always would be. He had looked at my body with a raised eyebrow, and made no comment, speaking, instead of friends he had made in Germany which included, coincidentally, Diana Mitford, Oswald Mosley's long-term mistress.

'Everyone has a secret life,' he had said, pointedly.

'And some not so secret,' I'd agreed. 'Did I tell you the King and Mrs Simpson came here?' I went on to talk about Colin's visit at Easter, the men who had come, my talk with Mrs Simpson, about Rose and Kenneth, and my new-found skill of bicycle-riding.

Afterwards we made love again, and in the aftermath I put my hand to his beard and cupped his emaciated face.

'You look like an old testament prophet,' I told him.

'I know,' he said. 'I was ill for a while - 'flu, and then a chest infection. It's what delayed my return.' He turned slightly and tilted my face up to his. 'But I prophecy this: a baby, at Christmas.'

'Well that's a novel idea,' I joked. 'I wonder if it will catch on.'

'Evelyn,' he cautioned.

I looked up at him, chastened and beset by quandary. There was no possible way the baby could be his, and he must have known it. The last thing I wanted him to do was to imagine he had a rival. On the other hand, to confess the truth would have been mortifying. 'Yes,' I said, at last. 'At Christmas, or just afterwards.'

'Very good,' was all he said. And then, in the morning, 'We will drive to town today, and see a doctor. And I think there will be no more bicycle-riding for you.'

THE AUTUMN AND winter of 1936 were momentous, both in the sequestered hollow of Tall Chimneys and out in the wider world. In October John heard through an acquaintance he had made in Berlin that Oswald Mosley had married Diana Mitford at a ceremony in Germany attended by the German Chancellor Adolf Hitler.[9] The regularisation of this socially non-conformist liaison gave me pause for thought; that they had felt it necessary, these two who had both made careers out of challenging the status quo. My general understanding of the outside world was that it was increasingly anarchic and chaotic; old norms clung on by their finger-nails and hardly anyone paid them more than lip-service. As far as my personal circumstances were concerned, I had stopped hoping to be able to marry John; as much as I might feel like he belonged to me, the fact was I was the marriage-wrecker, the interloper, and the law would never be on my side. And I was carrying another man's child. I had put myself beyond any shade of pale - social, religious, moral - which might still exist. The certainty of it - and the brazen swell of my stomach - made me oddly reckless, careless of social opinion even amongst the villagers and people of the little market town where I was now frequently to be seen in the shops and the library.

Some of the WI women had been less than kind about my pregnancy until a coalition of Rose, her mother, the redoubtable Mrs Greene and Patricia Coombes had silenced them all. Kenneth said nothing, either in congratulation or in condemnation, but I sensed disapproval, or, perhaps something even more - disappointment. From comparative loquaciousness - five or six sentences - he regressed to monosyllabic responses and eyes which refused to meet mine. I found I rather minded about his disapproval, but, regardless, I held my head up high and carried on as though nothing had changed, choosing not to see the

---

[9] This news was not in fact made public until 1938, on the birth of their first child.

disenchantment in his eyes. When out and about, I refused to hear the whispered comments of the townsfolk as I passed. John, as often as not, was with me. He took my arm and pointed out amusing or interesting things as we walked along the pavements, and tipped his hat to the women who stood to one side as we went by as though they might catch something noxious from our proximity.

Whatever the apparent orthodoxies of his private life, Mosley's political manoeuvrings continued unabated. He orchestrated a number of violent marches and protests, policed by his increasingly aggressive black-shirts, including the infamous battle of Cable Street, placing himself further and further beyond mainstream politics. I think it was from this time Colin and his cronies gradually separated themselves from the Fascists. The next time he visited us, which was in mid-November, there was no sign of the quasi-military uniforms and indeed these were outlawed by act of parliament the following January. He came, on that occasion, with Mr Baldwin, a number of governmental flunkies and a surprising flotilla of clerical gents including the Archbishop of Canterbury. There was much *sotto voce* conference and frequent use of the telephone, and a greater consumption of whisky than I would have expected for a gathering with such a marked ecclesiastical contingent. Giles Percy was one of the number. He had changed, in the months since I had seen him. His hair was brutally short but he was cultivating the sproutings of a nascent beard on his cheeks and chin. His eyes were hollowed with tiredness, his face almost cadaverous and a poor colour. He smoked voraciously; his fingers were yellow with nicotine. When he saw me and my obvious pregnancy his pallor blenched to an even paler hue, his bruised eyes widened but he managed to pull himself together sufficiently to hold out his hand and greet me.

'Mrs Johns,' he said, in an oddly strangled voice before, after a coughing fit, going on more levelly, 'Many congratulations. Your husband has returned to you safely?' He asked it as a question but I had the strong impression that it was more a statement of fact. He knew John was home; knew, I suspected, a good deal about our lives, John's work and professional connections, about my own daily comings and goings, than I would perhaps like.

'Yes, indeed,' I replied. 'He is working hard on a new installation, at present.'

The installation was actually a nursery, which we had converted from one of the old Butler's rooms across the corridor from mine. John was painting the walls with a frieze of outsized plants and fantastical flowers so that it looked like a prehistoric bower. Kenneth had drained and flushed out the ancient radiator in there and installed a wash-hand basin with dogged diligence, and said nothing about the room's intended purpose; I hoped he would get over his disapproval in time. My friend Ann was knitting a layette. Rose's father was making a crib. I was planning a trip to the attics where the old nursery equipment was stored, so see if anything could be brought back into service.

'Excellent,' Giles said. 'I heard his exhibition in Berlin was well-received.'

Mr Ratton did not accompany Colin on that visit. I was relieved. Even with John in residence, I feared Ratton's malign influence. I had no intention of asking after him but towards the end of the week Colin called me to one side.

'Our friend Sylvester is pursuing some business interests in this neck of the woods,' he said. 'He may need to use the house. He's to have full access, of course.'

'He's no friend of mine,' I declared stoutly. 'I hope he'll give me notice of his arrival?'

'Probably. Negotiations are on-going... An invitation here might swing it.'

I nodded. 'So there'll be guests? He brought...' I hesitated to say 'lady' in reference to the coarse, painted woman he had brought with him on his last visit, but alternative description evaded me for the moment.

Colin watched me struggle. 'Brought? Brought whom?' he asked, tersely, after a few moments.

'A companion. A female companion,' I got out, at last. 'When he came in the summer.'

'Did he, now?' Clearly, Colin hadn't known. 'The old dog,' he muttered to himself. He pressed his already thin lips together to make a hard, white line. His eyes glittered like frost shards. 'Well, no,' he said at last. 'No women, I shouldn't think, unless they're the wives of the people he's dealing with. He's buying up business properties in the area, mills and factories and so on. It's a thing we're speculating on together. As always, in this house,' his eyes flickered down to my stomach with a cold, speaking implication, 'discretion is the watch-word. None of us wants what goes on here generally known, do we?'

'What goes on at Tall Chimneys is nobody's business but ours,' I countered, boldly, more boldly than I felt. Somehow, Colin always managed to reduce me to a child, the unwanted, too-late baby, the supernumerary sibling. Of the seven of us Talbot children I was the only one to have produced a child who would carry our name into the future. Could Colin not be happy? Could he not offer congratulations? Could it not be a catalyst to some kind of family feeling and cohesiveness? I found myself engulfed by a wave of loneliness for something I had never really known, a sense of belonging which had evaded me almost all of my life. Only with Isobel and my niece Joan had I ever caught a glimpse of it, and with the Weeks, those kindly guardians at the gatehouse.

Colin had wandered away from me to poke at the embers in the fireplace. I could hear Mr Baldwin in the adjacent room, speaking into the telephone. Beyond the crazed, heavily leaded window, on the long terrace, Giles Percy passed by, smoking.

'Do you ever hear from our sister?' I burst out. 'Our sister Amelia?'

'She's in Germany with Diana Mitford - that is, I should say, Diana Mosley.' He replied, matter-of-factly. 'She's a celebrated beauty, much in vogue with the Chancellor's inner circle. She has her own room at The Berghof, I believe.'

He could not have described someone more alien to my humdrum, domesticated little existence. I felt small and contemptible in comparison. 'The Berghof?' I mumbled.

'Hitler's private country retreat. Much like here. A place where discretion is assured.' The idea made me shudder. Colin looked up from the fire. In spite of his proximity to it, his skin remained pale and waxy. 'She'll never come here,' he sneered. Could he read my thoughts? The tiny flicker of family connection which had suggested itself to me was snuffed. 'Unless... but no. It won't come to that.'

'To war?' I whispered.

He seemed not to have heard me. Next door I could hear Mr Baldwin concluding his conversation. Colin must have heard it too. He made for the inter-connecting door. 'But if it does,' he went on in a voice suddenly light, as though considering the likelihood of rain later, 'if it does, well, it's an ill wind which blows *nobody* any good, isn't it? I think we'll have tea, now, if you please.'

I went downstairs to ask Rose to prepare tea, and sat down heavily on the chair by the range while she assembled the crockery and cut the sandwiches and arranged scones on a plate. My only two relations in the world seemed so distant to me, utterly uncaring. I stroked my belly with a distracted hand. What kind of world, what kind of family, was I bringing my baby into?

But then John strode into the kitchen from the nursery, his hair unkempt and daubed with paint. He was still thin, the effects of his illness lingered, and occasionally he was overwhelmed by tiredness. But now his face was eager and at the same time satisfied, the expression he had when his work was going well, (and also, incidentally, during and in the immediate aftermath of sex), both energised and also gratified, the two feeding off each other in a creative, self-propelling engine of vision and experience. He snaffled a sandwich from one of Rose's meticulously arranged plates and plonked himself on the old rug at my feet. Rose uttered a cry of sham remonstrance and reached for the loaf to cut more bread. Kenneth announced himself at the door with an exaggerated scraping of boots on the mat and much snuffling and blowing into his handkerchief. Bobby, Rose's brother-child, who was with us for the day and had been helping Kenneth in the greenhouse, enacted a perfect facsimile of his actions, diligently wiping his little boots on the mat and rubbing his nose with his shirt-tail. And it suddenly dawned on me, like an illumination, here was the family who would greet my baby. Even Kenneth, who, I knew, frowned on me, would swallow his reproaches if push came to shove, and would never desert me in my hour of need. We gathered round the table and ate our tea, and it seemed to me to be enough.

Three weeks later, the outcome of Colin, the Archbishop and Mr Baldwin's labour came to fruition, and King Edward VIII abdicated.[10] We heard about it on the wireless. The King himself explained his action. 'You must believe me,' he said, 'when I tell you that I have found it impossible to carry the heavy burden of responsibility and to discharge my duties as King as I would wish to do without the help and support of the woman I love.' I did believe him. The idea of carrying on without John, in whatever context, was insupportable. I felt sorry for the King, that he had been made to choose; sorry that some accommodation could not have been reached that would have allowed him to have both. I was happy for Mrs Simpson, though, that poor, starved woman, hustled in and out of cars, driven miles through the night, stowed away in discreet sitting rooms until they could snatch five minutes together, always at hand but never by his side. Now she would take her place, I thought, and look the world in the eye. On the other hand the sacrifice had been all his. Would resentment, I speculated, regret, recrimination, make a bitter third in their relationship?

'And I want you to know that the decision I have made has been mine and mine alone,' the King went on. 'This was a thing I had to judge

---

[10] The involvement of the then Archbishop of Canterbury in manoeuvring Edward VIII into abdicating has only recently been brought to light.
Source: Cosmo Lang. Archbishop in War and Crisis by Robert Beaken London, I B Tauris, 2012, ISBN: 9781780763552

entirely for myself. The other person most nearly concerned has tried up to the last to persuade me to take a different course.'

'Ahhh,' Rose sighed, giving a worldly nod. 'She didn't want him to do it. She was holding out to be Queen, I bet.'

'I don't think so,' I replied. 'All she wanted was a hot bath and a whisky, when I met her.'

We had snow at the beginning of December and then the temperatures plummeted so it stayed on the ground in frozen drifts against the house and in hard sheets amongst the shadows beneath the trees. The bowl had a sense of stillness and waiting, the trees perfectly motionless in the arctic air. Everything was petrified, even the branches of the trees were encased in sheaths of ice; it tinkled and rang like steely bells when a snow-fall set the branches waving, and, in the stillness, it creaked and squeaked as it tightened its grip. The terrace was a sheet of ice, the cobbles of the yard like polished, pearlescent goose eggs. The steeply sloping drive was treacherous, its craters and potholes as sharp as jaws; Kenneth punctured his motorcycle tyre twice in as many days. A dense fog enveloped everything, we hardly saw the sun and from the drawing room windows I could barely make out the outline of the grey fountain.

Inside the house, in contrast, all was light and warmth, readiness and anticipation. The nursery was ready, a gloriously colourful arbour, all sunshine and vibrancy. The handmade crib, the bale of clothing and nappies sent down by Rose's parents, the beautifully worked blankets and shawls made by Ann all stood ready. I was ready, more than ready; sick of waddling through the rooms, unable to bend to put on my own shoes, eager to meet this little person who had been brewing and baking inside of me.

We had laid our plans. Rose would help me, boil water and assemble towels, make tea, rub my back, all of which - she assured me - would be necessary before the baby made its appearance.

'Mum will come, if you like,' Rose offered. 'She and I, we managed it between the two of us. We didn't need the doctor.'

I refrained from pointing out that, in their case, the muddier the waters over Bobby's origins, the better. Unless I could convince people I had found my baby under the gooseberry bush there would be little question about its genesis. I didn't have a convenient married relation I could palm it off onto. And, truth be told, I didn't want to deny it. I was past caring what people might think.

'It's all the same to the doctor,' I said.

The telephone stood ready to call him; for the first time it would be of some use to me. If the doctor was out on his rounds, John or Kenneth would go and look for him in the motorcar which Kenneth had primed and serviced. He had also overhauled the generator; we kept it purring, the furnace stoked up and the range lit.

John and Kenneth seemed to have come to a manly accommodation. John accepted Kenneth's authority at Tall Chimneys in all matters practical and technical, never questioning the freedom I had conferred upon him to make decisions on his own cognisance or his ability to do so. John never presumed to interfere with the workings of Tall Chimneys or undertook any remedial tasks unless under Kenneth's supervision. Like me, he did not treat Kenneth like a servant but as a colleague. In return, Kenneth seemed to swallow his resentment of John and to overcome his suspicion. Occasionally I found them having quite garrulous discussions and I was glad that John had managed to break through Kenneth's reserve even though I wondered why I had not. It was understood that they took a joint, equal and equally jealous interest in everything pertaining to Tall Chimneys, and that included me.

We had a lovely Christmas, John and I. We lit the candles in the dining room and dined in state to the strains of the wireless floating from the drawing room. We served ourselves; I had given Rose and Kenneth a few days' holiday. We ate well and John raided the cellar for a good bottle of wine. I drank of it pretty sparingly - it had, after all, been the cause of my flagrancy with Giles Percy - and we laughed about those agonisingly awkward meals with Ratton sitting at the head of the table, as ugly and objectionable as a goblin. Afterwards we took a careful turn on the lawn, the crisp, frosted grass crunching beneath our feet like sugar coating. John threaded my arm through his and held my hand. We looked at the skeletal rose bushes and limp, water-weighted heads of the hellebores, and breathed in the sharp-edged air. It smelt of polar-places, distant bergs and creeping glaciers, but also of our own home woodlands, pine-laced and peaty, and of the smoke which rose in sluggish columns from the tall chimneys but then fell back to meld itself with the vaporous mix of mist and gelid air. Overlaying it all was the smell of John himself, soapy and smoky and manly and mine.

'Don't you ever wonder,' I began, my voice surprisingly loud in the silent garden.

'No,' he said, shaking his head. I threw a glance at him. He had diamonds of dew in his beard which he had kept, though trimmed to tidiness. 'No, I never do, not for a moment.'

'*I* wonder,' I said, 'about what *you*...' but he cut my sentence off.

'I think of the baby as a sort of immaculate conception,' he offered, 'like Jesus.'

'I'm no Mary,' I laughed, but awkwardly, because the name Mary conjured the automatic addendum 'Magdalene' in my mind. *That*, perhaps, was more apt.

'You're Eve, though, aren't you? Did you know it means 'origin'? Earth mother. Primal woman. The whole population sprang from her loins.'

'Eve had her Adam,' I murmured.

'Perhaps that's what you'll call him, then? Adam?'

'The baby's father?'

John shook his head. 'No, the baby.'

'I don't think so. What were Eve's children called?'

'Cain and Abel, of course, but neither of them had enviable careers. Seth was the one who came after Adam in the great family tree.'

'I like Seth,' I said. 'Were there any girls?'

John laughed. 'It's a theological sticking point,' he said. 'Assuming God made no more people (a big assumption, in my view), who did Cain and Seth marry, since we know they produced children?'

'You don't have to be married to do that,' I put in, dryly.

'Indeed. Anyway, I read somewhere that Cain, at least, married his sister Awan. Cain was banished and went off to the land of Nod, fathered many children and built a city.'

'Awan,' I repeated. 'She was a sort of pioneer, then, forging into the unknown, making the best of what there was.'

The light was fading, turning from opaque pearl to smoky amethyst. We went indoors and stoked up the drawing room fire. John went downstairs to make tea, while I arranged all the cushions so as to ease my back and aching legs. Later, John read to me from A Christmas Carol and I stroked my belly, and wondered if the baby could hear the sonorous tone of his voice as he read. The three of us curled up together in the depths of the sofa, and the warmth of the room wrapped itself around us, and the whole house stood sentinel over us in that remote, hidden glen, swathed in mist and clamped by cold, under the dome of the sky and the eye of God.

John still used the upper room of the gatehouse as his studio but he hadn't spent a night there since his return from the Continent. It seemed a specious fallacy, now, a charade that fooled nobody. We usually slept in the housekeeper's room, and kept ourselves discreetly and decorously below stairs in all our daily comings and goings, but, that night, when it was time to sleep, we damped down the fire and switched off the lights, and climbed the stairs to Mrs Simpson's room.

Overnight the temperature rose, the mist dissolved and in the morning the house was bathed in pure, winter sunlight. The lawn and trees sparkled, drenched in dew like diamonds. John opened the curtains and immediately got that look in his eye which I knew presaged creativity.

'Go and paint,' I told him, nestling back into the pillows and resting the cup and saucer he had brought me onto my bump. 'Go, while the light lasts, and paint something glorious.'

He looked at me. 'I oughtn't to leave you,' he demurred.

'Nonsense,' I retorted. 'I'm going to go back to sleep in a moment, so I'll be no company for you.'

'Oh, alright,' he gave in.

I was as good as my word, back asleep within moments; I didn't even hear the motorcar as it pulled out of the stables and laboured up the slush on the drive. I slept in the filtered sunlight that came in through the half-drawn curtains until midway through the morning when a change in its quality woke me. The blue had been replaced by thin cloud. Above the amphitheatre of the trees I could see it moving, quite quickly, from the east. I got up and drew myself a bath. From its depths I could hear the telephone ringing, but it would have been impossible - and dangerous - for me to try and answer it. I wallowed on, and presently it stopped ringing.

By the time I got downstairs it was midday, and I set about getting together some food to carry up to the gatehouse for John, later. This necessitated a trip to the hot house, where tomatoes were still to be had from the yellowing, spent trusses. On my way I let the chickens out, and collected the eggs - not many, at that time of year, but enough for an omelette for supper, I thought. The hens came out cautiously, eyeing the air, placing tentative feet down on the chill, wet ground. As I re-entered the house I could hear the telephone again, ringing in the butler's pantry. I dropped the eggs and tomatoes into a handy basket and hurried through, but when I lifted the receiver there was only a click and a buzz like an angry wasp on the line. The only person I could imagine calling was the doctor, and I put a call through to him, but his telephone, too, rang on and on and nobody answered.

I continued to potter round the kitchen; folding laundry which had been drying over the range, getting distracted by a particularly delicious pie which Mrs Greene had sent down for us, opening one of the jars of pickled cabbage from the larder to eat with it. I dried and put away the glassware we'd used the night before. Time passed.

About three o'clock I locked up the hens. They had already retreated into the shelter and warmth of their accommodation, sensing, as I had not, the storm which was imminent. The air outside had turned bluish; the cloud overhead was much thicker, lower, and very dark. As I watched, fat flakes of snow began to float from the sky.

I packed up my basket and made ready for the walk up to the gatehouse. I would have to hurry.

The first pain came as I was bending to lace up my boots. It was sharper and much stronger than I had expected, and not in my back, as Rose had described, but in some hidden and hitherto unsuspected ventricle at my core. I took a sharp intake of breath and sat back on the settle, quelling panic. My instinct was to clench up the place where the pain had been, to resist the sense of prising pressure.

'Relax,' I told myself, 'probably just wind. Shouldn't have eaten that cabbage.'

But immediately it came again, more insistent, a sense of determined opening, the way I had seen Kenneth kick and rattle at a shed door which has swollen and warped over winter, breaking the seal which time and nature together have fastened shut. At the same time I was conscious of a trickle of warm liquid coming from me.

Clearly, the baby was on its way.

I rang the doctor again, and also the number of Rose's father's shop. There was no reply. Nobody else I knew had a telephone except Patricia at the Plough. I dialled it and some-one - a man - answered, but just then another pain gripped me and I couldn't speak. The man shouted over the din of the noisy bar, 'Hello? Hello?' and then put the receiver down. When I tried again the line was dead - I presume he'd left it off the hook.

'Be calm,' I told myself. 'John will come back soon. He can't paint in this light, anyway.'

I went through to the bedroom and changed my clothes. Outside, the piece of kitchen garden I could see from the window was blanketed, the air a choked maelstrom of snow.

The pains continued to come, each one more urgent than the last, and lasting longer. I paced the flagstone floor of the kitchen, counting my steps, counting the flags, counting the seconds until the next onslaught. When it came I braced myself, and clung onto the back of a chair or the edge of the sink, wherever I happened to be. Still, my overriding urge was to fight back against the invader, to tense up everything, to resist the advance.

Between pains I tried the doctor and Rose again. Still no reply. Well, what did I expect? It was Boxing Day. People were out socialising.

Four o'clock came and went, then half past. By now the contractions were coming thick and fast. They made me cry out. Not just that inner gateway but my whole body convulsed when they came. Surely, *surely*, I told myself, John would come soon. But then I began to imagine disasters. He had had an accident; the car had had a puncture, swerved off the drive and plunged him into the woods. He was unconscious at the wheel; suffering from hypothermia; dead. The more frequent and powerful the pains, the more fevered my imagination became until I was certain John was in desperate trouble. I wrapped a coat around me and staggered into the blizzard.

My idea - dimly caught - was that I would go to the foot of the drive and call to him. I could see the opening of the drive at the end of the gravelled forecourt. It was flanked by conifers and in the dusky light and my delirium it looked to me like the yawning mouth of a terrible beast. The snow had drifted into the throat of it, but beyond it was dark and forbidding. All around me the garden was foreign, disguised by snowfall, vague outlines of well-known shrubs and familiar statuary camouflaged and all-but unrecognisable. Behind me the house was unlit, its windows blind and uncaring. Another pain came and the noise I made was like the bark of a vixen.

I lurched towards the drive, peering through the murk to see if I could make out the outline of the car, or John himself, walking towards me. But the road was empty.

I listened. Nothing. Just the pump of blood in my own ears, and the gossamer fall of snow on foliage, as innocent and suffocating as feathers in a pillow.

I wished I'd brought a lantern or a torch, berating myself for being so stupid. But surely he couldn't be far away. If I just walked as far as the first bend...

The driveway took me into a kind of tunnel. The trees crowded to the edge and made a canopy above. Within it, the snowfall was less, the silence more, the darkness intense.

'John! John!' I cried out. But my voice was deadened by the congregating trees, or perhaps I was deafened. I felt like the world was shrinking; the sphere of my existence closing down to the smallest bubble whose membrane hovered only inches from my skin. Or that I myself was growing, expanding to fill the universe, the coming baby swelling and inflating me until I would explode. Whichever way it was, there was myself and only myself and the pain which was almost like a prisoner scrabbling with tooth and nail to escape.

The lane from Tall Chimneys snakes up from the house, switch-backing left and right through the steep incline of the trees. Even at the best of times and in temperate weather it is a challenging walk, but one which I had been doing hardly without a second thought for most of my life. But that late afternoon my steps were dogged and wavering. I found I could hardly keep in a straight line, zig-zagging like someone who is drunk, falling now into the undergrowth at the side of the path, then over boulders which mark out the precipice beyond the edge. At the first bend another pain racked me. I stumbled and fell onto the wet, slush-mired surface. Something squirted out of me, hot and wet, and I looked down to find my skirt red with blood.

I was dying, and every instinct cried out to me to get to the gatehouse, my place of sanctuary. As a wounded animal will limp and drag itself back to its lair; as a dying soldier asks for his mother, so I, then, desired only that one thing. I went on, on my hands and knees, filthy and drenched and frozen and bloody, another few yards, until it came again, a vast opening; a pressing, inexorable, unanswerable progress, like a hot glacier tearing me asunder.

My body took over. I was beyond rational thought of any kind; blind instinct and a preternatural knowing made my body convulse in rhythm with the contractions, pushing and expelling the burden from within. I tore aside my underclothes and crouched over my coat - filthy though it was - to deliver the baby. And when she came we both howled, like animals, at the horror and the joy and the wonder and the shock of it, and then I held her, tightly wrapped in my coat. Another pain, but less intense, and something else slithered from within, and then it seemed like we were both borne away on some ebb of a peaceful tide. The forest now felt benign, a kindly shroud, and I heard, as I had not, before, the quiet twittering of birds deep inside the woods, the distant trickle of water down a gully, the little snufflings and mewings of Awan as she wriggled in my arms.

And after a while I got up and walked up the drive to the gatehouse.

That's where John found me. He saw the light in the window as he drove back across the moor from the station. He strode into the room bringing a flurry of snow flakes, clods of snow falling from his boots. His hair was drenched and plastered to his head, the shoulders of his greatcoat dark with damp. What a sight I must have looked! Filthy, bloody, my hair matted and unkempt, but with a look on my face as serene, he later told me, as any angel. I gazed up at him and down at Awan, and smiled, and he came and knelt down by the chair.

'The baby came,' I said, unnecessarily.

'So I see,' he nodded, lifting an ironical eyebrow. Then he tilted his head to indicate the doorway behind him. 'So did Ratton.'

I raised my eyes to see my nemesis hovering in the little kitchen. Even in the gloom I could see his engorged face, livid with some emotion I couldn't quite read, his piggy eyes narrowed in spite and cold as star-shards. He looked sick, disgusted at the evidence of childbirth which was larded over everything - bloody smears across the floor, my own dishevelment, Awan herself - incontrovertible testimony to what had taken place. But there was also, in his mien, an element of affront, as though he, personally, had been injured in some way.

'I telephoned a dozen times,' he blurted out at last, and strode into the gatehouse parlour as though to demonstrate some kind of possession. 'Of course I see *now* why there was no reply.' He spoke as though I had been caught in some guilty or irresponsible act.

'I was preoccupied,' I said, coldly. 'Babies don't deliver themselves.'

Ratton gave a shudder. 'There is no need to be coarse,' he said. 'My companion is perished. Let us go to the house.'

'You will find nothing in readiness,' I told him, 'and no-one to serve you. The servants are on holiday.'

'You will stay here,' John said to Ratton, getting to his feet and taking charge. 'Bring your guest in here, where there is a fire. I need to take Evelyn and the child home, and then go out again and fetch the doctor. I'll round up the staff on the way.' Without waiting for any reply - the outburst of objection he must have known was coming - John threaded one arm beneath my knees and the other under my arms and lifted Awan and me off the chair. For a moment we were out in the blizzard - blowing strongly across the moor and already obscuring the tracks the car had made along the approach - and then in the warmth of the car, a rug unceremoniously yanked off the passenger within and wrapped round us.

'Get out,' John barked above the howl of the gale, 'and go inside. There's a fire, and things for making tea. I'll be back, presently.'

The car set off, passing the gatehouse and then down the steep, treacherous incline of the drive. At least, within the girdle of trees, the storm was muted, and John took the opportunity to explain his long absence.

'When Ratton couldn't get a reply at the house he telephoned the village. The Post-master's lad was on his way out with the message when he saw the car at the gatehouse. I decided to go to the station myself.'

'And not down to the house to see if I was alright?' I asked, with dry humour.

'No,' he bit his lip, guiltily. 'I should have done, shouldn't I?'

'Yes, and you should have sent Kenneth to the station,' I said, dreamily. The car, the drive, the day which had gone by, John himself, they were all beginning to seem more surreal with every moment that passed. Only Awan, solid and warm in my arms, sleeping now, seemed real at all.

'I know. But I'd been painting - oh Evelyn, wait till you see - and you know how distracted I get. I wish I had sent Kenneth, though. What a journey we had of it back from the station. The road was thick with snow in no time, and there were snow-drifts. I had to stop I don't know how many times to dig the car out. Ratton took pleasure in allowing me to do all the work, of course, treating me like a chauffeur.'

If I had been *compos mentis* this information would have struck more of a chord with me than it did. John's chest wasn't up to such exposure, or such exertion. But, as it was, it registered only a faint sense of disquiet.

The rest of the day, and indeed the following week, are lost in a fog in my mind. I later found out John got me safely home and settled me in bed, before going back out into the blizzard to find the doctor and bring Rose. Only then did he fetch Ratton and his companion. By the time they arrived at the house, I am told they were perished with cold (neither of them having the presence of mind to keep the gatehouse fire alight or to make tea with the equipment readily to hand there) and in high dudgeon. The house, as I had stated, wasn't ready for visitors; the beds not aired, the log baskets not full, the menu not planned. These matters manifested themselves in my mind in nightmarish proportions as I drifted in and out of consciousness. I was aware of Ratton as a malevolent presence, out of view, thankfully - he did not attempt to broach our quarters - but near enough to cause me disquiet. I was a little feverish for a few days following my exposure in the snow. I was aware of people - Rose, her mother, Mrs Greene, Ann - hovering in the room, cleaning my body, settling Awan in the crook of my arm, even putting her to my swollen breast to feed. Sometimes I woke to find John seated in a chair by the fire, the baby swaddled up and in his arms, and once, Kenneth, hovering in the shadows beyond the dim pool of light cast by a shaded lamp. But after a few days these visions faded, and where I thought I had seen John there was only the chair, and the figure of Kenneth melded into the drape of the curtain and the only person I could be sure of was the doctor, who seemed to be in constant attendance.

Then, one morning, I woke up properly. A bright, white light like a knife blade pierced the gloom of the room through a chink in the heavy curtains. My body felt weak, but well. From across the passageway I could hear Awan crying. Instinct as strong and irrepressible as the tide overwhelmed me, and I had pushed the covers back and crossed the floor before rational thought caught up with the compulsion.

John was really unwell. His exertions for Ratton in the snow had brought back his chest infection and the doctor had sent him to bed. Rose, Kenneth and their mothers had, between them, nursed us both. My friends Patricia and Ann had managed things for our recalcitrant guests, bringing food from their homes and taking away laundry, but Ratton's stay did not last more than a couple of days. John's illness lingered far after my brief incapacity had ended and I was up and about.

BY THE SPRING of 1937 John was well enough to get up, but the appalling weather made it impossible for him to get the fresh air he so desperately needed. He had lost more weight and his hair, which had always been lustrous and thick, began to thin at his temples. Once or twice I asked Kenneth to drive him up to the gatehouse to work on the canvas he had begun on the morning of Awan's birth. But often he tired before much time had elapsed, and Kenneth gave me to understand that when he went into the gatehouse to collect him he would find John sitting by the fire, staring into the flames. He had a persistent cough which never really left him fully and there were times, in that wet spring and late-coming summer we had that year, when it seemed no amount of jerseys and coverings could keep him warm. He made hundreds of pencil sketches of Awan, though, capturing her sleeping and waking, making studies of the creases in her wrist, the feathering of downy hair on her head, the curl of her tiny toes. I have them here, yellowed with age, but still exuding love and tenderness. It occurs to me perhaps he was trying to capture in his memory something he somehow knew he would not be able to see indefinitely with his eyes. How he lived with this foreknowledge I do not know. I had no suspicion of it, living blithely, day-to-day, all unsuspecting of what was to come.

I recovered well from the birth, after that small bout of feverishness. The doctor pronounced me fit in February and I resumed my work in and around the house. Apart from one solitary visit from Colin and some gentlemen we were left alone at Tall Chimneys. It was a good thing, really, as the house was hardly fit for guests. In spite of the allowance for fuel which we received from Colin, and the diligent efforts of Rose, Kenneth and myself, we had a hard time of it keeping the house in good repair. We had rainfall double what we would normally experience and dampness took easy hold unless we heated and ventilated the rooms. It was almost impossible to admit fresh air without letting in squalls of rain too, and mould bloomed on the cornices and all the linens took on a musty, unpleasant smell. Our gutters sagged and then broke under the weight of water that came down. Kenneth risked life and limb to repair them. It seemed the slightest storm could dislodge tiles from the roof and we had a number of severe thunderstorms in February, March and April.[11] Temperatures remained bitter; Kenneth struggled to get vegetable seeds to germinate, the raised beds were soggy, the vegetables which had over-wintered rotted in the ground. To add injury to insult a fox got into our hen house and decimated our flock.

It was a struggle, but none of it mattered to me. In my naïve understanding, John and Awan and I floated in a little bubble of happiness which the awful weather, the challenges of John's illness and the decrepitude of Tall Chimneys could not puncture. I stopped thinking about the outside world, about what other women were achieving, about how life was progressing, leaving me behind. It had all become irrelevant. John and I were both utterly and absolutely in love with the baby, whose sunny nature and goodness made her a daily delight. She looked like an angel, with all the blonde, cherubic looks of her father. Nobody, not the best intentioned or most diplomatic person, could have mistaken her for John's child, but she adored him from the first, and when the truth was cruelly and precipitately thrust upon her, she continued to love him and to think of him as her daddy.

1937 drifted by and we celebrated Awan's first birthday on Boxing Day, an overcast day without the sparkle and beauty of its predecessor but without its drama and trauma also. Rose and Kenneth - by then engaged, Mrs Greene clearly having gained her object - joined us along with their mothers and little Bobby. We made merry around the kitchen table and Awan's eyes almost popped out of her little face at the second tranche of gifts she had been presented with in as many days. I looked around the table and my eye fell upon John at its head; still too thin, still too pale, as he leaned forward to help Awan blow out the candle on her cake. Something in the way the candlelight illuminated him from beneath his

---

11 As far as possible I have tried to reflect the actual weather conditions which prevailed at the time by consulting historical weather reports.

chin exaggerated the thinness of his face, his sunken cheeks, the dark hollows around his eyes, and then I had a sudden sense - terrible but fleeting - that he was slipping away from me into some shadow where I would not be able to follow.

The weather for the first part of spring 1938 was exceptionally dry and warm, and John's cough seemed less troublesome, but we had awful rain in May and it came back again, stronger than ever. The doctor sent him to Leeds for a chest X ray and the results were worrying; a tubercle in the left lung.

'He needs hot, dry weather,' the doctor pronounced. 'God knows, Europe is a dangerous enough place at the moment but staying in Yorkshire is a death sentence.'

I gasped, and cried out. John frowned. It dawned on me that this was not news to him; but that he had rather it had been kept from me.

'I'm sorry,' the doctor said. 'But there it is.'

'Why?' I asked.

'The dry weather will help a scab form over the lesion,' the doctor explained. 'With luck, it will hold fast far into the future. Unfortunately many artists fall foul of this disease: Keats, Shelley, Kafka, Chopin. It's the bohemian lifestyle, poverty, living in close proximity in sub-standard conditions...'

'I did all of those things in Paris,' John said.

We spoke little in the car on the way home. Awan wasn't with us; Rose was looking after her.

'You'll have to go to France,' I said at last, the suggestion tearing itself out of me, bringing to the surface all kinds of rabid jealousies and ancient suspicions. 'You know people there,' I added, bitterly. 'You have people who will put you up, look after you.'

John glanced across at me. 'You don't know what you're condemning me to,' he muttered.

'No,' I retorted, 'I don't. You have never told me anything about your life over there, about your....' I choked on the word 'wife,' it wouldn't come past my throat for the sobs which were caught there.

John voiced it for me. 'My wife?'

I nodded, dumbly.

John sighed and pulled the car over on to the verge. It was at a particularly beautiful spot, elevated, over-looking the undulations of the neat countryside which rose up to meet the wilder, hardier line of the moors. Nestled beneath us, in a fold where a bright flash denoted the slow-flowing river, our local town looked safe and bucolic; the grey rise of the church spire, the squat square of the brewery in the elbow of the river, the arrow of the railway line piercing the age with a stab of modernity. We both climbed out of the car and stood near the hedgerow to survey the scene.

John lit a cigarette, coughing through the smoke as he always did. 'What do you imagine, about her?' he asked me.

His question surprised me. 'Oh! That she's beautiful, of course, sophisticated and worldly in a way that I will never be. Rather sultry and alluring, knowing in the ways of the world and proficient in the bedroom...' my description faltered to a halt as I noticed John's shoulders shaking. I thought for a moment he was coughing, but he was laughing.

'Oh, Evelyn,' he gasped at last, 'you are a prize ninny.' He put his arm round my shoulder and pulled me to him. 'She is old,' he whispered, 'bloated and lazy. She was thirty years older than me when I married her, and that's sixteen years ago, more or less. And she's virtually bed-ridden. She can hardly get out of bed, let alone turn a trick in one.'

I turned to look at him. 'Why did you marry her?'

He shrugged. 'She hasn't always been incapacitated. When I met her she was reasonably healthy if a little overweight. She was recently widowed, and rich - independent - without ties or obligations; she had no children. I was on my beam ends. No one was buying my pictures and I was overdue with the rent on my rooms. I was surviving on goodwill from a couple of café owners in Montmartre and what I could earn drawing portraits for passers-by on the Champs Elysée. She sat for me and I drew her likeness. Let's say I erred on the side of flattery. She was impressed. She invited me to her villa in St Germaine. You can imagine the rest, I suppose.'

I watched a bank of dark cloud advance towards us, throwing its shadow across the moor, and then over the town. 'It's going to rain,' I said, walking back to the car. John followed me, throwing the butt of his cigarette into the hedge before closing the car door. But he didn't start the engine. 'At the time,' he said, presently, 'it seemed like a life-line. She had money and she was prepared to support me while I painted. She was well-connected and she got me some commissions. But soon I realised it was a death sentence. She wanted to own me, to parade me in front of her cronies like a prize bull. She controlled the purse strings very tightly. I'd thought we'd be able to rub along like two reasonable adults. I'd even imagined that affection might grow, in time. But soon I began to hate her. I found her disgusting - not because she was fat (which she was) but because she was such a bitter, rancorous person; selfish and scheming, missing no opportunity to do anyone a bad turn. She was tolerated in society, because of her wealth, but nobody liked her.'

'You were trapped?'

'I was. Until we met your brother and his wife. George and Rita were doing the tour and we were introduced to them in Paris. George liked my work. More importantly, Rita liked it - she would be paying for it, after all. It was arranged we would all travel to London to meet other members of their artistic circle - the Bloomsbury group; Monique liked that idea a great deal - she had a yen to try something salacious and disreputable. Rita wanted me to work on a series of canvases for them. But at the last minute, Monique fell ill and couldn't go. She wanted me to cancel the trip, but I didn't. I caught the boat train with George and Rita, and soon afterwards came up here and met you.'

'I'll remember that night as long as I live,' I put in, 'you rescued me on the north landing.'

'You rescued *me*,' he replied, taking my hand.

We sat for a moment. I took in what he had said. His wife had never been any kind of threat to me, she was not my rival. She might have been the first, but I would be the last.

'You're my only wife,' John said, as though he had been party to my thoughts. 'And I have told her as much.'

I gasped. 'You've *seen* her?'

'Yes, of course. When I go to Paris, I have to visit her, to stay with her. There are appearances to keep up. I owe her that much, at least.'

'And she accepts me?'

John shrugged. 'She has no choice.'

'And...' I struggled with my next question, '...if you go to her, now, she'll look after you? She'll take you back?'

'Oh yes,' John sighed, his voice doom-laden, 'with open arms. She has a place in Provence, the perfect place for me, where the weather is warm and dry, and the scenery is good to paint.' He turned to face me. 'You'd like it there, Evelyn. Why don't you come?'

I was aghast. 'To Monique's house?'

He shook his head impatiently. 'No, of course not. But somewhere in the region. Or somewhere else? Italy? Spain? There's no earthly reason why we couldn't all go.'

'There is,' I said, snatching my hand away. 'There's Tall Chimneys and our life here.' I could almost feel the pull of it as I sat there, like a magnet of pride and need and refuge and honour. In contrast the world felt cold and inhospitable and a place of rejection. 'And I don't want to have to sneak and hide,' I went on. 'Awan would be in an impossible position. She'd be labelled a...' I couldn't say the word. 'Those are Catholic countries, aren't they? It would be even worse than it is here.'

John sighed. 'You and that house,' he said, 'what *is* its hold on you?'

'It's my home,' I said, in a small voice. 'And it isn't just the house; it's *us* and our... predicament.'

John nodded. 'I know, I know.' He reached for my hand again, and clasped it between both of his. 'Provence it is then,' he said, with a brave, resigned smile. 'No doubt we'll go there until...'

'Until what?' My voice was scarcely a whisper.

He plastered a wider smile across his features. 'Until I'm better,' he said, with forced brightness, starting up the car and putting it in gear, 'or until the war,' he added, over the roar of the engine. 'Either way, I'll come home.'

He left us soon afterwards, travelling light, as though for a short trip. The night before we made love ferociously, as though we were both famished for love. I took him into myself as deeply as I knew how, as though I might retain him; absorb him utterly into myself, leaving nothing remaining for Monique. John mistook my desire for him as pure lust; he brought me to climax again and again, with his mouth and his hands, his fingers deep inside me, finding a place which Awan's birth seemed to have made more sensitive than ever before. My last orgasm drenched us both and we lay, panting and satiated in the damp, tangled sheets.

The following day he flew to Paris and then on, as I soon heard, to Marseilles. Awan cried for three days, endlessly touring the rooms and calling for him down the empty corridors. I cried too, at night, and breathed in the scent of our lovemaking on the bedding, and wondered what sophisticated niceties of punishment the spurned Monique would inflict upon him. But soon Awan and I both took up the reins of our ordinary lives, she playing with her dolls and toys, running on the lawns and 'helping' Rose and Kenneth as they converted the old estate office and the rooms above it which were to be their married home.

Of course we knew that war was coming; it encroached across our lives throughout 1938 and into 1939 like a malevolent cloud which blocks the sun. We had newspapers and we listened to the news broadcasts on the wireless. Periodically Colin came to Tall Chimneys with a party of grey, grim-faced political and military cronies. The men's talk was always of appeasement and peace, but their actions were of rearmament and general preparedness. The size of the RAF, Army and Navy were discreetly increased; we lost many a local village lad to one or other of these organisations. An airbase was established across the moor from us and we frequently saw the 'planes practising manoeuvres across the dome of our sky. Those not young or fit enough to enlist were encouraged to form local militias. Rose's father, an ex-sergeant, exercised a gaggle of ancient worthies and loose-limbed youths on the village green, under the bristling eyebrow of retired Colonel Beverage who had moved into the old Rectory.

Kenneth played no part in these proceedings. There was no question of him being conscripted - he was nearing the upper age limit of 41 and his marriage would put him further down the list in any case. But the emotional trauma he had suffered in the first war would probably have rendered him medically unfit even if he had not been in a reserved occupation, which, thankfully, he was. He clammed up whenever war was discussed. I wondered if, at heart, he had become a pacifist, ideologically opposed to war. I asked Rose what he had told her of his time in the trenches, but she was unable to enlighten me.

'He never discusses it,' she said.

'He never discusses anything!' I said, lightly, 'not exactly a great conversationalist is he?'

'He says plenty, but not with his voice,' she said. 'You don't know him well enough, or perhaps you're not looking.' Then she gave me a narrow look, and said something odd which I didn't understand. 'Perhaps that's as well, for me and Bobby.'

Mills and factories which had been empty were suddenly busy, rattling with machinery, producing mysterious components and millions of yards of brown serge. Ratton was with us often, orchestrating the purchase and repair of these facilities. It became clear before too long, his business dealings had amply paid off. He got fatter and greasier with every new acquisition, also more smug and insufferable. Ratton's wealth seemed to increase with his figure; he no longer needed a car to fetch him from the station, he had two or three of his own, different models, and a driver. He boasted to me he had flown across the English Channel on several occasions. He began to sneer at our domestic arrangements, complaining about the lack of modern bathroom facilities and the homely nature of the food we served. He was amazed to find we didn't have a television set. He was haughty and officious, once telling me to 'keep the brats out of sight' when he saw Awan chasing Bobby round the parterre. I told him, coldly, Awan had more right to be at Tall Chimneys than he did, but without much conviction; I had long since given up my efforts to discredit Ratton in Colin's eyes and I knew our tenure at the house depended on both their goodwill.

Rose and Kenneth were married, very quietly, in a Registry Office ceremony in town. Rose looked beautiful, with a circlet of flowers on her cascading hair. Kenneth, in a new suit, had a collar so starched it had rubbed a raw line on his neck. He worried at it constantly with his finger as the moment for the ceremony approached, and, at last, threw me a look such as a drowning man might give to a rescuer who has failed to throw a rope. I smiled my encouragement and followed them into the chamber. He spoke the vows and responses well enough, quietly, but clearly, his face as flushed as his neck, his lip beaded with perspiration. Rose spoke hers through tears. Afterwards we had lunch at a hotel - a new experience for me - before the couple caught the train for their honeymoon in Scarborough. Three days later they moved into their new home, and I had neighbours for the first time in my life. Kenneth seemed different, in some way relieved or set free, when he came home from his honeymoon. He was less taciturn although he would never be garrulous. He walked with a more confident step and took up the position as the head of his household with quiet authority, kind, but firm. I assumed the release at long last - he was nearly forty, after all - of sexual tension had in some way discharged his social awkwardness. I asked Rose, discreetly, how things had gone in Scarborough. She smiled and blushed and said '*very* well.'

Bobby, of course, came to live in the newly converted estate house too. Awan adored him, and missed him when he started school, which he did in September that year.

**THE WAR SEEMED** a long way from us even though, at its outbreak, John was still in France without knowing how - or if - he would be able to get home. To be honest, the worry I had for him at the mercy of Monique's machinations was far more than the threat I perceived from marauding Nazis. But you must remember I had little recollection of the first war. It had taken my father and oldest brother from me, and also, tangentially, my mother, but these figures were vague in my mind, mere ghosts. When I'd returned to Tall Chimneys I'd missed the Weeks, more.

War impinged on our lives in many ways; we had our gas masks - they hung in rows on the hooks in the passageway - and Kenneth had fitted out the ice house - never used, in these days - as an air-raid shelter. Awan and Bobby liked to play in there anyway, and had gradually transported toys and old rugs into it to aid their games; I suppose it was spooky and spidery, dark and thrilling without being really menacing. We supplemented their provisions with some old garden chairs and an oil lamp or two. It was a token; we didn't expect to be the target of bombs, so far north and so far away from any conurbations. Rationing began early in 1940 but it didn't affect us too badly at first. Rose's father made sure we had meat and we grew most of our own fruit and vegetables. We had eggs. Somehow or other Kenneth's mother continued to be able to access flour and sugar and provided the children with cakes, which satisfied their longing for sweet things. The bartering system which has always flourished in the countryside became more prevalent, and, all in all, we didn't go without.

We got used to seeing aeroplanes in the sky; spitfires and Lancasters regularly crossed overhead, not in waves, heading for the Channel or France (we were too far north for that), but in ones and twos as their pilots were trained to fly. Throughout the long, hot summer of 1940 we could hear the engines, like angry bluebottles caught against a window, a high-pitched whine and then an eerie silence as they stalled, a coughing, stuttering re-start or, once or twice, a dull explosion as a plane fell to earth on the moorland around us. The airmen took to patronising our local public houses, very young men, many of them, hardly old enough to be able to hold their beer let alone be sent up aloft to fight the Luftwaffe. They would be there one evening, talking loudly with their fellows, flirting with the local girls, and the next night there would be an empty chair.

At Tall Chimneys we had more mouths to feed. Kenneth drove us to the station and we came back with four evacuees from Leeds, where Lancaster bombers and munitions were being churned out by the factories, some of which were owned by Sylvester Ratton. Kenneth and Rose wanted a boy because he would have to share a room with Bobby. A school-age boy would be ideal, as Rose was, by then, expecting a baby and didn't want an extra child who would be under her feet. They picked Malcolm. He was about Bobby's age but whereas Bobby was chubby and dimpled, Malcolm was thin to the point of being skeletal. He was filthy, ill-turned out in torn trousers and shoes so badly scuffed we could see his toe through the leather. He was snot-nosed and whiney, standing rather apart from the other boys waiting on the platform. Kenneth chose him in preference to the more appealing alternatives because he looked so frightened and Kenneth felt sorry for him. I went in search of the girls and spotted one aged about seven in the waiting room. She was holding the hand of a toddler perhaps two and also cradling a baby who was under a year old. They were all dressed in clothes which, though well-mended, were immaculately clean. The hair of the older girls was neatly braided and in ribbons. The baby wore a home-crocheted bonnet. As I approached the little group, the oldest girl shrank away from me and pulled the toddler behind her.

'We have to stay together, Mam says,' she announced, defiantly.

The woman who was supervising bustled over with a clip-board. She was hatchet-faced, prim and terrifying, without a shred of maternal instinct or kindness. The girls shrank even further into the grimy corner of the waiting room. 'Which will you take?' she asked me. 'Madam here says they're to stay together but I've *told* her nobody will have room for three.'

'I have room for three,' I said, quickly. 'I'll take them all.' The big girl's face remained stoical and determined, but a fat tear oozed from her eye and dribbled down her face.

'Oh!' The woman took a step backwards and looked me up and down. 'Mrs…?'

'Johns, from Tall Chimneys,' I said, picking up the small leather suitcase which was propped against a nearby chair leg.

The woman sniffed; she knew me, clearly, by repute. 'Regulations state…' she began, but I cut her off.

'This is no time to be hidebound by regulations,' I declared, stoutly. 'There's a war on. We all have to do our bit.' I reached out my hand to the toddler, who let go of her sister's and took mine. It was hot and sticky, as Awan's often was.

'I'm not sure I can…' the woman tried another tack.

'Have a heart,' I hissed, glancing at her chest as though I doubted she had such a thing - it was as flat as a board - and then at the pathetic sight of the three children. 'If you doubt me, Mrs Greene can vouch for me.' Kenneth's mother was a redoubtable figure in and of herself and a big mover in the WI world. Her name seemed to do the trick.

'Very well,' the woman leafed through her file of papers. 'You'll take Marion, Audrey and Kitty Blakney. Marion is the big one. It says here she wets the bed.'

The seven year old gave a little cry of outrage and shame. Her brave demeanour collapsed and she sank onto the bench behind her in a torrent of tears. The child whose hand I held - Audrey - began to cry also and the baby, naturally, followed suit. The harridan with the clipboard gave a satisfied smile. 'Good luck,' she said, nastily, stalking off to exert her authority elsewhere.

The three girls settled quickly into Tall Chimneys, after getting over their awe at its size and isolation. Kitty went into Awan's cot and I unearthed two truckle beds from the attics which had been used in the nurseries years before. These were for the two toddlers who were, to all intents and purposes, of an age. All three of them slept in Awan's nursery but I brought a proper bedstead and mattress down for Marion and set it up in the room next door, a mere anteroom, very narrow, with the smallest of windows which looked out onto nothing, but private and quiet - I hoped it would make her feel grown up and safe. She wet the bed every night for the first couple of weeks, but I made no fuss about it. She became my shadow, always at my elbow to help with the smaller girls, pass a trowel or grasp the corners of the sheets for folding. I told her a little about my own childhood, about the Weeks, exploring the grounds, about being sent to Isobel's, about the kindness and understanding I had met from everybody. I taught her to crochet and a little embroidery and in the evenings, when the little ones were in bed, she and I would sit by the fire and work, and listen to the radio. She wrote regularly to her parents and occasionally got letters back which were full of admonitions to behave, be polite and look after her sisters. On the advice of Rose's mother I gave Marion a spoonful of cider vinegar diluted with water every night at bedtime. I don't know if it was this remedy or just a gradually encroaching sense of security, but Marion stopped wetting the bed.

Marion, Bobby and Malcolm attended the village school. Goodness knows how Miss Eccles, the school mistress, coped, with a sudden doubling of her roll, an influx of children from the town with widely differing abilities and issues.

Like Marion, Malcolm settled after a while. He was an awkward, damaged little boy, socially inept and inarticulate. Rose fed him up, cleaned him up, eradicated the hair lice and provided him with clean clothes and an endless supply of clean handkerchiefs to deal with his perpetually snotty nose. Kenneth took him into the workshop to show him the basics of woodworking and mechanics. His quiet ways and easy temper and, most of all, his verbal reticence seemed to reassure the little lad. In time his closed, suspicious demeanour eased. He and Bobby never got on very well and I think, for a while, Bobby's nose was pushed out of joint because, with two new playmates, Awan suddenly had no time for him and then, to make matters worse, Rose produced a new baby brother who was no fun at all.

In spite of the dark shadows across the channel, things at Tall Chimneys were relatively bright; the children were happy and healthy, we had plenty to eat, the weather was fairly good. We didn't expect the war to last long - news reports were up-beat but often days or even weeks out of date. Later, the period became known at 'the phoney war', but at the time we believed the propaganda we were fed - that everything was going swimmingly well.

In June 1940 John came home. Leaving Provence and Monique - under what circumstances, I do not know and did not ask. He got away with the allied troops off the beaches of Dunkirk, one of the few civilians to do so. The trauma of the experience stayed with him - the desperation, the shoreline and dunes black with the press of men, men floating dead in the sea as he had waded out to the boats, the cold of the sea as he waited, up to his neck, the continuous bombardment of shells falling all around them, day and night.

As always with John, his anguish poured out on the sketch pad and onto canvas; he produced some harrowingly dark works on which whorls of greyish green and arcs of white spume were overlaid with dangling, awkwardly broken figures. They were painted thickly, almost violently, with ugly strokes. Fine webs of magenta spread like burst capillaries from a central slash.

The eye-witness view of the war he brought back with him was startling and sobering; France over-run, her troops in disarray, the British offensive stymied by the superior tactics and armaments of the enemy, the wholesale decimation of our troops. By the time he got his story out, France had surrendered to the Nazis and Mr Churchill, our new Prime Minister, was warning us not to consider the successful evacuation as any kind of victory.

I was careful with the amount of news I allowed John to see or hear; I feared for his mental, as well as his physical health, but, on that front at least, he did seem better. He was tanned, his hair very short and his beard gone altogether, lean, his eyes darkly shadowed and in some way hooded, as though hiding truths he did not want me to see.

He did not stay with us long. Precluded from active service because of his chest - thank goodness - he was co-opted into a unit which operated out of London, a secretive intelligence outfit whose work he could never explain to me but where his excellent French and German were apparently invaluable. He was away for long stretches of time and I missed him. When he did come home he seemed very tired and in some way distant and disorientated, as though he had been much further away than just London both physically and mentally. He didn't sleep well, tossing and turning in the night, as though troubled, but I could not get him to unburden himself to me.

I saw Colin's hand in John's appointment. Colin now played an important and influential role in support of the Coalition Government and seemed to be up to his self-important neck in officialdom. Ratton, of course, was always in his shadow, a hanger-on, basking in the borrowed glow of Colin's success and benefitting whenever possible from snippets of information carelessly dropped by loose lips or deliberately passed on by my double-dealing brother. London was a dangerous place; there were air-raids nightly and sometimes in the day as well; the damp, sooty, smoke-laden air was anathema for John's chest, the black-out encouraged ne'er-do-wells to rob anyone they encountered in the street. But London was safer than France or the further outposts of the conflict, and, for that, I was grateful, both for John, who seemed on the whole to enjoy his work and feel he was making a valuable contribution, and in terms of Tall Chimneys.

We had several visits from officers reconnoitring likely houses for use by the military. Already many of the county's biggest houses had been requisitioned; Wentworth, for example, was already housing a battalion, and rumour had it its gardens and park were to be torn up and mined for coal. Some houses were being used as schools, others as hospitals. Others still were being prepared for use as prisoner of war camps. Tall Chimneys was scarcely big enough for any of these purposes, our grounds too restricted for military training, and, crucially, we didn't have mains electricity, a must-have for most people in those days. I would often find a military vehicle on the gravelled drive, a Captain weighing the place up, but mention of Colin's name usually sent them away again. When they were more recalcitrant I would telephone Colin and put him on the line. I didn't know then what arrangements Colin had made for the maintenance of the house, or for the payment of death duties for George, to enable him to keep it. Perhaps he had made some deal with the government - we certainly had a number of governmental and diplomatic guests throughout the duration of the war, often at short notice - perhaps it was considered a sort of outpost for national use, like Blenheim, which became the HQ of MI5, Bletchley and Wilton. Whatever it was, for a long time, our peace and tranquillity at Tall Chimneys were not broached. Of course, it could not last.

The evacuees went home at the end of 1940, the threat of bombing or invasion being deemed, then, to be negligible. What blindness! Leeds was bombed in 1941, the town hall, markets, museum and station were all decimated. I wept for the children, especially Marion, Audrey and little Kitty, but also for Malcolm, not knowing what had become of them. I wondered if Marion might write to me - she had promised she would - but I didn't receive a letter. I just prayed they had escaped danger.

Of course it was terrible, *terrible*, to know what was going on in Europe. After Dunkirk all pretence in the news was dropped. The newspapers had graphic pictures and, I am told, you could see newsreels in the cinema depicting the mud and carnage. This war was mechanised in a way the first had not been - in the interim we had invented ways of killing many people from a safe distance with aeroplanes, tanks and submarines. We had become sneakier about war, using intelligence, radar and sonar to second-guess our enemies' movements. It was more effective but somehow less honest than the man-to-man combat of past conflicts.

From the spring of 1941 the government began to register women, list their occupations and offer them a range of jobs which would contribute towards the war effort. Later that year, unmarried women under the age of thirty could expect to be conscripted to do war work in munitions factories or operating the enormous bureaucratic machine which drove the war forwards. I escaped this, having turned thirty in 1940, although in some ways it might have presented me with opportunities to branch out of the narrow existence which had thus far contained me. Once again, fate seemed determined that the openings presented to other women should pass me by. My female contemporaries grasped the openings offered by the war with both hands; some of the younger women joined the ATS, trained as auxiliary nurses or went away to be ambulance drivers. The farming women took on the work of the men and supervised the women of the Land Army who arrived to help out, proving themselves just as adept at the management and planning challenges which farming presents as the men had in years gone by. The older women, and those who were married, were left to look after the children and keep the infrastructure of civilian life going; running shops, pubs and post offices, driving buses, sometimes stepping into the still-warm shoes of their conscripted husbands. Here, again, I had reason to suspect Tall Chimneys was considered in some way a satellite resource of the government; my role as housekeeper there went unchallenged and there was no suggestion I should be sent off to do something more useful. I was busy in the village and the wider parish - I felt I was 'doing my bit'. I was co-opted onto the committee of the WI in the village; we ploughed up the village green and the cricket pitch to grow vegetables and my long years' experience in the kitchen gardens of Tall Chimneys came to the fore.

On top of that, Colin brought frequent parties of gentlemen to the house for conferences and pow-wows - very secretive and business-like; there was little of the whisky-swilling of former days and the food I managed to serve up was necessarily rather Spartan. I cooked for these parties myself, having assimilated a wide enough repertoire to be able to satisfy house parties of seven or eight gentlemen for three or four days. Rose helped me and I brought in women from the village to assist with the laundry and cleaning. It seemed to be accepted this was my war-service and in all honesty it was arduous enough, at times; running the house and garden almost single-handedly hadn't got any easier, with the years.

Giles Percy never appeared at these gatherings, and I was glad of it - the older she grew, the more Awan resembled him. I enquired, casually, after him once or twice - had he joined up? Was he abroad? I gathered he was engaged in some vital but shady war effort but no-one was prepared to enlighten me further than that.

Ratton sometimes made one of the party. Although not connected with the government and having no official role, he seemed accepted by the military men, officious secretaries and Cabinet members who arrived by train or in their own motorcars. He wore some kind of uniform, non-determinate khaki emblazoned with stripes and other doubtful insignia, but then most of the men did in those days, even men who did no combative service seemed co-opted in some role or another, variously attached to numerous obscure branches of the military machine. Ratton looked ridiculous in his get-up, like an under-cooked pie filled with gristle and minced snout - offal trying to pass itself off as good quality meat. He was entirely bald by this time, but sported a bristly moustache which looked absurd beneath his snubby little nose. He wore spectacles, too, behind which his round, naked eyes looked even more like glass beads. He was fatter than ever, his round chin melding into the heavy column of his neck, and his breathing was laboured and stertorous; he needed to take a rest half way up the staircase while he caught his breath, although he pretended to be using the pause to survey the portraits of latter-day Talbots which lined the walls.

But that Ratton was, now, a rich and influential personage was beyond doubt. His mills and factories were churning out uniforms, boots, belts and knapsacks, all contracted to the government. He wore a flashy diamond ring on his little finger and drove a number of luxurious motorcars. He often brought a secretary with him, female, a thin, unsmiling individual, who walked a pace behind him, her shorthand pad at the ready. She seemed trained to anticipate his every need, equipped with a lighter for his cigar or a hip flask of brandy to stiffen his morning coffee, and sometimes a handkerchief discreetly proffered to polish the lenses of his spectacles or dab the dew-drop which periodically gathered on the blob of his nose.

Whenever I was in the room, bringing tea or adjusting curtains, Ratton watched me. His eyes seemed attached to me, as though by threads, and wherever I moved, they swivelled in pursuit, unblinking. I avoided being anywhere alone with him, and, at night time, I placed a chair against the handle of my door. Sometimes, in the mornings, I detected something awry in the kitchen - the pans were not as I had left them, perhaps, a pie had been partially consumed in the larder. One morning I found the back door standing open and the kitchen fire stone cold. Another day the kitchen clock had been stopped so if it hadn't been for my wristwatch I wouldn't have known if I was going to be late with breakfast.

I had no proof these annoyances were caused by Ratton although I could not imagine anyone else being responsible - they were just the kinds of sneaky, slightly threatening mischiefs he would conceive of as being amusing devilry, calculated to discomfort me and incommode the running of the house.

I told Rose about my worries who in turn, of course, told Kenneth. He appeared in the kitchen hot foot, flushed with annoyance. 'Should have told me,' he barked, 'that bastard. Fix him.'

'I don't *know* that it's him,' I warned.

'Rig something up,' Kenneth muttered. 'A bell, something, so you can let me know.' He spent the rest of the day stringing an electric cable between his place and my rooms and attaching a switch which I could press to bring him running.

'You're sweet,' I said, when it was done, 'and I do feel safer, knowing you're on the other end of this wire.'

'Wish I could attach one to him, and electrocute him,' Kenneth said, darkly, and stumped off home.

What we could not have anticipated, though, was that Ratton would switch his interest from me to Awan. She was almost five, very talkative and entirely confident - I had brought her up to have none of the shrinking insecurities and low self-esteem which I had suffered, as a child. She would converse without hesitation with anyone she met, be it the butcher's boy or the Prime Minister, it was all the same to her. She was almost ready for school, and eager to start; indeed I had already taught her the letters and numbers and the school mistress was encouraging her to read by allowing her access to the school library. Perhaps she was precocious? I don't know. She was happy, that was all I cared about, with full access to the entire house, the state rooms as well as the attics and cellars and dusty, unfrequented passageways and also the gardens and grounds. She was as at home in the woods as I had been - I had no fear for her, having shown her the secret byways, the best stepping stones across the tumbling streams, the concealed access behind the greenhouses and all the places I had played as a child. She knew her boundaries - the places where she was not allowed to go - the moor, the soggy, boggy grounds at the far side of the north wing where the foul water drained, Kenneth's workshops, the sty where the boar lived. More often than not, in any case, she was accompanied by Bobby in her games.

Ratton seemed amused by her, sometimes bringing her sweets (a rare treat) and toys. I might find him engaging her in conversation by the fountain while the men meandered round the gardens and smoked their cigars after luncheon, or taking an interest in a book she was looking at. One day she referred to him as 'Uncle Sylvester' and I corrected her, sharply.

'He isn't your Uncle,' I said. 'Uncle Colin is your Uncle, you have no others.'

'Uncle Kenneth is an Uncle,' she replied, pedantically, pouting her pretty little lip.

She had me there. I bit my own lips to supress a smile. 'That's different. He's an honorary Uncle,' I faltered.

'That's what Uncle Sylvester is,' she proclaimed, looking pleased with herself. 'He wants me to show him all the secret places.'

'But you mustn't,' I said, all amusement banished.

'Why not?'

'Because...' I stammered. How could I explain it to a four year old? 'Because he isn't to be trusted,' I said at last. 'He found out about *my* secret place once, and wanted to go there all the time. He couldn't *rest* until he'd been there. It spoiled it.'

Awan nodded, solemnly. 'That's bad,' she whispered.

One day, towards the end of November 1941, during a particularly protracted visit by Colin and his cronies, Awan disappeared. The weather throughout November had been wet and very windy and outdoor play had been almost impossible. But as the month drew to a close things had brightened, temperatures had dropped and on this particular day Awan had run off to play amongst the piles of frost-rimed leaves at the edge of the woodland. I saw her from a bedroom window at around eleven. Ratton was with her, draped in a greatcoat which dwarfed his diminutive figure although by then a weak sun shone. At one thirty I prepared a cold buffet luncheon for the men. Rose helped me lay it out in the dining room and then I sent her home. Rose and Kenneth took their meals in their own house now. Their baby, Brian, was a sturdy toddler with a voracious appetite who could not be kept waiting at mealtimes. When I was sure the guests had everything they needed I went in search of Awan. She was nowhere to be found.

I was calm at first - she had no idea of the time and had eaten a hearty breakfast - her stomach might not be telling her it was time to eat. I looked in all the likely places - the ice house, the stables, where one of the dogs had recently whelped and there were puppies to fondle, the glasshouses, where a few deliciously sweet late tomatoes still clung to the vines. No sign of her.

I roamed the grounds, noting a shrub which needed pruning, a silver birch which was being strangled by ivy. Still, I wasn't especially concerned. What harm could she come to here, at home, where she was safe?

Through the windows of the dining room I could see the men on their feet. Would the coffee still be hot? I went in to check if they needed more, hastily brushing twigs off my skirt and changing my shoes in the kitchen. Ratton gave me a peculiar look, his eyes unreadable behind his glasses.

'A pleasant afternoon for a stroll in the gardens,' he remarked.

The men finished their lunch and dispersed to their various occupations. I toured the house - the attics and back passages, the little-used bedrooms in the north wing, the library, where a fire and the books might well have enticed a chilly child to take refuge, but there was no sign of Awan. Her coat and stout boots were absent from the place where we always kept them. I went back out into the afternoon. The sun was sinking away behind the trees. Much of the garden was now an envelope of chill shadow.

I shouted in at Rose's door. Had she seen Awan? A muffled negative came back to me, no, not in the last couple of hours. Kenneth came out from one of the workshops, wiping his oily hands on a rag.

Kenneth was one of the few able-bodied men left behind by the war; he worked hard helping the lone women in the parish, maintaining people's vehicles and teaching women to drive them. He'd taught Rose and me, to our great hilarity; we'd taken turns burning the clutch out as we bunny-hopped up the drive, crashing the gears and having near-misses with tractors in the narrow lanes. What I had learned about him over the years was this: he was steadfast and stayed calm in a crisis. Of all men on earth he was the one I'd have chosen to help me deal with Awan's disappearance, an absolute stalwart of a friend and very fond indeed of Awan.

'Help you look,' he said, and I felt my anxiety subside just a little.

We wandered the periphery of the grounds, calling Awan's name, our voices weak and somehow ineffectual in the thin air. Kenneth employed a piercing whistle which he produced from between his teeth. It brought the dogs running immediately and also Bobby, who arrived pell-mell from school on his bicycle - was it really that time already? I wondered, distractedly. I checked my watch. Yes, it was half past three. How long, then, had Awan been missing? From inside the woods I could hear the faint, gelid splash of water as it slid down the mossy runnels and fell onto the accumulations of semi-frozen leaves. Boughs in the canopy creaked in the faint breeze. Very high up in the dome of sky above us, a buzzard circled and cried. An icy hand gripped my heart. Something was wrong; very wrong.

Rose joined us, Brian on her hip. 'We need to spread out,' I said. 'I'll go up through the woods towards the gatehouse. Bobby, could you check all the outhouses and sheds? Look with your eyes, don't just shout,' I admonished. 'She may be unconscious, ill... She may not be able to reply.'

He ran off, eager for the adventure of it.

I glanced behind me at the house. No smoke rose from the chimneys - the fires would need replenishing. A last slant of sun hit an upper window, gilding its leaded panes into amber mirror. From behind that burnished surface two round pennies of light reflected back even more strongly, winking and shimmering as their source moved his head, and I knew without a shadow of doubt Ratton was there, lurking, observing us from the shadows of the room. At that moment a French door below opened and two guests stepped out onto the terrace and lit cigarettes. 'Rose,' I said, 'the men will be wanting tea.'

'I'll see to it,' she replied, shifting the child to her other hip, 'and I'll telephone the village, just to make sure she hasn't wandered that far.'

Kenneth put his hand on my arm - it was unusual for him to make a physical gesture like this and I understood from it he was as deeply concerned as I was. 'We'll find her,' he said, looking at me intently from beneath his fringe (it had grey streaks in it, I noticed, distractedly). Then he turned and headed for the truck, urging the dogs into the back of it. 'I'll scour the moor,' he shouted, his voice thin and strained, and roared off up the drive.

I took to the woods. My voice calling Awan's name took on a shrill, anguished tone. I hurried along the by-ways I knew so well, and that I had shown Awan in our wonderful wanderings together, looking for - I don't know what. A shred of material, a hair ribbon, a discarded boot, a small body, prone and bleeding, its brains dashed out on a rock.

The light was fading, the short day hurrying to its close. Beneath the trees the air had a thick, almost tangible quality, a gloom you could almost grasp. It weighed down every sound making all the usual woodland noises maddeningly mute. In my fevered torment I imagined it would smother Awan's cries for help. I ploughed on, up the slope, dodging beneath branches and over boulders. The forest floor was thick with pine needles; there was no sign anyone else had passed that way. In the clearings the grass was wet with early dew, and unmarked. There was any number of ways Awan could have taken, always assuming I had guessed her destination. I knew where *I* would go, of course, if chased, or afraid, or bored or lonely. The gatehouse drew me like a lodestar. But there was no certainty that it would be Awan's.

Very dimly, down through the belt of woodland in the hollow where the house stood, I could hear masculine voices calling Awan's name; clearly, Rose had recruited the guests to the search. I imagined them, ineffectually thrashing through the undergrowth and getting themselves lost in the labyrinthine passages of the workshops, sheds and stables.

There was a place in a coniferous part of the woods where a serpentine track wove between the slender trunks; Awan had always liked it especially - the soft, needle-strewn floor, the strong scent of pine, the occasional fir cone which could be found. I looked carefully to see if there was any evidence that she had been here, but there was nothing. The light had dwindled to such an extent the trees themselves were only solid shadows in the more nebulous murk.

Sometimes I thought I could hear the soft tread of a little foot, or even a supressed giggle. 'Awan,' I said, sternly. 'This game is over. It is dark, and time to come home.'

But there was no reply.

Finally I reached the rim of the crater, a couple of hundred yards from the drive and the gatehouse. Several vehicles had joined Kenneth's on the short turf beside the road. Across the moor I could see lanterns and torches like fireflies, and hear dogs barking. It looked as though the village had turned out to help in the search, and I was conscious, even amidst my increasing desperation, of gratitude.

The gatehouse door was never locked, but an accumulation of leaves inside the little portico which sheltered it lay undisturbed. It yielded at my push. The scullery was dark and full of cobwebs; they caught stickily to my hair as I passed. I put my hand in the sink - it was dry - there was no indication anyone had been there for a drink of water. In the main room dust lay over the table - I wiped my hand across the old, scarred surface and it came away furred. The clock which we kept on the mantel was silent - long unwound. The air was chill and un-breathed. I stood for a long time drawing it into my panicked chest, deriving some unnamed comfort from it, as I always had done. The safe embrace of the walls around me, the familiar furniture and little bits of domestic paraphernalia which I could see in my mind's eye as clear as if it was bright morning, gave me succour. I fell into the chair by the cold fire, the same chair where I had collapsed with Awan in my arms when she was less than an hour old. I needed John, needed him more than I had ever needed him before and, heaven knew, my need of him on those other occasions had been dire enough. My soul sent out a sort of cry - I don't think I voiced it - it was more spiritual than a mere shout.

I rose from the chair and half stumbled across the room towards the door, my confidence in my surroundings gone. The sole of my boot hit the edge of a raised floor-slab and I fell against the corner of the dresser, jarring my hip and setting the crockery a-jingle on the shelves. As I steadied myself I felt, on my hair and cheek, the slightest possible brush of something, a falling mote dislodged from the wooden ceiling boards which formed the floor of the room above. All my senses tuned themselves to the room upstairs. My ears homed in, my skin was alive to any breath of air or vibration. My eyes, despite the utter darkness turned up.

Then I heard it. Hardly a sound at all, less than a whisper, the slightest slide of one material against another and the tiniest noise that lips make when they part, the susurration of a drawn breath.

Outside, the men of the village must have called their search off. I could hear voices calling farewell, dogs being urged into vehicles. I cursed them, as though their noise could cause whatever was upstairs to disappear into thin air.

Treading carefully, I crossed the room and put my foot on the bottom stair. All my old assurance in the room had returned to me. I reached out and found the banister under my hand, smooth and solid. I mounted the stairs, avoiding the creak in the middle of the third, the loose board on the sixth, the slightly proud nail-head in the next-to-top. Outside the engines of the cars and trucks coughed into life. Lights pierced the darkness. There was the sound of manoeuvring as they reversed off the grass and turned in the road to head home. Suddenly the lights of one vehicle shone straight in through the uncurtained window. It lit up the room and travelled across the space, illuminating John's skeletal easels and half-finished canvasses, his table of paints, the divan, covered with a heap of bedding, a small child.

She stood in the middle of the room like a marble statue, white and petrified, I saw her only briefly while the light remained. Lit up from behind, I must have looked to her like a dark, advancing monster. She could only have seen my silhouette, briefly, before the car's lights slid away and the total blackness of the room engulfed us both again.

Awan started to scream.

She continued to scream into my body as I wrapped her in a quilt and gathered her to myself, pressing her into the void I had felt earlier, filling myself back up with her. She had never felt so small and vulnerable to me since she had been a new-born and her cries, as then, were an out-pouring of emotion she could not articulate; the pent up anguish of her day finding release. She knew me, and clung to me, her granite stillness of a moment before collapsing at my touch; she could not stand, she was as limp as one of her rag dolls. She was cold to the bone, dehydrated, her little lips as dry as paper; I kissed them repeatedly as her screams blasted my face and penetrated my mouth and ears and heart.

Presently I wrapped her into the quilt and carried her downstairs and out of the gatehouse. All the cars but one were gone; Kenneth's remained. He had not given up the search. I knew he would never have given it up. Cradling Awan, I opened the door of the truck and leaned on the horn repeatedly, until first the dogs and then Kenneth emerged from the thick night of the moor. He was stained thigh-high in peaty water. He must have been wading through bogs in his efforts. At the same time a posse of guests from the house stumbled from the drive. They were not dressed for adventure; most were still in their smart uniforms and indoor shoes which were snagged and muddy from their exertions. Colin was amongst them of course, both relieved Awan had been found safe and well and annoyed about the drama and distraction her disappearance had caused. He would have chastised her, I think, if one of the elder statesmen had not restrained him.

Of Sylvester Ratton there was no sign at all.

The next morning there was something of an inquisition, which I was allowed to attend and, I must say, rather enjoyed. Awan's story had come haltingly out as I had fed and bathed her and put her to bed. 'Uncle Sylvester' had promised her a prize if she could hide in her most secret place until tea time without him finding her. A high-stakes game of hide-and-seek had seemed very exciting to her until midway through the afternoon, when hunger and loneliness had overwhelmed her. Once darkness had fallen she had been unable to do anything other than wait, frozen by fear and a sense of having been outwitted whether found or not. She had picked the gatehouse, she told me, because she knew that *he* knew that it was *my* secret place, and therefore wouldn't likely be hers. Also, from what I had told her, she understood Ratton had already trespassed there; even if he did find her, he would not be discovering anything he did not already know. Part of me marvelled at (and was rather proud of) this complex reasoning, the rest shuddered at the twisted mentality of the man. To play such a game was one thing - to set off in search of her, to do his part - but to send her off with no intention of even looking, and, worse, to feign ignorance and innocence while half the county had been raised, was quite another.

I am happy to say that, for once, Colin saw things through my eyes. He was fond of Awan in his cold, fishy way, and rather proud of her wit and confidence amongst the sombre-suited politicians and strategists he brought to Tall Chimneys. He and a small delegation of the gentlemen cornered Ratton in the dining room after breakfast the next morning. By arrangement, I was there clearing the breakfast dishes. At a discreet signal from Colin the majority of the men left the room and Colin closed the door. Ratton, who had been finishing his coffee and staring out of the window, turned at the sudden silence and realised what had occurred.

'What's this?' he blustered, placing his cup and saucer on the table. Behind his eye-glasses, his eyes blinked repeatedly, a spurious indication of innocence.

'My sister tells me that you were the cause of the child's disappearance yesterday.' Colin came right out with it.

An older man with a grey, nicotine-stained handlebar moustache muttered 'Very poor show.'

'Me?' Ratton laughed nervously, 'what could I have had to do with it? I know nothing about it.'

'You suggested the idea to her,' I said. 'You offered her a prize if she could stay hidden until tea time.'

Ratton shrugged, but a line of perspiration oozed onto his upper lip. 'She misunderstood me,' he stammered.

'Not at all,' I replied, 'she expected you to be looking for her. She thought it was a game.'

'I haven't got time for games,' Ratton spluttered, indignantly. 'The girl's a liar. I haven't spoken to her.'

'*You're* a liar,' I countered. 'I saw you speaking to her yesterday, by the fountain.'

'So did I, as a matter of fact,' said the moustache-man.

'The child's a damned nuisance, always in the way,' Ratton spat out. 'I may have told her to go away and stop bothering me.' He threw me a steely glare, 'You ought to keep her under better control, madam.'

'I find her a very pleasant child, and extremely well-behaved,' put in a balding man who remained seated at the table. 'A pleasure to have about the place, in fact.'

I gave him a grateful smile.

'Whatever your intention, whatever you actually said, it was very ill-judged,' pronounced a man with smoothly slicked-back black hair. 'I have two daughters at home. The idea of either of them being lost for hours...'

'She wasn't lost,' Ratton interrupted. 'In fact she boasted to me that she knew every inch of the woods and could hide for days if necessary. She still has some idea the Germans are due imminently.'

'There but for the grace of God...' the balding man said under his breath.

'So you *did* have some conversation with her!' Colin pounced.

'I *told* you the man's a liar,' I put in, bitterly. 'I've been telling you for years he isn't to be trusted.'

'Let's not rake up old grievances,' Colin said.

'No, indeed,' Ratton echoed. 'If I'm to be arraigned for misdeeds past and present, accused by a loose woman and her illegitimate progeny...'

'Sir!' the smooth-haired man interrupted. 'Remember your manners!'

'Yes, Sylvester,' Colin warned, 'remember of whom you are speaking...'

'Well,' Ratton threw his hands up, 'I'll not be party to any kangaroo court.'

'No more will I,' the bald man said, 'nevertheless, I think it's clear you gave the child the idea of hiding, and offered her an incentive to do so. At the very least you owe her some recompense.'

'Agreed,' the slick-haired man said.

Ratton's usually pasty complexion turned puce. He groped in his pocket and threw some coins onto the table cloth, 'A few shillings? Will that put an end to this ridiculous interrogation?'

'A few guineas would be more like it, I think,' the man with the moustache said, drawing his pipe from his pocket. 'The child's had a terrible fright, not to mention our lady hostess, here. As it turned out there's been no actual harm done, but potentially…'

'Oh, alright,' Ratton said, with ill-grace. 'I'll see the child is recompensed. What a fuss over nothing, when we have so many other more important things to occupy us.' He took out a weighty pocket watch and squinted at it. 'Now you must excuse me. I have a meeting in York and I'm going to be late.' He strode round the table and put his hand on the door knob. 'Thank you for your kind hospitality, Colin,' he said, through gritted teeth. 'I fear my business will detain me for a day or two. Kindly have my valise sent on to The Grand in York. I shan't have time to pack, now.'

He wrenched open the door and disappeared through it.

'Thank you, gentlemen,' I said, quietly, gathering dishes onto a tray.

'A pleasure, madam,' the man with the black hair said. 'Such an engaging child, with that cloud of blonde curls and those blue eyes. Reminds me of someone. Can't think who…'

'Can't you?' Colin asked, sharply.

I felt the blood rush to my face. I kept my eyes down, riveted to the greasy dishes and eggy cutlery. Even the men who knew about my association with John could never have supposed Awan to be his child - as dark as she was golden, his features as bold and full as hers were delicate and fine - and, it was true, the older she got, the more like her biological father she became. *He,* surely, was well-known to these men, and it would not take an Einstein to make the connection. Colin's question was virtually a challenge to them to do so. I could almost hear their mental processes considering men of their acquaintance.

'As Ratton says, there are more pressing matters,' the older man said, breaking the silence. 'Talbot, I want to go over those papers with you again...' The two left the room in deep conversation.

'And I must telephone Westminster.' The bald man said, getting up from the table and following them.

As I gathered in the breakfast things I heard Ratton's motorcar pull onto the gravel at the front of the house. I longed to hear it drive away; the man's malevolence always caused me to shudder. But the engine idled for a while and presently I heard raised voices. When I reached the open dining room window I saw Kenneth, dressed in his gardening gear and grasping a scythe, holding Ratton by the shirt-front against the bonnet of the car. Ratton was purple, struggling ineffectually against Kenneth's vice-like grip. I couldn't make out Kenneth's words but there was a torrent of them, more than I had ever heard him speak since we had been childhood companions. He spat words like bullets from a machine gun into Ratton's face. Kenneth himself was blanched white, even his freckles had paled. The contrast between the two men couldn't have been starker; Kenneth, slim and hale, as tough as hemp, and Ratton, soft and fat and as ineffectual as eider feathers. Kenneth leaned forward, Ratton cowered back. Kenneth was white-hot, powerful in his anger, while Ratton melted with fear, a pathetic excuse for a man.

After a while Ratton tore himself from Kenneth's grip, scrambled into his car and roared off up the drive. Kenneth remained on the gravel, his fist opening and closing around the handle of the scythe. I wrestled with the window catch and threw the window wide. The sound alerted him to my presence. We looked at each other and for once his eyes did not slide away but held mine in a steadfast gaze. We both smiled.

JOHN CAME HOME on leave at the beginning December 1941 and announced he could stay for Christmas. I greeted him rapturously but Awan outdid me in enthusiasm. That evening she refused to go to bed and in the end we took her in with us - a mistake, of course. Her presence in the bed put the kybosh on our usual blissful reunion after a separation, that night and subsequently, as, naturally, once she had been admitted to the big bed she refused to go back to her own.

John seemed physically well, although more tired than he usually was after a time in London. I questioned him, but he was as close-lipped as ever. He was thin; good food was possible to find in London despite rationing, if one had money, but the hours he worked seemed to preclude regular mealtimes and John was not one to eat while his neighbour went hungry. The blitz had ceased earlier in the year as Hitler had turned his attention to the Soviet Union, so threat of air-raids was less, but the situation in the capital was still dire, streets reduced to rubble, gas and electricity still very unreliable and unexploded bombs being discovered daily.

John sat and listened carefully as Awan and I described the day she had hidden in the gatehouse and why she had done so. I was glad to see her ordeal had not quelled her spirit; she was as brave and as adventurous as ever around Tall Chimneys, but she was more reserved with the gentlemen who came to stay; she had learned a hard lesson, I suppose, that not all men are to be trusted.

The incident seemed to ignite a gnawing angst in John - he was furiously angry with Ratton, of course - but there was something else, another quality to his reaction which I couldn't, at first, identify. Why had Ratton taken such an interest in the child, he wanted to know. Had he, on other occasions? Had I discouraged it? Or allowed it?

'Awan makes herself at home in the house,' I told him, 'and why wouldn't she? It's her home! She is used to having gentlemen stay here and she thinks nothing of speaking to them. Ratton is just one amongst many. I neither encouraged nor discouraged it.'

'But surely,' he fumed, 'Ratton, of all people, you would want to keep her away from. Unless...'

'Unless?'

'Well,' he gave me a sideways look, 'unless he has some right...'

'A right?'

It dawned on me, then, what was at the root of John's response. He was jealous of Awan. Although he knew he was not her father he was the nearest she had to one. He didn't like the idea of anyone usurping that role, let alone Ratton. And it had come to him in a blinding flash of lunacy that the one man I might allow to form a relationship with the child was her natural father.

In spite of myself, I started to laugh. 'You think Ratton might be Awan's father?'

He had the decency to look ashamed of himself.

'Over my dead body,' I declared. 'If you want to know, I'll tell you.'

'No,' he shook his head. 'I don't want to know.'

It was a thing that stood between us, a shadow. Like John's marriage to Monique, Awan's provenance was a closed book, something we could not share with one another. It separated us, an obstacle we could never over-leap no matter how we tried. I wonder if he resented it, as I resented his marriage. Did it haunt his dreams as he and Monique inhabited mine? And what did he imagine? A charming seducer? A romp under a hay-stack? An on-going affair which suffered a hiatus every time he came home? All I can tell you is that his umbrage - if he felt any - never showed in his dealings with Awan; he was never anything other than loving and true to her - the perfect father. And if he doubted my loyalty, he never showed that, either.

The Japanese bombed Pearl Harbour a day or so after John came home and we entered onto a new phase of the war; The United States joined the allies along with Canada, Australia and New Zealand. The theatre of war was wider than ever, being fought on islands and in seas which were so remote they were almost unheard of to many small-islanders. Certainly, for myself, as reclusive as I had been, they meant almost nothing; I could as easily imagine Jupiter or Neverland as those sweltering islands and dust-blown deserts, and yet I was as alive as anyone to the terrible hardships and devastating losses of men and ships. More and more villagers and townspeople had received news of killed, wounded or missing men-folk. One or two dreadfully maimed and disfigured men began to reappear on our streets, their trouser legs pinned up, their shirt sleeves empty, their eyes blank - blind, or haunted by some inner nightmare.

At first John thought this new development would mean him cutting his leave short, but we were reprieved - he could stay. He took Awan into town shopping before Christmas, a trip loaded with excitement and mystery in equal measure which had her almost incontinent with anticipation beforehand but which sobered her when she encountered the wounded men on the streets and in the shops. John told her not to stare at them, but also, not to ignore them. He instructed her to say 'good morning,' as she would to anyone, and to forgive them if they did not reply.

We enjoyed Christmas with Kenneth, Rose, Bobby and Brian, and had a small party for Awan on Boxing Day, her fifth birthday. The weather over Christmas was cold, with hard frosts and bright, glittering days. John went up to the gatehouse most days to paint. Sometimes he took Awan with him. Occasionally they would take their paints and easels outside, onto the moor. Awan's daubings were immature, of course, and she soon grew tired of sitting still and would wander off to collect things she considered interesting. John's paintings were bleak, wide expanses of featureless moor rendered in smears of grey and purple, dark boggy pools like gaping mouths, the sky as cold and hard as steel with a grey blade of cloud, knife-like, across the horizon. Only a smudge of cottage with a wisp of smoke rising from its indistinctly rendered chimney, or the hazy spire of the village church would offer any comfort in these forbidding landscapes, at all.

On these days Awan would sometimes fall asleep in the car on the ride back down the drive, exhausted by fresh air and exercise. John would carry her into the house and give me a knowing look over her nodding head. He would tuck her into bed fully clothed, creeping out of the room and closing the door with stealthy movements. Then we would throw ourselves into each other's arms, kissing and tugging at clothing, stumbling against furniture, scarcely making it to our own room before the first wave of pleasure hit us.

Even while John was at Tall Chimneys, despite it being holiday time, I remained busy. The house remained an unwieldy burden to maintain. Thankfully Colin's money continued to come and I could pay masons and roofers for repairs when required. The old generator continued to run thanks to Kenneth's ministrations and the plumbing creaked and shuddered, but worked. Kenneth, Rose and I worked hard in the kitchen gardens to provide food. We had chickens for eggs and meat, a pig and, that year, I recall, a few ewes in lamb. Many afternoons found me in the village, in the church hall or out on the old cricket pitch and village green, where we grew produce as a community. Conscription for all women had begun and many of my contemporaries had joined the ATS, WRNS, WVS and the WAAF in spite of being married with children. My own involvement on the Home Front seemed to satisfy the authorities and, indeed, I really threw myself into the work that had to be done 'keeping things going'. We were busy growing vegetables, bottling fruit and making chutney and jam. Nothing was allowed to go to waste. We knitted socks and scarves for the men serving abroad, and made up parcels to be sent away. We cared for the children, sharing out those whose parents were serving in the forces, volunteering or working in reserved occupations such as the munitions factories. We comforted each other when news came that a loved one had been lost.

On 5th January 1942 John and I took Awan to the village school, where she skipped into the classroom with barely a backward glance at us. I clung on to John's arm as we watched her go. He was dressed for travel, his packed bag in the car.

There was plenty of time before John's train. As we left the village I considered driving down one of the farm tracks or isolated lanes I had discovered; I itched for him, my sexual appetite by no means satisfied by the two or three hurried couplings we had managed while Awan slept or played out with Bobby and Brian. The idea of having him in the car, or on a blanket in the corner of a meadow, or both, made my juices flow. As long as we had been together I still found him irresistible. His hair was still very dark although much shorter than it had been when we had first met. He had retained his honed physique; he was well-muscled though spare of flesh. Nearer forty than thirty, he had developed creases around his eyes but the eyes themselves were as dark and deep as they had always been, velvet with lashes, and full of passion.

I wondered if his thoughts ran along the same lines as mine. If he hadn't spoken, I would have taken the initiative - there was a secluded track I knew of which led through a copse and would have afforded us privacy. But as the entrance came into view, he said, 'Do you think you'll always live here?'

His question startled me - I hadn't expected it - but it matched so ill with my mischievous plans I hardly took it seriously. I did think I'd always live there. I had never had any other life and, with its slight enlargement into the village and even occasionally into the nearby town, I wanted no other. 'At Tall Chimneys?' I asked, waggling my eyebrows suggestively, 'well, that depends.'

'On what?'

'Whether you'll keep coming back here,' I threw him a coquettish smile.

The tempting entrance to the greenway passed by, but there were others I knew of.

He smiled back, and reached out his hand to rest it over mine on the gear stick. 'Of course, as you're here, I will,' he said, with a resigned smile.

'So that will be always,' I said, with a laugh which came out forced and artificial. His air of long-suffering had put a stone in my stomach.

He said 'You know, Evelyn, there's a great big world out there. It might be in chaos, now, with war spread out like stain across its surface, but it's out there and in spite of what we're doing to it, it is beautiful. You ought to see it. You ought to take Awan and travel. You don't want, for her - do you? - the sequestered life you've had? And I think after the war things will change, very quickly. She - and you - must keep up.'

'This is sounding like a valedictory speech,' I said, tearfully now, all my roguish plans forgotten.

'No, no,' he soothed.

'Or that you're bored of Tall Chimneys, and of me.'

The world sounded like a frightening place to me. I knew I was parochial and naïve. The idea of sending Awan out into the bewildering unknown was terrifying to me and yet I knew John was right. She must have wider experiences than I, meet more people, see more, do more. This day - her first school day - was in every sense the first of the rest of her life. The question was - and I knew it was the question John was really asking me - would I go with her, or send her out alone?

We travelled for a while in silence. Then he said, 'The Royal Academy is staging its summer exhibition as usual, despite everything. I've been asked to submit something.'

'Really?' I turned to look at him. This was a wonderful piece of news. John's work was known and respected amongst a limited number of connoisseurs but was considered too outré by many. Sir Edwin Lutyens, however, the current President of the Royal Academy, was just the kind of forward-thinking person to appreciate John's modern style. 'Which piece will you submit?'

I considered John's recent works - the harrowing canvasses he had done on his return from Dunkirk, his desolate renditions of the moor above Tall Chimneys. The comparison with the exuberant botanical studies he had been working on before Awan was born, and the enormous experimental works he had been doing for George and Rita couldn't be more marked. It occurred to me for the first time that they reflected much more than what John saw, they reflected what he felt - the inner man; John was tortured, depressed and unhappy and it was my fault. How narrow and provincial my world must seem to him, after living in Paris and London. What a dearth of interesting artistic conversation there was at Tall Chimneys, where the year's carrot crop and some new recipe for pickle brine were sometimes our most fervently discussed topics.

'You'll be tremendously busy all spring,' I said, brightly, cranking down the window to let out an imaginary fly so he wouldn't see the tears in my eyes. 'I doubt you'll be able to get home, much.'

'So much of this war is being fought in secret,' John replied, cryptically. 'The battle fields are only the half of it. Intelligence will win the war for us, or lose it. And we're getting to a critical point.'

'Oh! With work, yes, but really I meant with painting. The exhibition might give you the impetus to do something entirely new. It will open up a whole new world of opportunities for you.'

'That's what I've been trying to say,' John sighed. 'The world out there offers opportunities for both of us. If only you'd come out.'

We pulled into the station yard. 'How can I?' I almost wailed, 'how can *we?*

'What do you think will happen?' John asked, witheringly. 'Do you expect to be put in the stocks? To have your nose cut off? Or a bolt of lightning to come down and strike you dead? The world isn't so medieval, now, Evelyn.'

I looked at him. The slaughter taking place across the globe felt to me exactly that - as crude and bloody as the Crusades of old. I felt the guilt of my unconventional life like a heavy weight around my neck - like Hester

Prynne's letter A. And yet, I told myself, I had made a world for myself where I was safe and even accepted. I had brought the folks in the village round to tolerate me - that was something, wasn't it? I had even brazened things out in the local market town. That had taken courage. But surely, out in the real world, I'd be spurned, wouldn't I? I imagined being turned away from decent accommodation, having respectable doors shut in my face, refused service in restaurants and cafes.

'No,' John said, reading my thoughts. 'People have moved on. Nowadays, when life is so precious, and often so short, nobody cares about who sleeps with whom. But you won't believe that, will you? Why would you, when you're so comfortable here? But do you ever wonder what it's like for *me?*'

The question haunted me as I waved John off on his train. He disappeared back into the world of secret communications, confidential intelligence and dark mystery he inhabited and left me feeling very far behind.

I drove home and, not able to face the house empty of both John and Awan, let myself into the gatehouse. It was dusty and cold. I lit a fire and drew some water to heat over it. The tea in the caddy was stale and I had no milk, but I drank it anyway, wallowing in my misery. I cried for a while, at first just an outlet for the tears I had not shed at the school or in the car, or on the station platform, but then in genuine anguish at my predicament, all of my own making, I realised.

Was I 'so comfortable' at Tall Chimneys? I had been in charge there, to all intents and purposes, my own mistress, independent, with the huge house and the encircling grounds to roam in as I had willed. But the truth was I had closeted myself at Tall Chimneys, too afraid to venture even to Leeds or York, let alone to London or abroad. My 'independence' had been a sham! Was it any wonder I was green and gauche? Why hadn't I braved the world? It was a self-fulfilling prophecy, I realised. I was green because I had not kept up with the times, and I had not kept up with the times because I was simply too old fashioned to fit in. How could I ever have thought that, small, mousey, unworldly as I was, I could hold a man like

John? And yet I had tied myself to him, knowing it to be an alliance which the world would always frown upon, knowing I would be a guilty shackle around his ankle. I might have told myself I did not care but, really, I cared very much.

Then, to make matters worse, I had recklessly slept with another man and got myself with child, adding to the burden John must carry and making my perpetual incarceration at Tall Chimneys even more certain. If I did not have the gall as a mistress to face the world, how much less could I do it with a fatherless child? My action had tied me even more securely to Tall Chimneys. I had walled up my guilty secrets there in the same way that I might have nurtured a monster, believing I would be free from prying eyes and wagging fingers, but as much a prisoner as the pig in the sty, and equally doomed.

John's final comment rankled most of all. Did I ever wonder what it was like for him, to be alone? What solitary hours he must pass, I thought, but then, another thought assailed me: what temptations might apparent singleness bring his way? How might he console himself for my absence?

I roused myself and took up a cloth and broom. I cleaned out the gatehouse, ravelling the cobwebs from the rafters and sweeping away the bloom of grey dust which coated the furniture. I shook out the covers from the ottoman and hung them out to air in the chill wind. I collected branches from the woods and stacked them under the eaves. I hid John's easel and canvasses behind a screen and tidied his paints and brushes away, throwing a lace cloth over the table where they had habitually been scattered. I worked automatically, without any thought, until the tolling of the school bell alerted me to the time, and I rushed out to the car to collect Awan.

Later, I settled her in to her own bed, and went upstairs to escape her cries of protest, wandering the state rooms until they had subsided. Not until she had quietened did I go back down to the echoing kitchen and at last into my own chamber. I felt the vast press of Tall Chimneys all around me like a suffocating weight, and the choking encirclement of the woods around the house, and the squeeze of the moor tightening in, and I realised the significance of my day's activity. Rather than reaching out into the world John was so keen for me to step into, I had been running further away from it, burrowing deeper in to Tall Chimneys. I had been preparing the gatehouse as my last bastion, an inner sanctum, a cell, a coffin.

I tossed and turned all night, all my old feelings of uncertainty clamouring to be heard. In the morning, early, I heard a footstep in the passageway. Kenneth greeted me with a grin. 'You're to come to breakfast, Rose says.' He nodded at the chair at the head of the kitchen table, the one John habitually used. 'You won't want to be staring at an empty chair,' he explained.

'Kenneth,' I cried, 'you're an absolute god-send. What would I do without you? I could kiss you.'

He blushed to the roots of his hair and his eyes slid to a point just above my knees. 'Come quick or the muffins will be cold,' he muttered.

'Ah,' I sighed. 'Where there are Rose's muffins, there is hope.'

1941 - 1944

The entry of the US and Canada into the war was another thing which provided hope although, from my point of view, they also brought the wider world uncomfortably close to my doorstep. Our morale improved because it evened up the balance of power - with such militarily superior troops and weaponry on our side, how could we lose? The talk in the village shop and along the assiduously tended rows of vegetables was up-beat. At first the talk was all fuelled by information from newsreels and the radio. We heard that they came equipped with fast, light jeeps, bigger planes, better guns and a business-like, 'can-do' attitude which made the slow machine of the British military seem woefully sluggish and old-hat. They were reputed to be a-brim with confidence; bigger and broader than our Tommies, and more attractively arrayed - their uniforms made the olive drab of the British regalia seem very homespun. With their pronounced swagger and characteristic drawl, they behaved like film stars, every one of them. They were gallant, we were told, their 'ma'am' so much more chivalrous than the 'missus' of the average Yorkshireman. They had seemingly endless supplies of money - the average GI earned five times what a British soldier earned and he was not shy of spending it, apparently; in areas where a US or Canadian encampment was established, business flourished.

Then, they were amongst us. In March a small Corps of US engineers came to occupy the RAF training camp which had existed for the past two years on the other side of the moor. They tore down the shabby wooden huts which had housed the trainee pilots and put up pre-fabricated buildings. These arrived in sections and only needed bolting together, providing roomy billets, a kitchen, mess-hall, classrooms and a shower block. They bulldozed the rough airstrip, making it wider, longer and covering it with cinder transported from various steel-works in the south of the county. They constructed an air-control tower with a modern radar installation. When off-duty the men converged on the local towns and villages, spending money in the shops and cafes, instigating dances and film-screenings in the long-deserted village halls and getting used to the local ale.

I didn't like it. Their modernity made me feel like a throw-back of history; I was out of step, out of place, out of time.

John did not, as I had predicted, come home at Easter time. He wrote to us fairly regularly. Of his work he said nothing, other than that it was more demanding than ever, and involving 'some travel', but he said he was painting in his spare time. I was glad of it, and wondered, with a bitter, jealous twist in my gut, what his work looked like, now he was back in his natural environment, and free of our constraint.

After a cold and wet start to the year, April and May were warm and sunny; the gardens looked splendid and we were hopeful of good crops of soft fruits and legumes. I kept myself very busy, adding occasional visits to my friends and the local market town to my schedule of activities, to keep my spirits buoyant.

Rose had her third baby - another boy, Anthony - in May. Kenneth brought him across to the house to show off, proud as a peacock but also endearingly shy when I teased him about his fecundity - perhaps he would rather I'd believed he'd found the baby in the gooseberry patch. This baby had his father's red hair and wary eyes. I took him gently into my arms. I ached for another baby of my own, for John's baby, but it was clear to me by that time such a thing was not to be. As I held the baby I was conscious of a sudden stab of envy that Rose's early fall from grace should have been forgiven and made good by the love of a decent man and the blessing of more children, while I seemed destined to remain forever cursed by mine. I wonder if Kenneth read my thoughts. He put a hand on my shoulder and gave me a look so filled to the brim with understanding and sympathy that for once it was me who blushed.

It might have been all of a piece with my sense that John was slipping away from me, but I had an abrupt sensation of vulnerability. It was abetted by my feeling that the world, in the guise of the Americans, was encroaching further and further onto what I thought of as my own territory. 'You won't move away?' I stammered, assaulted all at once with the idea they might abandon me and Tall Chimneys. The accommodation I had given them above the old estate offices and gun rooms would be too cramped for a family of five, as homely as Rose had made it. Bobby and Brian had to share a room and I knew this annoyed Bobby. Kenneth really needed more space for his repair and maintenance work which had flourished into a thriving business. I feared they had already outgrown Tall Chimneys in a way which I knew I never could.

Kenneth shook his head. 'Never,' he said.

While Rose was recovering from the birth she didn't help me in the house and so I didn't get the opportunity to gauge what she was thinking on the matter; I feared, though, that her desire for more space would outweigh Kenneth's promise to stay.

Colin did not visit at all, which was a relief. With Rose preoccupied by the baby and Awan at school, I put covers over the furniture in many of the rooms to save on pointless dusting and cleaning and took myself off into the gardens and up into the village as often as possible.

In June, I arrived home from collecting Awan from school to find a jeep parked haphazardly on the gravel sweep and two US Captains waiting for me in the library. How they had found their way there, I do now know. The idea of them wandering at will through the house, 'casing the joint' made me anxious and angry at the same time.

They both stood up as I entered the room. 'Good afternoon, ma'am,' they said in perfect unison.

Both men wore uniform; short jackets tapered to the waist, well-tailored trousers, black boots - stout but very clean. They kept their caps tucked under their arms. They were broad in the shoulder, their hair very short, chins clean shaven. They carried with them the smell of soap - pretty strong - and (stronger still) of spearmint.

I replied, stiffly, 'What can I do for you gentlemen? Perhaps I ought to inform you that, in England, it is considered polite to wait until invited, before entering a house.'

The taller of the two men proffered a document, a warrant, I supposed. 'Indeed, ma'am, we would have preferred not to trespass, but our orders do allow…'

I waved his letter away with a look of disgust.

The man summoned a palpable rush of bonhomie, calling it into himself as though from thin air. He spirited the paper away and held out his hand instead, a friendly gesture accompanied by a winning smile - very white teeth, a rather engaging dimple in one cheek. 'Captain Aloysius Brook, ma'am,' he gushed. I steeled myself to resist his blandishments and returned a withering look. 'And Captain Cameron Bentley,' he swept his spurned hand out in a seamless gesture to indicate his companion. '2nd Battalion, 503rd PIR,[12] at your service.'

'I thank you, I am not in need of a 2nd Battalion 503rd PIR,' I said, without a glimmer of a smile on my face. I knew what was coming.

Captain Brook widened his smile. 'Of course not,' he conceded, 'but the 2nd Battalion 503rd PIR is in need of *you*.'

'I thought as much,' I nodded.

'Next week our first trainees arrive,' he explained. 'The men will be accommodated at the camp, but the officers will be billeted on local homes.'

'Will they, now?' I raised an eyebrow. 'Mrs Coombes, at the Plough and Harrow, has comfortable rooms and cooks a wonderful breakfast,' I said. 'I am sure she'd be pleased to accommodate your officers.'

Captain Bentley took a notebook from his jacket pocket and flicked through the pages. 'Check,' he said, quietly. I noticed a tremor in his cheek. A nervous tic?

'She certainly was a very friendly lady,' Captain Brook agreed.

'Mrs Widderington at Clough Farm took in guests, before the war,' I suggested.

Captain Bentley leafed through his book. 'Land Army girls...' he muttered.

I ran through the other houses and farms in the village where there were rooms to spare, and where the payment of a billeting fee would be welcome. As I spoke the names, Captain Bentley gave an apologetic nod of agreement. 'We've visited everywhere, ma'am,' he said, avoiding my eye, 'and we still have four officers to place.' The twitch in his cheek continued to pull at the corner of his mouth. He rubbed his chin from time to time, as though to calm it.

---

[12] Parachute Infantry Regiment.

'The fact is,' I said, 'this house is already used for war purposes. I can't say too much, I am sure you understand.'

'Loose lips sink ships,' Captain Bentley said, sagely, staring at a faded flower on the library carpet.

'What kind of war purposes?' Captain Brook enquired, conversationally.

'Excuse me,' I replied, and went off to telephone Colin.

It took a while to get through. In the meantime, I served tea. The men drank from the delicate porcelain cups with great care, and hid their dislike of the beverage as best they could. I answered their questions monosyllabically. Only Awan provided any distraction from the stand-off which was, effectively, taking place across the library hearth rug. She brought an atlas down from a shelf and asked the men to show her where they came from. Captain Brook pointed to New York, Captain Bentley showed her a small town on the shores of Lake Michigan, 'St Joseph's,' he said.

The afternoon drew in and it was soon dark outside. I thought I was going to have to light the fire, perhaps even offer dinner, but at last the telephone began to ring.

To my dismay, Colin could offer me no support. 'The Americans are taking over the whole shooting match,' he told me, across a line alive with static. 'It would cause a diplomatic incident if I were to refuse them houseroom, Evelyn. You'll have to put them up.'

'But what if you need the place for one of your pow-wows?' I asked. 'We can hardly ask the Cabinet to share the place with a bunch of GIs.'

'It probably won't come to that,' Colin said. 'Put them up in the north wing, where it's cold and draughty, and don't let them into the cellar.'

I returned to the library with a heavy heart. 'My brother agrees to extend his hospitality,' I said, with a fixed, chilly smile, 'although I ought to qualify that term: we live frugally; the generator is unreliable and the plumbing very testy. Our victuals are by no means lavish. That said, I shall prepare rooms tomorrow.'

'Victuals?' Captain Brook turned a questioning eye on his companion.

'Supplies, I guess,' he replied, with a shrug.

The enormity of what was about to happen hit me in a sudden wave of anxiety. Four men - with aides? Valets? I didn't know what arrangements officers made for their personal care. Did four really mean eight? Or more? Or would I be expected to do their laundry, clean their boots, press their shirts? And these would be with me for the foreseeable future, permanent inhabitants, unlike Colin's guests, who came and stayed for three or four days and then went away again. My domain would be occupied, my little empire compromised. The idea made my chest squeeze with a kind of panic. 'My daughter and I live alone in the house,' I said, with a wobble in my voice which must have completely destroyed the Mrs Danvers impression I had managed to carry off up to this point. I didn't like the vulnerability it betrayed, but I felt it had to be said for Awan's sake, as well as for my own. 'There are no live-in servants either male or female. My...' I almost said 'husband' but caught myself in time; they might know I was unmarried - Captain Bentley's little book had seemed a fairly comprehensive inventory of the local houses and inhabitants. 'My daughter's...' Again 'father' was a stretch on the truth. 'John,' I clarified, at last, 'works for Military Intelligence in London. Can I assume my guests will respect our situation? And not expect to be waited on hand and foot? And the house,' I cast an arm out to indicate the neat if rather well-worn furniture, the artefacts in the cabinets, the gloomy portraiture, 'one hears such tales of disrespect and vandalism,' I concluded.

'Have no fear, ma'am,' Captain Brook said, rising to his feet and affixing his cap to his head. 'Captain Bentley and I will be two of the officers billeted on you. We'll ensure you and this wonderful old house are treated with the utmost respect at all times. On the matter of 'victuals', you'll have our ration books and I'll send our quartermaster to you.'

This, at least, was promising. Captains Brook and Bentley took their leave, and it wasn't until they were out of the door and on their way to their jeep that the tic in Captain Bentley's face climaxed into a broad grin. That he had been supressing laughter made me both angry and amused, and angry at myself for being amused. I shut the door on them with more vigour than I had intended, and a shower of motes shook from the chandelier and descended like infinitesimal snowflakes to the polished wooden floor.

Captains Brook and Bentley moved their things into Tall Chimneys the following day. I led them down the grim, bare-boarded corridors of the north wing and showed them into two of the four large but rather drear rooms I had selected for my guests. They had unprepossessing views over the stable yard and the kitchen garden. The furniture in each was by no means the best I had to offer. Both rooms had scarred, wonky-legged side tables liable to throw any object placed on them right off again. One had a chest whose drawers stuck immovably at a point where it was impossible to get anything in or out, another a wardrobe whose doors wouldn't close properly. The mattresses in all had seen much better days, the carpets were worn, the single arm chairs were as uncomfortable as it was possible to imagine. Earlier I had wrenched open the recalcitrant windows and swept a harvest of flies and desiccated moths from the window ledges, raised a cloud of dust from atop the armoires and collected up the soot fall from the hearths. I had made up the beds with fresh sheets, though, spread clean antimacassars on the spiteful armchairs and taken the rugs into the yard for a good beating. As a last minute offering I had placed bowls of fruit to hand, and added small vases of flowers from the garden. I thought the rooms looked welcoming in a resigned sort of way; 'Alright, stay if you must,' they seemed to say, 'but don't expect me to make much of an effort for you.' It was an attitude which uncannily reflected my own. The single bathroom I had allocated for their shared use was some distance away, round a corner and up a short, shadowed and notoriously unexpected flight of stairs, off a half-landing. Hot water rarely made it that far up the system. The toilet flush was unreliable.

'Wonderful, thank you,' the two men chorused, allowing no trace of dismay to show on their faces.

I showed them the dining room. 'Well *this* is very splendid!' exclaimed Captain Brook, looking around at the polished furniture and gleaming silver, 'we haven't anything like this at home.'

'What time will you require breakfast?' I asked. They cheerfully named an ungodly hour and my heart sank. 'And what kinds of things do you prefer?' I asked, dully.

'Oh, grits, eggs, biscuits and gravy,' Captain Brook said, 'the usual things, you know?'

I didn't know. Eggs, I could manage. I had a vague idea that 'grits' were a sort of porridge. But no combination I could imagine of biscuits and gravy could be suitable for human consumption. 'And dinner?' They said when on-duty they would eat dinner at the camp, which was a relief. But on other days 'whatever you're having will be just fine.'

Captains Brook and Bentley were my guests for the next few months. Other officers came and went, each staying only the two weeks allocated for their men to be trained up at the airfield, and they hardly registered with me. To be sure they were polite enough, respectful if brusque at times, preoccupied with their men and their mission I supposed. Amongst themselves they showed a comradeship which I rather envied, but, to me, they were a closed book and if any of them noticed me at all, they did not show it. They returned my cold, resentful hospitality with formal, lukewarm thanks. I did nothing to provide more than the most basic bed and board; hard beds, cold baths, unappetising food. I was sorry to see them come and glad to see them go and I made no secret of it to them, maintaining a haughty, dignified front. Whilst the British officers respected my reserve, the Americans were not a whit deterred, gushingly friendly and enthusiastic at all times, meeting my po-faced surliness with wide displays of their enviable dentistry. Perhaps they had been told English people were cold, rude and suspicious - well, all I can say is that I did not disappoint.

The nature of the visiting platoons' training soon became clear; they were to learn to jump out of aeroplanes wearing parachutes and it was the 2nd Battalion, 503rd PIR's job to teach them how. The men were schooled in the use and application of their various pack items, shown how to jump and roll on landing, instructed on the safe stashing of their gear in enemy territory. Then they jumped; first from towers of hay-bales and later from taller structures, then from planes. These, sometimes piloted by Brook and Bentley, took off several times a day with their green-gilled cargo. Men fell to earth on the moor and the surrounding farmlands, sometimes breaking legs and arms or giving themselves concussion, but more often bruised but safe. I heard reports of men falling through barn roofs, men landing in duck ponds, men suspended by loops of webbing from trees. One fool landed on the roof of the church and was there for hours while a steeple jack was brought from Sheffield. I got used to hearing the roar of the aeroplanes as they took off from the airstrip and climbed into the sky above Tall Chimneys. From time to time the jumps were at night; then the shriek of the aircraft would be followed by whistles as men combed the moor for airmen who had not reported back. Lights could be seen against the drab grey of moorland on those summer nights when it never properly went dark.

Occasionally the military personnel would be joined by others, very cloak-and-dagger, 'specialists' who were to be trained, flown at night over enemy territory and dropped in secret for some highly classified mission.

The officers caused a good deal of work; the laundering of their towels and bedsheets, cleaning their rooms, the preparation of their food. Where they got their personal laundry done I did not know and did not ask in case that, too, fell to my lot. They used one of the smaller drawing rooms for their recreation, bringing in bottles of beer from goodness knows where, and smoking endless cigarettes. The bottles were always neatly gathered for collection, the cigarette stubs never anywhere other than in the ashtrays or the grate, and yet I railed at their untidiness and resented their intrusion into my domain. They seemed constitutionally unable to plump a cushion or to draw the curtains properly. There was a certain table which was always out of place when I entered the room; it drove me half demented. At night their conversation, muted enough in volume, yet clearly high-spirited in nature, kept me awake. They found the gramophone and played their own records on it, strange music which pulled at the soul, and dance music which made my feet twitch.

Other houses across the country were being ruined by the military; priceless marble fireplaces used as target practice, banisters hundreds of years old ripped out for firewood, ancient books burned, grand pianos disembowelled, gardens ruined. Most of them were never to recover, their classical beauty gone forever, the homes they had provided to English gentry decimated beyond repair. Tall Chimneys got off lightly in comparison, and yet my resentment at these unwanted guests, these cuckoos in my private nest, felt like an equal outrage. I took to prowling the corridors, checking up on rooms I would scarcely venture into in normal days, casting jealous eyes over the faded furnishings and family collections to ensure nothing had been disturbed or gone missing.

At first I served the men their breakfast myself, and then hurried downstairs to rouse Awan and get her ready for school. I dressed in sober black, and waited on them without a smile in the blue dawn gloaming. But several mornings the eggs and porridge went cold; nobody emerged from their rooms to eat it, or returned from the base. By the time I'd realised there would be no partakers for breakfast that day, Awan would be downstairs helping herself to inappropriate foods from the larder, her hair a bird's nest of tangles, her face unwashed, her school clothes askew. Remedying these matters would make her late for school. On my return the food in the dining room would be congealed and useless for anything except the pig. My anger as I cleared away mounted like magma in a volcano.

On one of these days Captain Bentley caught me clearing the uneaten food away as he returned, and I unleashed my anger on him. What waste! Did he not know how precious food was? What rudeness! Could somebody not have telephoned, to let me know? What ingratitude! I had been up since four thirty, all for nothing.

Captain Bentley stood on the threshold of the dining room and looked at me steadily as I vented my spleen. His eyes, grey, calm and gentle, never left me as I stormed around the room crossly throwing plates onto a tray and scraping scraps into a bowl. He stood perfectly still, hardly bracing himself against my onslaught, but taking it full on, like a sturdy, determined boat withstanding the sea's cruel waves as they crashed onto its deck in a storm. Some part of me noted, but did not understand, the less than pristine state of his uniform - his flying jacket was flung casually round his shoulders, the bottoms of his trousers were dark with moisture. He wore no boots at all; a toe peeped shyly from a hole in his sock.

Presently my outburst ran out of energy and I fell silent.

'I am very sorry, ma'am,' Captain Bentley said. 'We had an incident this morning. One of our craft had engine trouble. There was an emergency landing. A small fire.' He pushed back the flap of his jacket to show me his left arm was encased in bandages.

I felt terrible. 'You're hurt?' I asked.

'A slight burn,' he shrugged, 'it's nothing much.'

'What can I do for you?' I asked, my anger of only moments before completely forgotten.

He hesitated, 'Well,' he said at last, 'if you wouldn't mind, ma'am, I could really use a cup of coffee.'

I took him down to the kitchen and made coffee to his instruction - nothing like the coffee I had been serving to them for the duration of their stay. As it brewed he told me a little of the morning's incident - a problem on take-off, an engine on fire, the troops in the body of the aircraft likely to suffer from the effects of heat, smoke inhalation, oxygen-starvation, panic. As co-pilot the job had fallen to him to tackle the blaze as best he could, hence the burn on his arm. 'Not too bad,' he said, ruefully, 'but I'll be out of action for a while.'

'And Captain Brook?' I asked.

'Back at base, filling out reports,' he said.

Captain Bentley sat at the kitchen table and drank cup after cup of the dark, bitter coffee as though it was the elixir of life. In spite of the stimulant the coffee must be providing he looked tired, his eyes shadowed and circled. His was a handsome face - broad jaw balanced by a wide, smooth forehead, the soft grey eyes I have already described, a good nose, full lips. He had a mole on one cheekbone, not round as these things usually are, but the shape of a sickle moon. In his pallor it was more pronounced than usual, its edges melding into the dark smudges beneath his eyes. It occurred to me in a blinding flash of clarity he had not been sleeping well - apart, I mean from working nights, long hours, instructing wave after wave of green recruits - he had found no comfort in the cheerless bed I had allocated him, the rattling windows had kept him awake, the argumentative furniture had made life difficult, the food I had served up had given no pleasure. I estimated his age - perhaps twenty eight or nine - and realised I knew absolutely nothing at all about him other than that he came from a small town in Michigan. I couldn't even remember his Christian name. In all likelihood he would be gone in a few weeks, part of the big initiative we all knew was being planned. For all I knew he would be killed, or horribly wounded. And what would his last memories be? Of a pleasant house in the English countryside? Of a friendly English woman? Of decent food and sweet dreams on an ancient bed? No. It would all be sourness and frugality, black looks and resentful silences. I asked myself how I would feel if John had been treated so, and felt ashamed.

Presently the coffee seemed to galvanise Captain Bentley. He sat up straighter and began to take an interest in his surroundings. 'This is a wonderful room,' he observed, eyeing the copper pans hanging from the beams, the huge old range - unlit now, it being summer time - but beautifully blacked and gleaming, the pots of herbs on the window ledge, the hand-made cushions on the comfortable chairs.

'It's seen some history,' I agreed, 'even in my time, and hundreds of years before that.'

'Our place is old,' he replied, 'but nothing like this.'

I asked him about his home - a fruit farm in the State of Michigan, where apples and pears grew in abundance in the summer months, and where cold cut like a knife in the winter, blackening the pruned trees so it seemed impossible they could survive. 'The wind comes over the lake from Canada, ma'am,' he explained, 'and beyond that, from the Arctic. Silver Beach - that's the beach in St Joseph's - it's beautiful in summer, and the town's folks like to spend time on the shore, but in winter it's like being at the North Pole. The houses all batten down, and many folks go to their winter houses in Chicago. They just can't stand it. But my family stays put on the farm, and we hunker down and see it out.' He spoke with such warmth and a wistful, heart-sore longing that I encouraged him to tell me more. He spoke of his parents (Ma and Pa) and his sister, and of his older brother, killed in a boating accident the previous year.

'Your mother must have been very unhappy to see you sign up,' I remarked, 'having lost one son already.'

He nodded. 'She was mad,' he agreed. 'But I had some flying experience, from the crop-sprayer - so few men have - so she knew I had to do it.'

'Do you write to her?'

He shook his head, sadly, and gave an apologetic little shrug. 'I'm not much of a letter writer.'

'I bet you write to your sweet-heart,' I said, teasingly.

'No, ma'am,' he said.

MY CONVERSATION WITH Captain Bentley marked a turning point in my attitude to and relationship with my guests. I announced that breakfast would no longer be served in the dining room, but in the kitchen. I showed the men how to cook bacon - when we had it - and scramble eggs, and left oats and bread, tea and coffee available for them to help themselves to at whatever time they liked. In turn they initiated me into the mysteries of biscuits and gravy (a salty, scone-like bake and a sauce made from the fat of cooked sausages, flour and milk.) They showed me how to make waffles, and, from somewhere, brought me a waffle iron and a bottle of Maple syrup whose sticky sweetness threw Awan into transports of bliss. Ground coffee arrived from the quartermaster's stores and I soon knew how to brew it to their taste and even to quite enjoy it myself. In the evenings I served their supper at the kitchen table, and Awan and I sat with them and listened to the stories of their day - the men who had jumped, the ones who had baulked, the daily roll-call of injuries and small triumphs. The officers with children at home liked to read to Awan, or to help her with her sums, and I would watch her halo of blonde curls press against the crew cut of a GI or the raspy cheek of a British officer in the last light of the day and hope that, for each of them, a lonely hole was being filled.

Sometimes, after Awan had gone to bed, they would bring the gramophone downstairs and play their music; black women with voices like treacle keening for lost loves, black men lamenting their lot, jazz music which jangled and confused and set the teeth on edge like a cupboard full of demented pans and crazed cooking utensils, dance music which energised tired legs and set them moving to its irresistible beat. They taught me to jitterbug, taking it in turn to whirl and twirl me on the kitchen flagstones, pulling me this way and that while my feet, of their own volition, skipped and swivelled beneath me. On these evenings it struck me once again that Tall Chimneys had provided me with a sort of family, a surrogate for the one I had never known, and these members of it, as temporary and passing as they might be, were gaining as much from our brief association as Awan and I were.

For some reason that I could not fathom, Kenneth took against the Americans. As men they were as unlike him as it was possible to conceive; whereas he was taciturn and self-effacing, they were garrulous and brash. Kenneth was loyal to his core, while the US troops had a reputation of being flighty and unreliable. They were known to be womanisers, something Kenneth would never be. But this divergence in character did not go far enough to explain his antipathy. I wondered if it was simply their military nature which had riled him, recalling a vague idea I had entertained that he did not approve of war. But then Rose let it slip that he had agreed to help in the rehabilitation of some wounded soldiers, teaching them car engine maintenance, so I knew his resentment of the GIs must stem from something else. In the end I told myself he was just jealous, too used to being the only man about the place. He and Rose declined my invitations to join in the fun in the kitchen during the evenings. He debarred Rose from any duties in the men's rooms, which was unhelpful, as it meant I had to shoulder the extra work myself.

'They're just men away from home,' I told him one afternoon, when a sudden shower had drenched the sheets on the line and I knew Rose would not help me put them all through the mangle again.

'They're men who'll take advantage,' he replied, 'mark my words. Rose will keep them at arm's length, and so should you.'

'You're jealous,' I laughed.

But he returned my humour with a hard look. 'Of course I am,' he said. 'I guard my own.'

Captain Bentley - Cameron, or Cam, as he liked to be called - remained grounded and on light duties for some weeks. His burned arm didn't heal well and at one point the scabbed skin got infected. When not at the base he made himself useful around the house. I found him one day repairing the drawers of the unco-operative chest from his room. It was an awkward operation, with one arm incapacitated, but he had managed to secure the drawer to a table using clamps. 'I hope you don't mind,' he said with an apologetic smile, looking up from his work, 'it'll work good as new when I'm done.'

'I don't mind,' I said. 'Where did you get those clamps from? Kenneth's workshop?' I knew Kenneth would not happily have lent Cam any of his precious tools.

'No ma'am,' he grinned. 'From camp.'

Cleaning his room a few days later I tried the refurbished drawers - they slid smoothly in and out as they had never done in my entire recollection. His clothes were folded up neatly inside. Seeing them there - tidy and in some way vulnerable, like a tucked-in child sleeping - made me feel as though I were spying, and I closed the drawer quickly. But the next day I asked him if he'd take a look at the flap-doored wardrobe. 'Only too happy to, ma'am,' he grinned.

That summer was balmy and kind, as though the weather had decided to give us a holiday between the horrors that had gone before and those that were to come. Oh, I know that abroad the war continued unabated. In the Western Desert Campaign Rommel was outwitting and defeating our troops at every turn, culminating in the defeat at Tobruk. At the beginning of July Sevastopol fell to the Germans, a bitter blow to the war on the Eastern front. We all knew the allies were gathering themselves for something big; plans were in train, preparations being made. No-one said what, or when, but we knew it, and relentlessly, day after day, the aeroplanes took off over the moor and dropped their cargo to earth, like sycamore seeds in autumn. In the meantime, we basked in days of warm sunshine, reaped the harvest of fruit and vegetables we had sown and took pleasure in little things.

John did not come home; his letters indicated great industry in the Intelligence Corps and some success at the exhibition. I wrote back and described our crop of peas and runner beans and the arduous watering regime needed to keep everything alive in this period of drought.

Throughout July and into August Cam laboured alongside me in the gardens and vegetable patch. He said it reminded him of home and I was doing him a favour by allowing it. He wore shirt-sleeves or even just a white vest, his trousers held up by braces. I remarked on them and he said 'Do you mean my suspenders?' making me burst out laughing. Kenneth, working at a distance, threw me a scowling look.

Cam's skin turned a beautiful peachy brown apart from on his arm, where the new skin stayed pink and wrinkled. The sickle-shaped mole became less obvious. He took it upon himself to fix things that were broken, proving himself skilful with wood in particular. He silenced floorboards which had squeaked for as long as I could remember, eased stubborn cupboard doors and oiled creaking hinges. He polished out scratches and steadied wonky legs; he glued and screwed and sanded. The more he did around the house, the more Kenneth seemed to resent him; I supposed he felt his toes were being trodden upon but these things needed doing and Kenneth had enough on his hands with his family, the general upkeep of Tall Chimneys, his business and his work with the wounded. Cam repaired an antiquated and long-defunct irrigation system in one of the greenhouses to ease the burden of watering the tomatoes, melons and cucumbers, and then rigged a shower pipe from some spare bits of it so the children could play in the cooling water. One day he came home from the base with a huge waxed tarpaulin, and made them a shallow bathing pool. The children frolicked and shrieked with delight, so glad to be able to cool off. Kenneth stood with his arms folded and his brow furrowed, wishing, I suppose, he had dreamt up the scheme himself. Once, when the children were in bed and Kenneth was visiting his mother, and we had sampled perhaps a glass too many of the GI's Scotch, Rose and I used it too, stripping to our under-slips under cover of darkness and taking it in turns to shampoo each other's hair. When I thought about it later, I realised our antics would have been in full view of those north facing rooms I had allocated the officers, and it seemed impossible they would not have witnessed the whole debauched, tipsy episode.

In the evenings I would cook food and we ate round the kitchen table unless we had what the men called a 'cook-out' which involved lighting coals in an old oil drum sliced in half and placed on trestles in the yard, and cooking food over the glowing embers. There would be laughter and fun, and I would ignore Kenneth's hunched shoulders and palpable disapproval as he tinkered in his workshop, waving away our invitations to join in. Usually, Captain Brook went off to the village (where, I suspected, he had at least one girl in thrall, which proved Kenneth's suspicions were grounded) but Cam stayed at home and made things for the children while I read, or mended, by the light of the lamp. Despite Kenneth's coolness towards the Americans, Cam included the boys in his industry, making little animals out of scrap wood for Brian's ark and a catapult for Bobby. He presented these to Kenneth, who received them with poor grace. Whether the boys ever got to use them, I don't know.

Some nights it was too hot to sleep, even with all the windows open. I was restless and wandered the house, as was my wont. I would find Cam sitting on the terrace in the moonlight, as still as one of the mossy old statues, the darkness of his form hardly distinguishable from the black mass of the house. When I sat down next to him his skin was warm and cool at the same time, the manly smell of him had a back note of wood-polish and beeswax, and it coalesced with the scent of roses from the arbour, the lavender along the pathways of the parterre, the sap-rich smell of the woods beyond. Sometimes we did not speak at all but more often he would begin to speak about his brother, the things they had got up to as children, the layout of their farm, his grandmother's baking. It was like being privy to the train of his thoughts; memories and impressions emerged like skeins of silk from his mind and wove themselves into a web of words. I felt privileged to witness the rare tapestry they formed. In response I found myself telling him something of my girlhood - my years with my sister Isobel and her daughters, my time at school - and earlier still, the Weeks at the gatehouse, as much as I could recall of the diaphanous form of my mother, the smell of the stuff my father used to put on his hair. Cam listened, occasionally nodding or putting in a 'Uh huh,' to encourage me along. I could hardly make out his face; he kept it turned slightly away from me. It had the effect of drawing my memories out, and my words poured into some dark pool of benign night rather than into the ear of a virtual stranger.

But then, as time went on, Cam began to feel less and less like a stranger to me.

It transpired as part of these nocturnal exchanges that I had never seen the sea, and, one morning, quite early, Cam arrived back from the airbase in a jeep with a hamper of food to take Awan, Bobby, Brian and me to Scarborough. I hesitated at first - I had never been so far since the days of my girlhood; John had never offered to take me to the sea but oughtn't it be him who initiated me? But the children were wild with excitement - Bobby gathering cricket bats and balls and buckets in a frenzy (Kenneth was working on a farm that day, so wasn't there to object) - and Rose was eager for them to have a holiday, hastily packing extra food supplies and changes of clothes. Before I had thought through the adventure it seemed we were off; I scarcely had time to find a sun hat for Awan or grab a bale of towels before we were motoring across the moor, the canvas top of the jeep pushed down, the children in the back singing songs at the tops of their voices.

It couldn't have been a more perfect day; the sky wide and blue, the sun unhidden, the countryside a gathered haberdashery of velvet and brocade, silken petals, iridescent feathers and lace-topped trees. It was rich, soft and inviting, and as exciting as a fantasy landscape in a children's storybook. Cam drove easily, with one hand on the wheel, the other resting along the sill of the open window, and that stifled smile played the flesh of his cheek so it quivered. We arrived in Scarborough and parked up, the children rushing ahead to the sands, casting aside their shoes and socks and outer clothes only just in time before plunging into the shallow waves in their underwear. Cam followed them while I set out the blankets and the picnic, and looked about me at the other day-trippers and at the beach, scarred by groynes to deter enemy aircraft, and at the blue, endless ocean. The children ran in and out of the sea, shrieking, and collected shells in their buckets. Cam helped Bobby fly a kite, and built a sand castle for Brian, and ran after Awan with a rag of seaweed. In between times they came back to me for drinks of warm lemonade or bites of sandwich. Then Cam organised a game - baseball, he called it, but it looked a lot like rounders - and had a dozen children flocking around him, clamouring to join in.

At last he flung himself down on the blanket in front of me, and flashed me a smile. 'Having fun?'

I nodded. Speech was almost beyond me. He had removed his shirt. His body was as perfectly sculpted as Michelangelo's David.

'In a while we'll go and find some tea and buns. Isn't that what you English people like? Tea and buns?'

I laughed. 'Tea and cake is a British staple,' I agreed.

'Like our coffee and doughnuts. You see? We're not so different after all.'

'I never said we were,' I commented, lying back on the rug and closing my eyes.

'We were given a little talk, you know, before we came over,' Cam said. I sensed he had lain down beside me. I could feel the warmth of his shoulder next to mine.

'Oh, yes?'

'About you folks being reserved. You don't strike up conversations the way we do because you think that's rude.'

'We like to mind our own business,' I agreed.

'That you like to talk about neutral topics like the weather and sports...'

I nodded. The sun on my body felt like honey.

'...rather than your feelings.'

An alarm bell sounded somewhere. It felt like a line had been crossed.

'We were told the women would be buttoned up, severe, very stiff, and up-tight...'

Is that how I seemed, to him?

'But you're not at all like that, are you?' Cam's voice sounded closer. He must have rolled over onto his side. If I'd opened my eyes, I would have seen him looking down at me, his hand supporting his head, lying next to me, like a husband next to his wife in bed. Something touched my arm - a sand creature? A flap of the blanket? A feather? I wanted to flinch, but didn't. 'At night, when we're talking, just the two of us. You're not buttoned-up at all.'

I opened my eyes. As I had expected, his face was inches from mine, his eyes soft and honest, the sickle birth-mark so close I could see the downy hairs which covered it. We were in a glass bubble, suspended in a moment in time; the laughing children, the crashing waves, the whirling sea birds above us were far away and almost unreal, simply a backdrop for this intensely amplified reality which encased the two of us. I felt I ought to speak, to say something either very flippant and witty which would shatter the spell like a hammer through glass, or something honest and instinctive, which would seal us in for ever. But before I could summon up a reply Cam went on, without a falter in the intensity of his tone or the directness of his gaze, 'and so, Mrs Johns, I hope you do not think you're going to leave Scarborough without a dip in the sea.'

I exhaled. I had not even known I had been holding my breath, but I breathed out in a long, relieving sigh, and sat up.

I indicated my stockings, 'Alas, I *am* all buttoned up,' I smiled.

Cam got to his feet. 'Take them off,' he said, and walked away to where the children were running on the sand.

After that day, I found myself often looking upwards at the impossible bulk of an aircraft as it passed overhead. It went over so slowly it sometimes seemed it was stationary in the high blue sky, defying all physics, even gravity itself. And I thought of Cam at the - helm? Wheel? - I didn't know how the thing was controlled, only that he was controlling it, his broad, strong hands coaxing that behemoth of metal into the sky, the faith of the hundred or so men in its belly placed in him alone.

In the late afternoons, or at the dawn hour if he had been on a night training session, I would realise I was listening for the spray of gravel under the wheels of his jeep, the careful tread of his feet across the hall floor.

After that day he started calling me Evelyn instead of ma'am. After that day we became friends. There was something about his company; he was like a favourite jacket - comfortable, the one you automatically reach for, but also warm and dry and reliable. Perhaps that isn't a very flattering analogy; he was also a deeply thoughtful young man, eager to please, kind, gentle; an exceptional soul. The current of mirth I had detected that first day, which twitched at his cheek and the corner of his mouth, and which had played on his face the whole day at Scarborough, was never far from the surface. He found life amusing, and me especially, I think; anyway, I often caused him to smile.

In September many of the Americans stationed up at the camp turned out to help local farms with the harvest and I recruited as many as I could to support my friend Ann Widderington at Clough Farm. The fair weather was due to break at the end of the week; a front of low pressure was expected, rain, perhaps even thunder storms. We laboured while the weather held fair, every ancient tractor pressed in to service, Kenneth and the camp engineers busy with repairs and maintenance. Awan, Bobby and Brian disappeared into the posse of farm and village children, who took advantage of the adults' distraction to paddle in streams and climb trees, romp in the mown fields and clamber on the haystacks. For me, who had spent a friendless childhood with only myself for company, it was a heart-warming sight. Baby Anthony was made much of, passed from arm to arm by the other women while Rose made sandwiches or dished out elderflower cordial; new babies were a rarity, most of the men being absent. We worked as a community, everyone bringing something; food, drink, a strong back, a song. I gloried in it. I belonged, this was my home and these were my neighbours.

The Land Army girls worked the hardest of all, but their labours were made more bearable by the flattery and flirting of the GIs. Of these,

Captain Brook was the worst; he schmoozed the women right and left, called them 'baby' and 'doll' and handed out chocolate and nylon stockings and cigarettes. Within his orbit, Cam, too, took the fancy of many of the girls, but he evaded their blandishments with shy courtesy.

'Has he got a wife? A girl at home?' they wanted to know.

I had to confess I didn't know. 'He never mentions one,' was all I could truthfully say.

Cam was clearly in his element on the farm, driving tractors and working machinery, hefting haystacks, hauling the grain to the silos. Apart from his crew cut and his US Army issue trousers, you might have taken him for a local.

On the Friday the sky was overcast. Bruised clouds closed in the sky, swallowing up the aircraft which took off from the airfield almost before they had cleared the tree tops. We redoubled our efforts, hardly stopping for food until the last bale was under cover, the final trailer-load of grain safely stored. Cam had been on duty that day and we had missed him. In the late afternoon we gathered for tea and cakes in the farm's cobbled yard. One of the GIs announced a 'harvest home' dance that evening, up at the camp. A thrill of giggling excitement shimmied through the girls; their talk immediately turning to hair-washing and clothing. I picked up baby Anthony, who had begun to grizzle in his pram, and walked him into the kitchen to find Rose.

'You should go to the dance,' she said, taking the baby off me and looking for a discreet corner where she could feed him.

'Oh, no,' I said. 'I'm too old for dancing.' At thirty two, I considered myself old.

'I've *seen* you dance,' Rose retorted, 'too old my foot.'

'There's Awan,' I said.

'I'll mind Awan,' Rose said. 'Kenneth won't want to go, and I won't go without him.'

'I don't know,' I demurred. 'I'll see,'

We drove home under a sky so heavy and angry it had brought the day to a premature close. Awan fell asleep in the car, and I carried her into the house and put her straight into bed. She had straw in her hair and streaks of dirt on her face. Her hands were as grubby as a street urchin's. Her dress was torn on the back.

'What a wonderful day you have had, my darling,' I said as I pulled a sheet over her.

The house seemed to be deserted. I went to Mrs Simpson's room and drew myself a deep, cool bath. I looked at myself in the long mirror while it was drawing; I looked like a scarecrow, every bit as dishevelled as Awan. I soaked for a long time, vaguely aware of the officers returning, the thump of water in the pipes, music from the gramophone. As I dried and put up my hair, I heard wheels on the gravel as a car disappeared up the steep driveway, and then silence. Outside the window, the day had turned purple with portent, the outline of trees barely visible against the indigo sky, the air alive with electricity which made my hair stand on end when I brushed it.

I slipped on a clean dress and descended the gloomy staircase into the dark well of the hall.

I noticed his smell before I saw him; that assimilation of Tall Chimney smells - good earth, soap, wax polish, sap. Then I made out a figure standing by the half open door, a ghost against a slice of shadow surrounded by impenetrable dim.

'There you are at last,' he said, turning as I descended the last stair. The white of his smile opened up an envelope in the dusk. 'Ready?'

'Ready? For what?'

'The dance of course,' he said. 'I've waited behind, to take you.'

'Oh!' I exclaimed, 'that's kind, but I'm not going.'

There was a beat. 'Not going? Why not?'

'There's Awan,' I began, but he interrupted me.

'Rose is in the kitchen. She's listening out for her.'

'And then there's...' I looked down at my dress, pretty enough, but not my best.

'Your dress is just fine,' Cam said, reading my gesture. 'Now come on. This storm's gonna break any minute and the roof of the jeep leaks.'

Time took me by the elbow and propelled me forward three or four minutes. Before I knew it I was in the jeep beside him and we were speeding up the black throat of the drive.

'But I haven't got my bag!' I cried, 'my...' Lipstick, I had been going to say.

'You don't need it,' he shouted back, over the roar of the labouring engine.

The dance was being held in the mess room. Before we even entered it I could feel the heat which billowed from it in gusts like dragon's breath. The noise inside was deafening; the four piece band, the shriek of the women, the pounding of feet on the wooden floor. Soon it was augmented by the pelt of rain on the corrugated roof. The air was thick with cigarette smoke and beer fumes and almost saturated with cologne - the men must have doused themselves in it. I had the fleeting impression of a machine, a turbine of bodies in frantic generation of the electricity which crackled and hummed in the storm-laden air. Then I was swept onto the floor and something - I don't know what it was - some restraint which had held me since I had been a child - slipped away and I was swept up in a coil of an entirely different ilk, a twitching, throbbing, primeval thread of movement which attached itself to my feet, and looped itself around my spine and burst out through the top of my head. I danced like a marionette, without thought. My body obeyed the music and became one with the crowd. It submitted to whatever beat the band played, followed where my dance partners led, drank the beer which was pressed into my hand. I grew dizzy with it, intoxicated perhaps, as the room whirled out of my control, and my body gyrated on the lifting pulse of trumpet, drum and double base like a piece of flotsam on a flooding tide. And always, within that maelstrom of music and heat and beat and pleasure, Cam's hand was there to steady me. I felt it in mine, a solid anchor point, or in the small of my back, spinning me this way and that but always at a safe centre of gravity. His face remained in focus while all others were a blur.

Presently the rhythm of the music slowed and Cam put his arms around me. In the periphery of my vision I could see other couples clasped and swaying, like us. Some of them were kissing, careless of who might see. I saw hands kneading breasts and scaling stockings. It was shocking, and thrilling, both.

The floor had emptied; only two dozen or so people remained. Two girls were slumped across three or four chairs at the edge of the room, fast asleep. A few men who had failed to secure partners were leaning on the bar looking sour. I could see the barman polishing glasses.

'It must be over,' I thought, and my sadness was overwhelming. Cam pressed me closer into him, but he didn't attempt to kiss me, and I was glad. 'We couldn't *be* closer,' I thought, or perhaps I spoke the words out loud. In any case, he took my hand and led me from the room, out into the rain.

The shock of the cool night and the pouring rain made us both laugh, and we ran for the jeep.

The roof of the jeep did indeed leak. Water collected on its canvas roof and then poured in streams from various places depending on the speed and trajectory of the car. Consequently we were deluged first from one place and then from another - on our laps, down the backs of our necks, on our feet - and we shrieked every time it happened.

In the tunnel of the drive we were more sheltered, the soakings stopped and our mood sobered, but something else, something which I suppose had been there all along but which I had not recognised, took the place of the frenetic energy of the dance and the hilarity of the ride home. The water sloshing around our ankles and soaking our clothes turned into something potent, like neat spirit, a sort of ectoplasm of sexual tension. It positively hummed as we drew into the courtyard and Cam switched off the engine and the lights.

'Rose will be inside,' I said, my voice trembling.

'Yes,' he said.

We climbed out of the car and dashed through the bucketing deluge across the yard to the door. My hair was plastered to my head. My frock, I suppose, was transparent with wet.

When we got into the kitchen the easy chair by the fireplace was empty and the lights were off. I had no idea what time it was.

'Perhaps she went across to feed the baby,' I whispered.

'Yes,' Cam replied, and he was very close to me, I could feel his breath lifting the wisps of hair on my cheek, 'perhaps she did.'

And then he kissed me, and one hand was under my chin, gentle, as though cupping a flower-head, and another between my shoulder blades. So proper, so respectful was his embrace, so clean and correct; there was no hint, no suggestion of the pawing and groping I had seen on the dance floor. But his kiss. He kissed me with warm, moist lips, gently, slowly. At their nudging encouragement I opened mine. On a screen in my mind there played a film of our association: the quiver of laughter which twitched at his lip, a toe poking through the seam of his sock, his injured arm, his neatly packed drawer, his shirt-sleeved body working in the garden, the furrow which came between his brows when he concentrated on a fiddly task, his face in the crowd at the dance, his lips, now, on mine. His tongue was soft but incredibly sensual, tasting my mouth as though sampling a new and exotic fruit; exploring in such a way that the idea of it on other parts of my body couldn't help but suggest itself. A current of desire coursed through my body. I felt my knees sag. My skin cried out for his touch. A distant part of my mind cried 'Stop! Stop! Remember what happened with Giles,' but my heart and some syrupy valve in my belly silenced it. I lifted my hands to place round his neck; I wanted to feel the warmth of him, the texture of that close-cropped hair on his neck, the corner of his mouth where his smile simmered. His tongue probed deeper and I opened my mouth wider and tasted him as he tasted me.

Then, suddenly, the room was all brightness. Cam pulled away from me. A man's voice said, 'Good evening, Evelyn,' and I turned to see John standing at the entrance to the corridor which led to our rooms.

JOHN'S RETURN HOME was of some duration, but it was not all pleasure and holiday. He had come, ironically, to be trained at the airfield. My understanding of his role in the Intelligence Corps took a seismic leap. I had imagined him translating German transmissions, listening in and reporting back on Axis radio and telephone communications, perhaps making the occasional mischievous or misleading broadcast. I had had no doubt that it was arduous and stressful, but I had always assured myself it was safe, anonymous, miles away from any bullet or bomb. But now he was to be trained to parachute and there was only one conclusion to draw: he was to be sent behind enemy lines.

'I need to be prepared, that's all,' he assured me. 'All the chaps who are able-bodied are being trained. The war in France is going under-ground. We're forming a network of agents and informants who can operate to frustrate the Nazis and we need to be ready to support them, if necessary.'

'But surely,' I insisted, 'no-one expects *you* to...'

'Why ever not? I'm not entirely incapacitated, you know.'

'Your chest...'

'Has been much better, of late, and anyway it wouldn't be a physical impediment. As a matter of fact I'm rather excited by the prospect.'

'Of throwing yourself out of an aeroplane?'

He gave me a slanting glance. 'Indeed. It seems it gives one a certain kudos. I hear all the girls in the village are *mad* for the airmen.'

'I think it's the stockings, chocolate and cigarettes they provide,' I suggested, dryly.

'Do you, now?'

Nothing had been said about the episode in the kitchen. How much John had seen, I did not know. John didn't seem to object to the airmen and officers in the house, accepting their coming and going in what had become our private space. He took it as read they would join in our meals and family times and welcomed them, including Cam, participating in the jocular talk.

But after John's return home, Cam spent more time at the base, flew extra sorties and, when he was home, tended to spend time outdoors rather than with us. From time to time our eyes would meet. There was so much unsaid between us, unfinished business on a number of levels. I felt confused and perhaps also a little ashamed at my behaviour at the dance, and afterwards. What had I been thinking? I told myself my body had betrayed me - I had spent too many lonely nights. I even blamed John: what did he expect, leaving me alone for so many months? But, if I was honest, I knew Cam had touched more than just a sexually frustrated nerve. My relationship with him - if it was a relationship - was nothing like my association with Giles Percy, who had simply provided an outlet for sexual angst and envy. No, I liked Cam, I really liked him. Perhaps I was even a little in love with him. The idea of him brought a glow to my mind, warm with affection. When he flew, I scanned the skies. When I knew he was jumping, I worried.

Awan went back to school and John began his training, returning each evening bruised but full of enthusiasm. He was precious of his hands and arms, for obvious reasons, wearing layers of extra padding and several pairs of gloves. Having said that, he did little painting, preferring to take long walks despite the weather, which was unsettled, often wet with sudden, drenching downpours. He engaged on lengthy telephone conversations with people back in London, his voice hushed; I could just hear the drone of it from the butler's pantry, where the below-stairs telephone extension was connected. We did not argue but there was an atmosphere between us, our conversation was bright and rather brittle, our comments tended to have an edge which was flippant to the point of sarcasm.

'I suppose you wouldn't like to go to the pictures?' he said to me one afternoon in late September.

'In York?' It was nearest picture-house that I knew of.

'Yes, indeed, Evelyn, in the wild and far-flung metropolis,' he replied, caustically. 'They do speak English in York, you know.'

'Of course I know that,' I retorted. 'I'm only thinking of the time it will take to get there and back again.'

'An hour and a half each way.' He stroked his chin and pretended to contemplate the enormity of such an undertaking, 'Do you fear your body will spontaneously combust in the attempt? It *is* quite an expedition, but no so far as Scarborough.'

Word of our outing had clearly got to him; Awan, I supposed, had regaled him with the details. And why not? It had been a perfectly respectable day out even if I had returned home without stockings. 'Don't be ridiculous,' I snapped. 'I simply wonder who will iron these sheets and prepare supper while I'm gone.'

'Or if Tall Chimneys can remain standing, in your absence,' he muttered, *sotto voce*, before adding, more forcefully, 'as you know, people have outings, Evelyn, they go out and enjoy themselves. It's normal. They eat meals, they drink port and lemon in pubs. They even have holidays. It's allowed. As you *now* know, the sky will not fall.'

I realised then he was jealous, and I should have laughed at him and collected my hat and gone to York, but I didn't. My day at the sea was precious and unique, and another outing would reduce it to just one in a sequence, something I didn't want. So John collected Awan from school and took her to the pictures instead. I spent the afternoon fuming with annoyance and resentment. Awan would be too late in bed; she would never get up for school the next day. Something would happen in York - I had no idea what, but in my imagination the city was a dangerous place, dirty and full of traffic. They would have an accident travelling across the moors, without lights in the blackout; what foolishness to contemplate such a thing! Really, I suppose, I was angry at myself. Why hadn't I gone with them? It would have reassured John and put my seaside adventure into its proper context. It would have broken for good the artificial and perhaps even dangerous precedent which Scarborough had tested.

While they were gone I came across Cam in the greenhouse, draining the watering system he had installed earlier in the summer. 'It will freeze and burst the pipes if we leave water in there,' he explained, over his shoulder.

'It's very good of you,' I said, more formally than I had intended.

Cam shrugged his shoulders. 'Where's Awan?' he asked. 'I promised her a tour of the airfield and I've never gotten round to taking her.'

'She's gone to York with her... with John,' I said, 'to the picture-house.'

'The movies? And you didn't want to go along?'

'I wasn't...' It wasn't true to say I hadn't been invited, and to suggest I hadn't been welcome would have been petulant. 'Free,' I said at last.

Cam nodded sadly. 'You're not free,' he echoed.

The truth of it felt like a stone in my gut. I fiddled with something further along the bench, the air loaded with all my fulminating over John, my unresolved affair with Cam, a new and frustrating sense of entrapment.

'Did Aloysius tell you that we've been posted?' Cam threw out.

I felt as though I'd been shot. 'Posted?' I stammered. 'Where?'

'Somewhere pretty remote. Land's End? And then we'll be deployed. I don't know where, yet.'

'Abroad?' I asked, stupidly.

'That's where the war is!'

I couldn't keep the tremble from my voice. 'And... and when will you come back?'

Cam gave me a rueful smile. 'That isn't the way war works, Evelyn, you know that.'

John and Awan got home quite late in the evening. As I had predicted Awan was shattered and querulous. The film, called Bambi, had made her cry, and I gathered she had snivelled all the way home, to John's annoyance.

'So much for the happy family outing,' I quipped, darkly.

In bed, at night, John and I slept apart, keeping scrupulously to our own sides of the bed, except once or twice, between sleep and wake, when I found his hands on me, and my automatic response was to pull him close. We spoke no words. Our sex was urgent, somewhat combative, and soon over with. I resented him access to me but could not deny him. I resented my own desire which rose to meet his. In the mornings, after these encounters, I felt strangely guilty if I met Cam in the kitchen or coming down the stairs, as though I had in some way betrayed him.

John's training finished but he did not return to London. Instead, he started painting, walking up to the gatehouse each dawn and staying there until the light had faded, which was early; October was almost upon us. I couldn't help thinking of the times in the past when I had walked up there to take food to him, eager to be with him; the pleasure and welcome I knew would greet me there, the sense of companionship which would sink into me as I sat in the chair by the fire while he painted above. Now I couldn't be sure if I would be welcome; he certainly never suggested I call in on my way to collect Awan from school. He didn't tell me what he was working on, but then again I didn't ask. Many evenings he didn't return until quite late, well after I had served supper to Awan and the officers. Several nights he did not come back at all, and I lay in bed wondering what was happening to us, where the fiery passion had gone to, and all the more drawn to Cam's draughty bedroom on the north wing.

October came, and the leaves in the woods turned golden and bronze, and fell to ground. Kenneth drained the fountain and serviced the generator, ready for winter. In the surrounding farmland, land was ploughed, cattle brought in for over-wintering. The boys in the village began collecting wood for the village bonfire and Awan, Bobby and Brian began work on their Guy. The world of Tall Chimneys was turning as it always had, and always would, I thought, a comforting ritual of seasons and celebrations; Advent would follow Guy Fawkes' night, Christmas would follow Advent, then Easter, Summer, Harvest and so round to Guy Fawkes' again, and so on, *ad infinitum*, down the years.

The 2nd Battalion 503rd PIR began to pack up at the airfield. Red-eyed girls were to be seen in the village. Cam and Aloysius started talking about 'Our last week' and then 'Just a couple of days before we move out,' and then, at last 'Our last night at Tall Chimneys.' That night I cooked two chickens I had killed especially, and made an effort with pudding, and raided the wine cellar for something special. I invited Kenneth and Rose and the children in. My idea was we would make merry, and send the boys on their way with cheer. But in fact the atmosphere at the table was awkward with things unsaid. Kenneth was particularly aloof and Anthony querulous. Our toasts were forced and falsely up-beat. John did not make an appearance and his empty chair at the table cast a pall like Banquo's ghost.

Awan kept on asking 'Where's Daddy?' 'Aren't we going to wait for him?' 'I don't want Daddy to miss the party,' which kept his absence in the forefront of everyone's minds.

After dinner Rose and Kenneth took their children home and I put Awan to bed. Aloysius Brook made his excuses and took the jeep up the village; I presumed he had fond farewells to say. Cam sat on at the table while I cleared the dishes. This in itself was unusual; normally, he would have helped me. The fire cackled and spat - the wood was too green, I suppose. The radio played in the background.

The silence between us was unnatural; we had never, since that morning he had been injured, been stuck for things to say. I stood at the sink and washed plates and pans, desperately trying to think of some subject to raise other than the thing that was upper-most in my mind. Suddenly I felt a hand on my sudsy arm.

'Leave that, Evelyn,' Cam said, quietly. He handed me a towel and while I dried my hands, he pulled the tie of my apron to remove it. It was the most natural, but also the most intimate gesture. He slipped it from my waist and the sensation could not have been more erotic if he had taken off my slip, my bra, my knickers. Indeed, I felt naked and vulnerable before him. He must have felt it, but, fine, respectable young man that he was, he took no advantage. He guided me to the chair by the fire and placed me into it, and then squatted down on the rug.

'Evelyn,' he began, but I interrupted him. Pandora's Box must not be opened.

'Oh! Please, don't...'

He shook his head. 'I *have* to. *We* have to. You know it. I can't go without speaking.'

I nodded, dumbly. I knew he was right.

He lowered himself onto the hearth rug and faced the fire. Perhaps it was going to be easier to speak the words if he didn't have to look at me. His shoulder was on my leg. His hand rested on my foot. It was familiar and comfortable to have him seated thus; close, relaxed, unguarded.

'At home,' he began, and it was by no means a subject I had expected him to embark upon, 'my family has a farm - I think I've told you about it. My Ma and Pa took it over after my Pa's parents got too old for it. They built a second house on the plot. My grandparents lived there until Grandpa died. Then Grandma moved in with us. She's elderly now; she needs looking after. So the new house is empty.' He gave a little laugh, a private joke. 'We call it the 'new' house, but in fact it's fifteen years old. It needs up-dating, some. We all thought my brother would marry and settle there. He had a sweetheart, you know, Eileen, a girl from St Joe's. They were set to marry but then there was the accident...'

'Poor girl,' I murmured.

'Ma and Pa are still pretty hearty,' Cam went on. 'But the farm, well, it's really too much for one couple. They were relying on the help. Really, you know, it's a lot like here. Chooks, a couple of pigs, a vegetable patch. You'd like it.'

'It sounds lovely,' I said, automatically.

'But more open,' he went on, as though I had not spoken. 'A fine view of the lake, from the rise behind the house. And in summer time we cross our neighbours' land to swim and have cook-outs on the beach.'

'Tall Chimneys can feel rather claustrophobic, at times,' I admitted. 'From the gatehouse, though, there's a view of the moor, isn't there?'

My mentioning the gatehouse seemed to stop Cam's flow, for a moment. I suppose it brought to both our minds the man who, at that very moment, was ensconced there.

But presently he took up his thread once more. 'I'm not going to pretend it isn't hard in winter, Evelyn. It's bitter! The water freezes - well, everything freezes. I mean, you think it gets cold here but you ain't seen nothin'!

'What kind of place is St Joe's?'

'A small town. A friendly place mostly. But our farm is quite a ways out of town. Quiet. Nobody comes by, hardly. And if you don't want to go into town much, you don't have to. Pa goes in a about twice a week, he can run any errands. And, of course...' he hesitated. I sensed a leap. 'Of course, I'd take Awan into school myself, every day, or at least to the school bus, so you could stay cosy and snug on the farm, if - that's if - if you wanted to.'

I stiffened. 'You're asking me to..?'

He turned, then, and looked up at me. One side of his face, the side which had been close to the fire, was red, the other white with strain, his birth mark standing out more prominently than I had ever seen it before. His grey eyes were direct, his face absolutely serious. 'Yes, Evelyn, I am. If I come home - if I survive the war - I want you to come home with me, and marry me.'

'I'm...' I began, but it was automatic.

'No, you're not. I asked Rose - quietly, very discreetly - and I know you're not married. You're free.'

'I might not have been to church,' I said, stiffly, 'I might not have the certificate or the ring, but in my heart, and in my mind, I *am* married to John.' Saying the words aloud sealed their truth. Why did it feel like a death sentence? How could it, at one and the same time, feel like a matter of honour, a stake in the ground, a thing worth dying for?

Cam screwed himself round on the rug and got to his knees. He took my hands in his. 'I'm sure it felt like that when you were younger, but the truth is there's nothing holding you to him other than your sense of duty. You can un-marry yourself,' he urged. 'As honestly and sincerely as you connected yourself to him, and as easily, you can separate yourself. He can't offer you what I can. He can't give Awan what I can. A proper family, a home, a love which isn't - I don't know how to describe it - complicated, compromised - as John's is, as it must be, else, why hasn't he taken you to church?'

'He's married already,' I said, tears brimming, testament to how much I had been hurt by that situation. 'I didn't know it when I... when we...'

'He didn't tell you?' Cam scrambled to his feet and began to pace around the kitchen table. He was angry. The flush on one side of his face had spread right across it. 'He didn't *tell* you?' he almost shouted. His moral outrage on my behalf took me aback; no one, not even my brothers, had taken such a stance.

'He told me he would if he could,' I stammered. 'He wasn't specific about the impediment and I trusted one day he would get round it. And in any case,' I concluded, 'it wouldn't have made a difference. It was too late. I was too far gone.'

'He took advantage of you.' Cam's perambulations had brought him back to the rug. He faced me from it, square on.

'No. He protected me. There was a man - an associate of my brother's, he was very predatory, he...' I swallowed, 'he molested me. John saw him off.'

'And then did the same thing.'

'No, no,' I cried. 'It wasn't like that! We had already... before, and I was... willing. More than willing.'

'But he wasn't free, Evelyn. He had no right. And since that day, neither have you been. Hiding here, ashamed, hemmed in by your guilt while he travels the world, comes and goes, picks you up and puts you down again just as he pleases. You're worth more, Evelyn, so much more.' He squatted down in front of me and took my hands once more. 'Let me give it to you, darling girl. Let me set you free.'

He pulled me to my feet and took me in his arms. His kiss was every bit as delicious as I remembered and had recalled to mind on numerous occasions, his tongue soft but more urgent, setting off a chain reaction of snapping synapses and oozing chambers which made my knees buckle. Still, his hands were respectful; they did not stray, as I wished they would. I pressed myself to him and felt his desire firm against my belly. I slipped my arm from around his neck and put a tentative hand there, but he disengaged himself. His lips were hot, his eyes burned, but he was master of it. 'No, Evelyn,' he said, hoarsely. 'I will not do what John did. I will take you to church and have you as my wife, or not at all.'

The next day, when he had gone, I stripped the sheets from his bed with heavy, languorous arms, and toyed with the smoothly-opening drawers in the chest. The idea of his investigative fingers probing its hidden recesses, his soft, careful hands spreading wax, was charged with erotic connotations and bitter regret. I felt myself flush. I glanced into the mottled mirror; the skin of my face was pink. If John had walked in at that moment he would have read my aroused sexual state immediately, as easily as he would have seen that I had been crying from my red, swollen eyes. I wondered if he would mention it, whether I would tell him what had taken place, pour out my feelings to him, if he would comfort me, and say he understood. It was ironic, I thought; he was the first person I turned to in any emotional crisis, my automatic harbour, but, now, in this situation, he was the last person I could tell.

The house felt empty as I couldn't recall it ever had done before. More officers would come; another battalion would replace the 503rd and continue the training program. But even when they did, I could not imagine they would fill the void that Cameron Bentley had left behind him.

For a time, the skies over Tall Chimneys were silent, empty of the lumbering aircraft I had grown used to roaring above our trees. The silence and vacuity weighed heavier than the thunderous engines and unwieldy monsters ever had. It was unnatural; the stillness like some kind of dream-state. I wandered in it, lost.

I thought over what Cam had said to me, that last evening. Had John, as Cam asserted, taken advantage of me? Was I just one of a string of women? For all I knew he might well have had other women, in Germany or France, perhaps, or, even right now, in London. But if that were the case, I had to ask myself, why on earth would he keep coming back here? What could I offer him, over and above those others? What, here, made the tortuous journey and the, frankly, rather acrimonious association we seemed locked into, worth the bother? The fact was, for whatever reason, John did always come back to me, and I still saw, in his eyes, behind the confusion, beyond the frustration, the truth of the promise he had made to me all those years before.

Was it really guilt and shame which kept me at Tall Chimneys? At first, I admitted, yes. I had felt the stigma of my situation. I had seen myself as a mistress, an adulterer, fallen. I had worn my sin like a hair shirt, a badge of iniquity, keeping away from others lest my proximity taint them. But then, gradually, guided by Rose and Kenneth, vouched for and shielded by their families, I had shaken those feelings off. If others did not seem to be conscious of the stain, why should I? I'd told myself I had brazened out the world's disapproval. But my world was so small! A tiny village, an insignificant market town! Such a small amphitheatre of defiance! In the face of a larger arena I knew my rebellion would be instantly strangled, smothered by deeply inbred coils of self-accusation and rendered to jelly by my sheer naivety. Only marriage, I realised, could shrive me. Only a husband could guide me. Without those two things, I would never be free.

I had made no promise to Cam, but I felt in my heart that if he came back, I should go to America with him. The terrors of such a journey were immense, the idea of starting afresh in a foreign land left me palpitating with anxiety. Equally, the prospect of leaving Tall Chimneys, my friends, this comfortable, sequestered pocket of Yorkshire where I had dug myself in, filled me with despair. I knew I ought to wrench myself free. I was like an animal caught in a trap. I might have to gnaw off a limb in order to survive. I would be free, but oh! How I would limp.

The idea of deserting Tall Chimneys caused as large a weight of guilt as the notion of turning my back on John. This house, without me in it, would be only so much stone and mortar. The rooms would bloom with dust and mould, the smokeless chimneys would fall. I had tried to save and sustain it, to protect the tradition and history for which it stood. As much as it had sometimes felt to me that the house was a burden as heavy as that borne by Atlas, and as often as my arms had ached as much as his must have done, I felt it would be a terrible abdication of responsibility to walk away from it. For the first time I really understood what a terrible dilemma the old king had faced, how torn he must have been between his desire and his duty, and what he must have suffered in the choosing of one above the other. At the time I had been all for the choices of the heart, unthinking of the lasting scars a dereliction of duty might inflict upon the psyche. I asked myself if Tall Chimneys was my pride or my prison, and I did not know the answer.

The sheets smelt of Cam, and I did not launder them; I put them in a box under my bed, and when John did not come home, I pulled them out and wrapped myself up in them.

John worked feverishly for a week or so after Cam had gone. I knew he was in the throes of some great inspiration - the signs were all too familiar to me; disregard of food, irregular hours, a distant, pre-occupied light in his eye, a lack of attention when anyone spoke to him of mundane matters. Without these tells I might have assumed he was giving me time to adjust to Cam's absence, or even allowing me space to make a decision about my future, but I am afraid at that time I did not credit him with so much sensitivity.

We attended a concert at Awan's school (she was in the choir, chirruping tunelessly but with great gusto along with the other five and six year olds) but John's eye kept wandering to a point beyond my shoulder where dust motes danced in the light from the high window. He kept leaning past me to see the pattern of shadow cast on the far hall wall by the gymnasium equipment. He was twitchy and unsettled, and asked me to drop him at the gatehouse on our way home, even though it was almost dark.

Then, in the second week of November, the hectic light in his eye died, the rush seemed to calm and he came back to us. I assumed the great surge of inspiration had manifested itself on canvas, but he did not ask me to see his work, as he would have done in the past, and, again, I did not ask him. He remained at home during the day, reading the newspapers and smoking. I noticed for the first time his cough had returned.

'I'm sure those things don't help,' I remarked as he lit another cigarette and started spluttering.

'They do,' he wheezed, 'they clear the tubes.' He returned to his newspaper, where something seemed to catch his attention. 'Evelyn,' he said, with a casualness which came across as somewhat false, 'have you read the paper today?'

'No,' I replied. 'I haven't had time. Is there news?'

'Oh,' he mumbled. 'Just the usual.'

It was lunchtime. I put bread on the table and began to ladle soup into bowls. 'I wonder when the new cohort of officers will descend on us,' I mused. 'I don't think I can put them in the north wing this time. It was one thing for the summer, but during winter, it's barely habitable.'

'Have you heard from the last cohort?' John asked.

'No,' I said, too quickly. I was expecting a letter daily although Cam had made no promise to write.

'How did you leave things, with Captain Bentley?' John got up from the easy chair and approached the table.

'What do you mean?' I returned, again, much too sharply.

'Evelyn.' John gave me a rueful smile. 'After all these years, do you think I can't read you like a book?'

My shoulders sagged. I gave him a baleful look. 'We left things,' I sighed, 'in the air.'

He nodded, sympathetically. 'Delicious soup,' he said, and began to eat.

Afterwards, he took up the conversation again. 'I suppose it's like Monique and me,' he observed, 'slightly, anyway. My sense of duty to her, my feeling of being honourably bound, no matter how I might feel about you. It's the battle of the head and the heart, isn't it?'

Afterwards, it occurred to me he had been trying to be sympathetic, to let me know he understood how I felt. But, at the time, it felt as though he was turning the rack, and the fact his train of thought ran so exactly along the same lines of mine made me feel trespassed upon.

'It isn't like you and Monique,' I shouted. 'You hate Monique. I don't hate you!'

'No, I know,' he said, kindly.

His kindness broke me. I confessed everything. 'I'm torn between you,' I burst out.

'Of course you are.'

'I don't know what to do! Cam can offer me...'

'Marriage, children, a home,' John enumerated, reasonably.

'Yes, yes, all of that! But I'd have to leave Tall Chimneys,' I wailed. 'And you. I'd have to leave you!'

John nodded. 'Of course. He'd want to take you to America.'

'But this is where I belong, here, at Tall Chimneys, with Awan and you.' I put down my spoon; all pretence of eating lunch abandoned. I faced him across the table. 'And that's the problem, John. I belong with you. But you don't belong with me. You go off, and you have a life, and there's Monique, and it's all so complicated and so compromised...' Unconsciously, I used Cam's words to describe my relationship with John. Their very utterance felt like a betrayal of all John and I had been to one another.

Perhaps John felt it too. He stood up, abruptly. 'We never pretended it would be otherwise,' he said, coldly. 'But in spite of that, I have asked you repeatedly to come away with me. We could have lived discreetly in London.'

'Discreetly? Discreetly!' I yelled. 'Is that to be the story of my life? Kept quiet, hidden away where I won't enrage the public sensibility? Am I always to be the Talbot's disreputable daughter?'

John laughed; a cold, cynical sound. 'Only in your own eyes, Evelyn. And even the most august families have their skeletons. Look at the Mitfords!'

'I don't care to look at the Mitfords, much less be numbered amongst them,' I said. 'Hasn't the one who married Oswald Mosley been interned?' Another of the daughters had tried to take her own life, I recalled. The way I was feeling at that moment, I sympathised with her. She must have felt torn in two by the declaration of war as I did, now.[13]

'You make my point for me. Indeed she has, and yet she is by no means shunned by the rest of her family or by society in general,' John fumed. 'Victoria is long-dead, and with her the harsh moral values she enshrined. People are liberated, now. They are deciding for themselves what is right and proper.'

'Then why is the Mitford woman in prison?'

---

[13] Diana and Oswald Mosley were both interred during the war. Unity Mitford is reputed to have vied with Eva Braun for the love of Adolf Hitler. She attempted suicide in Munich after war was declared and was allowed to return to Britain. She died in 1948.

'Politics. Not morality.' He gave me a cold, withering glare before turning away and lighting a cigarette. 'With or without the society of people like them,' he muttered, through the smoke, 'we could have been happy'.

'Happy?' I snatched at his word. 'Have you not been happy then? And if not, why have you kept on coming back?'

We faced each other across the room. I had never seen John so angry, even with Ratton. 'Because you wouldn't come with me!' he thundered. 'If you had only come then I wouldn't... I wouldn't have had to...' Suddenly he brought his hand up to his mouth and pressed his lips closed, sealing whatever confession he had been about to make securely inside. What had he been about to admit? I imagined the worst; numerous concubines, several bastard children.

John took a few deep breaths and gathered himself. Then he moved round the table to stand behind me. 'You *know* why I keep coming back,' he said, hoarsely, all trace of his former angst evaporated as though it had never been. 'Surely you do. Don't you?' My soup had gone cold and my tears spilled into it. He put his hand on my shoulder and squeezed. 'But look, don't torture yourself,' he said. 'Things will become clear. Just remember, Evelyn, whatever happens, whatever you decide, I love you, and I understand.'

I heard his footsteps down the long, stone-flagged passageway to the back door. I waited for the creak of the door hinge, the rasp of the catch where it always stuck, but there was nothing, only the echo of our angry words.

'As if that helps,' I said, bitterly. I waited for his reply, but none came. Presently I turned, expecting to see him hovering in the shadow in the corridor, but the place was empty. Then I recalled Cam had oiled the hinge and repaired the catch.

Later, in the evening, I picked up the newspaper John had been reading and scanned it listlessly. A small paragraph caught my eye.

Soon after dark on 7 November, the 503rd PIR battalion took off from Land's End. The thirty-nine C-47s headed for La Senia, Algeria,

constituting the first wave attack c
scattered battalion suffered casualties,
the battalion re-grouped at Maison Blan.

John and I did not discuss the matter agai.
kept his distance, showing his care in sma
morning and cycling up to the village to
newspaper, which I read voraciously, looking for n.   .c
I did so that he had already read it, and was in   _n as
information which I dreaded.   . of the

Day followed tormented day; the radio was silent on the subject of the
situation in Algeria, the newspapers a blank page. The more stretched out
my uncertainty, the greater my sense of panic, the surer I became that,
should he survive, I would go with Cam to America and marry him. It was
almost as though I hoped my resolving so might keep him alive. I burned,
I yearned to know that he lived. I would leave Tall Chimneys; it would be
worth the sacrifice, I told myself, if Cam would only live. I would embrace
the church, even the shrivel-lipped women who looked at me askance in
the village street. I would ask God to wash my sins away. I would wear
white, and make my vows, and look them all in the eye.

But then I would catch sight of Kenneth working in the gardens or scaling
the old stone walls to repair a window or re-point the masonry. His
dedication to Tall Chimneys was absolute, selfless and enduring. He was
Tall Chimneys, as much as I was. The house encompassed his past and his
destiny as surely as it encompassed mine. What would he be, without it?
What would happen to him, and Rose and their family if I left, and where
on earth in the world did I belong but here, with them? And all the while
John waited diffidently for some word or gesture from me, as unsure as to
his fate as I was. His dignity and faithfulness further overbalanced my
resolve. How could I leave him? It would break his heart, and I would
rather break my own. How could the love we had shared be called sinful?
And what did I care about frowning looks from people whose opinion I
did not respect, or the judgement of a God in whom I did not believe?

ted between my options, and day followed day, and no news came. John took Awan to school and brought her home again. Together they went into the woods and selected our Christmas tree. The temperature plummeted. We had snow. It was very cold but we had to ration our use of fuel to run the generator. More officers came. Automatically I prepared rooms in the east wing for them, and cooked, and smiled as they discussed their training. The aeroplanes flew lower and lower over the moor and the woods, sometimes seeming so close their under-carriages might brush the tops of the trees. The men jumped from lower and lower altitudes, surviving plummets of only 143 feet, the lowest ever attempted. I watched them with distracted eyes, their tiny black forms against the steely winter sky, imagining other airmen falling through air which was searingly bright onto parched, unforgiving earth.

Then, on Christmas Eve, a parcel arrived from the new quartermaster at the camp. I decanted the contents without much interest; chocolate, coffee, a bottle of Scotch. At the bottom of the box, there was a letter. I tore it open. It was from Captain Brook.

'Cameron and I survived the attack on 8th November, In spite of our losses, spirits were high.   Cam's were especially high; he talked a good deal of home, improvements he meant to make on the farm,   fixing up the house. You will know better than I the significance of this. On 15 November   approximately   300 paratroopers jumped into an open area near Youks les Bains on the Tunisia - Algeria border. The ensuing thrust east to cut off the German lines of communications required a third   airborne drop of 30 paratroopers and heavy equipment to destroy an enemy railroad bridge. Cameron   and I volunteered to lead the attack. I am sorry to have to tell you that of the 30 paratroopers to descend   on the objective only six returned to friendly lines. Cameron was not amongst them.[14]

---

[14] This is a true account of the heroic engagement of the 2nd Battalion 503rd PIR in Algeria.

1943 was a terrible year in Britain but nowhere was it darker or more dreadful than in my heart. I wallowed in my sadness, drinking the loss of Cameron Bentley like hemlock.

The year passed - as I had predicted it would - but my complacency about the permanence of things at Tall Chimneys was utterly shattered. The seasons turned without purpose, like a mad dog chasing its own tail; the futility of it gaped like a yawning chasm at my feet. My heart felt so heavy within me, like a boulder, and I edged closer and closer to the lip of the abyss willing it to topple me over. I moved through the days like an automaton, mechanically washing and dressing, preparing food, washing sheets. I was barely conscious of other people; their conversation was like the drone of a fly in an empty room. Occasionally I felt John's arms around me, or Awan's little hand in mine. On several occasions, I think, Kenneth found me wandering in the gardens without coat or shoes, and brought me home. I have blurred recollections of Rose steering me to a chair from where she had found me staring glassily out of a window in one of the far rooms of the house. She would chafe my hands, and place a cup to my lips. At night John would put me to bed and draw the curtains, and I would sink into the oblivion of sleep, and hope never to wake.

That year is all shadow in my memory; parched of colour, flavour and sensation. What remembrances I have are fragmentary; a rabbit thrashing helplessly in a snare, the percussive thud of axes at the base of a sycamore on the edge of the woods. One night in April John hurried Awan and me to the ice house while a gale tore limbs off trees and threatened to topple the swaying chimney pots and bring them down on our heads. It was like a dream to me, his sense of urgency a distant and unsubstantiated imperative.

He implored me to follow him. 'The chimneys are swaying, Evelyn!' he cried into the teeth of the wind, but I watched him disappear into the lashing rain with Awan in his arms and remained behind with the wind. I looked on with distracted curiosity as it rampaged round the yard overturning planters and scattering logs from the log pile and sending slates cascading off the roof to shatter like porcelain all around me. Then other voices joined the cacophony as Kenneth and Rose hurried from their accommodations, and I let them hurry me to safety without acknowledging there had been any danger at all.

I remember voices always muttering just out of earshot; people whispering, a low drone of secrets a perpetual soundscape at the back of consciousness. Periodically I might wonder what they were saying, and instantly realise that I didn't care.

That spring was wet, but I don't recall the runnels of water which would have spouted down the by-ways of the crater between the mossy stones and gnarly tree roots. I have no recollection of the sun which, I am told, was so generous for the rest of the year. My world seemed rendered in the grainy monochrome of newspaper photographs; grimy and unpleasant to the touch - I shrank from engagement with it in any form. Its details at the time and in hindsight are indistinct and in some way unimportant, as though not connected to me at all; third or fourth hand, obsolete, scenes from an insignificant archive.

Food tasted like wet newspaper in my mouth; as often as not I left whatever had been put before me untasted.

Of course I recovered. Bereavement does not kill us even when we lose the companion of a lifetime, how much less when our connection with the lost is only of a few weeks' duration. Life goes on, as they say, and indeed it does, however hard we might will it to end. Sonnet writers might have it otherwise, but nobody ever died of a broken heart and no more did I. Looking back on it now, so many years later, I can see my reaction to Cam's death went much further than mourning simply the cruel and pointless death of a beautiful young man. In taking him, life, fate, God (call it what you will) had snatched from my grasp a chance - oh so briefly dangled - of freedom, a freedom I had not even known that I wanted until that moment. I had spent my life telling myself I was free, within the safe parameters of Tall Chimneys, free to be loved by John, to bring up my child, free enough even to make a contribution to our sequestered rural society. By showing me an alternative Cam had pulled back the veil to reveal my freedom had been a specious facsimile; Tall Chimneys had in fact been a gilded prison and I its complicit captive. I do not know to this day whether I would have taken the opportunity he offered, gone to America, become his wife. I only know that it presented a choice, something I had never had before. I mourned his death, I missed the man. I lamented the opportunity I would never now have. But most of all I found I grieved for the illusion of liberty and security which had been stripped away. I would never feel entirely free at Tall Chimneys, or completely safe within its boundaries, ever again. My sense of it as an impenetrable domain had been shattered; life could and would impinge. But far from making me abandon its crumbling masonry I clung all the more desperately to it; if life here could be compromised, I reasoned, how much more vulnerable would I be beyond it?

WITH THE ALLIES now firmly on the offensive, the airbase on the moor ceased operations and the stream of billeted officers stopped. A skeleton crew maintained the buildings but very few flights came or went. John went away on some occasions but he was never away long; I did not know what arrangements he made with the Intelligence Corps and assumed (wrongly, as it turned out) his period of usefulness had come to an end. He painted and his work was in demand. Our financial situation commensurately eased but ironically there was nothing to spend any money on; no luxury goods or nice clothes.

We had seen virtually nothing of Colin for almost eighteen months and I had, perhaps, become a little lax in keeping things in readiness for his visits. Then, one afternoon in the early autumn of 1943, there he was, rolling down the drive in a swanky black motorcar with two companions in tow: Sylvester Ratton and Giles Percy. John was with me in the rose garden when they arrived and to my surprise Colin announced it was John they had come to see. So he helped carry the men's few bags into the house and then waited, a thing he would never under ordinary circumstances have done. I thought Colin looked thin and rather ill, very pale. His nose was sharp and beak-like, his suit hung off him. He disappeared to make a telephone call almost immediately, leaving John, Ratton and Giles, a triumvirate of awkward associations and rattling skeletons as far as I was concerned, in the hall. John greeted Ratton with a curt nod of greeting but, to my surprise, shook hands warmly with Giles. That the two of them were acquainted separately from me seemed incongruous, like two worlds colliding.

Giles was a grotesque iteration of the young man he had once been. He had put on weight, his body thickened and ponderous; he had the corpulence of good living. His youthful skin had coarsened and there were broken veins on his cheeks. His teeth were yellowed from smoking. But his hair, previously very closely cropped, had grown out, restoring the characteristic - and now rather anachronistic - halo of blond curls around his head and his eyes were as intensely blue as I remembered them. These positives failed to outweigh the negatives in his appearance and in comparison, I thought John by far the handsomer of the two even though he was some years older.

Ratton bore comparison with neither; very stout and entirely bald, he had done away with the mean little moustache so his head looked more than ever like an unbaked loaf. He had swapped his rimless spectacles for ones with a heavier, tortoiseshell frame. They didn't fit properly and were constantly slipping down his tiny nose. Nevertheless he was still clearly very successful; his suit was hand-made and his shoes hand-tooled. The diamond in the ring he wore on his little finger was larger and more sparkly, set off by another in the pin on his silk tie. He seemed to take delight in the encounter between Giles and John, watching them both with a bright, anticipatory light in his eyes. Rather than strolling at ease round the hall or through the rooms, or going upstairs to unpack his bag, he remained stubbornly in front of the unlit fire and looked from one to the other of us, his rosebud mouth wet with anticipation.

Giles, John and I made desultory conversation about the war and the weather while Colin could be heard speaking in a low tone on the telephone.

Presently, Ratton asked, 'Is the child at school?' John bristled visibly, recalling, I suppose, Ratton's mean trick on Awan at their last encounter. But I could see at once what was fuelling his devious excitement.

I looked at my watch. Rose had agreed to collect the children that day and they would be home at any moment. I thought to rush downstairs and head them off, to prevent a face-to-face encounter between her and Giles. Giles might be bloated and blighted, as far removed from Awan's fresh-faced litheness as it was possible to imagine, but no-one, not Giles, not John, perhaps even not Awan herself, could possibly ignore the unmistakable likenesses of eye and hair between father and daughter once they were in the same room. But fate was unkind and, at that moment, I heard Awan's light tread on the servants' stairs and her voice calling our names. She burst through the baize door and stepped into the hall, her uniform all askew from a day's work and play at school, her blonde curls rampaging free of the neat plaits I had made for them that morning, a slab of pie in her hand.

'Mummy, can I eat this…' she began, holding the pie out in front of her. Then she saw the company and fell silent. 'Ooops,' she whispered, looking from John to me and back again, and casting a shy glance across the hall at 'Uncle' Ratton.

Giles gasped - it must have been like looking backwards in time at a younger version of himself. He paled, visibly, and then flushed. His eyes widened. He took a step back and almost stumbled on the lip of the hearth. John threw out a hand to catch his elbow, lest he fall entirely, and guided him into a chair. Then John too looked across the hall to see what had so utterly spooked the visitor. Of course he saw it immediately - how could he not, with such an eye that he had for both the outward appearances of things and for their underlying structures? The blue of their eyes, the curl of their hair, the hue of its tresses - these were the least of it. How much more the matters of proportion, limb-length, the quality of flesh and bone? They were exact facsimiles of each other and you didn't have to be a painter to know it. It was as though threads of genetic connection looped across the space between them like skeins of cobweb. John gave a sort of grunt of surprise, and turned to me with a raised, questioning eyebrow. I gave a slight nod.

'Well,' Ratton burst out, rubbing his fat little hands together, '*this* is interesting, isn't it?'

'What is?' Colin asked, stepping back into the hall.

'Three gentlemen visitors, and only one slice of pie,' I said, quickly. 'You'd better eat it, darling,' I turned to Awan, 'before they start to squabble.'

Mercifully, Awan seemed not to have picked up on the atmosphere. She disappeared back downstairs to eat the pie.

Giles recovered himself enough to say 'Perhaps we might talk, later?' His voice was tight, hardly more than a rasp.

'What's the matter with you, man?' Colin barked.

'His birds have come home to roost,' Ratton chuckled, nastily.

Not understanding, Colin turned to me. 'Is there a problem about food? Can you find us some dinner, Evelyn?'

'I expect so,' I said. 'How long are you staying for?'

'Just tonight. As I said, we need to speak to Mr Cressing, here.' He turned to John. 'After dinner, perhaps?'

John nodded. 'Of course.'

'Or...' Colin seemed to consider something, briefly, 'why don't you dine with us,' he turned to me, 'both of you? What we need to discuss, it's - well - a family matter, partly.'

Ratton let out a shout of laughter. 'Family!' he repeated, 'how apt!'

'I can't cook, serve and dine,' I said, shortly. 'John will come up after dinner.'

While I prepared dinner, John and I quizzed each other about Giles. They had encountered each other in the Intelligence Corps, I discovered, but not frequently enough for John to take much notice. He had 'a reputation' apparently, and not as a womaniser.

'He's the last man I would have suspected, let's say that,' John remarked, 'so if I'd been making a list of possibilities, he wouldn't even have figured.'

'I must have been an aberration, then,' I said, through thin lips, 'a thoughtless moment of madness, as he was, for me.'

My words hovered between us. They were the truth, and I hoped they would give John comfort.

'Who would have been on your list?' I asked, presently, with what I hoped was a mischievous smile.

'Kenneth,' John said immediately, 'he's devoted to you, you know.'

'He's devoted to Tall Chimneys,' I clarified.

'Isn't that the same thing?'

John insisted I accompany him upstairs. We entered the library where I had put out a drinks tray. Nobody seemed to object to my presence and I took a discreet seat away from the lamp. The evening had turned chilly but the men had not lit the fire or drawn the curtains. The room was cold, therefore, and I shivered, and accepted the glass of brandy Colin poured for me. His hand, as he held out the drink, was claw-like, his wrists thin and without flesh. As I looked up at him, in the muted light, his face was quite cadaverous. I put my own hand on Colin's and began to speak. God knew there was no love lost between us, we had never been close, but he had allowed me a home all these years and over-looked my unconventional life style and he was, after all, my brother. But he shook his head and moved back to an upright chair by the table, and my words faltered on my lips.

Ratton occupied his habitual place by the fire, his balloon of brandy perched on the mantel. He threw me a significant look and I knew he remembered, as I did, that night years before when he had attempted to abduct me. I returned his look with cold disdain.

Giles slouched on a low settee. He was flushed and it looked, to me, as though he had drunk more than his fair share of the wine at dinner. John stood on the hearth rug and waited for them to speak.

'What I am going to tell you now,' Colin began, in a tone which would have been impossibly pompous if not for the dark note of genuine tension which undergirded it, 'is top secret. No whisper of it must leave these walls.'

John and I nodded. John seemed unfazed by the announcement, and I wondered again what the nature of his work in the Intelligence Corps might have been.

'As you know,' Colin went on, 'the war in France has gone underground. The Vichy government is in charge, visiting brutalities on those found to be supporting the Allies in any way. France is a very dangerous place to be if you have any anti-German sympathies whatsoever. Nevertheless, we do have there a network of courageous operatives who are foiling the Nazi war effort at every turn; passing information, facilitating the escape of stranded airmen, sabotaging weapons and disseminating propaganda. Some of these are native French, others our own operatives, agents we have placed to oversee and co-ordinate operations. Then there is a small number who have, for a long time, seemed to ally themselves with the Nazis but who have actually been our eyes and ears. Double agents.'

I sipped my brandy, wondering what this could possibly have to do with John or me.

Ratton piped in from his place by the fire, a comment so random I couldn't relate it at all to what Colin had already told us. 'I am sorry to tell you that Mme Cressing is very unwell.'

I could hardly suppose that John's corpulent, bed-ridden wife was an active fifth columnist but I couldn't make any other sensible connection to the previous conversation. 'Is *she..?*' I stammered.

John threw me a satirical look. Colin murmured a deprecating, 'No, no.'

'But it would be a powerful inducement for Mr Cressing to return to France,' Ratton suggested.

'Not *very* powerful,' I demurred, but John looked down at the rug.

'Her villa is on the coast, an easy place to gain access to,' Ratton went on.

'But less easy to escape from,' I remarked.

'Indeed,' Giles, who, up to this point had spoken not a word, put in, 'Madame Cressing lives such a very sequestered life there - she is quite the recluse, these days. The Gestapo have no interest in her villa and it isn't watched. I have that on good authority. But in any case, given your previous relations with the Germans...'

'Previous relations?' I queried.

John gave me a look full of meaning I couldn't interpret.

Giles went on as though I had not spoken. 'You would naturally reassume your former role.'

'However you choose to play it,' Colin concluded, 'having gained access, you would be contacted.'

I stood up. 'What on earth are you suggesting?' I asked. 'John has no relations with the Germans. He does not care about Monique and has no intention of putting himself in her power again. He is too ill to undertake such a journey in any case, and couldn't possibly make any contribution to the underground movement in France.'

'Evelyn,' John said, 'don't you remember what Colin said, earlier?'

'Monique isn't family,' I spat. The acrid burn in my throat was nothing to do with the brandy; it was jealousy, hot and sour.

Once again, the men - Colin, this time - went on as though I had not spoken. I found the habit quite maddening. I might just as well have not been in the room, but I sat back down in my chair as an act of defiance: they would not squeeze me out of the conversation. 'The position of the villa will make getting into France very easy. John will have a safe haven, a place where Gestapo eyes never look, but, if they do, he has a valid reason to be there; his wife is dying, the perfect cover. *And* (contrary to what some may believe) he *does* have a history of co-operative relations with the Germans which will stand him in good stead, if necessary. One of our operatives is in danger, grave danger. Only John can extricate her. Without him, she is lost.'

'It's a woman?' I gasped.

'It's our sister,' Colin said, and he looked at me, properly, for the first time.

'Amelia?'

'None other.'

'She has been working for us for the duration of the war,' Ratton explained, as though he had been privy to Ministerial secrets and covert operations instead of just a carpet-bagging opportunist who had made his fortune from the suffering of others. 'She went to Germany with the

Mitford girls but unlike them she didn't swallow the Party rhetoric hook line and sinker. She went along with it, and reported back.'

I turned to John. 'You met her, in Berlin?'

He nodded. 'Many times.'

'You were her…' I struggled to find the term.

'Contact?' Ratton supplied it for me.

'Yes,' John confirmed it.

Suddenly I wanted to be alone with John. To have Colin and Ratton observe how thoroughly I had been hoodwinked by John Cressing was humiliating in the extreme. I wanted to question him in an arena where my obvious ignorance wouldn't be so embarrassing.

'So,' I attempted a tone of mild curiosity, 'when you were in Berlin, it wasn't entirely because of an exhibition?'

'There was an exhibition,' John admitted, 'but, no, it wasn't the only reason for my stay there.'

'It was just a cover,' Ratton crowed, as though anyone with half a brain could have known it.

'And she introduced you to..?'

'John made a number of valuable contacts while he was in Berlin,' Giles confirmed, 'but mainly, what he did - what they both did - was establish the appearance of a connection between them which the Germans then believed they could exploit.'

Light dawned. I gave a dry laugh. My lover, the double agent! 'You've been providing them with information? Ever since?

'Mis-information,' John qualified.

'Peppered with enough truth to make it stick.' Giles lifted his brandy glass to his lips but discovered it was empty. He waved it hopefully at Colin, but Colin, either wilfully or actually, failed to recognise the gesture.

I was astounded. I gulped down the brandy and held out my glass for more, a request which Colin did not ignore. 'The two of you have been working hand in glove,' I fathomed. 'She passing real secrets back from what she could gather in Germany, in exchange for false information from you in return.'

'You have it exactly,' Colin said.

'But the Germans think you're both on their side.' The deviousness of such an operation, not to mention the danger of it, was stupefying. And here was I believing he had been occupied in translating boring documents or perhaps listening in on mundane radio transmissions.

'Amelia has been an invaluable source of intelligence throughout the war. She is trusted. I should say: she *was* trusted. But recently...'

John looked uncomfortable. 'My contact has been less frequent, these past few months. It must have stretched our cover too thinly.'

That was my fault, I realised. My depression had distracted John from his work. Had it in some way left Amelia exposed?

'They think you've gone off her,' Ratton chuckled.

'Gone off her?' I blurted out. 'What basis of relationship do they imagine exists between you?'

Ratton gave a sort of guffaw which he turned into an artificial cough at a glance from Colin.

'They believe we're lovers, of course,' John declared, 'what else? Or they did do.'

The upshot of the meeting in the library was John was to depart with the men in the morning. He would be smuggled somehow into France and hole up at Monique's villa until he could make contact with Amelia, form a plan and get her to safety. The men agreed it in the face of my arguments and in the end I simply had to give in.

Neither John nor I saw a wink of sleep that night. I railed at him as I had no right whatsoever to do, with the father of my child upstairs in the house and the ghost of my would-be lover an ever-present spectre between us. Were he and my sister really lovers? Or had that been just a front? How much time had they spent together? Under what circumstances? In company with others, or alone? What was she like? Did he think her prettier than me? Had she asked, at all, about me? My jealousy knew no bounds.

'A fine time you've been having of it,' I flung at him, 'fucking Cinderella *and* the ugly sister! Perhaps you'd have liked us both together!'

'Don't be ridiculous, Evelyn,' John said. He answered each question like a man under Gestapo interrogation; effectively name, rank and serial number, neither confirming nor denying. That the man I loved could be such a stranger to me, and could withhold the truth with such patient stoicism, appalled me, and although he comforted me, and reassured me, and held me while I wept, it was in the mildest, most non-committal terms, and I felt further from him than I had ever felt before.

In between placating me, John began to pack a few belongings into a bag, and stifled paroxysms of coughing.

'See! *See!*' I crowed, as he hacked over his handkerchief, 'you aren't well.'

But nothing I could say would deter him. 'I am doing it for your sister,' he insisted, 'she is a brave woman, in terrible danger which only I can rescue her from.'

His remark only made it worse. In my head Amelia was the other 'me', my alter-ego, the person I might have been if I'd been born higher up the family tree. She was the worldly, sophisticated, courageous woman I would never be - not because I did not have it in me, but because she had had all the opportunities. Now she would have John, too.

'Why?' I wailed. 'Why does it have to be you?'

'And then there's Monique,' he went on, adding fuel to the already burning fire. 'If she's really ill, (and I have no reason to question it) I really ought to go to her. I owe her something...'

'You owe her nothing!'

'Evelyn, darling, you don't understand.'

'You're right,' I sobbed, 'I don't.'

By this time it was almost dawn, and I was putting together the makings of a scratch breakfast. My sleepless head swam with that unreal sensation that all this was a dream or would prove to be a terrible joke.

John sighed. I could feel him summoning patience from a cache which was almost empty. He stood behind me at the table while I smeared a parsimonious amount of margarine onto bread, and put his arms around my waist. 'If I'm caught, we have a ready-made cover story,' he explained, as though to a child. 'They think we're passionately in love. Our communiques are coded as love letters. According to them I'm a man so far gone I hardly need the excuse of Monique's illness to rush back to Amelia's arms, as they believe. If I didn't use it as a pretext, I think they'd be suspicious. They think I'm one of them, so they won't intern me. Colin will provide me with a dossier of information to take with me. It will be so nearly true, so hard to prove or disprove, by the time they find it's a smokescreen we'll be home and dry. But probably they won't even know I'm in the country. I'll wait at Monique's villa and Amelia will get to me one way or another, and a boat will pick us up.'

'In which case, why do you even need to go?'

'In case, *in case*, Evelyn,' he said, unable to prevent a note of exasperation from sounding in his voice. 'These things are so layered in deceit and lies, half-truths, whole truths, different agendas. Different people know different things; one lie does not fit all. How can I explain it to you? You just have to trust me.'

'Trust you?' The notion was laughable. But then, John's arms around me were almost all that held me up.

'Yes,' he said.

The men gathered on the gravel in the first glimmer of dawn after a light breakfast, and began to stow away their bags.

Giles took the opportunity to pull me to one side, and we walked on the lawns below the terrace where, I recalled we had walked before.

If I expected complaints and recriminations, I was not to have them. Giles looked peaky, despite his fleshiness. His hand trembled as it held his cigarette. I wondered whether he had become too dependent on alcohol - he certainly looked as though he could use a drink now. But his tone was gentle and conciliatory. 'I ought to thank you, really,' he began.

'Thank me?'

'You could have made things awkward for me,' he went on, 'about the child, of course, I mean.'

'Why would I have done that?'

'Well,' he hesitated, awkward, unsure how to continue. 'I presume I imposed myself on you. At the very least, I don't suppose I behaved like a gentleman.'

'Don't you remember?'

The blush of dawn spread across his cheek. 'I thought at the time something had happened, but I had been very drunk, nothing was clear to me. When you didn't make any sign I decided I had dreamed it, imagined it. It suited me to believe so, I suppose.'

I smiled, 'I took the blame - if there was any - onto myself. I certainly had no intention of causing you embarrassment or of being a burden.'

'Ironically,' he said, 'though it would have caused tongues to wag in some circles, it would have stilled others. But that's by the bye. Let me say this: if there ever is anything the child needs, you must tell me. She seems a nice little thing - very pretty, like her mother. I don't suppose I'll ever have children of my own. I'm not the marrying kind.' He threw me a look, and I sensed confidences he would offer, if he could, but a slamming car door brought our conference to a close. 'I won't impose myself now, even if I did then. But that isn't to say I absolve myself of responsibility.'

'You're very good. But Awan thinks John is her father, and he has been a father to her in every way. She needs no other.'

On the drive, the motorcar roared into life. It was time to say goodbye. Giles gave an old-fashioned bow. 'Nevertheless,' he said, 'remember what I have said.'

John kissed me before he got into the car, and then it drove off and into the throat of trees at the bottom of the drive, and I was alone at Tall Chimneys once more.

Although, of course, not absolutely alone. Kenneth and Rose and their boys were like hawsers; they anchored me and kept me safe. If John felt increasingly like a stranger, they felt more like family than ever and I clung to them.

The weather that autumn was mild and dull, much like my life at Tall Chimneys while John was away. I worried about him but nursed, also, a bitter resentment against him; he had kept secrets which might have been in the national interest but which had not been in mine. The more I found out about him only went to show how much more there was I did not know. My failure to get to the hidden heart of the man infuriated me. And yet. And yet. Again and again he came back to me. In times of crisis he had not deserted me. If he gave me reason to distrust him then there was ample evidence also that he was reliable.

For the foregoing months of the year my depression had lent me a leaden indolence which would scarcely permit my limbs to stir or even the smallest modicum of enthusiasm to be generated for anything at all. But now I found myself restless and ill at ease. I took again to the woods, meandering beneath the dripping trees and forging carelessly through the rivulets and spongy bogs of the woodland. I walked to the village on occasion, and bought things I did not need from the village shop just to have an excuse for the journey, to use up time which had never seemed to hang so heavy on my hands before. There were several new babies in the village, nine months or so since the departure of the airmen. Did their mothers, I wondered, cringe with shame at the evidence of their licentiousness, as I had done? Would they suffer the withering looks and tart accusations which had been levelled at me? At one time I would have felt a sort of kinship with them, a kind of sisterhood of defiance, but now I felt utterly out on a limb, separated off from any association we might have shared. It reminded me with a pang, though, that but for the honourable behaviour of Cameron Brook, I too might have had another baby to take care of.

Work in the house was very spasmodic. I prepared meals for Awan and myself, did our laundry and kept our quarters clean, but Kenneth did all the work in the garden and Rose looked after the rest of the house, airing rooms and lighting fires as the weather dictated. They both did their best but things did deteriorate; a smashed window in an upper room went undiscovered for weeks, a soot-fall from a sitting room chimney was left un-cleared, a leaking pipe in a room above caused a brown stain on the library ceiling, some of the plaster cornicing fell down and the topmost row of books were ruined beyond saving. I just didn't seem able to summon up enough energy to care.

Awan chattered away as usual, played with the boys, did the reading and spelling tasks her teachers sent home and threw herself with enthusiasm into the Christmas Carol Concert, being selected, to her special joy, to sing a solo. She went out, as she always had done, at weekends to play and was often missing from early morning to dusk, which was early. I never questioned her as to where she had been or what she had been up to; she came home often dirty and ravenously hungry but perfectly safe and that was all that mattered to me. But amidst all these signs of normality I detected an underlying restraint which had never been part of her character before. She was particularly well behaved, careful about table manners (something I had always had to pick her up on, especially when she had been spending a lot of time with Rose and Kenneth's boys) and didn't cross or contradict me. One of the dogs had a litter of puppies and we didn't have our usual argument about her being able to keep one, or have them all sleep with her in her bed, or be allowed to dress them up in her dolls' clothes. At nearly six it seemed to me these were natural signs of a developing maturity but it occurred to me also they were the result of my own odd behaviour and distraction over the past year. I had not been *my*self. How could I expect her, in response, to be *her*self?

These thoughts occupied but they did not obsess me. Like my body, my mind did not seem able to concentrate on one thing. Random, contradictory and irrelevant ideas seemed to flit in and out of my brain, jostling each other and going nowhere in the same way that I might set out in the morning to clean out the hen coop, get diverted half way across the yard by a blocked gulley and end up rummaging in a lean-to for something whose purpose or necessity I had forgotten before five minutes were up. Usually I gave up even the pretence of rational thought or purposeful behaviour, and simply roamed about.

One day my meanderings brought me to the gatehouse. It was months since I had been there but the door yielded to my push and, inside, I found things fairly well ordered. A vase of rather desiccated holly leaves and sprigs of hawthorn stood on the table and there were some books which I did not remember having taken there. One of my cake tins stood on a shelf and inside I found the remnants of a seed cake I had baked some weeks past. I assumed John had brought these things when he had been painting at the gatehouse although the books were old ones of Awan's and the foliage arrangement rather clumsy for his artistic hands. Perhaps Awan had kept him company at some point during my bleak, mourning months?

Thought of John's work took me upstairs. As usual with him there was a chaotic mess of paints and brushes on the table under the window and a number of half-finished canvasses propped on easels around the room. Sketch books were flung onto the divan, amongst the blankets and quilts we kept there, and some pages of correspondence from what seemed to be gallery owners and agents in London. John's writing identified these commissions as 'shipped' or 'sent by carrier' or 'sketches awaiting approval'. There were bills and receipts also, from artists' suppliers of various kinds, and across these John had scrawled words like 'paid', or 'wrong pigment sent. Awaiting credit'. These evidences of commercial interaction gave me fresh pause for thought; further areas of John's life about which I knew little. I felt more estranged from him than ever.

Feeling that, for once, the gatehouse would not give me the solace I needed, I had turned to go back down the stairs when a group of canvasses stacked behind a screen caught my eye. They were shrouded in a sheet and their being doubly hidden excited my curiosity. I whipped off the sheet and brought the pictures into the light.

They were a series of three portraits of a woman, painted from unusual, even unnatural, angles, with light illuminating features which would not normally form the focus of a portrait-painter's eye. One showed simply the side of the woman's head and the tip of her ear brightly lit by a shaft of light perhaps from a partly opened curtain, the rest of her remained in deep shadow and no facial feature provided identification. For an artist given to modernist impressions and experimental uses of colour and texture, the style here was rather naturalistic, the individual strands of the woman's hair and the silken sheen of it so finely rendered I almost felt I could reach out and comb it. The flesh of the ear looked alive, flushed and warm with blood which flowed through tiny veins, and I could see the velvet of downy hairs which are usually invisible to the naked eye with a clarity which made me feel as though I were viewing it through a magnifying glass. The familiarity of the rendition, and the closeness of observation gave the picture an intimate quality, and there was a sense, too of voyeurism - I got the impression that the woman did not know she was being so personally observed, or, that if she did, she did not care.

The second canvas showed a woman's arm draped along the back of a sort of chaise. It was a sorry-looking piece of furniture, from what I could make out of it, the row of rivets dull, some missing, a rip in the material showed a mess of stuffing. The colour of it was impossible to make out; greyish purple, perhaps, its nap worn smooth. The wood of the frame was scarred with scratches. Again, the angle of light left much to be conjectured in the setting and detail - this time a dull lamp or perhaps even a candle, burning low on the floor beyond the frame of the picture, threw a muted glow over everything and cast many distorted shadows.

The arm was bare from the elbow, the material above a froth of lace which suggested sensuous lingerie. But something about the drape of the arm made this ironic; rather than elegantly arranged the arm was carelessly flung, the hand hanging down, the fingers empty and dispirited, and without adornment. John had painted the skin of the arm with biological exactitude; every pore and hair was visible, the network of blue veins at the wrist clear to see and even those beneath the skin of the finger-joints - more purple in hue and as fine as ink lines on paper. The hand was a capable-looking hand, a hand which could work or save or nurture. Somehow this made the indolence of the arm's posture, the emptiness of the hands and the overall sagged hopelessness in the drooped shoulder unbearably sad.

By this time the light was fading and I had to move closer to the window to examine the third canvas, pushing aside John's litter to set it onto the table. Ironically, this, the smallest of the three pictures, encompassed the largest scene, a disordered bed, painted from its foot, where a few casually strewn garments had been flung. The rumpled layers of the sheets and blankets and their various textures were very well done; I could see the sheen of silky eiderdown, the tufted ridges of candlewick, the nap of flannelette sheets. From this nest, a foot protruded, thrust out, its sole and the underside of the toes facing the artist, the rims of untrimmed - and rather grimy - nails just visible. In this perspective, the foreshortened heel disappeared into the ankle and shin of the woman, and then was absorbed into the tangled bedding. A curve of thigh and buttock and the hump of turned back and hunched shoulder could be made out in the contours, and, almost at the edge of the picture, a messed mop of hair spread on a pillow.

This scene I did recognise, or I thought I did, and in recognising it I recognised them all. They were pictures of me. Me in my depression, in my mourning for Cameron. How often had I been found in a room lit only by a slightly opened curtain? The arm, idle and bereft, when it should have been busy, was mine. And this bed had been my refuge; I had refused to leave it on many occasions, seeking oblivion in sleep. The hair was mine, the skin too, but, more than that, the emotional state was mine, and that mattered more and made the pictures so much more than mere likenesses.

That John had observed me so closely, and seen, in my drooping posture and distraction, the very depths of my despair, moved me beyond words. No matter what his life had been away from me, with me, he had been mine, absorbed in me and empathetic to my mood, and for that I ought to be eternally grateful.

The next few days saw a transformation. I had a bath and washed my hair, something I had not done in many weeks. I washed bedding and curtains, and scrubbed floors, and called in repair men to restore those areas of the house which needed it. I cooked, and told Awan to invite her friends. I called in on Patricia and Ann, and attended WI meetings.

I talked to Awan, one evening, when she was bathed and ready for bed, and sat at my side reading the book she had brought from school. 'The gatehouse,' I said, quietly, the smell of her hair in my nostrils, 'it's a special place, isn't it?'

She turned her face to me, a mixture of anxiety and relief in her eyes. 'It's your special place, Mummy, but, I've been sharing it.'

'I know,' I replied, hugging her warm little body to me. 'I'm glad. Do you know I took you there when you were born?'

'Yes,' she sighed, and snuggled closer, pushing the school book off her lap, 'tell me that story again.'

I thought about John almost all the time; where he might be - my feverish imagination had him cowering in the keel of a boat, lashed by gales, or hovering close to Monique's bed administering medicine or comfort, or socialising with a gang of heel-clicking Gestapo officers, or tied and beaten in an interrogation cell. Sometimes the images were hugely romanticised - closer to fantasies; he a dark and handsome figure, courageous in the face of the enemy. At others they took on the stuff of nightmares - he was ill and broken, and needed help I was utterly unable to supply. Either way, they reignited a spark which had been dead for a while. I found I was hungry for him, for the smell and touch of the man, and I kept myself in readiness for his return; my hair nicely ordered, my underwear the best I could muster, the bed clean and turned down in preparation for our falling into it in each other's arms. I cooked his favourite meals, as far as rationing permitted, and kept his favourite cardigan warm near the range.

Few vehicles called at Tall Chimneys these days, and my ear was constantly pricked for the sound of wheels on the gravel but the night he came home there was a lashing squall, and the sound of rain like pebbles on the kitchen window obliterated the noise of the car approaching. It was December. Awan had been long in bed and I had been working on a cardigan I was knitting her for Christmas but it had got late and I was beginning to think about retiring too, banking down the range fire and rinsing a few dishes at the sink. All at once the dog by the door stirred and gave a warning bark. Then the door at the end of the passageway flew open and a cloaked figure entered, bringing with it a howling gust of rain-sodden wind and a flurry of leaves which had accumulated on the outside step. The passageway was unlit, and the figure frightened me, dark, indeterminate and very large, it occupied the whole space and seemed to be fighting with some invisible force. The door was, with difficulty, wrestled shut, and a hand shot out to grope for the light switch. The cloak fell to the floor, revealing John, almost doubled over, soaked through, pale and coughing, a handkerchief clasped to his mouth. And next to him, emerging from the same cloak, almost seeming to be supporting him, my sister, Amelia.

AMELIA WAS PRAGMATIC and brisk, wasting neither time nor words on effusions of delight at meeting a long-lost sister. She helped me get John out of his wet clothes and into bed; he was in a terrible state, shivering but hot to the touch, and his cough seemed to rack his whole body. At last, when he was settled, she declared that she was 'tired to death' and took herself upstairs. When I caught up with her she was in Mrs Simpson's room unpacking her valise.

'This room isn't prepared,' she observed, tersely.

'No,' I agreed, 'but it won't take long for me to make the bed.'

'Where are the servants?'

'We only have Rose, who helps me in the house, and her husband who does the outside work. The house is run on a shoe-string; I do most of the work myself.'

'Good God.' She crouched by the fire I had hastily lit and stared into its meagre flames while I found sheets and towels which were not too threadbare. 'And you sleep..?'

'Downstairs, in the housekeeper's rooms,' I informed her, and then, feeling it necessary to establish my claim beyond any misunderstanding, 'where we put John.'

'You sleep with John,' she confirmed, 'yes, I understand.'

'I suppose this used to be our mother's room?' I said, more by way of filling the awkward silence than because I really wanted to know.

'No,' Amelia shook her head. 'It was kept in perpetual readiness for our Grandmother Harris - Mother's mother. She liked to arrive unannounced and outstay any lukewarm welcome she might have received, if I recall. We were all terrified of her.'

'I don't remember her at all,' I said.

'She was dead by the time you were born.'

'Of course. You're - what? Seven? Eight years older than me? You were at school by the time I was born, anyway.'

'You and Colin were both spared her denigrating remarks and endless cataloguing of our failings.'

'Oh?'

'Oh for God's sake, let's not talk about her now. I just want a hot bath and a decent night's sleep. Is that too much to ask, after all I've endured?'

I ran her a bath and took her tea and toast on a tray while she languished in it, stoking up the fire and turning down the bed on my way out. Any rush of affection I might have hoped for, any meeting of sisterly minds, totally quashed.

For the next few days she kept herself to herself, never getting dressed and coming downstairs only to forage for food in the kitchen once she had established meals would neither be served in the dining room for her, nor carried up to her on trays.

'I have John to look after,' I told her, after she had querulously complained about the lack of hospitality, 'and Awan.'

John was very ill, coughing constantly, feverish and sometimes delirious. The doctor visited daily.

'The little girl ought to stay elsewhere,' he frowned. 'The spores in the sputum are infectious.'

'She can stay with my neighbour,' I replied.

'Surely there is room in the house?' he questioned. 'Just so long as she doesn't come in here.'

I thought about the draughty corridors and comfortless rooms above us. It crossed my mind to suggest she share with Amelia, but my sister had shown scant interest in her niece. At least with Rose and Kenneth I knew Awan would be loved and cosetted even if conditions would be cramped.

'No,' I said, 'she can stay next door.'

I brought John warm soup which I dribbled into his mouth spoonful by spoonful, and cool water which he sucked from the corner of a cloth, and bathed his heated body. In a moment of lucidity I asked him about Monique.

He shook his head. 'Dead, before I even got there,' he croaked, through parched lips.

'Ah,' I sighed, feeling as though a gremlin which had dogged my back for as long as I could remember had suddenly fallen away, leaving me to stand up straighter. 'Well,' I added, and it was the truth, 'I am sorry. I don't think she had a happy life.'

'It was an unpleasant death, I gather,' John gasped, 'and she died alone.'

'God defend any of us from that,' I said.

I lay on top of the bed and cuddled into his back during the night. It wasn't the passionate reunion I had envisaged, but I was satisfied. John was home.

After a few days' recuperation, Amelia appeared downstairs dressed, with her hair washed, and announced she was going to town to buy clothes. 'The ones I have are unsuitable for this rustic, bohemian existence,' she said, pouring coffee from a pot on the stove. 'My sequined cocktail dresses will be out of place here, I surmise. I don't suppose the Vicar holds many soirees?'

'None whatsoever,' I confirmed. 'But you? Even during the war, you've been enjoying cocktail parties?' I was astounded by the idea of such frivolous luxury. Life in Britain had become grim and grey indeed, leached of colour or pleasure; a doleful daily grind. I cast my mind back to the last time I had really enjoyed myself and my memory slammed against its recollection of my day in Scarborough with Cameron Bentley. The idea of shimmering evening dress, cocktails, canapes, the tinkling of a piano, all seemed wildly exotic and also trivial and wasteful. Given my day's holiday again, I would not spend it at a cocktail party.

'Indeed. Hob-nobbing with the higher ranking Gestapo officers and members of the Party elite was my raison d'être; they let things slip, you know, when their minds are loosened by Martinis,' she gave me an unpleasant wink. 'I make an excellent Martini.'

'You have been a spy,' I said, with a shudder. Even though she had been on our side, it still felt, to me, like a disreputable occupation, dishonest and double-dealing.

Amelia laughed. 'Poor little Evelyn,' she said, and her remark made me wither inside.

When she came back from town she was laden with bags - how she had bought so much with clothing coupons I did not know, but then, I realised, she probably had cash or some governmental authority which would allow her to buy whatever she wanted. 'What a God-forsaken little town,' she complained. 'Hardly any Christmas decorations and no Christmas cheer whatsoever. In Germany, even with the war on, they know how to celebrate Christmas.'

'Perhaps the Fuhrer's entourage do,' I replied. 'I suppose the ordinary Germans have it as bad as we do. The Jews, I understand, have it a whole lot worse.'

Amelia ignored my barbed remark. 'Come upstairs with me,' she said, airily, as she passed through the kitchen, 'and see what I have bought.'

She laid her purchases out onto the bed and I saw immediately why she had made such a good spy; she was a chameleon, able to blend seamlessly in to whatever background she found herself in. The clothes she had bought were much like mine - conservative, practical, hard-wearing. 'Suitable for a daughter of Yorkshire, do you think?' she asked, holding a woollen skirt up against herself, and layering it with a thick cotton blouse and long-line cardigan.

'You'll blend right in,' I said.

'That's the idea,' she smiled. 'I've bought vests too. This place is freezing - you do know that, don't you?'

'Fuel is rationed,' I said, 'so we can't use the furnace.'

She laid down the skirt ensemble and picked up a two-piece suit. 'This is a horrible colour,' she observed (it was brown), 'I'd have liked it better in dove grey, or pale blue, but there wasn't any choice.' She turned back to the mirror, to admire the effect.

'There's plenty of wood for the fires, though,' I went on, 'assuming someone gathers it and chops it up.'

Amelia had her back to me. Perhaps she didn't realise I could see her face in the mirror, but she gave an exasperated eye roll at my comment, and inspected her nails, 'Well,' she said, 'I think I draw the line at *that*.'

'Someone has to do it,' I retorted.

'I've done enough for King and Country, don't you think?' She looked up and our eyes met, through the silvered surface of the mirror.

'This is nothing to do with King and Country,' I said, with a bitter note to my voice which I couldn't conceal. 'This is family. Everything I do is to make sure that the people and the place I love survive.'

She smiled. 'We're not so different, after all,' she said.

And looking at us both, there in the mirror, she was right. Physically, there were several similarities between us. We had the same hair colour - light brown, with golden highlights - although hers was cut shorter than mine and she wore it loose, I could see we shared the same thick tresses and curly habit. Our eyes were the same shape - mine perhaps a shade or two darker brown - and our eyebrows had the same arch. Our skin tone and texture was identical, but Amelia's bone structure was more sculpted, her cheek bones having a greater prominence, and she had a sharper chin and nose. She was a few inches taller than me (but wore boots with heels) and was several pounds lighter; in fact she was slim to the point of thinness, not only on her waist and hips but also her arms and shoulders. But then, I considered, she had borne no children - the end of many women's waistlines - nor had she done physical work, as I had, preserving her from developed muscles which were perhaps not very feminine.

'Isobel was fair, and very slight,' I said. 'She is the only other sister I remember. I lived with her, you know, when I was small.'

'She took after Father,' Amelia said, 'like Colin.'

'And we look like our mother?'

Amelia nodded. Now I thought about it, George had also had our colouring. Of our oldest brother, the one who had died in the first war, and our older sister, I had no memory of at all.

'William and Josephine were unlike either mother or father,' Amelia said, as though she had been privy to my thoughts. 'Both thick-set, with wiry hair and an over-bite. No beauties. They took after Grandmother Harris' side of the family. Thankfully Mother - and therefore we - escaped it.'

We both smiled. Perhaps there could be, I speculated, briefly, some sisterly accord between us? Did I mind so much if Amelia didn't pull her weight around the house? What was one more mouth to feed, when I had catered for the airmen with relative ease? It would be good for Awan to have a woman around who had travelled, a worldlier woman than I would ever be. Maybe, in time, Amelia would take Awan to London or even further afield.

'John has had to pretend to be in love with you,' I said, raising a subject which we had hitherto not broached. I said it with an amused tone, as if the thing was absurd in itself but also very clever, since it had fooled the enemy so successfully.

'Pretend?' Amelia almost shouted, and turned from the mirror to rummage in her handbag for a cigarette. The confidential moment was broken. 'Well, it wasn't so difficult. After a few years we both got quite used to the subterfuge. At times, I almost believed it was true.' She threw herself onto a chaise longue and looked at me narrowly through the haze of smoke from her cigarette.

'And how far...' I began, faltering, now that I was on this dangerous ground. How much did I really want to know?

'Oh, *you* know,' Amelia said, archly, 'the usual things, what would have been natural, in the circumstances. We went at it very...' she flicked ash onto the hearth. It missed, and cascaded onto the carpet, 'professionally, let us say,' she concluded.

I swallowed down a lump in my throat. The absolute certainty I had had in John since seeing his pictures at the gatehouse began to melt. After all, it came to me, with a sickening clarity, those pictures could as easily have been of Amelia, as of me.

John did not improve. The doctor expressed grave concern. 'Without an X ray it isn't possible to be certain, but given his history, I'd say the TB is back with a vengeance,' he said. He suggested transferring John to a specialist hospital. 'The journey alone, though,' he warned, 'will be dangerous.'

'Then, of course, he should not undertake it,' I reasoned.

The doctor sucked on his pipe. 'I've already told you the air here will never be conducive, even if we manage to shake this infection. Long term, Mr Cressing cannot remain here at Tall Chimneys. As before, he needs dry air, a warm climate, as well as medication which, unfortunately, doesn't come cheap.'

I gave a hard swallow, but Amelia said, 'Whatever it costs, we can pay.'

'We *can't.*' I corrected her.

'We *can,*' she repeated.

I devoted myself to John's care, sitting by his bed through the nights, wiping his mouth after the dreadful coughing fits, changing the pillowslips which were often dark with blood and mucus. His breathing was dreadful; bubbling like a subterranean geyser. Kenneth helped me move him off the bed and into a chair while I changed the sheets and several nights he came in unasked and ushered me off to bed.

'I'll watch him,' he said in a low voice. 'You can trust me.'

I stood against him for a moment, my head drooping with tiredness, resting on the flat of his hard chest, and felt as though I was resting in the lee of a massive and ancient tree. I felt sheltered, momentarily, from the onslaught of John's illness and what I feared would come. I could trust him, just for a few hours, to relieve me of the burden of it. Kenneth placed his hands on my arms and lifted me away from himself. 'Go to bed,' he whispered.

To be fair, Amelia also took her turn. Whereas I sighed and wept, and stroked John's hand, she sat impassively, doing what was necessary for his care but showing no sign of emotion.

One night, as we sat in his room watching over him, she said to me, 'I think we'll have to take him to America. I can't think of anywhere else where the climate and the medical help will be good enough, or where we can get to in safety.'

'I shouldn't think we could get to America, could we?' I replied, dully. 'Surely ordinary people can't cross the Atlantic? And anyway, it isn't safe. What about the U boats?'

She shook her head with irritation at my naivety. 'We will fly,' she said. 'John isn't an 'ordinary' person, he has military clearance, and so do I. I can arrange transport on an aircraft for us.'

'For... the two of you?' My heart felt like a stone in my chest.

Amelia gave me a straight look. 'Let's be honest with each other, shall we? John is dying here. If he goes to America and gets the best treatment he may survive. He might not survive the journey, it might be too late for any treatment to save him, but at least there's a chance. If he stays here, he'll have none. This infection or the next one. It will carry him off. Even if the TB doesn't. But it will.'

I began to cry. 'You put it so baldly,' I sobbed.

'Of course,' she nodded, reasonably, 'what other way is there?'

The room suddenly seemed very small and suffocating. A single lamp burned in a far corner of the room so as not to disturb John but the darkness which overlaid the rest of the space and the heavy curtains across the window seemed to smother me. The heat from the fire in the grate felt overwhelming. My sobs became more laboured, my chest rising and falling but seeming to bring no air and no relief. In a far, arbitrary part of my brain it occurred to me that this must be how John felt - asphyxiated, fighting for air. I was desperate to get out but the thought of leaving Amelia and John alone was equally unsupportable. I felt if I walked out now I would never see him again.

'Couldn't Awan and I come with you?' I gasped out.

'I don't think so,' Amelia said, indifferently, as though considering a trifle. 'And even if you could, *would* you? I mean, aren't you rather...' she gave a dry smile, '*rooted* here?'

'I have had to be,' I said, bitterly. 'Life has offered me no alternative.'

'Life has plenty of alternatives to offer,' she countered, 'it is you who have not grasped them. Evelyn, what do you image the world out there to be like? Do you think of it as it was when you travelled to Isobel's when Mother fell ill? When was that? 1915? 1916? Were you taken in a pony trap to the station, and collected at the other end in a hansom cab? Did Isobel wear corsets and a dress to the floor?'

I stared at her. She had described exactly the world I remembered.

She went on, rubbing salt into my wound. 'Were there bobbing servants and dainty sandwiches and little girls being seen and not heard? I suppose church-going was obligatory, and tea with the Vicar, and modesty and maidenhood placed on the altar along with the chalice and holy wafers? A girl's 'reputation' was as precious as her actual virginity - more precious, probably.'

She stopped to light a cigarette. In the light of the match her face was angular and ugly. 'That was thirty years ago!' she muttered, almost to herself. 'My God, the hypocrisy of it!'

She smoked for a while in silence, but then burst out again. 'I know plenty of girls who screwed the footmen but wore white to marry earls in

Westminster Abbey! But Evelyn, those thirty years have seen indescribable changes. The world of now is unrecognisable! Life is hectic and noisy. It's fast and exciting. Women have broken free. They are working alongside men, outside the home, going to university, living alone. They have their independence and they use it to live how they damned well like. Think of that, will you? A woman with a lover is nothing - lots of women have lovers, several lovers! And children too. You aren't as special as you think. It isn't easy, sometimes, in practical ways, but it's done and no one turns a hair. You could have lived out in the world, Evelyn, with John, and although some few old-fashioned, small-minded people might have judged you privately no one would have done so publicly; they understand that the world has moved on. You would not have been shunned, as you seem to imagine. In some circles, you would have been respected, held up as a positive example, even, of what emancipated womanhood looks like in this day and age.' Her soliloquy ended, Amelia threw her cigarette butt into the fire and leaned back in her chair with the air of a woman who has at last got something off her chest.

Her tirade had brought my tears to a halt. 'It's too late, now,' I said, tremulously.

'Too late for you,' Amelia said, shortly, and, with a glance at the bed, 'and for *him*, more's the pity.'

A few seconds passed before she added, almost to herself, with a shake of her head, 'The life you have led him.'

Her doleful judgement on the deleterious impact I had had on John's life caused me to lift my head up, presenting her with, I suppose, a tear-streaked face. 'He talked about it?'

She gave a snort of derision. 'He spoke of little else, in connection with you. His frustration at your stubbornness, your shrinking timidity, a sense of being pulled in two.'

'Oh!' It was too much. I thought my heart would break. I had ruined John's life. 'I thought he loved me. Whatever compromises we have had to make, I thought it must be worth it for him, because of that,' I cried, 'because at least, despite everything, he loved me.'

Amelia stood up. In the shadowy room, lit from behind by the lamp, she seemed enormous to me, towering over the bed, the prone figure of John and myself, perched round-shouldered like a defeated bird on a hard chair, a balled up handkerchief clutched in my fist. 'You ninny,' she jeered, and I thought, for a moment, I heard something else in her voice, more than just derision, more than sneering rebuke, but another, sourer note, something caustic which burned her as much as it did me, 'he *does.*'

Amelia spent the next few days organising things on the telephone. It wasn't easy. Christmas was almost upon us and it seemed the people who could help her had already left for the holiday. In desperation she caught a very early train and travelled to London, returning late at night but clutching a sheaf of paperwork; Visas, letters of authority, medical certificates and the like.

Meanwhile John's fever broke and he seemed better, although very weak. The doctor came and listened to his chest and took samples of sputum away for analysis. He shone a bright light in John's eye, and frowned.

John had no energy at all, even walking from the bed to the chair seemed to exhaust him, so he gave up on it. I washed him and dressed him in clean pyjamas each morning, and propped him up on many pillows, which seemed to ease his cough. I gave him books to read, but they lay unopened on the bedside table. Sometimes a programme on the wireless would interest him, but usually his attention would stray before ten minutes were out, and he would doze. He liked having the curtains open so he could see the kitchen garden, bare of interest as it was, and the sparrows in the trees. Awan came to show him some of the things she had been making at school and to sing carols to him from the other side of the French windows, which she did so loudly that the rooks on the chimneys all took off in fright. John smiled and applauded and I hoped Awan could not see the tears which coursed down his waxy cheeks as he did so.

Christmas Day came. I went across the yard to give Awan her gifts in the morning, and later again to eat my second Christmas dinner with Rose and Kenneth and their family. Earlier, Amelia and I had shared a scrawny chicken and some vegetables. The atmosphere between us was leaden. She drank most of a bottle of champagne.

After the meal she got up and picked up the bottle. 'I'm going upstairs,' she said, heavily. 'We leave on New Year's Eve. It's all arranged.'

I took John his meal on a tray. He ate very little of it; next to nothing, in fact.

'Amelia is going to take you to America,' I said. 'You'll get better, there.'

'So I believe,' he said, wanly.

'You don't want to go?' It was craven of me to ask. 'I don't know,' I went on, with an attempt at hilarity, smoothing down an already smooth bedsheet, 'I seem to be perpetually sending you off abroad into the arms of other women!'

John threw me a look. 'My neck is sore,' he said, by way of rejoinder.

I ran my hands over it - it was clammy to the touch although the room was warm. His hair was long again, as it had been the day I had first seen him, but silvered now with streaks of grey and lacking the lustre it had had then. I pushed it to one side. There was a lump beneath the surface of the skin, the size of a quail's egg, quite hard and red.

'A boil,' I said. 'I'll get you a dressing.'

As I dressed the lump, I said, 'I found your pictures at the gatehouse. You caught me unawares.'

'You were not at all aware, when I sketched them,' he said, quietly, 'altogether in another place.'

'They are nothing like your work of late,' I remarked.

'You are like nothing I have ever painted,' he said. 'No style I tried could capture you.'

'You needed no style to capture me,' I replied, in a quiet voice. 'I was yours from the moment you appeared on the north wing.'

'And I was yours.'

I kissed him, very gently.

The effort of talking had tired him; his eyes were dull with fatigue. 'We can get married now, if you want to,' he murmured, but he was more asleep than awake, and I did not reply.

We celebrated Awan's birthday quietly. It would have been a boring day for her but that it snowed heavily in the late morning and she spent all afternoon out with the boys building a snow man and throwing snowballs. Being a girl seemed no hindrance to her, and buttered no parsnips with the lads, and why should it? She was hale and strong, had a good throwing arm, was equal to climbing any tree and could whittle a decent stick - all essential attributes for being in Bobby's crew. (She also, I heard much later, from Bobby, had a convincing right hook and a ribald line in swear words.) I watched them playing on the whitened surface of the front lawn. The sky above was purple with more snow, the trees absolutely still, as though playing musical statues with little crystalline peaks of snow balanced on every limb and twig. Above, behind and around me, the house was silent, as though deserted, although I knew that in Mrs Simpson's room Amelia was packing, (lamenting her lack of wardrobe for January in Texas) and John was listening to a concert on the wireless. I felt as though I, the house, the whole of our weird little depression in the Yorkshire moor, had been frozen in time, or perhaps were echoes of a myth, smoky reflections of an enchantment intruded upon through some trick of mystery by these children, to play in the charmed grounds in make-believe snow.

As unreal to me was the concept that John would go away and never come back. I would never see him again. As long as the weeks and months of waiting had been in the past, they had always been alleviated by the sure knowledge that - for whatever reason - he would return. But this time he would not, I knew it. I supposed it must be the way a condemned man must feel, convicted and destined to die. The days creep inexorably by, then the hours, then the minutes until he is brought to the scaffold. And nothing he can do or say will avert what will be; no last minute reprieve will come, no friend will ride to the rescue, no dexterous twist or act of derring-do will snatch him from his fate.

My heart fluttered like a frightened bird. But outwardly, I was calm. I was resigned. I walked back to John's room. I thought he was asleep, at first, propped up on the pillows as I had left him, but slumped slightly to one side. But he did not wake when I shook him, and, when I lifted his head, a mess of yellow pus streaked with blood spurted from beneath the dressing on his neck and splattered the pillow.

He did not regain consciousness. His breathing became more and more laboured, bubbling and stertorous, his stomach rising and falling to fill his lungs with air which could not penetrate the liquescent mess which his lungs had become. A secondary infection had attacked the lymph nodes in his neck. The next stage, the doctor advised, would have been an infection of the meninges, a brain fever producing rages and hallucinations, distressing for all concerned. Thankfully we were spared it; John passed away in the early hours of 29th December. I was with him. He was not alone. That, at least, is a comfort.

Amelia helped me wash John's body and lay him back innocuously in bed, so Awan could come and say goodbye. 'You don't seem disturbed by death,' I commented.

'I've seen plenty of it, and much more untidy than this,' she said, matter-of-factly.

'You knew John as well as I did,' I reasoned. 'Better, I sometimes think. Aren't you... sad?'

'Of course I am, you little idiot,' she said, and looked up at me. Her eyes were bulging with unshed tears. 'I'm heart-broken. John was a good man - better than you ever knew, and more talented than the world knows.'

She finished tidying the bed, gathering up the cloths and linen to take to the laundry.

Later, I held Awan on my knee until she had cried herself to sleep. 'It would have been better if you'd taken him,' I whispered to Amelia, who occupied the chair across the fire, and sat staring into the flames. Awan was used to John going away, and being away for long periods. She could have coped with that long stretching out of their relationship, its gradual numbing, its gentle separation and sinking into memory. This was too sudden, too cruel.

'I tried,' Amelia said, cryptically, before I could expand my meaning.

The following day the undertaker came and took John away. The snow turned to ugly slush and the children's snowman became a grey stump on the mushed-up lawn. I stripped the bed and washed the sheets, even though they had been clean on for the laying-out, and opened the windows. The air was sharp and cold. It scoured the room of death.

In the afternoon, Amelia's suitcases appeared in the hall. 'Will Kenneth drive me to the station?' she asked. She was dressed for travel, the unflattering brown suit made rather nice with a silk scarf and an amber brooch.

I goggled at her. 'What? You're leaving? *Now?*'

'Of course,' she said, checking her handbag.

'But...' I was flabbergasted. 'What about the funeral?'

'The plane won't wait. I have to get to the airport by first thing tomorrow. There won't be another opportunity. These passes aren't transferable.'

'What? You're going to America anyway? Without John? How crass!' I shouted, 'how crass and unfeeling you are! He saved your life! Doesn't that count for anything?'

'A great deal. But what's done is done. John won't miss me.'

'*I* might miss you,' I cried. 'Don't you think, just for this once, I might need the support of my family?'

'Oh,' she said. Clearly, she hadn't given it a second thought. 'You'll manage,' she said, airily, 'you always have.' She turned to a mirror and tweaked her hair.

'I haven't heard from Colin either,' I wailed.

'Oh I don't think Colin will come,' Amelia informed me, without turning round. 'He isn't well, you know.'

I looked at her aghast. 'Talk about kicking a person when they are down,' I spluttered out. 'I have just lost my husband. Now you tell me I might lose my home as well. If Colin dies, what will happen to Tall Chimneys?'

Amelia shrugged. 'You'll be alright. You can sell John's work. You have a stash of it, do you?'

'Some pieces,' I mumbled, thinking about the portraits in the gatehouse. Nothing on earth would persuade me to part with them. I had an idea there were some other canvasses in one of the north wing rooms.

'You should contact John's agent,' Amelia advised. 'I could see him if you like, while I'm passing through London. It will be tight, time-wise, but if it would help...' She was pulling on her gloves.

I mumbled something about being grateful.

'And you should *move*,' Amelia said, gathering her belongings. 'For God's sake, get out of this crumbling mausoleum, take the child and go somewhere and *live.*'

'What *on?*' I cried.

'On your wits, if you have any. That's what I've done, all these years.'

'I'm not you,' I said, dropping into the hall chair, 'I wish I was.'

'Isn't that ironic?' Amelia said, pausing by the door. 'I've spent the past nine years wishing *I* were *you.*' She pulled open the front door and stepped out. She left without saying goodbye.

'It will be a sorry send-off for poor John,' I said, to the empty house.

It was not, though. The village turned out to see John interred in the church graveyard. Rose and Kenneth and their boys walked behind Awan and me, and behind them their parents, my friends from the WI, Ann Widderington and the land girls and Patricia from The Plough. Colonel Beverage came with his wife. The rector's family was there, and the commanding officer from the airfield. Miss Eccles brought some of Awan's classmates. They made a solemn procession through the sodden cemetery and gathered round the grave, and Awan and I threw Christmas roses onto the casket.

Afterwards I invited them all back to the house for refreshments, and threw open the principal rooms to their slack-jawed amazement. None of the villagers had ever stepped inside Tall Chimneys; it must have seemed a curio to them, a museum of a place occupied by an odd woman and her child. Whether they imagined we lived in the rarefied splendour of bygone times or floated round in the imposing rooms wearing crinolines, I do not know. I do not suppose that in their wildest imaginings they conceived of the regime of soot-fall clearing and bucket-emptying which was the actuality of life at Tall Chimneys. None of them made enquiry. They stood in respectful huddles under the heavy crystal chandeliers, in awe of the faded grandeur, eyeing the gilt-framed mirrors and the cabinets of ancient artefacts while Rose and I served them tea, and I was suddenly overwhelmed by gratitude to them; they had taken me as I was into their community, and Awan too. White with grief as she was, she chatted to them quietly, and took their hands to show them the books in the library and the frowning portraits on the walls, and helped me circulate with plates of sandwiches, and I was immensely proud of her.

1944 - 1949

Colin did not return to Tall Chimneys, but Sylvester Ratton came quite frequently during the remainder of 1944 and throughout 1945, bringing parties of business people with him. Due to rationing, and the general shortages of everything, our hospitality would have been lack-lustre. My stock of preserved foods was woeful - I had paid no attention to the garden since Cameron had left - and the cellars at Tall Chimneys had long since been decimated. But Ratton's visits were always presaged by a delivery in an unmarked van of wines and spirits, and often of food-stuffs too. Where he got these riches, I do not know and did not ask, I simply made sure that some was hived off to benefit my friends in the village, many of whom were really suffering. I employed as many of them as I could to help out during Ratton's visits, and I hope the gentlemen rewarded them with handsome gratuities.

Colin continued making payments for the upkeep of the house from his own purse but these were less than formerly and more sporadic. However, I kept the house comfortable enough and the men Ratton brought seemed impressed by it. I surmised they were a new generation of tycoons, men who, like Ratton, had taken advantage of the war to make money. They were often loud-mouthed and full of their own self-importance, and spoke with accents which did not suggest a public school or university background. A few of them were veterans, sporting various limps and scars, but most had been in reserved occupations or had otherwise evaded active service. None, I thought, were frequent visitors to country houses even of the calibre of Tall Chimneys, which, in the scheme of things, was not grand. Their chief concern now seemed how to manage the change from supplying the government with armaments, uniforms and equipment to manufacturing goods which would find a market with the general public both in Britain and abroad; I supposed they could see the gravy train of government contracts was coming to an end. It seemed to me that Ratton, at least, need have no worries. He had clearly made a fortune.

Ratton never brought any women to the house, even his prim secretaries seemed to have been abandoned. But if I had feared John's death might lay me open to a renewed assault, I was wrong. For some reason Ratton treated me with a new kind of respect and ensured his guests did likewise. I did not find him lurking in the kitchen, he made no sneering remarks, he maintained a studied civility towards Awan. He offered his condolences on John's death and I could see in his eye no glint of cynicism or cruelty. I found his presence in the house more tolerable and did not dread his visits as I once had.

April and May of 1945 saw momentous events; 1,500,000 Germans were taken prisoner by the Western Allies; the horrors of Hitler's concentration camps were exposed by journalists travelling with the advancing forces. Mussolini was executed and four days later the Germans in Italy surrendered. The following day, Hitler took his own life and by 2nd of May Berlin had fallen. It took four more days for their utter capitulation across all theatres of war.

We celebrated wildly in the village, the women bringing food they had hoarded, the men breaking out home-brew, the children cavorting in the pouring rain. There was hopeful talk of reinstating the green and the cricket pitch, of getting back to normality. Three or four girls who had struck up relationships with Airmen spoke of travelling to America, the beginning of the wave of what would become known as GI brides. They made me think of Cameron, not as a substitute for John but as an alternative. Part of me hoped Captain Brook had been wrong, that Cameron would be discovered alive if not well in one of the many internment camps for POWs which were being discovered, but it was a vain hope.

Across the moor, on the periphery of the airbase, some-one had built a bonfire and lit it, as a beacon of hope and jubilation, I suppose. But it sent up more smoke than flame - the weather had been so wet - and I gazed across at the rising tower of smoke and thought of the towns and cities across Europe and the whole world, razed to ashes. It was a day of mixed emotions. While our faces ached from laughter, our eyes brimmed again and again with tears for the ones who would never return; sons and brothers, husbands and fathers. We shared our grief as we shared our joy, without words. What words were there? Peace. But at such a cost.

Life went on, but it was hard, and tragedy had not finished with us.

In 1946 Rose was killed in a road accident. She had been in town, attending a lunchtime concert at Bobby's school. The event had gone on longer than expected and the mayor had taken the opportunity to make a lengthy speech. Rose, fearing she would miss the bus back to the village, had stepped onto the road without looking properly. A heavy wagon hit her, killing her instantly.

The first we knew that something was wrong was when Mrs Greene arrived with the children from school. I was taking down the washing from the line when they arrived, in a neat and orderly crocodile, from the shadow of the drive. Kenneth emerged from his workshop, wiping his hands on a rag. That Rose should have left the children waiting without good cause was inconceivable to us all. We threw each other white-gilled looks of alarm and concern whilst placating the children with drinks and biscuits and reassuring them that all would be well.

Later, a police car arrived and took Kenneth away to identify Rose's body. I fed the children and got them bedded down for the night. Bobby, of course, had arrived home before that and without giving me time to break the terrible news to him, reported an accident near the bus station which had excited ghoulish interest on the school bus. He gave me chapter and verse on the police cordon, the ambulances, the wagon cab which had ploughed into a shop front and its load which had spilled across the High Street. I remained tight-lipped until Brian and Anthony and Awan were asleep but my face must have betrayed me because immediately after we had put their light out and crept from the room he asked me what the matter was.

'Oh Bobby,' I stammered out, tears spilling down my cheeks, 'oh Bobby, your dear, lovely mother... She's dead. I'm so sorry, Bobby. I'm so sorry.'

When Kenneth came home, he was a shell of a man; stooped and broken. He sat limply in a chair while I made him tea and something to eat, but both went untasted. Bobby sat by his side and held his hands - those large, clever, capable hands which were never still and never empty but always busy with repairs, coaxing machinery, scattering seed, slick with oil or black with soil - they lay unresisting and hollow. Bobby had cried and his eyes were red and bloodshot, but Kenneth's eyes were dry and dull, without glimmer or spark.

I tidied the room and set the table for breakfast, and mopped my streaming eyes again and again, and still the two of them sat like frozen statues by the dying fire and said nothing. I wondered whether some currents of converse were passing between them that I couldn't hear, just through the connection of their hands and I wished I could be part of it. I feared for Kenneth. He had always been my rock. Would this unhinge him? I did not think I could bear to lose him as well.

After a while Bobby got up and went to bed. Kenneth sat on for a while and I settled myself on one of the kitchen chairs to make vigil. I must have fallen asleep. When I woke up the room was dark, the fire was out and no moon shone through the open curtains. From behind Kenneth and Rose's bedroom door I could hear a noise; a dry bark of grief which extended itself into a low, suppressed wail. It drew fresh tears from me - his pain was as hard to bear as her death. I didn't want to intrude. I felt that to do so would irritate, not salve, the pain of such a private man. But neither could I endure to do nothing. I dropped to my knees and crawled across the wooden floor to his door, and leaned against it with all my weight, pressing my care towards him as though it could penetrate the timber. There was a gap beneath the door and I slipped my fingers through it. The chokes of his anguish went on, but I felt the brush of his fingertips against mine and I felt sure, then, that he would not disappear beyond my reach.

IT WAS INEVITABLE that Kenneth would move back to the village. He couldn't manage the three boys by himself and his mother had plenty of room for them in her house behind the shop. I suppose the accommodation they had occupied since their marriage held too many memories of Rose for him, too; the evidence of her care and industry were everywhere, from the curtains she had stitched and hung at the windows to the preserved fruits which were stacked on their kitchen shelves. On the other hand, Kenneth had been intimate with Tall Chimneys and all its environs since he had been a small boy - his life was as entwined with it as mine was, and I could only imagine the wrench it must have been for him to leave it behind.

He packed up their belongings and loaded them into the back of a van, quietly and calmly as he did everything, but with an additional stiffness and rigid solemnity which I interpreted as a sign that he was struggling to restrain his emotions.

'Will you be able to continue to help me?' I asked him. 'I know it's hard,' I qualified, 'every square inch of the house and garden holds such memories. But you belong here as much as I do.'

He replied with an agonised expression, his hazel eyes limpid with grief. They met mine for a brief moment before sliding away. 'A labour of love,' he mumbled, fussing with a tangle of string. And then, in a voice so low I could hardly hear him, 'But I never belonged here.'

'You *did*,' I said, putting my hand on his arm. 'You *do*.'

'No,' he shook his head. 'I shouldn't have wanted both. Mistake to stay. Should have made a new start. Rose felt it, resented it.'

I started. Had the house, then, been a cause of friction in their marriage? In truth I knew I had paid Kenneth and Rose little enough for their work, perhaps Rose had begrudged it? Providing them with a home had probably hardly recompensed them for the hours and effort they had selflessly put in to keeping the house in order. I had thought of us as friends, as equal sharers in the pleasures and the difficulties of living at Tall Chimneys. Had she felt differently? Had he?

'So,' I faltered, fighting tears, 'you'll make a clean break now, will you? A new start? I do understand, you know.'

He pressed his lips together for a moment. His hands, the while, continued to tease and tug at the knot of twine he held. 'The closer it is, the more impossible,' he said, cryptically.

I frowned. 'You mean,' I interpreted at last, 'the closer you are to Tall Chimneys, the more impossible it is to believe that she's gone?'

He threw me a wild, exasperated look and shook his head. 'You don't understand,' he almost cried.

'Of course I do,' I replied, 'with John's ghost in every room. If I don't understand, who can?'

He shook his head again. 'You don't understand at all,' he said again, and stalked away.

Without him and the family across the stable yard, I felt bereft indeed. I missed Rose's help in the house, her cheerful company and friendship. I missed the sense of safety and protection I had gained from Kenneth's quiet, reliable proximity. Awan was lost without the boys for company. She moped around the house and gardens finding amusement in none of her usual pursuits, and in the end I gave in to her requests to be allowed to cross the moor and visit the village. She had turned ten at the tail end of the previous year and would soon be contemplating the move to the secondary school in the local town. I felt she was ready for a wider sphere of adventure.

Throughout '46 and '47 Tall Chimneys continued to host the occasional weekend party for Ratton and his associates and I was glad of it in spite of the effort of having to prepare the house on my own, the poor quality 'gentlemen' he brought and the ribald, boisterous goings-on I sometimes heard from below stairs. The supplies he provided ameliorated very considerably the deprivations we would otherwise have suffered along with everyone else in the country. How he was able to source such luxuries I did not enquire too closely into, but could guess - there was a lucrative black market for rationed goods. For ordinary people like us, the meat ration was reduced to one shilling a week and the meat itself was poor quality, always supplemented by corned beef, which I grew to loathe. Coal supplies were adulterated with shale, flour was often half chalk, tea was almost impossible to get at all, likewise sugar, petrol, margarine and soap. America had ceased to supply Britain with meat and vegetables and the goods we got from Commonwealth countries were diverted to the starving in Europe, from where we heard stories of people reduced to eating grass, cats and dogs. I took to pressing a list of commodities I needed into Ratton's hand as he departed with his friends, and he rarely failed to supply me with what I needed. I was not selfish with the booty of Ratton's nefarious dealings - I saw to it they were shared around in the village. Heaven knows, we all needed a lift where we could get it. Day by day, life was a terrible struggle 'mending and making do' as the phrase of the day was. I had expected peace to bring a kind of inner rest to us all - we might be at rock bottom but could comfort ourselves that the worst was surely over - but in fact the struggles we had endured during the war years just went on and on. Depression was wide-spread - everything seemed broken and hopeless.

It took all my effort to resist the temptation to sink back into the slough of despair I had experienced after the death of Cameron Bentley, and take up my life once more. With a heavy heart, and missing Kenneth's benign company, I took up my gardening tools and went into the kitchen garden. If we could grow fruit we would have jam and cordial, I thought. Potatoes were in short supply, but if I could get seed-stock I could grow our own. Ann Widderington had hatched some chickens and gave me four of them, so I had eggs to eat and to barter until the dreadful winter of 1947 when two of them died of cold and one went mysteriously missing. That winter was terrible. The arctic conditions killed virtually everything I had planted, brassicas were frost-scorched and withered and it was almost impossible to get root crops out of the iron-hard ground. Our coal supplies were scant. Together Awan and I scoured the woods for fallen branches we could burn, but we were not alone; I often found evidence of others who had had the same idea, and even of trees felled and dragged away for firewood, but no amount of wind-fall wood seemed able to banish the chill which gripped the house. Awan and I hibernated in the kitchen and my bedroom, where she began to sleep, wash and dress. I unravelled old woollen jumpers to knit back into warm cardigans and socks for her. The house suffered with ingresses of damp, burst pipes and an infestation of mice who, like everyone else, wanted shelter from the cold. The rooms above stairs were uninhabitable without heat, but fuel could not be spared. Ice rimed the windows inside and out. Upholstery was spongy with damp, wallpapers peeled away and plaster crumbled. Above our heads I could hear the creak and groan of the towering chimney pots, and frequently their decorative brickwork shattered, sending cascades of shards rattling down the roof.

Ratton's visits stopped and with them the occasional supply of food and any little luxuries that sometimes came with them. I heard nothing from Colin and his payments abruptly ceased. My letters of enquiry went unanswered. I was often hungry, passing my share of our rations to Awan to make sure she had enough. I grew thin, and my hair began to fall out in clumps.

Spring of 1948 brought little relief, even though the cold abated. Utterly alone, I wrung my hands in despair at the garden. It was rank with weeds. The hedges were wild and tangled with inveigling briar and bramble. The terrace was slick with moss, the fountain only a bowl of decomposing leaves and greenish slime. Ivy ran riot up the east wing, choking the gutters and downspouts so when it rained water gushed down the walls, washing out mortar from between the stones, pooling on the window sills and soaking into the window frames. I longed to call Kenneth and ask him for help but something - pride? - prevented me. I heard he was very busy doing general repairs as well as in great demand for fixing motorcars. Awan told me Bobby was being trained in car mechanics at the weekends. I asked her if she'd like to help me around the house a little more, but she made a face and ran off. Personally, I didn't blame her. I had run out of energy or enthusiasm for keeping the house clean and aired. It stood all but ruined, its furniture shrouded, the shrouds themselves bloomed with dust. Cobwebs coated the curtains and laced the chandeliers. Water dripped into buckets, mould grew everywhere. The books in the library swelled with moisture, grew pulpy and then began to disintegrate on the shelves. Every surface - every table-top, shelf and mantel, and all the floors - developed a gritty, greasy coating. I could feel it under my fingers and beneath my shoes, like ash or old skin. I didn't know what it was or where it came from. It felt as though the house was decomposing, subject to some degenerative wasting disease born of age and neglect and death. I struggled to keep body and soul together, and sometimes failed. Evenings would find me shivering in front of a fire which threw out no heat, crying into my empty hands. Sometimes I felt as though the house was weighing down on me. I could feel the press of its stones on my shoulders and crushing my heart. From being a monument of family pride and a place of personal refuge, it felt like a burden, an impossible, unwieldy encumbrance. Sometimes I hated it with an impotent, helpless passion. At other times I feared it would suffocate me, crush me, kill me. I soldiered on, day to day, doing my best to endure for Awan's sake. But when she was at school, or playing in the village, or, at night, in bed asleep, I longed to lay my head on the old kitchen table and sleep, and never wake up. I wondered if, somewhere beyond the veil which divided life and death, John or Cameron waited for me. I pictured them bathed in light, warm and well-fed, and smiling to me with beckoning hands. The urge was hard to resist, and only the idea of Awan coming home to find me smashed on the cobbles of the yard, or swinging from a high beam in the stables stopped me from answering their call.

In April I had an unexpected visit from Sylvester Ratton. He arrived in one of his sleek motor cars and instead of pulling up on the gravel sweep, he drove round to the stable yard at the rear of the house. The first I knew of him was the sound of his footsteps down the passageway and a knock on the door which was surprisingly timid. I whirled round to find him standing on the threshold.

Time had not improved Ratton's looks and no amount of expensive tailoring could ameliorate for his essential ugliness. He looked more like the Michelin man than ever. His tiny eyes were sunk into folds of flesh so they seemed to peep out from behind curtains. These were similarly shielded by thick-lensed spectacles with heavy black frames. His nose was a ridiculous pudge of flesh now discoloured by purple thread-veins. His teeth, from a lifetime of smoking cigars, were yellow. Nevertheless there was something in his demeanour and expression which caught my attention.

'I wasn't expecting you,' I said, hastily untying my apron.

'I know,' he said, through lips which were strangely rigid.

I ran a hand through my straw-like hair - not that I cared what I looked like, for his benefit, but I knew I presented a woebegone sight. 'Have you come to stay?' The idea was appalling - the house was in such a terrible state.

'That depends,' he muttered. He indicated a kitchen chair. 'Do you mind if we sit down?'

I shrugged. 'Do you want some refreshment? Tea? It will be weak, I am afraid, I haven't much left.'

'I'll get you more,' he said, and I slid the kettle across the range.

'Thank you. We've seen nothing of you for months, and Colin does not answer my letters.'

Ratton left my remark in the air, but only said 'You ought to have an electric one,' nodding at the kettle and unbuttoning his jacket. He took a seat on one of the wooden kitchen chairs gingerly, as though afraid it might collapse under him.

'Not much good without the generator,' I said, lightly. Without petrol, and without Kenneth to coax it for me, I had not even tried to run it. 'We're still not on mains electricity, you know, not that it makes much difference. I hear there isn't any at peak periods. I suppose it affects your production.'

'Yes,' he said, heavily, and looked around the kitchen with a bleak, almost daunted expression. 'There is much to be done.'

I poured the tea into the pot and set it with two cups and a jug of milk on the kitchen table. Ratton motioned towards a chair at the head of the table. 'You sit down too, if you will.'

I took the chair cautiously. Ratton did not speak, but continued to look around the kitchen like a man who had never seen it before, eyeing the rows of saucepans, the stacks of crockery on the shelves, the windowsill where spindly herbs struggled from their pots, the worn flags on the floor, the peeling distemper on the walls, anything at all, in fact, but me.

Presently I coughed, and poured tea into his cup, adding two spoons - but miserly ones - of precious sugar because I knew that's how he took it. 'So,' I said, into the silence. 'To what do I owe this pleasure?'

Ratton gave a wan smile. 'I am afraid I am the bearer of bad news. Your brother Colin has passed away.'

I let the news sink in. It wasn't a surprise. I had known the last time I had seen Colin he was unwell, and Amelia had confirmed it. I hadn't liked Colin much. But he was my brother, the sibling with whom, for good or ill, I had had the most contact. He had given me a home when he could have sent me packing. 'How... how did he die?' I asked, in a small voice.

'A growth - cancer - in his gut. It has eaten him away from the inside out.'

'Poor Colin. The end, was it..?'

'Peaceful? No, sadly not. I believe he suffered a great deal.'

'You weren't with him, then?'

'Not at the last, no. But I had visited a month or so beforehand and we had concluded some business which, I know, set his mind at rest on one question.'

I nodded, not really taking in what he said. 'Good,' I said, thinking of Colin as a child in short trousers, teasing me by threatening to torture my dolls, his vicious accusation that my birth had hastened our mother's death, his refusal to side with me against Ratton. Despite these perfidies, I would not have wished a painful death on him. 'I suppose Amelia will come home for the funeral,' I mused. Would I attend it? I presumed it would be in London but if Amelia were to meet me there, I might brave the journey, I thought.

'Alas, the funeral has already taken place,' Ratton said, stiffly. He fixed his eyes on me. I got the impression he was not expecting this news to go down well. I did not disappoint him. 'What?' I shot up from the table, 'with no family present? Why was I not even informed? I'm his nearest relative, after all!'

Ratton put out a podgy hand and laid it on mine where it quivered on the scrubbed table. From where I was sitting, I could see a tiny scar in the curl of his ear, where I had bitten him all those years ago. The sight of them evaporated my ire and reminded me I was dealing with a dangerous man. 'There was a memorial service in the chapel at the House - very well attended, the great and the good turned out in force; Baldwin, Churchill, even Atlee[15] was there. But there was no funeral as such; Talbot gave his body to science. It's quite common now; people have had enough of graves.'

I sat back down and removed my hand from beneath Ratton's. The enormity of his news crashed upon me like a cold wave. I was alone - entirely alone. Amelia was far away in every sense, and could provide no help or support. The fleeting question as to whether Tall Chimneys would become mine was swamped by practicalities. There would be death duties, which had recently been increased to 75% of a person's estate. I had John's paintings, but I had already determined that any income from their sale would be saved for Awan's future; it is what John himself would have wanted. I thought of the dozens of other country houses being demolished by bereaved families who could not afford to pay their taxes, of houses which could not now be staffed, in any case, of estates which

---

[15] Clement Atlee was the leader of the Labour Government which had come to power in 1945.

represented a way of living and a stratum of society which did not exist any longer.

My dread must have shown on my face. Ratton moved his hand as though to cover mine once more, but thought better of it and instead pushed my cup towards me. 'Drink your tea,' he said, and, for the very first time, I saw a light of human sympathy in his eye. It was the first, the very first gesture of kindness he had ever shown me in our twenty year acquaintance.

'I'm done for,' I said, dully, 'aren't I?'

'Not necessarily,' Ratton said, and I saw a spark, a stiffening in his whole body. This, I realised, whatever was coming next, this is what he had really come to say.

Maddeningly, he lifted his cup and gulped his tea before speaking. When he had finished there were wettish reservoirs of milky tea at the corners of his child-like mouth. As he began to speak, they glistened, and in spite of myself I was as fascinated by their revolting, slightly greasy refusal to dry or be licked away, as by what my visitor had to say to me.

'You recall I mentioned a moment ago,' he began, 'that your brother and I concluded some business before his death which set his mind at ease?'

I nodded.

'Currently, you may know, death duties stand at 75%. Colin's estate was not enormous but was considerable. He had business interests with - certain other parties...'

'You mean, with *you*.'

Ratton pressed his lips together. The drops of tea squeezed into creases at either side of his mouth but did not dissipate. 'Amongst others, yes. But the contracts were prepared in such a way that we need not bother the probate office with these matters.'

'You mean you'll just appropriate for yourself Colin's entire share of the business. I expect it was his money that set you up in the first place' I put in indignantly.

'That's partly true, but your brother was amply repaid for his initial investment many years ago. His support has been taken into consideration in the transaction I want to explain to you, if you'll let me.'

'Go on,' I said, stiffly.

'This house constituted the lion's share of the estate,' Ratton said. 'The super-tax on large houses imposed in 1942 has had a serious impact on Colin's finances. The London house went years ago, you know, to cover the death duties for your father and oldest brother. Colin sold the Scottish shooting lodge to cover George's.'

'I didn't know we had a shooting lodge,' I murmured.

'Indeed? Colin knew this one too would have to be sold to pay his death duties or knocked down to avoid them. Selling to a stranger was unacceptable. Even if he could have found a buyer which, to be honest, was a very remote possibility, he would not have entertained it. He had *you* to think of, of course. It may surprise you but he felt responsible for you. The burden of your continuing security weighed heavily on him. So,' Ratton took a deep breath, 'he sold the house to me.'

I felt sick. 'To you?'

'Yes.' He licked his lips. 'I'm now the owner of this house.'

The tea on his mouth melded with his spittle to form globules of greyish matter. I forced my eyes away from them and searched his face carefully, for a glimmer of triumphalism or sickly gloating, but found none. He was sincere. My throat contracted. I was sure I was going to vomit. The nausea was accompanied by a violent chill which made me shudder.

'You're cold?' Ratton stood and reached for my cardigan which I had thrown over the arm of an easy chair. He draped it awkwardly round my shoulders. 'It is rather raw, today,' he observed.

I swallowed. 'I cannot conceive,' I said, shakily, 'how Colin thought that selling Tall Chimneys to you could in any way provide me with security.'

'Can you not?'

I shook my head. 'No.'

Ratton sighed. He had not resumed his seat and he took a turn or two around the room, an exercise which I suppose was designed to give me time to work things out.

'No?' he asked again.

'No,' I repeated, but I was lying. I saw exactly his plan. He had manoeuvred himself into a position where he could control my whole life; I would be beholden to him, his housekeeper, a prisoner, at his beck and call for the rest of my life.

He lowered himself back onto his seat and leaned across the table towards me. 'Let me explain, then,' he said, quietly. He laid his hands face down on the table. His fingers were inches from mine. As he spoke, without seeming to move at all, they slid infinitesimally nearer and nearer like a line of pink slugs. I watched them, fascinated. How could they seem to remain so absolutely still and yet slide, imperceptible iota by undetectable smidge, across the table towards me? 'When you first came here,' he said, his voice low and somewhat hesitant, 'I behaved very badly towards you.'

He waited, but I neither spoke, nor raised my eyes.

'I had no right to do so. You were a member of the family. I was only the estate manager. I lived here above my station. I took advantage of the family's absence and, when you came, I took advantage of you.' I heard him swallow, a dry gulp. 'I know I threw away any possibility that I might... that we might...' he trailed off. Indeed, that possibility was beyond articulating. 'But,' he went on, more firmly, 'I must tell you, Evelyn, that although I knew I could not expect it, yet, I did, in my heart, always hope for it. Always. And still.'

'Still?' my voice came out as a whisper. His fingertips were half an inch from mine. Both our hands, I realised, were trembling.

'Still. I bought this house from Colin in the hope that you might become what you should always have been - its mistress. That is your rightful place, and I want you to take it up, properly.'

'As *your...*' I could hardly speak the word, 'mistress,' I got out at last.

'No.' Ratton leaned forward. The action brought his fingertips to mine. They were clammy, the nails bitten to the quicks. 'As my wife.'

I recoiled, snatching my hands from the table and throwing myself against the backrest of the chair, but before I could speak Ratton went on, in a rush of reasoning which, I got the impression, he had rehearsed many times. 'There will be no more living in the servants' quarters,' he said, throwing his arm out to indicate the shabby kitchen and the tired rooms beyond where Awan and I slept. 'You will occupy the principal suites,' he said. 'The house will be fully staffed, and redecorated, of course, refurnished, repaired: mains electricity, water, sewage, telephone, a television, if you like. Every modern comfort will be supplied.' In his enthusiasm, he got up from his chair and walked quickly from one end of the room to another. 'We'll have parties. You're starved of respectable company, here. I know women who would fall over each other to be your friends.'

'Stop,' I croaked.

But he rushed on, pacing, pacing, up and down the room, 'Or we'll live quietly, just as you prefer. And, naturally, we will travel, once the embargo is lifted. Private yachts, exclusive hotels, a safari...'

'Stop,' I said again, more loudly.

He didn't seem to hear me. 'Surely, you'd like that?' he asked, 'it will be as though your life is beginning all over again. The child can go to school - Bedford, I hear, is very good - she will be denied nothing at all. And other children, should they come, they will lack nothing that money can buy.'

'Please, *please*,' I begged.

It was as though I was mute. There was no stopping him. 'Because there is money,' he gushed, 'lots of money, more than even I ever dreamed! But more importantly, there is me. I know I began badly, but Evelyn, I loved you from the first, and I love you still.' His perambulations had brought him back to the hearth - a favoured spot of his - where he turned to face me. 'I have watched over you, all these years. It was me who persuaded Colin to re-open the house. I suggested using it for private meetings and so of course it had to be repaired and maintained - that was for *your* benefit. My idea. You see? All these years I have been your guardian angel. Even when they brought in that crucifying super-tax, I used all my powers to persuade him to find it, somehow. I even paid it, on more than one occasion!' In spite of his pacing and his animated speech, he was pale, his eyes, within their thickly-fleshed sockets and behind their inscrutable lenses, were dark flints of passion. He breathed quickly.

'*Please*,' I said again, and held up my hand to stop him from going on.

'No,' he said. 'I've needed to say this for so long, just hear me out.' He took a deep breath. 'Please, Miss Talbot, do me the honour of becoming my wife. There, I've said it. Whatever has happened in the past I forgive. I don't care about your history or your reputation and you need have no fear of it; no one will dare impugn the wife of Sylvester Ratton and no word of reproach will ever pass my lips. Don't you think fate has brought us to this? I do. All these years, we've led parallel lives and now, at last, our paths have joined.' His tirade came to a halt at last. 'There,' he said, with a satisfied smile. 'I've finally said it. Now you.'

But now I had the opportunity I was lost for words. My mouth flapped uselessly. Ratton misinterpreted my silence. 'You're overwhelmed,' he said. 'Let me pour you more tea.' He reached for the pot.

'No,' I said, quickly.

He held his hand, 'Oh, very well, if you're sure. Something stronger?'

'No,' I repeated.

So many thoughts were going through my head I couldn't order them. Colin was dead. Would there really be nothing left of the Talbot family wealth once his affairs had been settled? Ratton implied as much, but could I trust him? Tall Chimneys was Ratton's. The idea of it felt the same as if the whole house had been swept away in a tornado or burned to ashes. His ownership, his influence, would defile it. The prospect of having no home was terrifying; what, I wondered, assuming I could get work, could I afford to provide long-term for Awan and myself? I did not know. I was woefully out of touch with such things. Could I possibly accept his offer? For the sake of Awan, for our future security, could I endure his sloppy kisses and sweaty pawings? Everything in me revolted against it. But how could I live otherwise? Panic rose in my chest. Would Ratton, I wondered, wildly, consent to a celibate marriage? Perhaps, I reasoned to myself, if he would agree to that, I could endure his society, preside at his seedy business dinners, manoeuvre things so that we spent as little time in each other's company as possible, as I had done, I recalled, at the beginning. He would be away a great deal, I told myself, on business. He must have another home. He could live there and I could remain here - he might only visit at weekends, or less often... On the other hand, the world of the respectable married woman - a wealthy married woman - brought me into touching distance of the shimmering, mirror-image of myself that I had sometimes day-dreamed. As revolting as things might be behind closed doors, publicly I could hold my head up high. Ratton might even agree to my studying, taking up a career. I could educate myself, socially and intellectually, so that I would hold my own in any society, host fund-raising lunches, invite the foremost women thinkers to Tall Chimneys...

'I can see you're giving a great deal of consideration to my proposal,' Ratton broke into my thoughts.

I found a handkerchief in my pocket and brought it to my mouth. 'Indeed,' I said. 'I am so taken by surprise. And the news about Colin is so sudden and so sad. And I am trying to envisage what life as Mrs Ratton would be like.'

'Oh,' he smiled, 'as to that, it will be splendid. I have a house in Leeds but it isn't a place for a lady. We'd need somewhere new - Roundhay, perhaps. In London I tend to stay at my club but we can find an apartment. Having said that, I expect my dealings with the government to decline, so I won't need to be in London very often.'

'We wouldn't live here, then?'

He shook his head. 'I don't see myself as the country squire.'

The bubble of my day-dream burst. 'You used to,' I replied, with an acid note in my voice. 'I assumed...'

'Things have changed. I have changed. I'm now a respectable and successful businessman. I have my various enterprises to consider. I couldn't live so far from them. It would be out of the question.'

I felt the mass of rooms above me, the press of furniture and oaken floors. They teetered on my shoulders and clamoured in my mind, they clawed at my heart for purchase. 'Wouldn't it be better,' I asked, with a smile I hoped wouldn't be interpreted as patronising, 'that things continue as they are? I will manage the house for you, as I did for Colin, and provide for your guests. You will be free to pursue your business interests. I mean,' I gave a faltering laugh, 'I presume, when Colin sold you the house, with, as you say, my welfare in his mind, he did not do it on the *condition* that we should marry?'

Ratton blanched. 'He knew it was my heart's desire. He did not expect you would do anything so foolish as to refuse.'

'But if I did? Surely, in your new, softer self, you could see your way...' I was wheedling, I knew it.

So did Ratton. Perhaps he feared he might succumb to my obsequious blandishments. 'I will not allow you to take such a reckless step without due consideration,' he said, sharply. 'You should consult your friends - if you have any. They will advise you to do what is best.'

I stood up. My knees were shaking so violently I did not dare take a step away from the table. 'Thank you,' I said. 'I will do as you suggest.'

'And we will talk again.'

Ratton walked stiffly to where he had left his hat, and took it up. He turned it in his hands a time or two, smoothing the nap with his fingers. Then he said, 'I will be a softer self, Evelyn. Kind and gentle and generous. I will be a different man from the one you think you know.' He gave me a look so piteous with hope it almost broke me.

'We will talk again,' I said.

He nodded and turned away.

As poor and dependent as I had been all my life, I had never felt as insecure as I did as I listened to Ratton's car drive away. His timing, I thought, was absolutely impeccable. He had waited until I was at my lowest possible ebb, and pounced.

Ratton himself had suggested I consult my friends (if I had any) and I went first to Patricia Coombes. Her husband had returned from the war minus an arm and had all-but retired, taking up a position on a stool close to the end of the bar adjacent to the cash register, where he jealously watched every transaction whilst sipping from a bottomless glass of beer. Patricia did all the work, including hefting barrels, replenishing stocks of bottles and cleaning the urinals. Like many families, she had also taken in extended family members who had returned from war to find their homes bombed to rubble; her brother and sister in law had brought their young family to live above the pub. Neither did a stroke of work that I could see. Several houses in the village were in a similar situation, housing two or even three generations and while we had been promised (again) 'homes fit for heroes', none had yet been built in our locality. The poor woman was run off her feet, but she made time for me, and listened patiently as I poured out my tale of woe.

'Well you can't marry the man,' she opined, when I had done, 'but I don't see that you can stay in that crumbling pile of masonry much longer, either. Those chimneys'll fall round your ears before another winter is out.'

'There isn't a third option, though, is there,' I said, wanly. 'What can a woman with a child do to support herself?'

'Plenty, if she's the mind and the skills,' Patricia sniffed.

'I have no skills,' I replied, 'I'm fit for nothing.'

'I wouldn't say that,' my friend smiled. 'I think you need some legal advice. Why don't you visit Colonel Beverage? He'll be able to recommend someone.'

'You won't tell anyone about this, will you?' I asked, gloomily, as I got up to leave.

'Of course not,' she said.

The Colonel was a man with whom I had had little to do since he had come to the village and moved into the abandoned Rectory. Whether this was due to my ambivalent status at Tall Chimneys or my disreputable situation as an unmarried mother, or whether it was more to do with Colonel Beverage's impatience with all things female, or the character of his shrinking wallflower of a wife I do not know. Where there was no warmth of friendship, however, there was certainly no animosity either, and I recalled with comfort their attendance at John's funeral, so I decided to consult him as a man worldly-wise who would be able to advise me.

It was a long time since I had set foot in the Rectory but it was largely unchanged - still draughty and dark. But I was shown into a small study lined with intriguing bookcases where a bright fire burned. The Colonel's wisp of a wife served anaemic tea and then retired to a hard chair in a chilly corner and took up some embroidery. Briefly, I explained about Colin's death, my resulting predicament and outlined my request.

'Poor woman,' he said, to the room in general (he could have been referring to either of the women in the room). 'I know Ironmonger of Shackle, Dogwood and Ironmonger. Thoroughly sound man. I'll write you a letter of introduction. Will, probate, terms of contract etcetera - he'll be able to steer you, and an accountant will help you with the pounds and pence, Mrs... er, that is, Miss...'

'Evelyn,' a disembodied voice issued, rather than spoke, from the chilly corner. It was so quiet and self-effacing it might have been a whisper of a draught from the window, a shift of coal in the grate.

'Indeed, Evelyn. I'll have it with you by morning.'

The Colonel was as good as his word and the following morning I found a letter commending me to the firm of solicitors. I enclosed it in my own missive asking them to examine Colin's Will and advise me regarding Colin's affairs. What, if anything, remained of the Talbot estate? Could they look into the sale of contract which had transferred Tall Chimneys to the ownership of Mr Ratton; were there any clauses which catered for the needs of sitting tenants, incumbent family members or long-standing family retainers at the house?

With a sense more acute than it had ever been that I had, now, to look after myself, I wrote also to Giles Percy about John's affairs and asked him to pass any information to Shackle & Co. I had searched John's papers without finding a Will. I assumed, as Monique's surviving spouse, he would inherit her estate although I doubted there would be anything left of it once the various governmental and diplomatic channels now operating had dealt with it. I didn't know where I would stand legally in regard to anything John might have left but I assumed my claim would be shaky at best, unless there was a Will. I wrote also to John's agent, whose details I discovered on papers in the gatehouse. I had some early canvasses of John's, the work he had done on return from Dunkirk and afterwards and several sketch books.

The wheels of commerce turn quickly and I heard back from John's agent quite soon; unfortunately the market for art was in the doldrums, but I should preserve the paintings I had until such time as things looked up.

Giles also wrote, condoling on Colin's death and telling me all members of Military Intelligence were obliged to lodge a Last Will and Testament with their commanding officer. He promised to request sight of John's and forward it as I requested. He asked after Awan and enclosed a five pound note - untold wealth, in those days.

The wheels of law turn more slowly indeed and, apart from receiving an acknowledgement of my enquiry I heard nothing from Shackle, Dogwood and Ironmonger for some time. In the meantime Ratton called several times, urging his offer and further outlining the benefits to myself and Awan should I accept. He brought tea, as he had promised, and other necessaries. I prevaricated as to my response, pending a reply from the solicitor but I felt utterly at his mercy. I had no other options, and he knew it. I searched minutely for some sign of an underlying scheme, some dastardly machination by which he would reduce me to ruin and then stand by and crow with triumph. I saw none. He was restrained and courteous, seemed genuinely concerned for our welfare and discussed, in vague terms, projects which would repair and improve the house.

A warm, dry May was followed by a wet June - perfect for fruit and vegetable growing, but I had made a mess of the pruning the previous autumn and our crops were not promising. The soil in the greenhouse became infected with some kind of fungus which blighted the tomato plants. All the raised beds were infested with couch grass. Inside the house, too many unused rooms and a lack of proper heating meant it was a work of diminishing returns, and the havoc wreaked by the preceding winter was almost impossible to make good. One of the rooms had been so badly damaged by ingress of water that the floorboards were spongy and I had to lock it up for fear someone might fall through. Everywhere wall paper peeled, curtains mouldered and tiles bloomed greenish slime.

I struggled on.

IN SEPTEMBER I received a visit from Mr Ironmonger. He wrote a note to inform me he was coming, and arrived, on foot, down the tunnel of driveway, wearing tweed walking attire, thick boots and bearing a rucksack. He was thin, immensely tall, but rather stooping in posture, with narrow shoulders and arms so long that his cuffs barely reached his bony wrists. His trouser-bottoms, similarly, ended well short of his boot-tops, revealing thick, army-issue socks and, when he sat down, an expanse of thin, hairless leg. He had fine, greyish hair, which, due to the breeze or the exertions of his walk, was rather untidy and revealed rather more than he might have liked of bare scalp across the crown. His eyes were very blue under beetling grey eyebrows. They were kind, and his smile appealing in a lop-sided way. He was probably in his mid to late forties, I thought, and a bachelor (no self-respecting Mrs Ironmonger would have allowed him out without lengthening his cuffs and hems). He looked nothing whatsoever like a man of the law. I took to him immediately.

I offered him 'formal' tea, in one of the drawing rooms of the house, or 'informal' tea, in the kitchen with me.

'Oh, informal, every time,' he said, looking woefully at his dirty boots and burr-infested jacket. 'I'm not fit to be seen above stairs!'

'Neither am I,' I laughed, indicating my old trousers and gardening cardigan.

'I'm on a walking holiday,' he explained, unlacing his boots and resting them on the hearth (a long toe poked through a hole in his sock - more evidence that he was unmarried), 'so decided to combine business with pleasure and call in.'

'I'm glad of it,' I admitted, placing scones on a plate. 'I've been anxious for advice.' I did not know how much longer I would be able to hold off Sylvester Ratton.

He rummaged in his rucksack and brought forth a file of documents. He placed them on the table and put a reassuring hand on them. 'All in good time,' he said, eyeing the scones, 'pleasure first, I think.'

'Taste the scones, before you pass judgement,' I said, ruefully, pushing the plate over to him. 'Goodness knows what's in the flour, and I only passed the sugar packet across the mixing bowl.'

'You have jam though,' he remarked, helping himself to it.

'I have something red in a jar - once again, I had to be sparing with the sugar, but the fruit was naturally sweet, so that's something.'

He began to regale me with stories of his holiday - the difficulties he had had, to begin with, even finding accommodation - everywhere seemed to be booked up. The less than comfortable rooms he had endured, the unreliable bus timetables, the local character who had told him his eighty four year life story in a pub one night, in return for three halves of mild. I found him interesting and entertaining and almost forgot to go and meet Awan from school at half past three.

'Have a look around the place,' I told him as I shrugged on a coat, 'feel free. Despite what you'll hear in the village, there are no ghosts. I hope you'll stay and have dinner, and spend the night. I have plenty of spare rooms! Unless you feel your reputation would be compromised? I can enquire if Mrs Coombes at the Plough and Harrow has a room if you like.'

'What about your reputation?' Mr Ironmonger raised a quizzical eyebrow.

'Oh!' I waved, airily, 'shot to pieces already. Quite beyond the pale!'

Mr Ironmonger clearly took me at my word and gave himself a very thorough tour of the whole house. It took Awan and me a while to find him, but bedroom doors were left open which were usually closed, curtains pushed to one side, a cloud of dust hovered at knee level where he had disturbed it in passing. We found him in a far attic, straining to look through a high window, presumably at the roof which, no doubt, was in a parlous state of disrepair.

'Here you are!' I cried, looking around me. 'This room used to be for the maids. Poor things, I expect the wind scared them rigid. Nobody has set foot in here in years.'

'That chimney is unsafe,' he declared immediately, indicating one visible from the window, 'and the roof needs work.'

I peered where he indicated. He was right; the mortar round the decorative brick work had crumbled away and a buddleia had rooted itself in a gap beneath the pot. 'It *all* needs work,' I said, with a note of exasperation, 'but unless I sell my soul to the devil, what can I do? Let me introduce you to Awan.'

The pair shook hands and we all retraced Mr Ironmonger's steps. I noted with some satisfaction that, as he went, he reclosed curtains and pulled doors firmly to after him.

'You have some lovely pieces of furniture here,' he commented. 'Those Chinese lacquered cabinets, for example, the Hepplewhite chairs, the Chippendale desk in the library. And some of the curios in the cabinets - they're probably very valuable, you know, to the right collector.'

'And now belong to someone else,' I remarked, dryly. 'In any case, they probably have rot or worm.'

Mr Ironmonger made a humphing noise, but did not reply.

The sausages I cooked for supper tasted of nothing at all but Mr Ironmonger ate them with apparent relish with lots of fried onions and some stringy greens from the vegetable garden. I opened a bottle of beer to wash the food down with. Afterwards I produced a semolina pudding, one of Awan's favourites, sweetened with honey from a bee-keeping friend in the village. Awan gobbled her portion down in an instant. Mr Ironmonger pretended to be full and took only a very little. Awan gladly finished the rest of his share. His kindness endeared him the more.

When Awan had gone to bed, I cleared the table. Mr Ironmonger pulled his file of papers towards him and put on a pair of spectacles. As the evening progressed he repeatedly put them on and took them off again depending on whether he was referring to his notes or speaking to me, or alternatively, looked at me over the tops of their tortoise-shell frames. He made quite a comedy business out of it, the only light note in an evening of doleful tidings.

'To business,' he said. 'Firstly, let's deal with the estate of Mr John Cressing. Your friend Mr Percy has been most helpful. It seems likely Mr Cressing was the sole beneficiary of his late wife's Will, but, things being as they are, I have had no joy in gaining any information whatsoever on that front. We can assume that any chattels were seized either by unprincipled looters or by the Vichy government which, you may well argue, are one and the same. Monies likewise will be held permanently in Escrow for the convenience of Mme Cressing's legal representatives, banker or any other highwayman who gets his hands on them. There may come a time when we can unravel this mess, but, sadly, that time has not come. However,' Mr Ironmonger took a sip of his beer, and smacked his lips, 'I am happy to say Mr Cressing's Will is far more transparent. Miss Awan is named as his sole beneficiary. Therefore anything you have of his becomes hers. This includes (specifically, I may say) any and all unsold works of art, sketches, part-works, studies etc. She has both actual and intellectual copyright of these, which means they may not be reproduced without her permission and a royalty would, naturally, be due. As her parent and legal guardian one would assume you would hold these things in trust until she comes of age.'

'His agent says there is no market at the moment,' I replied with a sigh.

'Indeed,' Mr Ironmonger sighed. 'And unfortunately what market exists is being flooded with works purloined illegally in the aftermath of war. Greek sculpture, Italian frescoes, works of the French and Dutch masters are all to be had on the black market.'

'What kind of world did the Allies fight for?' I wondered.

'Now, to your late brother's affairs. I'm afraid it has been very difficult to extract information from the Executor.'

'Let me guess,' I said, rolling my eyes, 'Sylvester Ratton?'

'None other. I had to contact a friend in the probate office and make all kinds of other 'casual' enquiries to find out much at all.'

The long and the short of Mr Ironmonger's findings was that, essentially, Ratton had correctly reported things. There was virtually nothing left of the Talbot money. What there was would go, rightly, to Amelia as the oldest surviving child. 'We can be glad the estate was not entailed[16],' Mr Ironmonger declared, 'or some forgotten cousin would have been the beneficiary. As it is, I have corresponded with your sister.' Mr Ironmonger extracted a hand-written letter from amongst his papers, 'Have you?'

'Other than to let me know she arrived safely in Texas, I have heard nothing,' I said. 'To be truthful, we didn't really get on.'

'Then I have happy news to impart,' Mr Ironmonger said, 'she is to marry, a Texan rancher by the name of...' he scanned the lines of writing, 'Charles Wyman Jr. She tells me they intend prospecting for oil on their property and will use the funds for that.'

'Good for her,' I said, through clenched teeth. 'I will lose my home while she drills holes in the ground.'

Mr Ironmonger removed his spectacles and made a steeple of his long-fingered hands. 'This house,' he said, in a tone of someone delivering necessary but unwelcome news, 'would be an albatross around your neck, my dear. I know it's your home, the only one you've known and you have had all the trouble of managing and maintaining it. But you have not borne the cost. And as the years go by, that cost is going to become more and more prohibitive. These old places are beautiful, some of them are historically significant, but in these modern days they are untenable as mere houses. Across the country they are being turned into schools, hospitals, prisons, or being demolished. Whatever Mr Ratton decides to do with the place, he has, in a way, saved you from the burden of it.'

---

[16] A system which means that estates pass only through the males of a family.

I stood up and walked to the range to feed in a few precious shovels of coal and move the kettle onto the hob. I wanted to cry. I knew he was telling me the truth - but the truth was painful to hear.

Mr Ironmonger busied himself re-ordering his papers and slipping them back into his file while I marshalled my thoughts. When he had finished he removed his glasses and waited patiently for my mind to settle. Whatever dream I had entertained - of finding myself a rich woman, of being able to buy back Tall Chimneys and renovate it myself, of securing a home for myself and Awan which would always be ours and which no one could take from us - was over. These things only happened in novels and this was real life.

'I'm done for, aren't I?' I stated at last. 'I shall have to marry Sylvester Ratton.'

Mr Ironmonger beetled his eyebrows. 'There's the National Assistance Act,[17] have you heard of that? It's new... '

'But where will I live?' I almost wailed. 'Would I get a council property? They're going to build some in the village, I'm told, but there are whole families on the waiting list. What chance would I stand? How much does it cost to rent one anyway? What about a room in a lodgings house? Could I afford that? I know they're awful, and I wouldn't mind if it was just for myself, but with a child... I've never worked, Mr Ironmonger. I mean, I have worked, like a Navvy, but I haven't a profession. I can't type or teach. Perhaps someone would employ me as a maid - it's all I'm good for.' I rummaged for my handkerchief to stem the tears. 'Even that, I suppose, would be impossible,' I sniffed. 'There must be a thousand former parlour maids looking for work.'

---

[17] The National Assistance Act 1948 came about as a result of the Beveridge Report 1942. It replaced the Poor Laws and covered those cases like Evelyn's (single mothers) who had not paid National Insurance and were not entitled to assistance from other Welfare Acts. She might have expected to receive something like 40 shillings (£2) per week.
Source: https://en.wikipedia.org/wiki/National_Assistance_Act_1948.

Mr Ironmonger closed his file of papers and placed his hands on the table, his work completed.

Later, I showed him to his room and, for the first time ever, felt ashamed of Tall Chimneys. I had chosen one of the 'good' rooms off the East landing, but saw it through his eyes; a threadbare carpet, the wall-paper darkened by mould in a draughty corner, a shutter so swollen with moisture I could not get it to close properly, a drip of greenish ooze from one of the taps. One of the lamp shades was scorched from where a bulb had blown - I hadn't noticed it before, and when I turned the bed down the sheets felt damp. I would not want to sleep in here, I thought to myself, and when I looked at Mr Ironmonger's face I caught a baleful expression, although he was quick to mask it with an easy smile.

'It isn't very comfortable,' I burst out. 'You should have gone to The Plough.'

'Not at all,' he said, placing his bag on the faded chair cushion.

'There won't be any hot water,' I said. 'I'll bring you shaving water in the morning. What time?'

'Eight? Will that be convenient?'

I nodded. 'Certainly.' I fiddled with the counterpane. It was so long since I'd had company that, although it was late, I didn't want to say goodnight. 'You know,' I said, 'the thought of not living at Tall Chimneys feels like looking in the mirror and not seeing my own face there: utterly, utterly *wrong*. But, suddenly - I don't know if I can explain it - I feel as though if I could see myself, I would look like a stranger.'

He nodded. He had such an innately empathetic air about him; I instinctively sensed he knew what I meant.

'Before I turned to the law,' he said, 'I dabbled in Architecture. In fact I did two years of Architecture at King's before I switched horses. And I've visited a number of houses like this - so many of our clients are people in your situation - impoverished descendants of once-landed families - I mean no offence, you know.' He looked at me from beneath his bristly eyebrows.

'I take none,' I murmured.

'Even in a brief tour of this house,' he went on, 'I see issues. The stonework is crumbling. The masonry of the famous 'tall chimneys' is particularly bad - if you weren't so protected by this odd little hollow, I'm certain at least one of them would have crashed down by now.'

'There was a storm,' I told him, 'in the winter of 1942.' I remembered John trying to get us to the safety of the ice house that wild and stormy night. I had stood in the yard, I recalled, dazed by my grief and depression. 'John said the chimneys were swaying.'

'I'm not surprised. There's more, I'm afraid. You have mice, and your wiring is very old. A fire could break out in the attics and you might not know about it for hours - these things smoulder, you know. I notice you have no fire-escape. Anyone in the upper rooms would be trapped.'

I clapped my hand to my mouth. The thought of fire was too terrible to contemplate.

'I know, I know,' Mr Ironmonger said. 'I'm sorry, but I feel I have to say these things. You have damp. You probably have dry rot - all those rooms which never get ventilated. It's fungal, you know. And wet rot. Imagine the floorboards giving way...'

'Oh please,' I cried.

'I know it's awful. You must feel as though I'm telling you your best friend has some incurable disease, but what I'm trying to tell you is that, now, none of these things is your responsibility. Even if Mr Ratton manages to win your heart, he's looking at years and years of works and thousands, hundreds of thousands of pounds. In the meantime the house will scarcely be habitable.'

I hardly slept that night. Of course I had seen the dulling of wallpapers, the yellowing of paint, curtains faded into stripes by the sun, carpets losing the thickness of their pile and the richness of their pattern. Worse, I knew about the leaks, the spongy floor boards, the flaking plaster, the ruined artefacts and soggy books. Now I knew the very fabric of the building was crumbling around my ears. I did indeed feel as though a dear friend was dying. As I had said goodbye to Cameron and to John, to Rose and to Kenneth, I would have to say farewell to Tall Chimneys.

In the morning Mr Ironmonger ate bread and drank tea but refused a precious egg. He claimed to have slept well, but dark shadows under his eyes made a liar of him.

We made desultory conversation about the itinerary for the remainder of his holiday. Meanwhile he packed his bag and laced his boots. I felt jaded from lack of sleep. I didn't want him to leave but knew he must. At last he was ready, and held out his hand to shake mine. Like him, it was long and bony, but warm. I took it and held on to it for longer than was necessary. 'You'll be alright, you know,' he said, seeing the doubts and fears which must have shone in my eyes. He placed his other hand over mine and squeezed. 'I'll be in touch very soon,' he said, but we both knew he could offer no hope, no solution to my parlous situation; none whatsoever.

I watched the loping figure of Mr Ironmonger stride off up the drive and then went back inside.

The telephone was ringing. I picked up the receiver. It was Sylvester Ratton. Over the telephone his voice was gasping, his breathing laboured, as though he had climbed several flights of stairs to make the call. He enquired, briefly, after my health before arriving at the purpose of his call.

'I'm going abroad,' he announced. 'I have business prospects in Hong Kong and Singapore. I've been invited to join a Ministry of Trade delegation.'

'What an honour,' I murmured.

'Indeed. I rather hoped you'd have an answer for me, my dear, before I went.' Ratton's coquettishness made my stomach turn. It was glutinous and unpleasant. 'I could buy wedding clothes, jewels and so on, while I'm away,' he went on, smoothly, as though those things could possibly butter any parsnips with me. 'And I could contract a builder to begin repairs on the house. If you agree. You understand, Evelyn?' For the first time since his proposal I glimpsed beneath the veneer of his false charm. I could see his selfish intent, like streaks on glass which had always been there but were only shown up by a certain angle of the sun.

'Perfectly,' I said, coldly. 'If I agree to marry you, you will repair Tall Chimneys. But I have to tell you, even if I don't agree, the house is going to need considerable work.' I listed the issues Mr Ironmonger had pointed out; crumbling masonry, wet rot, dry rot, faulty wiring, 'and sooner, rather than later.'

'Have you had someone there?' Ratton's jealousy rose up, razor-sharp.

'Yes, actually, a friend with architectural experience.'

Ratton struggled to resume his composure. 'I didn't know you were in the habit of entertaining personal friends. Who are they? Anyone I know? In any case, you're not telling me anything I don't know already. Anyone with eyes can see the house is in a terrible state.'

'You'll want to protect your investment,' I suggested.

'My investment can go to hell,' he barked. '*You're* what I want, Evelyn. You. You're what I bargained for, when I paid Colin for the house. I don't know how I can make my feelings plainer.'

'An attitude like that is hardly likely to thaw *my* feelings towards *you*,' I retorted. 'There are some women you can "buy"; I'm sure you're well acquainted with many of them. But I'm not one of them.' I put the receiver down sharply and stalked from the Butler's pantry with a sense of enormous satisfaction.

Three days later I received a letter from Sylvester Ratton. It was conciliatory, full of mollifying sentiment and regret.

I can see I must be patient (the letter concluded). *I have waited this long for you and must resign myself to wait a little longer until you see that I am a changed person. To this end I propose to leave you in peace for six months. My trip abroad will be of at least that duration as we will travel by sea and make stops at commercial hubs en route. In the meantime I hope that you will come to truly appreciate the life which could be yours as Mrs Ratton.*

It did not occur to me until some weeks later what Ratton really meant; he sent no money and there were no further deliveries of groceries. He had left me to stew and, if necessary, to starve, in the hope it would concentrate my mind.

In a way, it did. I began to read the situations vacant section of the local paper, and applied for jobs: as a housekeeper, a matron at a school, a companion to an elderly lady and a governess to two boys. I described myself as a widow with a young daughter and stated accommodation would be required for both of us. Of course I could provide no references and any account of my experience to date was sketchy, to say the least of it. I was summarily rejected for all the posts. The wording of the letters wounded me, words like 'unsuitable', 'unqualified' and 'unthinkable' but, in truth, I had had little expectation of even being invited to interview, and the prospect of actually travelling, of arranging accommodation, of presenting myself to a stranger, had been appalling to me. Perhaps my reluctance had shown itself in my letters. My heart was not in them.

I took the bus into town and went to the bank, but when I passed my cheque across the counter the clerk scrutinised it, excused himself and went into the manager's office. After a while I too was summoned thither. The office was large, shabby, with a cracked leather chair behind a scratched but ancient desk. The bank manager was similarly scarred, from the first war, I imagined - he was too old to have served in the recent one. One side of his face and head was pink and ridged and hairless and did not move when he spoke or frowned or smiled - not that he smiled much, during our conversation. The eye stared ahead of him at a fixed point above my head, and did not blink. The other side of his face was grey and haggard, with a tired grey eye deeply set into a saggy socket beneath a woolly brow. His left arm seemed weak and shrivelled; for the duration of our interview it rested on the desk like a forgotten umbrella. Before him, on the blotter, a huge ledger was open, laced with neatly calligraphed notations and columns of figures. The number at the bottom of the column was very small, and underlined, twice.

'This is your account,' the manager said. 'There have been no deposits for some time.'

'My brother has passed away,' I told him.

'Withdrawals have continued sporadically,' he went on.

'I try to call on the account as rarely as possible,' I said. 'I live hand to mouth. I have a daughter to feed.'

'Indeed,' he said. 'Times are very hard.'

'Can you cash my cheque today?' I asked, more sharply than I had intended.

He pulled the cheque towards him and looked at it. 'Today, yes,' he said, 'but unless there are deposits in the future, I fear the account will be closed.'

From the bank I passed down the street and across the market place to visit the Council offices to enquire about accommodation. The woman there led me to a desk in a large room where several of her colleagues were interviewing other applicants. She was corpulent, her chair creaked as she sat down on it and her thighs, in their cheap dress, spilled over the edges of it. Her fat fingers were crammed with tacky, paste rings. She licked her thumb and finger with a wet tongue and lifted a form from a stack at the edge of the desk. 'Name?' she carped, 'marital status?'

'Widow,' I told her. She glanced at my hands. I wore no wedding ring. She made a cynical face and I avoided her eyes.

'Current address?'

I told her.

'Sounds grand,' she remarked. 'What do you do there? Housekeeper?'

'Sort of,' I stammered. 'The house belongs... belonged to my family. It's been sold now, so I have to move out.'

'I see,' she scribbled something on the form before moving on to the next question. 'Occupation?'

'I… I have none,' I croaked.

She wrote something in the box. I could read it, upside down. It said 'lady.'

'I'm not a 'lady'!' I remonstrated with her. 'I work. I cook, I clean, I grow vegetables.' I held out my hands as evidence. They were calloused, the nails rimmed with dirt.

'Not a lady!' the fat woman declared, catching the eye of a colleague on the next desk.

'You know what I mean,' I said, sulkily.

'Means?' she ploughed on. 'Savings, property?'

Her colleague, in the next desk, added, *sotto voce*, 'Jewellery, works of art, houses in Scotland?'

'None,' I said, firmly.

'Nothing?' She gave me an exasperated look. 'How will you pay the rent, then?'

'I'll find work,' I said, in a small voice, 'cleaning, in a factory, anything.'

'But at present, you have nothing; no job offer, no savings. Family?'

'I have a daughter.'

'Oh! For heaven's sake,' she burst out. 'Why didn't you say so? That's a different form altogether.'

But, it transpired, whichever form we filled in, my chances of gaining council accommodation were zero.

'Your situation isn't a housing issue, it's a welfare matter,' the woman told me finally, folding her fat little hands. 'We don't deal with those here.'

'But I'll be homeless,' I insisted. 'How can homelessness *not* be a housing matter?'

'Because of your daughter,' she said. 'We could offer temporary accommodation for a single homeless person, but only in an emergency. But when children are involved, we hand it over to Welfare. She'd probably be taken into care.'

'I wouldn't allow it,' I said, through thin lips.

'You would have no choice,' she replied.

Outside the building I paused to pull on my gloves. A man who had been seated at another desk approached me and asked me for a light for his cigarette. He was thin, his face lined and sallow. He had a beakish nose and irregular, brown teeth.

'I'm sorry,' I said. 'I don't smoke.'

'Looking for work, are you?' he asked, placing the unlit cigarette behind his ear.

'Y... Yes,' I faltered. I threw a glance behind him, back into the vestibule of the council offices. If I had employment, a means to pay the rent, perhaps the woman would relent and put my name on her list. 'What is it? In a factory?'

He shook his head. 'Comfortable work, for a woman like you,' he said. 'Three or four evenings a week. Easy.'

'Bar work?'

He smiled. 'In a bar, yes.' He lifted the cigarette off his ear and put it in his mouth, and took a box of matches from the pocket of his grubby gabardine. 'But not behind the bar. More in the hostessing line.'

I took a step backwards, appalled. 'You don't mean...?' I struggled to speak the word, 'in a *brothel?*'

'No!' he shook his head, 'it's a reputable club, private, for gentlemen. You'd be an escort.' He struck the match and looked at me, narrowly, through its guttering flame. 'All quite respectable.'

'Oh no,' I stuttered, stepping away from him, 'oh no, thank you.'

'Call me, if you change your mind,' he cried after me. 'Ask for Clive at the Admiral Rodney.'

The whole day shook me considerably. Avenues I thought might be open to me were turning out to be closed tight. Others, opportunities I would never consider, were proving all-too prevalent. My hands were shaking on the bus back to the village, and I almost dropped the money for my fare as I handed it to the conductor.

I got off the bus at the church and passed through the lych gate into the grave yard. John's grave had been marked by a simple stone with his name, dates and the word 'artist' chiselled in plain lettering. I tidied away the desiccated remains of the flowers I had left a few weeks previously and crouched on the lush grass with my hand on the warm stone.

'I wish I could join you,' I said to the empty air. 'I wish I could lie down and melt through the earth and lie next to you.'

The wind rippled the grass around me and sparrows in the hedgerow squabbled amongst themselves. Across the churchyard I heard the school bell toll the end of another day, but no comfort came.

Awan and I walked together across the moor. The exercise, and Awan's eager chatter about her day at school, calmed me. Also, the closer I got to home, the safer I felt, although I knew this to be specious; I was not safe at Tall Chimneys, not really.

The gatehouse was shut up. I hadn't been there since John's death. Some part of me had felt by leaving the door and the shutters tightly closed I could keep some part of him contained within. I thought of him, there, staring out of the upper window and across the moor, capturing the texture of heather and the colour of cloud in the prism of his eye and reaching for his palette and brush. I craved his body and visited his grave from time to time because I knew that his remains rested there, but his essence was elsewhere, at large, in everything beautiful and, a little, walled up in the gatehouse.

We passed by and entered the leafy tunnel of the driveway. Our feet knew the topography of the pot holes and crumbling kerbs so we did not stumble even in the semi gloom of the forest shadow. Our voices always dipped as we walked beneath the cathedral of trees; a feeling of reverence stole over us as we walked. We followed the switch-back down and down. Brambles were encroaching onto the driveway, and a fallen tree which lay partially across it would make access difficult for a motor vehicle, but none ever came and went in those days and Awan and I stepped around it, as we always did. Then the ground levelled out and we came into the sunshine of the gravel sweep and again I was struck by the enchanted situation of Tall Chimneys, lost in its hidden dell, apart from the world and left behind by time. The air was still, as though holding its breath or under a spell. The familiar gables and loved mullions welcomed me like old friends, the crazed glazing of the windows glowed like mirrors in the afternoon sun and the chimneys stood sentinel over all.

Awan ran ahead and went into the house. I stood alone where the edge of shadow met the pool of light.

We were all interwoven, Tall Chimneys and me. My sense of self and my family heritage wandered along the echoic landings and glinted like the sun on the flaking plaster of the staterooms. My lifeblood flowed along the woodland byways where I had played with Kenneth as a child or limped behind dear Mr Weeks; they were as familiar to me as the pattern of veins on my wrist. John, and the love we had shared, towered like the chimneys, bringing warmth and life. The hidden doors and secret passages of the house reminded me of Cameron and the furtive, deliciously naughty passion he had awoken in me, and the possibility he had offered of escape. Awan was the corner stone and crowning glory. They all wrapped themselves round the fabric of Tall Chimneys like ivy, inveigling into the very stones, imprinted on the façade for all eternity. We were one. The place was myself - old fashioned, unworldly, of a time and place now obsolete. We could serve no useful purpose, except to one another. I could no sooner leave any of it than I could step out of my own skin.

The months of Ratton's absence wore on. Christmas then Easter. I knew I could expect his return any day but I was no closer finding an alternative to his proposal. Some days I contemplated the prospect with equanimity;

he had said that he loved me, and, whatever skewed idea he had of love, I believed him. Surely he would not behave brutishly? Other days I recoiled from the very idea of it, and maintained a fiction in my head that, if it came to it, he would not evict me if I refused him but allow me to stay on.

Week followed week and he did not return, or write, and we struggled by. I grew thinner than ever, and spent my evenings taking in my clothes. I hardly knew the face that looked back at me from the mirror. I had wrinkles under my eyes, a deep score between my nose and my mouth's corners. My skin was an unhealthy colour. I was often hungry and always lonely. Depression dogged me like a whining puppy but I kicked it away and soldiered on.

Spring came, and Awan sat the entrance examination for the local Grammar school. I begged spare onion sets and thinnings from other people's vegetable gardens and also seed potatoes. Although these had come off ration the previous year it was still cheaper to grow them. I set myself the task of clearing the choked raised beds and fumigating the greenhouse, determinedly ignoring the prospect that I would not remain in residence long enough to see either bare any kind of crop. As I worked I thought about Ratton, indeed, he was an ever-present spectre in my mind. My imagination entertained notions of him dead in Hong Kong from some exotic malady, or attached to some wealthy (but not very choosy) Eastern woman, all idea of marriage to me forgotten. I fantasised everything from his elevation to High Commissioner to his shipwreck - anything which would mean that I could stay at Tall Chimneys, all the while knowing it was in vain.

THE SUMMER WORE on. We heard that Awan had passed the examination to attend the Grammar school in town and although I was immensely proud of her I groaned inwardly; how would I afford the uniform? Then I recalled Giles Percy's promise, and wrote to him requesting assistance. It hurt my pride to do it - it felt like begging - and even as I held the letter in the mouth of the post box I hesitated still. But what choice did I have? I thrust the letter through the slot and walked away.

Ann Widderington invited us to help with the harvest in late August. Her husband had returned from war unscathed. From the capable and assertive woman she had become in his absence, Ann had reverted to cowering skivvy. One of her sons had died in the conflict but both the others were married and had brought their wives to live at Clough Farm where they seemed to create more work for Ann, rather than less. She lived at the beck and call of her bullying husband, her loutish sons and her querulous, demanding daughters in law, both of whom were expecting babies. I didn't want to help out that year, the cloud of my own future hung round me like a pall and I wasn't sure I would be able to keep my troubles to myself. But I wanted to give Ann any assistance and encouragement I could, so Awan and I went along on the appointed day. Awan ran to meet the hoard of children hovering by the farm gate. All their talk was of new school in September, and I quailed when I thought of how I would break the news that the Grammar could not be afforded after all.[18] It occurred to me, if I married Ratton, Awan would have to move schools anyway, to one near Leeds, or even go to boarding school. Nothing could be decided until I had come to a conclusion concerning his

---

[18] Since Butler's Education Act 1944, most Grammar Schools had become state-funded and so there would have been no fees payable. However uniform, sports equipment and fees for peripatetic tuition (such as music) were costly. Some Grammar schools offered bursaries or scholarships for pupils from poorer families.

proposal, and time was running short. I sighed and set my shoulders as I made for the bustling kitchen; I would not think about that today.

As always, Kenneth was crucial to the success of the harvest. I saw him at a distance driving a tractor, and later squirming under a baler to make some adjustment to the mechanism. He raised his hand to me in greeting, and smiled, but we had no conversation then. Miss Eccles, the school mistress, who usually left the area for the duration of the long vacation, had presented herself to help in the kitchen, and I heard murmurings she and Kenneth were walking out. I was surprised; she was older even than Kenneth and had been thought a confirmed spinster. On the other hand, I knew her to be kind and loving towards children, a quiet, self-effacing individual who might suit Kenneth to a tee. Bobby was present in his capacity as apprentice, much-grown and sporting a shadow of fuzz on his cheeks. He eschewed the other children, considering himself too grown up for their childish amusements. He and Awan had some converse and then he stalked away, clutching a fistful of spanners, and the dismay on her face made my heart sink further.

'You're quiet,' Pat Coombes observed, as we stood at a trestle table which had been set up in a corner of the yard, spreading margarine onto bread for the lunchtime sandwiches, 'what's up?'

'Oh,' I said, busying myself with the bread knife so I wouldn't have to look her in the eye, 'you know.'

'Still bothering you, is he? That Ratton?'

'He's gone away, but his proposal is still on the table,' I muttered, looking round to make sure we couldn't be overheard. 'You haven't told anyone, have you?'

'Of course not,' she replied, stiffly. 'I know how to keep my mouth shut.'

'I know, Pat, it's just that I'd be mortified if I thought anyone knew there was even the possibility...'

'But there *is*...' Pat interrupted, 'isn't there? You haven't said "no".'

'Lots of people make sensible marriages,' I said, in spite of myself. 'In the past, every marriage was arranged for the mutual benefit of the families. It can't all be about reckless romance and dancing.'

Pat humphed. 'You don't believe that,' she sneered. 'If there isn't love there has to be liking and respect. You marry that maggot and you'll end up like her,' she nodded across the yard to where Ann carried a cup of tea to one of her daughters in law, basking in the sunshine on a bench. 'Did you see the bruise on her arm?'

'Yes. She said she did it in the dairy.'

'Dairy my eye!'

'I know. But I wouldn't stand for that kind of behaviour from Ratton.'

'I expect Ann said that, at first.'

We were silent for a time, making the sandwiches.

'God, I hate corned beef,' I remarked, after a while.

'So does everyone, but what else is there? What else troubles you?'

I brought it out in a rush. 'I can't afford the uniform for Awan,' I wailed. 'I've written to her... godfather for help, but had no reply.'

She turned to face me. 'Are things really as bad as that?'

I nodded. 'I have no money. None. The account Colin used to pay into is empty.'

'Isn't there anything you can sell?'

'I have some of John's work but that is Awan's and anyway, I can't bear to part with it,' I said. 'The contents of the house were sold to Ratton.'

'He won't be familiar with every stick of furniture,' Pat advised. 'You could sell a few pieces, surely?'

'That would be stealing,' I shuddered, 'but in any case, dismantling the house would feel like the beginning of the end.'

'From what I hear, it's dismantling itself.'

The men began to troop in from the fields for their lunch. As I handed out sandwiches and slices of pie, Awan came and stood next to me, her face a picture of misery.

'What's the matter, darling?' I asked her, giving her a quick hug.

'Bobby won't speak to me,' she muttered, pressing her face into my side. 'He says he's too old to play kids' games, now. And he says people at his school don't mix with Grammar school people.'

'I'm sorry,' I said, wishing I could protect her from the hurt the world inflicts, 'but you have lots of other friends here. Here. Have a sandwich.'

She made a moue. 'Is it corned beef?'

'No,' I replied. 'It's cheese. I kept it back for you, specially.'

That cheered her, and I wished my predicament could be solved as easily. Presently she went off to join the other children and I got busy clearing up.

Later, Pat said to me, 'About the uniform, I think I can help you out, if you don't mind hand-me-downs.'

'Of course not,' I cried, thrilled.

'The Methodist minister's wife has twin girls two years ahead of Awan. She has two lots of everything, all grown out of but perfectly good. I'm sure she'll let you have them.'

I could have wept with gratitude.

Towards evening, when the crop was all undercover and the stubble fields peppered with birds foraging for stray kernels or macerated rabbits, I found Kenneth half-lying, half-propped against the bole of an old oak. His shirt was undone, filthy with dust and oil, the sleeves turned up to the elbows revealing forearms reddened by the sun. I recognised the trousers he wore - heavy duty cotton, much mended - I could even see Rose's neat stitching around a repair. I sat down next to him and it was like falling into a familiar and very comfortable chair; his grunt of welcome, his slight adjustment to allow me some support from the tree, his earthy, wholesome smell.

'Good job, today,' I said, nodding towards the neatly cut fields.

'Nice food,' he replied.

'Boys all right?'

He nodded, ''Cept for Anthony. Terrible hay-fever. Had to leave him with Mother. Doing all right are you, down at the house?'

I shrugged. 'It's a mess. I can't keep up with everything. The roof of the tool shed has fallen in and there's a wasps' nest in the greenhouse so I lost all the grapes and tomatoes.'

'You should have told me,' he chided.

'I know. But you're busy.'

'I'm never too busy to help you,' Kenneth growled.

'There is something you can help me with,' I told him. 'Bobby's upset Awan.'

'Oh?'

'He says he's too old to play with her, now. Quite the little man, isn't he?'

Kenneth frowned. 'I'll have a word,' he said. 'They're like brother and sister, those two. You don't grow out of that.'

'Like us,' I said, with a laugh, giving him a playful push.

'I wouldn't say that, exactly,' he replied, quickly, sitting up to pull strands of straw from his boots.

'You were as old as Bobby is now when you took me under your wing, all those years ago, and I was younger than Awan. What must I have been? Four? Five?'

I saw the corner of his mouth twitch. ''Bout that. You were a lonely little thing,' he muttered, and then, so low I could barely catch the words, 'you still are.'

'I hear that *you're* not so lonely,' I joked. 'Miss Eccles?'

All at once Kenneth scrambled to his feet and began to button up his shirt. 'Better get the lads home,' he said.

'It's all right, Kenneth,' I said. Looking up at him, the evening sun was slanting into my eyes and I had to put my hand over them like a visor to make out his expression but, with the sun behind him, his face was shadowed. 'It's perfectly natural and Rose... Rose would understand.'

'Rose always understood,' Kenneth said, so savagely it took me by surprise.

'I know, I know,' I soothed. Clearly, I had touched a raw nerve.

Immediately, his ire evaporated. I saw his shoulders relax, and I saw the glint of his teeth as he smiled. 'Mother's doing,' he said. 'Don't believe everything you hear. She doesn't always get what she wants.'

He turned and walked away into the lowering sun, and gave that piercing whistle which Bobby and Brian would know was designed to bring them running.

'She usually does, though,' I called after him.

It was late when Awan and I arrived at the gatehouse, but not entirely dark. A low moon hung in the clear sky casting an ethereal light over the moor; the tufted heather, spiny grass and soft mosses looked like intricate fretwork on a sheet of antique silver, the work of an ancient craftsman from days of yore. Everything, in fact, had a ghostly hue; the lane was a pewter ridge between indistinct embankments, the trees were steely spires, unnaturally still, and everywhere a miasmic vapour hung over the land as the cooling air met the hot earth. We dismounted from our bicycles and entered the driveway, a throat of misty darkness. We knew the way as we knew our own faces but we both quailed a little at the prospect, so disorienting was the fog which hung beneath the canopy of the trees and coiled itself around us. The narrow, yellowish beam of my bicycle lamp failed to penetrate the cloud of murk and, worse, cast outlandish shadows on familiar boulders and contorted ordinary shrubs into demons. The fallen tree looked like an elongated body with broken limbs all awry. We stepped around it as though it was a veritable corpse.

At the second hairpin Awan hesitated. 'Perhaps we ought to go back, Mummy,' she said. 'I don't like this.'

'Back to the farm?' I said, my voice too loud and falsely confident. 'They'll all be a sleep, by now.'

'Back to the gatehouse, then,' she suggested. 'There are things there. We could manage, for one night.'

It was awkward, wheeling our bicycles over the pot-holed drive, keeping ourselves away from the precipitous edge which, no matter how I tried to navigate a line away from it, kept throwing itself under my front wheel. 'Let's leave our bikes here,' I said, laying mine down at the side of the route. 'We can collect them in the morning. Then we can hold hands and keep each other safe.'

'All right,' she agreed, in a brave, thin little voice.

I unclipped my lamp and we went on together, hand in hand, through the clinging mist.

About halfway down the driveway the quality of the fog changed. I don't know if Awan felt it too. The air, which had been damp and cloying but fresh before, laced with botanical scents, clean and natural, changed. It became thicker and smelt woody, and caught the back of the throat so I was suddenly conscious of a raging thirst. It made me think of the trees, sweltering all day in the summer heat, their sap liquefying like treacle in a saucepan and the distinctive thick, sugary, sticky smell which rises when you have left it just that second too long.

I swallowed, trying to find some saliva to slake my dry throat, but my mouth was as arid as bone.

When we came out of the shelter of the driveway we only knew it by the falling away of the skirt of trees. The whole hollow of the basin was filled with thick fog. It boiled and churned around us. Rather than emanating from the earth it seemed to pour from above, like thick cloud weighed down by water which it cannot release. I could scarcely see the house through it; the outlines of the roofs, the columns of the chimneys, the jutting gables and overhanging eaves were blurred, a pencil sketch which has been smeared with a greasy thumb. The woody smell which had intrigued me in the woods was much stronger and more acrid, and in spite of the dryness of my throat, my eyes began to water. At last I realised.

'Fire,' I croaked. 'The house is on fire.'

At that moment a breath of breeze dispersed the smoke just enough for me to get a clear view of the house. I could see no flame, but thick smoke poured from the gap between the slates and the gutters and fell like a dirty grey curtain down the front of the house. Tendrils of smoke snaked from between the slates, as though a thousand cigarettes were being smoked within. Then the fug closed and I could see nothing.

Awan's face was white with panic, her mouth an open maw. She gripped my hand with super-human strength.

'Go to the icehouse,' I told her, gently disengaging my hand from hers. I knew there were blankets there, and candles, left behind from when we had equipped it as an air raid shelter. Everything would be damp and dismal, but she would be safe. I handed her my bicycle lamp. 'I'm going to telephone for help, and then I'll join you.'

'You mustn't go into the house,' she warned.

'I won't,' I promised her. 'I'll use the telephone extension in Kenneth and Rose's place. But you must go to the icehouse.'

She looked like she might refuse. 'On your way,' I told her, 'check the outhouses.' Our last dog had died in the terrible winter of '47. We had no poultry or livestock. But a wild creature occasionally bedded down in the old stables, and a feral cat had had kittens there earlier in the year. 'Make sure the cat and her kittens are gone.' I knew they were long-gone, but giving Awan responsibility for another creature's safety would serve my purpose.

'All right,' she agreed.

No doors at Tall Chimneys were ever locked and the door to the old estate office which had served as the entrance to Kenneth and Rose's house opened at my push. We had had no electricity for months and months, unable to afford fuel for the generator. I dismissed the idea of looking for candles or a match. I groped my way to the corner of the room where the telephone apparatus sat on the floor, and dialled the operator.

The fire brigade was stationed in the local town and it would take them at least half an hour to reach us. Then there was the driveway to negotiate - I thought of the tree which lay across it, and berated myself for leaving it there. They would have to cut it up, I thought, or at least drag it to one side, that would waste extra time. In the meanwhile, Tall Chimneys was on fire. A bile of panic rose in my chest, bitter, jealous, my home was being consumed from within. Forgetting my promise to Awan, I stepped across the yard and went into the house through the kitchen door.

The air inside was strangely still and tomb-like. I listened carefully, for the crack and snap of burning timber, for the crash of falling roof beams, for the shattering of glass, but could hear nothing. The old clock above the mantel ticked doggedly, the tap dripped.

Perhaps, I thought, I had made a mistake?

I climbed the back stairs to the hallway, my hand trembling as it gripped the worn rail. The room was impenetrably dark, the furniture mere shapeless shadows. No light shone through the windows, which were charcoal rectangles in a sea of dim. I walked as though on shards of glass, as though to avoid disturbing a burglar at work above, as if my presence there would make him redouble his efforts of pillage and devastation.

The smell of smoke was unmistakable, but not overpowering.

I placed my foot on the bottom step of the wide staircase and began to climb. On the large landing which overlooked the hall below, the smell of smoke was stronger, faintly sour, like a garden fire in autumn, but still I could hear no roar or crack. The house was deathly still, as though holding its breath, and I realised that I, too, had stopped breathing. My hand gripped the carved balustrade and the house clung around me, as though for succour. I could feel it pressing, as Awan had done earlier, and the weight of it was almost too much to bear.

I surmised that the fire was in the attics. I had been up there only a few days before, and my mind homed in on a specific lumber room which was stuffed to its rafters with boxes of mildewed books and crates of mouldy, moth-eaten linen. It had been a routine check, one which I carried out every month or so, looking for leaks or signs of rodent infestation. In point of fact I had found signs of water ingress and had stuffed some material into a gap which had appeared at the side of the roof-light. In pushing between the boxes I had dislodged a precariously balanced chandelier, broadcasting crystal drops everywhere. It came to me with blinding clarity that one of these had formed a lens, intensifying the sun's light until the dampened floorboards had begun to smoulder. The room was airless, and a lack of oxygen would inhibit the fire. But not indefinitely. The heat, in time, would crack the glass of the roof-light, and once the fire had air to breathe, it would be an inferno.

Time was short. I might have one, at best two opportunities to save artefacts from the upper floor of the house before the fire made it impossible or the arrival of the firemen made everything chaotic. What might be the most valuable? What could I easily carry? I thought about the silver dressing table set in Mrs Simpson's room, the little trinket box, said to be *Fabergé*. There was a small Constable in one of the dressing rooms and antique glassware in the cabinets. But all those things were Ratton's, now. Why should I risk my life to save them? My thoughts flew instead to the north wing, and the room where John's canvasses were kept. I set off into the gloom of the north landing. I navigated the awkward chicane of unexpected steps and the sharp turning without difficulty, my feet seeming to have in-built memories of them. The smell of smoke was much stronger. I cocked my ear at the bottom of the stair which led up to the old servants' quarters in the attic; a strange, other-worldly whisper drifted down to me, like spectres murmuring secrets to one another. The place was smouldering, heat seeping like molten metal through the age-old beams. It would only need a stray draught or a pocket of stale air in a cavity between floorboard and ceiling laths to ignite it.

I hurried to the end of the corridor to the room where John's things were stored. The room was pitch black inside, for the shutters were kept tightly closed. The air smelt dry and musty, and hot; it seared the inside of my nostrils.

John had used a large leather satchel to transport his paintings. I groped for it in the darkness and began to fill it with as many sketch books and small canvasses as I could. When it was full I picked up a large canvas with my other hand, and hurried back the way I had come.

Passing the attic stair, the whisperings above had become more strident, like an exasperated delegation complaining in a library. Smoke was pouring thickly down the stairs, now, the stuffy attic must have reached its capacity and the lath and plaster eaves must not be allowing enough to escape; it needed another way out.

I fled along the landing and down the main stairway as though hounds of hell were chasing me. The air in the kitchen was still smoke-free but I could smell it anyway - coming from myself. I dumped my treasures on the table and went back for more.

By now the smoke on the landing was quite palpable. It hovered in a grey pall beneath the ceiling like clouds in purgatory. The acrid tang of it caught in my throat and made me cough, and I clapped my handkerchief to my nose and mouth. The heat at the end of the corridor was almost searing, as though from an oven. Above my head I heard the crack and shatter of glass, and the patter of broken shards on the floor overhead.

All at once the fire roared into life. I heard it whoosh and leap like a ravenous animal, fed by the air from the broken window. A patch in the ceiling darkened, the paint curling and withering before my horrified eyes.

I dashed back into the room where the paintings were kept and snatched as many as I could carry. The larger works were too big for me. I tore the heavy curtains from their poles and threw them over the artworks in the forlorn hope they might be spared, and then stacked the smaller, experimental canvasses on top of one another until I could barely see over the top of them. I lifted them and staggered from the room, pulling the door closed behind me. The ceiling above me was fully ablaze, a roiling mass of bluish flame and orange tongues rippling across the old distemper. I could hear my hair singe as I passed beneath it, my eyes pouring, each breath a choking lungful of bitter ash. I saw the curtains of Mrs Simpson's room ablaze as I passed the door of that room. At a distance I heard the crash of something heavy falling. The house resonated with the busy burn of a million enraged bees conscientiously consuming every sweet morsel of vintage beauty and priceless antiquity to be found.

The kitchen was cool and dark, mercifully free of smoke. I retched into the sink and scooped water from the tap into my acrid mouth, coughing and gasping until I thought I might expel my own lungs, almost swooning over the cold hard draining board. I had a sense of the house above me buckling and folding like a box, the pressure in my ears was immense, I could almost feel the ceiling above my head pressing down. When I moved again it was in a half-crouch, so vivid was the feeling that the house was collapsing on top of me. I scurried to open the strong room and hastily pushed the paintings inside. The tarnished silver platters and candelabra glowered at me from their dusty shelves. I slammed and locked the heavy door on them.

In my bedroom I threw the contents of my drawers onto the bed, and gathered up the corners of the quilt to form a makeshift sack before hauling it along the stone floor and into the chill of the boot room which was closest to the outer door. I went back and did the same in Awan's rooms, remembering her favourite dolls, the bits of furniture for the dolls' house which Cameron had made, her books and box of precious trinkets where she hoarded feathers and interesting stones picked up over the years. I cast an agonised glance at the lush mural of flora and fauna which John had painted. If I could have torn it from the wall, I would have done so.

Overhead, the sounds of a riotous party resonated; intoxicated gentlemen played an unruly game of rugby. Cabinets of curios exploded as if in applause. Furniture hurled itself into the fray. With a last, woebegone look at the dear, familiar kitchen, I dragged my bundles out into the night.

The sky above the house was lurid with orange light. Every upper window shone brightly as though a thousand candles burned within. I didn't recall ever seeing the house so animated and alive. It looked like a jolly party was in progress, every room occupied with high-spirited guests, the crash and smash of priceless glass like careless footmen indiscriminately dropping trays of cocktails and platters of canapés. The north wing roof was fully alight now, sending showers of sparks up. Smoke and flame both spurted from the chimney pots. Before my horrified eyes first one and then another tall chimney tottered. They seemed to hesitate, and then began to lean. Further and further they tilted, with infinitesimal slowness and grace. Their decorative masonry seemed illuminated from within, incandescent, their very bricks melting back into the sand which had formed them and then regressing further to a molten, primordial floe until the structure was impossible to recognise, and they sank with a sigh into oblivion. My own cry of distress melded with theirs and rose up into the implacable night.

Of course, the following day, amid the devastation fire and water and the tramp of auxiliary fire-fighters had caused, Ratton returned.

I met him on the gravel sweep, my hair and face crusted with soot, my clothes singed, almost dead with fatigue. I looked, I suppose, quite dreadful. But he greeted me with a chaste kiss, and said he was happy that I was safe, and enquired after Awan, who had gone with Patricia Coombes to be bathed and put to bed in one of her guest rooms.

We surveyed the remains of Tall Chimneys together. The entire crater reeked of ash, soot, sodden plaster and charred wood. The wet-hot, desiccated dampness was a contradiction it was impossible to assimilate. The sturdy stone of the old house was blackened and compromised, the filth and greasy residue of smut a stark anachronism to the freshness of the forest and the heartless blue of the sky.

The whole of the upper north wing had been destroyed; the attic storey was gone altogether, the roofless bedrooms stood open to the elements, blackened stumps of age-old purlins pointing impotently at the sky. The heavy joists still smoked. It was shocking to see what had been private for so long now exposed; in some way shameful and dissipated. The odd tattered remnant of brocade bed-hanging flapped carelessly in the light breeze. The beds themselves were reduced to tortured springs and twisted frames. The rest of the furniture was charred beyond recognition; eviscerated armoires gaped, their doors warped all out of shape. In places the heavily figured wall-paper was just visible beneath thick brown scorching; peeled, shrivelled, in some cases even melted. The windows had smashed in the inferno leaving jagged edges round the burnt frames. The stain of last night's flames was imprinted on their weathered mullions. Hand-woven silks - shredded and ruined, and once-lustrous velvet hangings seemed to have attempted to evacuate themselves from the building - they dangled from the apertures, snagged on the sharp edges of glass like hanged children. The shattered remains of the roof tiles and the decimated chimneys littered everything like scree.

The rooms on the ground floor had fared better; most of the furniture was untouched although everything reeked of smoke and there was much water damage. But the joists which supported the rooms above were suspect, weakened, and we had been told not to venture inside until they could be shored up. Fortunately these rooms held little of value, opening as they did onto the stable yard and kitchen gardens - the accommodations Kenneth, Rose and I had occupied, larders and laundry rooms, the kitchen and other areas of mere utilitarian purpose.

To my amateur eye the east wing was largely untouched. Even the chimneys which had collapsed had done so over the north wing. The three remaining ones seemed intact, blackened of course, like the attics below them which had been impregnated with smoke and desiccated by heat. The east wing bedrooms appeared structurally intact and also the ground floor staterooms. Heat had caused considerable damage, smoke more, water from the hoses had perhaps caused the worst ravages of all but architecturally, as far as I could see, the east wing could remain even if the rest had to be demolished.

'I'm sure I can make something of it,' I said, turning to Ratton. 'The east wing, at least, seems...'

He shook his head, and put a gentle hand of my arm. 'No, my dear,' he said. His tiny eyes, through the prism of his thick-lensed glasses, glinted with genuine sadness. 'It's finished. You must marry me, now, don't you see? What else is there for you?'

I cast around me. The garden remained, though churned and ploughed by the tyres of the engines and puddled with water from the hoses. The trees still stood, the kitchen garden and greenhouse remained. I turned again to the house. 'I can live here, still,' I asserted. 'There is still furniture, a roof. The kitchen can be shored up...'

'It isn't safe,' he said, smiling sadly. 'Why would you stay here when I can offer you so much more?'

'Because it's my *home*' I cried out. 'It's all I've ever known. It's all I want to know. I can't leave it, I *can't!*'

Ratton sighed. 'Look at you,' he said, not unkindly, and raised his hand to my singed, straw-like hair. I allowed him to weigh a tress of it in his palm. 'Look at your face,' he went on, running a finger from my brow to my jaw. 'You're tired and thin and hungry,' he said. 'Wouldn't you like a hot bath? A good meal? A comfortable bed with clean sheets?'

I started to cry. He had described my heart's desire. 'No, no, no,' I sobbed.

'Yes, yes,' he said, and gently took my arm. His car was parked up the drive and he began to lead me towards it. We passed some pieces of furniture supposedly salvaged. They stood around haphazardly on the sweep like people waiting for a funeral to start. They were variously scratched and scored. I didn't know if they had been damaged the previous night or if they had always been so shabby, their dilapidation hidden by the gloom of the house. Two fire tenders remained, one half on and half off the rose-bed, the other slewed across the lawn, hoses snaking from their bellies. Inside the house, firemen roved from room to room dampening the last smouldering remnants, careless of their muddy boots on the carpets, shoving furniture around, shouting to one another like costermongers. From the corner of my eye I could see the two bundles I had hauled from the house. They were pushed against a hedge which shielded the stable yard from the drive. I had stashed them in a panic when the fire engines had arrived, and forgotten about them in the ensuing chaos. They had been kicked around and trampled on in the melee, and looked woebegone and filthy. Our precious belongings peeped from their folds as though ashamed. I allowed Ratton to lead me past the carnage, towards his car.

Then a shout went up from inside the house, panic and alarm. Two firemen rushed down the steps from the front door, another shoved up the casement of the drawing room window and scrambled out of it, a fourth put his shoulder to the French windows in the dining room and burst out as though pursued by demons. A deep moan echoed from inside the house, inhuman and yet perfectly intelligible, articulating despair, resignation, a final letting go. The firemen rushed away from the house, across the lawn towards the sloping woodland, urging us to do likewise. Ratton took a firmer grip on my arm and began to hurry me across the gravel, past his car and into the shade cast by the inner rim of trees. I resisted him, and looked back, over my shoulder. High above the house, at the topmost chimney pot, two crows gave cries of alarm and launched themselves into the sky. The noise from the house intensified - how can I describe it? It was like I imagine ships' timbers to sound in a storm - tortured, stretched, twisted and pressured by the onslaught of elements. It was the noise a volcano might make as the last plug of rock gives way to allow the molten magma to flow. Two of the remaining chimneys shuddered, and began to descend, gracefully, like opera singers taking a final curtsey. The roof tiles shattered, began to slither towards the gutters and then cascaded in a fountain onto the terrace. The house seemed to implode, to collapse in on itself as the supporting trusses gave way. Through the broken windows I could see furniture jostling, sliding crazily across the rooms. A manic cacophony of breaking glass and splintering wood emanated forth. Plumes of dust - or smoke - issued from the windows and doors and rose from the fractured roofs. The massive stones of the east wing appeared to crumble as though made of pumice and the Talbot family crest, which had adorned a panel above the door since 1620, fell away and smashed into a hundred smithereens on the steps below.

I felt as though my own skeleton had collapsed, melted, and would have sunk onto my knees had Ratton not caught me.

'Come,' he said, and carried me to his car.

HE TOOK ME, not, as I had half expected, to a seedy hotel or even to his own house, there to be sequestered until such time as the marriage lines could be attained, but to The Plough and Harrow, where my friend Patricia looked after me. He helped me from the car and into the lounge bar of the pub (a place I had never set foot in before) and handed me over to Patricia's brisk but kindly ministrations. Before leaving me he took my hand and gave me a direct and unambiguous look. 'It is agreed, then?'

I nodded, and lowered my eyes. 'Yes, it's agreed. As long as you...' I thought of Tall Chimneys, decimated. How much would it cost, now, to repair? But this was the price I demanded.

'Yes,' he said, nodding once. 'I know the condition. It will be done. So?'

'Yes,' I whispered.

'Good. You will hear from me soon.'

Patricia made me a cup of tea and presented me with food which she insisted I ate, and then ushered me upstairs where a hot bath had been drawn. I sat in it listlessly while she shampooed my hair and washed the smut and grime from my body. It was greasy, stubborn, and she scrubbed at me with a loofah until my skin was raw. All the while she kept her mouth pursed in a harsh line.

'Don't judge me,' I wailed, at last, as she pulled one of her nightdresses over my head. 'What else can I do?'

'Go to sleep,' she said, showing me into a twin bedded room where Awan slept. The curtains were drawn against the bright summer day but the window was open, and I was glad. The soft, fresh air was intoxicating after the acrid stench of burning. 'Things will seem better in the morning.'

'It *is* morning,' I corrected her, pedantically.

She narrowed her eye, and shut the door.

I slept all that day and the following night. From time to time I was aware of Patricia in the room, or others, perhaps. I was given water to drink and led like an automaton to the lavatory. At some point I felt Awan kiss me and tip-toe from the room. The room was quiet and cool, the sheets comfortable against my skin, and when I dreamed of burning timbers falling around me, or of being choked by ash and fumes (as I did), their softness and safety was a welcome reassurance, soothing my troubled brow, and I slept again.

In the morning I ate breakfast in Patricia's parlour while Awan bottled-up in the public bar under the direction of Patricia's incapacitated husband. I eyed the piles of clothes, toiletries, bedding and kitchen requisites which had been delivered for me.

'Ann went round the village,' Patricia told me. 'Most people donated something. You'll have to start afresh,' she said, 'they know that. They want to help.'

'People are so kind,' I murmured, thinking their kindness would be wasted. I wouldn't need these things as Mrs Ratton.

'It's no more than you would have done,' Patricia said, 'if *their* house had been burned around their ears.'

'I suppose...' I began, stirring my tea, 'I suppose there's nothing left, down there?'

Patricia shrugged. 'The gates have been locked.'

'Locked?' The gates had never been closed, let alone locked, in my lifetime.

'Yes. There's a sign saying the place is unsafe and trespassers will be prosecuted.' She paused, tweaked a wisp of her hair back into its chignon. 'So naturally, the world and his wife have been down to look. School children in droves, a proper village picnic, if you ask me. Ghouls.'

'Awan?' I didn't want her to be confronted with the waste and destruction, and if the place really was unsafe...

'Oh no. I've kept her here, with me.' Patricia straightened an antimacassar. 'She's been trying on her new uniform, though,' she said, brightly, to change the subject. 'Looks really smart in it. I had to take in the skirts - those Manse girls eat like horses - but everything else fit perfectly.'

'You're very kind,' I said, picking at an invisible thread in my hand-me-down skirt. Awan's Grammar school debut would be cancelled, I supposed. Ratton had mentioned a boarding school. Perhaps that would be best, I mused. I didn't think I wanted Awan to witness my ultimate humiliation.

A soft tap at the outer door announced Mrs Greene. She stepped into the parlour and shut the door in a way that suggested to me she had done it many times before. She brought a cake, still warm, and laid it on a table, along with an envelope. 'This came in the post for you,' she said. 'Not the cake, of course...' she tittered a little, at her own joke.

'I *can* bake, you know!' Patricia laughed.

'I know dear, but not very well,' Mrs Greene replied, not unkindly. 'And, my dear,' she turned to me, 'I wanted to say, how very sorry I am. I don't know *how* you must feel, and I'm sorrier than I can say, truly I am. And Kenneth says... well, Kenneth sends... Oh! *You* know Kenneth, he doesn't say anything much but I know he's devastated for you. I've never seen him so white as when he came back from - you know, he thought he'd better have a *look,* just to see.'

'To see if he could fix it all up?' I smiled, sadly, and patted the chair next to me. She came and perched on it, like a little bird. 'That would be just like him. I can't think of anything in my life he hasn't fixed, or improved, or had a hand in one way or another. I seem to recall, after I'd had Awan, he was there, in the shadows, watching over us. And when John was ill, he helped...' Suddenly I was crying, and Mrs Greene put her small, capable hand on my shoulder.

'There now, dear,' she said, as she might to one of her grandsons. 'Things will look better, in a day or so.'

But I knew that no matter how many days went by, things would look just the same, and I would have to marry Sylvester Ratton.

I didn't look at the letter until later that morning. It was from Giles Percy, and was written on prison notepaper.

You will see immediately [it read] *that my circumstances are not of the best. There is no way to sugar the pill so I will tell you plainly that I am incarcerated pending trial for committing acts of 'indecency' with another man. I shall plead not guilty since there is no evidence to prove that an indecent act was committed, however, I have small hope of being acquitted. I shall be imprisoned, fined or subjected to chemical castration.*

My resources are inaccessible to me and so I am unable to supply funds, but I have not been behind-hand in ensuring my responsibilities can be met and have made arrangements with an old acquaintance of mine from Bletchley[19], now Headmistress at Casterton School, near Kirkby Lonsdale in Lancashire, so that, if necessary the girl can be placed on the roll. The school is of good repute, founded for the daughters of impoverished clergymen and the like, closely associated with neighbouring Sedbergh (my alma mater). I am told it has a homely and gentle ethos and that girls do exceptionally well there academically and personally. It is in a part of the countryside not unlike your own.

Naturally these arrangements will make no financial burden on you and are entirely at your discretion to take up or pass by.

The letter lay in my lap as I considered this possibility. To send Awan to school would be a terrible wrench for both of us - we had hardly spent a single night apart. But it was no good thinking things would mend themselves - they wouldn't - and this opportunity was one I didn't think I could pass up. To have Awan at a school of *my* choosing, paid for by a means which owed nothing to Sylvester Ratton, would mean that she, at

---

[19] Bletchley Park was requisitioned and used by a team of top secret code-breakers - both men and women including Alan Turing, who managed to break the Enigma Code and turned the tide of intelligence in the war. Like Giles, he was arrested for 'indecent acts' and subjected to chemical castration. He sadly took his own life as a result.

least, would be free of his manipulation and influence. Casterton, although in Lancashire, was hard against the border with Yorkshire; only a very few miles away. I imagined I would be able to visit often. She would be independent, she would make friends, she would have openings which had been denied to me. She would be able to go out into the world, as John had always said she ought to. And if mine was to be an uncomfortable, awkward life of compromise and compliance, she would not have to see it.

All I had to do now was break the news to her.

It turned out not to be the only unpleasant tiding Awan was to receive that day.

Patricia kept Awan busy all day, helping in the bar before opening time and then very properly shooing her into the kitchen once the bar was open. She helped make sandwiches and plate up ploughman's lunches. In between she stroked the cat which slept on the kitchen window ledge in a patch of sunshine, and chatted to Enid, Patricia's girl-of-all-works, who washed the dishes, made up the guest room beds and sluiced out the urinals as occasion required. Enid was a simple soul, not well endowed with discretion or imagination but very voluble; a constant stream of inconsequential chatter issued from her mouth from morning till night. Whether she repeated gossip heard elsewhere, or took it upon herself to inform Awan I do not know, but towards two o'clock Awan came into the parlour looking white and trembly.

I pulled her onto the sofa next to me thinking that she was finding herself subject to sudden vivid flash-backs and repeated heart-stopping reminders that our home was gone, as I was. 'Tell me,' I said, settling her in the crook of my arm.

'Enid says you and Daddy weren't married,' she burst out. 'That isn't right, is it Mummy?'

I quailed, but took a deep breath. 'We didn't go to church,' I told her, 'and we didn't have the certificate. But we were married in the most important way two people can be married.'

'What way is that?' Awan asked me, her little face looking up into mine.

I thought about it for a moment. 'Some marriages are made from the outside in.' I said at last. 'The couple's parents decide it will be a good thing for their families to be joined, and an alliance is agreed. The minister at the church lays his hands on theirs and declares that they are wed. The registrar writes the certificate, and signs it, and makes it so. All those things can happen without the couple loving each other or even knowing each other very well. They agree, because they see it's a good thing and they decide to make a go of it. And that's all right. Many, many happy marriages have been made that way in the past: from the outside in. But some marriages are made from the inside out. The couple have a connection - there's a spark between them. Something - I don't know what - lights them up from the inside, both of them; they are two branches of the same candelabra. They make each other laugh, they have the same thoughts, they feel the same way about things, they share the same values. It's as though their hearts beat as one heart, almost that they are one person. It may be their families don't approve, or the minister won't speak the words, or the registrar sign the paper, but it doesn't matter. In their hearts - in their *hearts,* Awan - they are married. That's how it was with your daddy and me. We lit each other up in that way. We knew each other inside out and we loved each other through thick and thin. We were true to each other...' I gave a fleeting thought to Giles Percy and Cameron Bentley, and to Amelia and Monique and the other women who may or may not have been part of John's life when he was away from me. '... in the way that really matters,' I qualified. 'In the end, he always came home to me, no matter what, and I was always there waiting for him.'

Awan nodded, and mulled over what I had said. 'And if you loved each other like that,' she said, fiddling with her hands in her lap, 'why didn't you get properly married so that you were outside-in *and* inside-out? Wouldn't the minister say the words?'

'No,' I said, through thin lips. 'No, he wouldn't.'

'Why?'

It was a fair question, of course, a natural question, and I had to answer it. In doing so I felt I was laying down a foundation for the future as well as explaining the past, throwing out loose ends which Awan would one day be able to join, providing something she would be able to build on, when the time came.

'Many years before he met me,' I said, 'your daddy made the other kind of marriage, an outside-in, one. He was poor and very hungry, in a foreign country, and he had no friends. Then he was offered nice food and shelter in a pleasant home, and the chance to paint (which, you know, was the thing he loved doing best of all), if he married a lady and kept her company, and took her out to parties and behaved politely to her friends. So he agreed. They both understood exactly what the arrangement was and they were both happy with it.' I turned Awan's face up to look her in the eye. 'That's all right, isn't it? I mean, you can understand, can't you, why he did it? It was sensible and quite agreeable. At the time, and in the circumstances, it was a very natural and proper thing for him to do.'

'But then he met you, and he wanted the other kind of marriage?'

'Yes, darling. So he had both kinds, in the end. Lucky man!' My voice sounded hollow in my own ears, and perhaps Awan caught the timbre of it.

'I... I suppose so,' she faltered, 'if *you* didn't mind...'

'Not at all,' I said, breezily, 'and neither would he, if it were ever to happen the other way around.'

I did not tell Awan that day that she would not be going to the Grammar school with her friends. I wanted to make sure Ratton concurred. Not that I needed his permission, but I needed him to understand that I was placing Awan outside of his jurisdiction.

He called the following day, bearing neither flowers nor a ring (as I had feared) but wearing a smart suit and driving his most ostentatious vehicle. He looked out of place in Patricia's homely parlour, like a fat kestrel that has found itself in a budgerigar cage.

I took a narrow chair by a small table and motioned him to one of the more comfortable seats by the fireplace, but he took up instead a rather proprietorial stance on the hearth rug. I explained my decision to send Awan to Casterton.

'Suit yourself,' he merely shrugged. 'Bedford is better, I'm told, for girls, with a natural progression to Oxford or Cambridge.'

'But so far away,' I said, 'and I have determined on Casterton. I haven't told Awan yet. I haven't told her anything of our... plans.'

'You do quite right to consult me first. I shall make the necessary arrangements.'

'I am not consulting you, I am informing you,' I clarified. 'You need not concern yourself with anything that appertains to Awan. She is outside the scope of our... understanding. The school will be paid for by Giles Percy.'

'That degenerate?' Ratton spluttered. 'I am amazed you want any connection with him. He is utterly disgraced, you know.'

'I know he is facing trial,' I replied. 'I believe our judicial system allows people to be innocent until proven guilty.'

'Pwah!' Ratton ejaculated. 'I always knew there was something suspect about the man.'

'I remember,' I said, ironically. 'You wanted nothing to do with him when he was rubbing shoulders with the governmental great and good at Colin's house parties. No, nothing at all.'

'Hah!' Ratton gave a guffaw of laughter. 'I had forgotten what good sport you can be. We are going to have fun, you and I, sparring off one another again.'

'I don't remember it being much fun,' I demurred.

'It will be, this time,' he said. 'Now, my dear, about the arrangements...'

'Yes,' I interrupted him. 'I have been giving them some thought as well. I want to wait until Awan has gone to school.'

'You don't want her there?'

I shook my head. 'I want nobody there. A quiet ceremony in a registry office. Just us two and whatever witnesses we need.'

'Really? You don't want a church? Bridesmaids? All the trimmings?'

'Emphatically not.'

'Oh.' It looked as though I had really nonplussed him. 'May I ask why?'

'It's obvious. At our time of life, such fripperies are ridiculous. And, let's be honest, ours is going to be a practical arrangement...'

'Practical?' he burst out. '*Practical?* Good God, woman, how many times do I have to tell you?' He took a pace towards me and raised his hand and I thought he was going to strike me. I ducked my head and hunched my shoulders in anticipation of it but what he did was reach for my arm and hoik me to my feet. We stood nose to nose. His breathing was rapid; I could feel the draught of it on my face. He took my shoulders and gave them a little shake - not violent - but enough for me to know a violence of passion simmered very close to the surface. 'I *love* you,' he said, hoarsely. 'I have *always* loved you. I want you for my wife.' He looked hard into my eyes and it was all I could do to meet his gaze. 'There's nothing 'practical' about this for me,' he went on, his voice low and choked with emotion. 'This is my heart's desire.'

I dropped my eyes then, and stared at his diamond tie pin. 'I know,' I said, in a small voice. It was humbling, the strength of his passion, and frightening also - I knew what atrocities his passion had led him to commit. On the other hand I had to have it clear between us that my feelings were different. I raised my eyes once more and took hold, in my turn, of his elbows. 'But, you do know, don't you, it isn't the same for me? I don't want to deceive you. I don't want you to deceive yourself. You are offering me security, a home, respectability. More importantly you have agreed to rebuild Tall Chimneys. That's *my* heart's desire. I don't love you, Sylvester. I will never love you.'

I thought he might cry. His little eyes began to swim. His nasal breathing became moist. His face was pale, stricken. Then he gave a hard swallow and took a pace back. Both our hands dropped to our sides. He turned away from me and rummaged for a handkerchief in his pocket. He busied himself with it for a while, blowing his nose, polishing his glasses, and then he stepped across to the parlour door and opened it enough to call, 'I wonder if we might have some coffee, Mrs Coombes, if you please?' before returning and taking the seat I had offered him at first. He smiled. It was as though the whole of our foregoing meeting had not taken place. 'I have sent a man down to the house,' he announced, in a business-like voice, 'to see what can be salvaged. Anything of value will be removed, repaired if possible, and stored, pending renovations. You see? I am already active on the business. Matters are already in hand.'

'That's good,' I said. 'Thank you. A man?'

'An expert, I should have said. Somebody who knows his Hepplewhite from his Chippendale.'

'He will find both, I believe.'

'I fear he will find just so much charcoal and ash,' Ratton observed, 'but I am determined we shall save what we can.'

I nodded. 'In the strong room,' I said, 'there are some things of mine - of Awan's, I ought to say. Some of John's paintings and sketch books. They were specifically left to her, in his Will.'

'Very well,' Ratton nodded. 'I will make sure they are stored securely. Is there anything else you particularly wish to have by you?'

I thought of our sorry little bundles, kicked and trampled. Awan hadn't mentioned the fate of her things. Perhaps it was best to draw a line under it all. 'No,' I said.

Patricia brought in a tray with coffee and some homemade shortbread. She served it in silence, her lips stitched closed, but throwing acid looks at Ratton as she did so which made her opinion abundantly clear.

'Oh dear,' Ratton mused, as he poured coffee for us both, 'I don't think Mrs Coombes approves of me.'

'No,' I agreed. 'I don't think she does.'

Ratton stayed for about an hour, drinking his coffee and speaking of his business, his search for a house in Roundhay, his ideas for a honeymoon tour. 'Europe is a mess, still,' he opined, 'as much as I might like to take you to Rome and Florence. I wondered about America? You might like to call on your sister.'

I shuddered. The idea of Amelia seeing what I had descended to was appalling. 'We are estranged,' I said, 'and I don't think Texas has much to offer in the way of culture. Only beef cows.'

'And oil,' he appended. 'I hear your sister has found some on her husband's property.'

'You are better informed than me,' I said.

He gave a smug little smile. 'I keep my ear to the ground.'

'Perhaps the Great Lakes?' I suggested. 'There's a little town on Lake Michigan I wouldn't mind visiting - St Joseph's?'

'Certainly,' Ratton said, affably.

Presently Awan returned from where ever she had been in the village. She burst into the room without knocking. Her cheeks were flushed with exercise and rude good health. Her hair was an unruly nest and she had green stains down the front of her donated frock. Whatever trauma and forfeiture the loss of Tall Chimneys had caused her seemed, temporarily at least, forgotten. She pounced on the shortbread. 'Such fun,' she said, through the buttery crumbs, 'Bobby and I have made friends. We've been climbing trees. Later, we're going down to the pool to swim. Is there a swim-suit, in the donations? Oh!' she said, noticing Ratton for the first time, 'hello.'

At her entrance, Ratton had risen to his feet. 'Good morning, young lady,' he said, looking her up and down. 'How you have grown.'

Something about his tone disturbed me. I looked at Awan. She was normally developed for an eleven year old. The slightest possible swell at her chest presaged the breasts which would grow there. Her hips were widening, creating a curve from her waist which would be voluptuous. Her childhood loveliness was already metamorphosing into the beauty which would characterise her adult face. Ratton seemed to appraise these things, even as I did. I didn't like it.

There was no sensible reply to Ratton's comment and Awan made none. Ratton was of no interest to her and she gave him a vague smile before turning to me and asking again, 'Is there, do you know? If not, I can probably borrow one.'

'Donations?' Ratton enquired, before I could answer.

'People have brought things for us,' Awan explained. 'Mostly jumble, really, and what Mummy calls their unwanted chattels - some of it really made us laugh, didn't it, Mummy?'

Indeed it had. We had become almost hysterical the night before, going through the clothing that well-meaning neighbours had thought we might need; men's vests, shrunken woollens, a cardigan with all its buttons snipped off, knickers with no elastic.

'We have been the recipients of our friends' charity,' I explained to Ratton, indicating my hand-me-down skirt and oversized blouse. 'This,' I added, perhaps unwisely, 'is what we have been reduced to.'

'We're destitute,' Awan announced, cheerfully, to put the severity of our predicament quite beyond doubt. 'At the mercy of any villain who decides to take advantage of us.'

These were not words Awan would have come up with on her own and I knew immediately she had overheard them spoken by someone else - probably Patricia - without understanding their import. She could not know, of course, what inference Ratton would take from them or what embarrassment they would cause me.

'Awan!' I said, sharply. But it was too late, the words were out.

Ratton stood up and drew himself to his full height, which was not substantial, but might have seemed so, to her. She paled and turned to me, awareness flooding her mind that she had done or said something very wrong.

'Villain? Take advantage?' Ratton roared. 'Is that what you have told her?' he asked me. 'Is that what you think?'

'No,' I stammered. 'We understand each other well enough, I think, and there's no question of that. I believe she's repeating something heard elsewhere.' I looked hard at Awan, who, from being deathly pale, had now blushed crimson.

'If you're going to live under my *protection*, young lady,' Ratton spat, venomously, 'you will have to watch your tongue.'

'No! *No!*' I cried. I didn't want Awan to find out this way.

But Ratton would not be stopped. 'You will see and hear things which are not to be repeated. You need to learn discretion.'

Awan threw me a puzzled, panicked look. 'What does he mean?' she asked.

'Look at me when I'm speaking to you,' Ratton snarled.

Awan shrank back. No one had ever spoken to her like that.

'Discipline is what you need,' he went on, less angrily, but with equal puissance. 'Boarding school will do you good.'

'What does he mean?' Awan asked again, more urgently this time.

My mouth flapped uselessly. It was the last thing I had wanted, to have to explain things to her like this, with him present. Indeed, I had thought to tell her nothing at all until the deed was done.

'Mummy!' Awan cried, tears erupting from her eyes.

Her tears seemed to satisfy Ratton. He nodded, and got out his handkerchief to wipe his hands, as though he had just completed a dirty but necessary job of work. He took his seat again and smiled, speciously benign.

'Awan,' I said, and reached out for her, but she swerved to avoid my hand.

'Tell me!' she shouted, deathly pale once more. Even her lips were bloodless. I thought she might faint.

'Later,' I croaked, throwing a desperate look at Ratton. 'Later, when we're calmer, and just the two of us together...'

'Nonsense,' Ratton waved an imperious hand. 'It isn't a secret and we're not doing anything to be ashamed of.' He addressed Awan as though speaking to a simpleton. 'Your mother and I are to be married. She will have wealth and luxury and be waited on hand and foot. Nothing shall be denied her. I am very rich, you see, and I want to look after her. She has had a wretched life, so far, don't you think? I am sure you want what's best for her, don't you. And you shall go to boarding school.'

Awan considered his words, wondering which element of his announcement to address first. At last she turned to me and said, haltingly, 'I don't think you've been wretched, have you Mummy?'

'No,' I frowned, 'of course not. But things have changed...' Everything had changed.

'And this...' I could see her struggling with it, trying to get it into some kind of shape in her mind that she could handle. '... this is what you want?'

I nodded. 'It seems to me to be for the best.' I wanted to say, more truthfully, it was the *only* option I had before me, short of the seedy precincts of the Admiral Rodney and the greasy, grey man I had met outside the housing office. Even *this*, I thought, was better than *that*. But then again, I considered, perhaps the two were not so different.

'I see,' Awan said. 'It will be an outside-in?'

I thought my heart would melt. What a clever, brave, sensible girl she was! 'Yes,' I said, 'that's right.'

'An 'outside-in?'' Ratton queried.

'It doesn't matter,' I said. 'Awan and I understand one another.'

There was a long pause. Perhaps Ratton considered objecting to my daughter and I having understandings he was not party to, to being excluded in that way. If so, he decided not to raise the subject at that moment. I was relieved. The atmosphere was balanced on a knife-edge, the air taut around us, incendiary with latent conflict and juxtaposing agendas. One more off-key remark from any party would ignite it.

He rubbed his hands together. 'Excellent, then,' he crowed, falsely up-beat. He got to his feet and took a step towards Awan. Even that, it seemed to me, was risky. He smiled, the rubbery mask of his face seeming unaccustomed to the contortion. The small, yellow teeth revealed between his stretched lips glinted unpleasantly. He raised a hand and placed it on her shoulder, self-consciously avuncular.

Then, like a spark in a gas-filled room, he said, 'What about a kiss, then, for your new daddy?'

Awan was convulsed with utter revulsion at this idea. I saw it take hold of her and shake her in its slimy, abhorrent fingers. 'No!' She tore herself away from him and bolted for the door. 'You can do what you like, Mummy,' she shouted. Her voice, her hands, her whole body was shaking. From looking faint she now looked sick to her stomach. 'But he will never be my daddy! You,' she addressed him directly, now, 'are nothing like my daddy.'

'You know nothing about that perverted individual,' Ratton sneered.

'Stop!' I shouted, throwing myself forward at Ratton. If there had been anything to hand I would have bludgeoned him into silence, but the fire irons had been removed for the summer and I could see nothing else which would serve as a weapon.

'How dare you!' Awan yelled. 'My daddy was a fine, good man. He was loyal and true. He always came back to us, didn't he, Mummy?'

'Yes,' I cried. 'Yes, he did. Go now, Awan, go back and find Bobby and play.' If I couldn't shut Ratton up, I was desperate to get Awan out of the room.

But Ratton just would not let it go. 'Your father is in prison, my girl, for indecent acts.'

'STOP!' I shouted again, putting my hands across Ratton's despicable lips, 'just *shut up* will you?'

He thrust me aside. 'She needs to know the truth, Evelyn. Better to come from us, than from a malicious gossip.'

'My father is *dead*,' Awan said, her voice breaking. 'He isn't in prison.'

'Oh!' Ratton jeered, thrusting his jowls forward, 'you mean John Cressing! *He* isn't your father! Dear me, Evelyn,' he turned to me with a look of bogus shock on his face, 'what tales have you been spinning the poor child?'

'He...?' Awan looked at me, her eyes huge with questions, her mouth agape.

'Awan,' I faltered, wringing my hands, my eyes flooded with misery and self-recrimination. This, a small, prosecuting voice whispered to me, is what you have brought upon yourself.

'Tell me he's wrong!' Awan screamed. 'Tell me! Tell me, Mummy.'

My poor child. I wanted to run to her. I wanted to hide from her. Her whole world had disintegrated into a million fragments and it was my fault. I held my hands out, palms upwards. I was all out of prevarication. 'I can't,' I said.

She wrenched at the door handle and fled.

I threw myself again at Ratton. 'How could you?' I spat, beating my hands on his chest, flailing at him like a mad woman. 'How *could* you?'

He caught my hands to still them. 'Evelyn, Evelyn,' he crooned, 'darling. She'll be all right.' He let go of my hands and tried to put his arms around me. I leapt from him as though electrocuted.

'Don't touch me,' I said, coldly.

His face, from a study of concern and compassion, became bland, utterly devoid of any expression at all. 'Someone had to, and it was better coming from us,' he announced, as though the matter was a detail of business, now effectively dismissed.

'From *us?* From *you*, you mean.' I couldn't let it rest. Then something, I don't know, a light in the depth of his piggy little eye, a quiver at the corner of his plasticine mouth, something reminded me of the fact that underneath the veneer of earnest restraint there lurked the Ratton I had always known. How could I have forgotten? How could I have been fooled? 'You enjoyed that, didn't you?' I said, in a level voice.

'Well,' he turned to the mirror which hung above the fireplace, picked a thread from his lapel, 'it seems sensible to establish a stake in the ground at an early stage,' he said. 'There has always been that skeleton in her cupboard, Evelyn. *I* didn't put it there, *you* did. But now she knows about it, that's all. So, like you, she stands at a fork in the road. She can walk one way, and trust me to lock the door on it forever, or she can walk another, and allow it to dog her steps and put the kybosh on her hopes for the rest of her life. And mark my words, it *will* do.'

'You mean, you'll make sure it does?'

'These things have a habit of getting into the public domain. Being illegitimate is one thing if your father is a member of a bohemian artists' set - all very avant-garde and glamorous, I'm sure, to those who aren't too picky. But to be the bastard of a disgraced queer, (who, by the way, will be buggered senseless every day of his life if he gets a prison sentence), I mean, that kind of stain never washes clean, does it?'

My legs were shaking so much I had to sit down. I collapsed into the chair behind me.

'There now, darling,' Ratton said, seeming to notice my distress for the first time although he must have seen how his words assaulted me, syllable by syllable, as he had spoken them. 'Don't worry. I've told you, I'll look after you - you and the girl. You have nothing to fear.'

His utter callousness astounded me, his calculated extortion was amazing, and yet I was as limp and helpless as a puppet.

He looked at his watch. 'Look at the time!' he declared, 'I must go.'

He crossed the rug, leant over me where I sat and tilted my chin up with his finger. His mouth on mine felt appalling but I did nothing to resist him. When he prompted me I parted my lips and he thrust his tongue inside. It was thick, and too wet. I endured it. His breathing was quick. One hand slipped inside the neck of my blouse and pushed inside my borrowed bra. His fingers found my nipple and he made a guttural sound in the back of his throat. His other hand groped for mine where it gripped the arm of the chair and forced it to his crotch. He was very hard. He lifted his mouth off mine long enough to croak, 'Do it.'

It was easy, and very quick. He was so engorged only the least touch was required. He came with a spasm which shook his whole body and made him cry out so loudly he had to remove his hand from where it clutched at my breast to clap it over his own mouth. At last he slumped against me, over my shoulder, spent and weak. He rested there for a few moments until his breathing became more regular, and then lifted himself off me to straighten his clothes. He smiled down at me, a beatific smile, and said, 'Next time, I will pleasure you. I am not a selfish brute. I understand a woman has her needs too. But today we didn't have the time or privacy we needed, did we?'

I muttered something - I don't know what - and the next thing I heard was the door closing softly behind him.

When I looked at the coffee tray on the table beside me he had left a scattering of coins. I wondered if they were for Patricia, to pay for the coffee, or for me.

I sat on in Patricia's parlour all afternoon. At a distance I could hear the murmur of conversation in the bar and the thump and pump of the beer engines. Presently these melded into the soft clash of glasses being collected and the rush of water. Finally I heard the whinge of the heavy outer door and the solid shot of the bolt being sent home. Then the building fell silent. I knew I ought to move, vacate the little room so that Patricia and her husband could put their feet up, but I felt nailed to the chair, my limbs flaccid and feeble. My future rolled out before me in dreadful detail; Ratton's fist-like grip on my comings and goings, his jealous hand on my arm or in the small of my back, guiding, pushing, controlling. I could see the rubbery sneer of his smile - a thin veil of courtesy masking malevolent intent. I felt the triumphant glint in his watchful eye as though it bored into me even now. What nightly horrors he might visit on me I could only imagine but I expected an onslaught until the years of pent up lustfulness had purged themselves.

And all this I would have to endure. He knew too much about me; my secrets were like knives in his hand which he could use to sanguineous effect, or keep sheathed.

It was much later when I came to myself and realised Awan had not returned. How could I have forgotten about her? She must be terribly distressed, I thought to myself. She will need me.

Without stopping to look at myself in the mirror to so much as tidy my hair, or consider the spectacle I would make in the ill-assorted garments I was wearing, I went through the back door, across the pub's yard and into the village street. It was deserted. At the school, the playground was empty. The shop was closed - so it must have been after five - and Kenneth's workshops behind it all shut up. His vehicle was gone - he must be out on a job. I asked at the farm if anyone had seen Awan but the answer came back in a negative. Then I recalled the plan to go swimming.

The pool was on Clough Farm. The lane to it had never seemed so long or arduous to walk along. Dust rose off it and went into my shoes, which were too big for me. I took them off and went barefoot. Ann was in her yard, sweeping wisps of hay into a heap. Was it only three days ago that we had brought her harvest home?

'Did the children come to swim?' I asked her. 'I've lost Awan.'

'Some children came, but they've long gone home again now. That pool falls into shade early on, you know. It gets too cold.'

'Was Awan with them?'

She shook her head. 'No, I don't think so. Will you come in and have a cup of tea? It's Jethro's day at the market. He won't be home until late.'

'I haven't time,' I almost shouted at her. 'I must find Awan.'

At the top of Clough Farm lane I saw Bobby, riding idly on his bicycle. I hailed him with my hand. 'I've lost Awan,' I told him. 'She's upset - very upset - have you seen her?'

'Not since morning. We climbed trees in the knoll.'

'I know,' I raked my hand through my hair, my mind a whirlwind of thoughts; places she might be, people she might have turned to, dangers she might encounter. 'She said she'd enjoyed it. Could you go there, Bobby, and see if she went back?'

He pedalled off at top speed. Back on the village street a few men were making their way to the Plough and Harrow - it must be opening time. What would that make it? Six? Seven? I had no idea. A chill breeze sprang up. I only had on the thin, second-hand blouse and my skin puckered into goose-bumps. I approached the men. 'Please,' I asked them, desperately, 'have you seen my daughter? She's blonde, with curly hair, about this big?'

They all sucked their teeth and stroked their chins.

'Have you seen her or not?' I barked out. For God's sake, they must know, mustn't they?

'No, missus,' they chorused.

I pushed in front of them into the pub and rushed up to the room we'd been using. It was empty, the curtain flapping at the open window. I checked the parlour. The coffee tray had been removed but there was no sign Awan had been there. I stepped into the bar to speak to Patricia, behind the bar. 'I've lost Awan,' I said. 'She was upset. Ratton told her... but it doesn't matter. I'm worried, Patricia. Where has she gone?'

Patricia lifted the telephone receiver with one hand. 'You lot,' she said, to the gaggle of men who were waiting to be served behind me. 'Get out and look for this child. The beer will be free once she's found but not a drop will I serve until then.'

There were shouts of dismay and grumbled complaints but they turned tail and shuffled back out into the street.

I hammered on the back door of the shop. Mrs Greene opened it quickly, her hands floury. 'I know, I know,' she said, before I could open my mouth. 'Bobby called in on his way. The other two lads are out looking, and Kenneth too. He's gone down to the old house to see if she's there.'

An hour, two, went by. Men searched farm buildings and haylofts. Children toured stubble fields and hollered through thickets, delighted to be allowed up so late. The women stood at their garden gates and discussed the matter, their arms folded, their foreheads creased in a communal frown. Someone set off in a motorcar to drive the road which led to the local town, to see if she was walking there, perhaps to the railways station, although I could think of no earthly reason why she might do such a thing; we hadn't a friend in the world outside these parish boundaries. Colonel Beverage gathered a group with dogs and began to search the moor. Bobby returned from the place he called the knoll to report there was no sign of Awan there. I sent him down to Clough Farm pool - I hadn't, in my panic, actually checked it. I wanted to go everywhere with everyone, but somebody told me to stay put at the pub so that, when Awan turned up, we could be reunited immediately. That little parlour seemed smaller and stuffier than ever. Somehow Ratton's aura remained there, and I found myself staring at the chair where the day's outrage had been enacted as though it represented the sum of all the calamitous parts which had made up the last thirty six hours.

It suddenly came to me that Ratton might have taken Awan. Perhaps he had overtaken her on the road and persuaded her - or even forced her - to get into the car. I had no way of knowing how to contact him, but when the local police constable came in to tell me that he had nothing to report, I mentioned the matter to him and he hurried off to follow it up.

It was almost dark when Bobby threw his bicycle down outside the pub and came in to report Awan was found. 'She's at the gatehouse,' he panted. 'Dad is with her.'

News travelled fast. As I ran down the street to the entrance of the drive, I passed men hurrying for their free beer.

'Thank you. Thank you,' I said to them as they went by.

There was no moon that night. The road across the moor was only the dimmest strip across the black heather and bog on either side of it. Faraway I could see pin-points of light, and hear the whistle which told the searchers there that the quarry had been found. I rushed on, my breathing laboured, tears running down my face. I had forgotten to ask Bobby if Awan was all right - unharmed - I had no idea what I would find at the gatehouse. I still wore no shoes. The sharp stones of the gravel hurt my feet but I forged on. I had to get to Awan. I had to know that she was safe.

The gatehouse stood as it always had - as it does today, as I write these memories down - solid and dependable at the place where the moor meets the trees. At its back the forest whispered and swayed. Over the moor the coarse grasses and tufted moss quivered. But the gatehouse was rock-steady, the grey of its stalwart stones coming from the very earth that anchored it; timeless, faithful, a bastion against the cruelties of life.

I pushed at the door and it swung open. Someone inside stirred. No lamp shone and the interior was impenetrably dim. Even so I could make out the nebulous shape of the old table, the friendly silhouette of the dresser against the wall, the hazy form of the chairs which flanked the fireplace, and Kenneth, standing square and solid between them.

'Evelyn,' he said, quietly. 'She's safe. She's asleep, upstairs.'

'Oh God!' I cried, breaking down. 'Oh! Thank God. Should I go up to her?'

He took my arm and guided me to one of the chairs. 'No,' he said. 'She's sleeping.' He took the chair opposite to mine, and let me cry until my tears were spent.

The room was alive with ghosts; they hovered in the gloom. John, energised by some artistic idea, daubed with paint, his unruly hair falling to his shoulders. I could almost hear the echo of our love-making, that first time, and many times since, and recalled how the building had seemed too small to contain our passion. Awan was there, as a tiny baby - I had sat in this very chair with the mess of her afterbirth still larding my coat - and that other time, when she had gone missing, and the motes falling from above and the twang of some deep and resonant instinctive string had told me that she was above. Through my tear-blurred eyes I could almost see myself, as a child, kneeling on the rag rug before the fire while Mr Weeks filled his pipe and his kindly wife wrote the alphabet in the soot on the hearth.

'This place,' I said, in a low voice, 'seems to be a sort of crucible - all the important things have happened here. When there has been nothing else in my life, there has been this.'

In the gloom, I felt Kenneth nod.

It was interesting, I mused, that although my words had sprung from my foregoing thoughts and could not have made any kind of sense to him, yet, he understood.

'Is Awan safe?' I asked him. 'Was she down at the house?'

'No, she was right here.'

'I should have known. Is she all right?'

'Quite safe,' he said. 'Tired... confused. But I explained things.'

'*Did* you?' I wondered how on earth he had made coherent to her the tangled mess of unwelcome news and revelation she had been subjected to.

He nodded again. 'She understands, now, about her father.'

I sighed. 'How on earth did you explain it?'

The gloom shifted fractionally, and I knew he had shrugged, as though nothing had been easier. 'It's just the same as with Bobby.'

Of course, I thought. Whoever had fathered Bobby, Kenneth would always be his Dad. How had I not seen this parallel? 'And...' I cringed in the dark, 'she told you... everything?'

There was a pause. Perhaps Kenneth was too disgusted with me to discuss it. The notion of him knowing just how low I had fallen - what extremes of desperation I had come to - was unbearable. His disapproval made me feel almost as sick as the thing itself. Oh! I didn't blame him, I was disgusted with myself. And yet, through that mire of self-loathing, I could still make out no alternative. Now that Ratton had both me and Awan in his clutches, I could see no way of placating him other than by becoming his wife.

'*You* tell me,' Kenneth said at last.

'I can't,' I burst out. 'Don't make me. It's too awful, too shameful.'

He gave his head a shake, irritation, I supposed. 'Tell me,' he said again.

And so I did. Out it poured. I told him everything, from the very beginning. How Ratton had pursued and assaulted me when I had been a girl and how John had rescued me. I spoke of John at length; my great love for him and my crippling insecurities also, and how pique and envy had taken me to Giles Percy's room that night. I talked of Monique, of Amelia, of the others I suspected had entertained John's fancy while he had been away and I told him about Cameron Bentley - that great opportunity which had been snatched away. It was easy, speaking in the dark like that, surrounded by the benevolent spirits in that comfortable stronghold, pouring my life story into the endlessly patient and reliable vessel that was Kenneth. He sat in the dark and listened and said 'I see, I see,' from time to time, immobile in the chair across from mine. He remained implacable in the face of my anger and my tears, but nodded, and stretched out the receptacle of his understanding until it encompassed my whole life.

My story brought me at last to the recent months and my struggle since Colin's death. I don't know how many hours had passed. From far away the church clock struck, but I did not count the chimes, and after a while the slightest lifting of the heavy darkness told me that dawn was coming. 'There's no money in the bank,' I said, calm now after the turbulent retellings of the night. 'I visited the housing office but they said they can provide no shelter for us, and Awan might be taken away. I applied for jobs but no one wants me except one man who said he would give me work hostessing in a gentleman's club. Maybe I should have taken him up on his offer? How awful could it have been? But I ran away from him. The truth is I am unfitted for any career; I was born to be a gentlewoman in a time when gentlewomen are obsolete. And now the house has gone!' The truth of this statement impacted me strongly. I think, up until that point, I had been in a sort of denial over it, but saying the words out loud made it irrevocably so. 'I can't even hide there, I can't wall myself up in it because the walls are all rubble,' I moaned. 'I can't even throw myself from the roof!' More tears, but short-lived. My well was dry. 'No,' I went on, sniffing. 'This is where life has brought me. I have nothing at all except myself - here, the sorry scrap you see before you, in borrowed clothes and barefoot - and Ratton stands ready to take me, bare feet and all! My self is all I have to bargain with, to pay over in exchange for anything at all. He'll take it, and in return, he will give us everything.'

In the hoary dawn, Kenneth materialised in the chair opposite mine. His sandy hair was the colour of silver-gilt, his face milk-pale in the surrounding dimness, his hazel eyes shadowed, yet I knew they were riveted to my face. He sat perfectly still, his elbows on his knees, his chin on the steeple of his fingers, and I knew he had sat thus, without moving, for the duration of my story, his eyes fixed on mine even through the darkness.

'Yesterday,' I said, dredging the last malodorous bucket of silt and slime from the cesspool, 'Ratton told Awan that John was not her father - you know this, she has told you - and that the man who *is* her father, Giles Percy, is discredited, in prison. I had hoped by sending her to school at Giles' expense I could keep Awan from Ratton's controlling influence, but he has made it clear that he will save or ruin us both.'

Kenneth sat on, and said nothing. I tried to fathom his response to all I had said. Shock? Surprise? But his body language suggested neither. Indeed it suggested to me that all I had told him he had already known. I concluded that he, like me, could see no escape for me other than as the wife of Sylvester Ratton. The thought strengthened me. If Kenneth, who, all my life, had fixed and made good and directed all his strength and skill to restoring all that was broken for me, if he could see no alternative solution, then there wasn't one.

When he did move it was to fetch water and a towel from the kitchen. He knelt on the rug and bathed my feet, which were crusted with dried blood and dirt. He worked in silence, and by then I was all out of words. All the while the dawn crept in upon us, squeezing past the shutters with insistent beams, sliding itself beneath the door. The silver air warmed to palest rose, the blurred shadow of furniture became solid wood and in the ivy outside the window, a sparrow began to trill. Kenneth went to the window and pulled back the shutter. A sticky mat of cobweb stretched and tore; he wiped it away with his hand. The sun poured into the room illuminating the gathered dust and ancient grime, but banishing all the ghosts.

'Now,' he said, turning to face me. 'Listen to me. Awan can go to this boarding school if she likes. I will take you both and you can look it over. But you won't be marrying Sylvester Ratton.'

'But Kenneth,' I protested. 'How will I live? I haven't a job. I haven't any money. I can't even afford to pay Patricia for the room at the Plough.'

'You can have a job, if you want one,' he said, as though it was the most obvious thing in the world. 'Mother needs help in the shop. She wants to retire. You'd know this, if you'd come to visit.'

I felt as though I'd been slapped. 'I didn't think you wanted me to come,' I said, petulantly. 'I thought I reminded you of Rose too much.'

He rolled his eyes in vexation. 'How could any remembrance of her be too much? And we wanted you to visit, for yourself.'

'I'm sorry,' I stammered.

He waved this away. 'You should sleep now,' he said, motioning upwards with his eyes, indicating I should do so at the gatehouse, and not back at the Plough. 'Then come and see Mother and she'll show you the ropes.'

He began to cross the room, making for the door.

'But Kenneth,' I said, twisting in my chair. 'My situation can't be solved that easily. Haven't you been listening? I have nowhere to live.'

'Everything in good time, Evelyn,' he replied.

I got to my feet. They were painful. Standing on their lacerated soles made me wince. But I couldn't let him go off with the idea he could fix this as easily as if it was a shed door or a leaking pipe. 'You don't understand,' I cried, 'you don't understand at all.'

He stopped in his tracks and swivelled to face me. His face, despite being in the full sun now, was dark with anger. 'Don't understand?' he croaked. 'I understand enough. All *this*...' he swept his hand at arm's length to indicate the room, not the room itself but all it contained, all I had deposited there through the dark watches of the night; my tears and dilemmas and inadequacies, my mistakes and compromises, my failures and bitter recriminations - all that I had poured out. '*All* this, I could have spared you, I *would* have spared you, if I had only been given the chance.'

'The chance?' I was stunned. What did he mean?

He made an impatient movement. 'Time, fate, circumstance, class. They all stood in my way.'

342

'Stood in your...' I echoed, stupidly.

'Yes,' he said. 'Do *you* understand, at last?'

He turned and disappeared through the low door.

'Kenneth?' I shouted. 'Kenneth!' And then, in wonderment, 'you never said.'

I heard the crunch of his feet on the gravel fading to distance, and out of the morning air, as fresh and good as she had been herself, Rose's voice came to me. 'He says plenty, but not with his voice,' she had said. 'You don't know him well enough, or perhaps you're not looking.' I realised she had been right, I had never really looked at Kenneth, only seen him at a distance or from the corner of my eye, tinkering with this, hammering that, digging, pruning, his feet sticking out from underneath a motorcar. He had been at one and the same time a peripheral addendum to my life and the absolute mainstay of it. Always ready to step in but willing, also, to hold back. What had they been telling me, all those years, those skilful hands, those capable arms, that strong back? What message had been written in that diffident, watching brief I had so signally failed to decipher?

All at once I was overcome with tiredness, and almost dragged myself upstairs to where Awan was curled up on the old divan. I snuggled in next to her and she pressed herself to me, and wrapped her arms around my neck, and we held each other like that for many hours.

In the morning, when we descended the stair, someone - Kenneth, I presumed - had been there. The fire was lit and the kettle hung over it, steaming. On the table were a tea pot with tea-leaves, milk, bread rolls and butter and two hard boiled eggs - untold luxury in those ration-straitened times. Placed on the two chairs before the fire were the things from our abandoned bundles: our clothes and bedding, Awan's dolls and trinkets. They had been washed and dried and carefully folded. We fell upon them as though they were old friends thought to be lost but now restored. Putting our own clothes on felt like finding ourselves again.

I MANAGED TO avoid Sylvester Ratton for two weeks. He looked for me, I know, but some village conspiracy kept him away from me. When he called at The Plough Patricia told him I had 'gone to town', or 'had gone to visit a friend.' Other enquiries he made around the place were met with head-scratching bewilderment as though Evelyn Talbot had never been heard of in that parish. Awan and I moved to a less salubrious but much more discreet room at the top of the building where our light at night could not be spied from the road. We came and went through the back door, always on the look-out for the sleek, predatory outline of his motorcar. Meanwhile I worked at Mrs Greene's shop, a place Ratton would never have dreamed of entering. She showed me how to arrange the shelves and deal with the ration books. She initiated me into her very efficient ordering system, explained stock control and bookkeeping. She shook her head over my efforts at baking, though; my scones were declared inedible and my pastry only fit for the pig. 'I'll continue to provide the baked goods,' she declared. 'You concern yourself with the shop.'

It was a bargain I was happy to comply with.

It seemed a sort of dream, the antidote to the nightmare I had been living within for the past weeks. The shop was busy and I was on my feet all day. The boxes of tins and packets were heavy and my back hurt, sometimes, from lifting them. But the parade of folks coming and going, the little snippets of chat, the genuine sympathy I received for my loss was so affirming it compensated for the physical hardships. I felt supported and encouraged and sincerely liked. I felt like part of the community. I felt happy. It was an emotion that had been a stranger to me for so long it took me a while to recognise it. In identifying it, my regret for the confining walls of Tall Chimneys grew less acute. In the evenings Awan and I had our meal with Mrs Greene and the boys. Kenneth was always absent, off on some urgent building job, I was told. It was merry, sitting around the table with Bobby, Brian and Anthony, eating the good fare provided by Mrs Greene. I enjoyed the company. My recollection of our solitary meals at the too-large table in the cavernous old kitchen became less rosy.

I did not know what the future held, where I would live, if my wages could support us. But I had taken the first step, thanks to Kenneth and his mother. It was the narrowest foothold on an almost vertical slope, but it was a beginning and, with the support of my friends, I did not feel that I had to climb alone. The question of Awan's schooling lay in abeyance. We had agreed we would make no decisions, but let the aftershock of the fire and Ratton's inflammatory meddling subside. The Grammar school term could start without Awan. Casterton did not commence lessons for another fortnight.

Of course Ratton found me in the end. He burst into the shop, setting the little bell above it jangling in alarm. He looked flushed, broiled in a three piece suit far too hot for the weather, which remained glorious. A film of sweat beaded his bald head and upper lip. 'Here you are,' he declared, laughing, but his laughter was hard-edged with annoyance. 'Have you been avoiding me? A very coy bride, you are! I wouldn't have expected it, in the circumstances.'

Of course I had always known that this moment would have to be faced, but I had not bargained on doing so unsupported. 'In what circumstances?' I asked, fighting the tremor in my voice, wiping my sweating hands on my apron.

He glanced around the little shop and peered through the door into the rear kitchen. 'Well,' he said, confidentially, shooting the bolt closed across the shop door and stepping up to the counter, 'you're not quite the blushing virgin, are you?'

I felt the blood drain from my face. I gripped the edge of the counter with both hands. 'That's not very chivalrous,' I said.

He smiled, self-deprecatingly. 'I'm not exactly the shining knight, either. We know each other, you and I, don't we? No need to pretend.'

I made no response to this assertion, and presently he went on, 'What are you doing here? Helping out for the day?'

'Mrs Greene will be back any moment,' I stammered. 'She has only stepped out for a minute.'

'She is gossiping with the coven of women at the far end of the street,' he sneered. 'She won't be back for a good while. So! I have the attentions of the pretty lady shop-keeper to myself, which is just how I like it. I am not averse to playing games.' His inference was as revolting and unsavoury as possible, the salacious glint in his eye made me want to retch.

'I am playing at nothing,' I told him, drawing myself up. 'I am working here. Earning a living. To support myself.'

His colour deepened, the flesh of his jowls becoming mottled and purple. 'What?' he hissed. 'What are you trying to do? You will put me to shame! My wife has no need to *work!* Look at your hands!'

I did so. They were indeed dirty as I had been decanting potatoes from a sack into a display basket. 'There is no shame in honest work,' I said.

'Evelyn,' he snapped. 'You must stop this charade immediately, and come away with me. It isn't seemly. I have made all the arrangements for the wedding, as you required. There are clothes to be purchased and decisions to be made about furniture.'

'The furniture from Tall Chimneys?'

He made a dismissive gesture. 'No, of course not. New furniture, for our house. I have made arrangements for you to stay in a suite at The Grand in Leeds. You will marry from there. It is to be at the Registry office, as you wished, although it's a grim enough building. And afterwards, we will go away.'

'What about Awan?' I was prevaricating, hoping against hope that someone would come to my aid.

He made a grimace of irritation and distaste. 'She will be at school by then, *as you required.* I have arranged it all as you wished. You try my patience, Evelyn, you really do. Come now. Come away with me.' He lifted the flap at the end of the counter and stepped through it. He held out his fat, bejewelled hand. 'Come along.'

I took a step backwards. 'I can't leave the shop,' I said, 'and anyway... and in any case...'

'Yes? What?' he barked.

I looked at him, my mouth flapping uselessly. Now that it came to it, I didn't know how I would speak the words. His reaction - emotional breakdown or violent explosion - would be terrible.

While I hesitated, whatever restraint he had been exerting on himself gave way. He lunged towards me. I was pushed against the shelves at the back of the shop. A hook where we hung paper bags gouged into my back. His hands roamed over my breasts and down between my legs, he mouthed my face, his breathing fast and hot. He was everywhere, it was impossible to fend him off. 'Stop, it! Stop!' I cried, writhing to free myself, but the space behind the counter was small and he blocked off escape via the kitchen.

'You try my patience,' he hissed again, pressing himself against me with his shoulder, wrestling the while with the fastenings of his trousers. 'You're a prick-tease, giving me such a little taste when I want it all, I want *you* all.' He caught my hand and forced it down to his groin. 'Feel that?' he grunted, 'this is what you do to me. But I'll bring you to heel, woman. I'll break you like a dog. Now open yourself, before I explode.'

I cried out, nothing articulate, just an anguished sob. My nightmare was back. I was amongst the trees in the darkness. His hand was under my skirt and pushing aside my under-clothes. I reached with my teeth for his ear again but he landed me a swift slap which made my head ring. 'Oh no, lady, you don't get me that way twice,' he snarled. His fingers were pushing. I could feel the scratch of his ring on my soft parts.

'Oh God, no!' I cried out, shrinking away from him. He forced himself between my thighs. But then the back door of the kitchen slammed open, heavy boots took four or five steps across the room and Kenneth burst into the confined space behind the counter. He grabbed Ratton by the scruff of his jacket and hauled him off me. The force of his action was so powerful Ratton was lifted from his feet and sent rolling across the counter top scattering six or seven dozen eggs from the display onto the floor of the shop. His trousers and under-clothes were round his ankles, larded with raw egg and dirt from the floor. He struggled to right himself, to stand up, dragging his trousers back to his waist. Kenneth vaulted over the counter in an easy leap and picked Ratton up bodily, one hand grasping the collar of his shirt, the other the loose waistband of the still-unfastened trousers. Then Ratton was hurtling through the plate glass of the shop window. He arrived on the pavement in a flurry of glass shards and egg shell and exposed privates.

Kenneth stood within the shop, breathing heavily, his hands on his hips. 'Evelyn won't be marrying you,' he stated. 'Leave her alone.'

'Oh! Ratton crowed, staggering to his feet and pulling his trousers up once more. 'The love-sick swain has found his manhood, has he? Have you been ploughing her too? I suppose you know all her dirty little secrets?'

'There's nothing about her I don't know,' Kenneth said, quietly, 'and none of it is dirty.'

The women at the far end of the street, alerted by the sound of breaking glass, were hurrying to see what was happening. A few had rallied their husbands along the way. Bobby, who, I guessed, had gone to fetch Kenneth as soon as he had seen the black car parked on the road, was standing across from the shop with the other teenaged boys of his gang and Awan. He had his arm around her shoulders. I gave her an encouraging smile, through the shattered shop window and decimated window display.

'Well,' blustered Ratton, seeing he was out-numbered. 'She'll be sorry, that's all I can say.'

'She will not,' Kenneth replied.

Ratton took in the approaching crowd of villagers, the gaggle of youngsters on the far side of the street. He looked past Kenneth at me. His eyes bored into mine. His expression was pure malice and wounded pride, his voice bitter with recrimination. 'Your precious house is empty,' he crowed in a voice calculated to carry to everyone in the vicinity, 'every stick of furniture has been sold. Everything I could salvage has gone, sold to the highest bidder. That includes the pitiful daubings of the man you called your husband although,' he raised his voice still further to ensure the crowd on the street could hear him clearly, and even turned to them to include them in his tirade, 'the world and his wife knows you were only his whore. Tall Chimneys will be a derelict hull until hell freezes over. How the mighty are fallen!'

Kenneth stepped coolly through the gaping window frame and took Ratton's arm roughly. He began to frog-march him towards his car.

But Ratton had not had his pound of flesh. 'Oh! I forgot to mention,' he cried, theatrically, over his shoulder. 'The gatehouse is sold. That precious place of your deflowering - Colonel Beverage has bought it for his deranged sister in law. Little did these good people here know it was your couch of vice and depravity! Well, it will house a lunatic now - how do you like that?'

I flinched in the shadowed recess of the shop. The gathered crowd gaped at his words. Kenneth bundled Ratton unceremoniously into his car and leaned in through the window to say something I could not hear. Then the engine started. But still Ratton was not done with me. As he drove past the shop he wound his window down to shout, 'And as for Giles Percy, your bastard's father, I'll see he is convicted of every unnatural and bestial act, and everyone shall know who his daughter is.' He waited to watch the effect of his words, a thin smile on his lips.

'This was your plan from the beginning.' I croaked, whitely.

He could not have heard my words but he inferred my thought. 'Yes, it was always my intention,' he bragged. 'You would have sold your soul for nothing.'

Then his car roared away up the street. My legs gave way and I sank to the ground. But my spirit did not fail me. 'I have not sold my soul,' I whispered to myself, 'I have saved it.'

'Yes,' Kenneth said, helping me to my feet, 'you have.'

August turned in to September. I was busy in the shop and in the evenings Awan and I sat in our attic room at the Plough together. We read books or sewed, and were content. The weather remained clement, warm days and nights with a thrilling chill of autumn. We kept our window open. The breeze from across the moor was fresh and clean, and made us realise how stagnant and confined the precincts of Tall Chimneys had been. We did not go there, it held nothing for us. What devastation the fire and then the roof collapse might have wreaked was beyond my imagination. The wanton destruction Ratton's men might have caused salvaging the furniture and chattels could only have made a bad thing worse. I mourned the gatehouse, but wished Colonel Beverage's sister-in-law happiness in it; it was indeed a peaceful tower, a refuge for a woman battling demons if ever there was one.

Awan and I visited Casterton School and met with Enid Makepiece, the headmistress. She was a thin, upright person, her hair scraped unbecomingly into a small bun at the back of her neck, her clothes dour, but she engaged Awan in eager conversation, probing her gently to assess her level of competence, favourite books and particular enthusiasms. The girls at the school all seemed happy, the facilities good. It was situated in a small hamlet not unlike our own village, hard against the soft hills of the Yorkshire Dales. In the afternoon we walked to Ingleton falls, and Kenneth and Awan and I took off our shoes and stockings and paddled in the icy, gem-strewn water. The action awakened memory for both Kenneth and me. We exchanged a knowing glance across the tufted grass.

'I think I'd like to try it,' Awan said, on the journey home, 'only, I'd be worried about you, Mummy. Won't you be lonely?'

'I will miss you,' I said, 'but I won't be lonely. I'll have Ann for company.' Ann Widderington's two sons had been offered council accommodation for their wives and families. She had offered me the rooms above the lambing shed where, in the war, the Land Army girls had lived.

Kenneth gave an odd cough, and said, 'Give it a try, lass, if you like. If you don't like it, you can come home.'

The following week Kenneth came back early, just as I was shutting up the shop and pulling the blind down on the newly puttied window. 'Come for a walk with me,' he said.

We walked without speaking along the village street, past the neat cottage gardens and the tidy yard of the farm. We came to the church and the gate into the graveyard.

'Shall we visit Rose and John?' I asked him, putting my hand on the catch.

'Not today,' he said, and motioned that we should continue. We passed the grey school and the playground. The Rectory looked deserted. 'I wonder when Mrs Beverage's sister will come,' I mused.

'I have been making the gatehouse ready for its new occupant,' Kenneth offered.

'Have you? Are there to be bars at the windows?'

He shook his head. 'The new tenant has been imprisoned long enough,' he said.

'Does she come from an asylum, then?' I asked, genuinely curious, but Kenneth just smiled.

We came to the entrance to the lane which led to the gatehouse, that ribbon of road across the narrow neck of moor. I hesitated. 'I'm not sure I want to go that way,' I said. 'Why don't we go down to Clough Farm?' Its gateway stood almost opposite. 'We can survey the old Land Army girls' quarters,' I said. 'I might need you to do some repairs.'

'Come this way,' Kenneth said, motioning towards the gatehouse. 'It will be all right.'

'I suppose you want me to confront my ghosts,' I remarked, following him along the rough track.

'No,' he said, and took my hand. It was an act both unprecedented and extraordinarily natural. His hand was firm and cool and surprisingly soft, considering the nature of his work. Mine, within it, felt small but very comfortable. We walked on together, along the road to Tall Chimneys, not speaking. We looked at the myriad colours of the moor, the soft olive of moss, the golden glory of bracken and the dusky purple heather. Tufted spikes of moorland grass fringed black bog, and granite cairns were peppered yellow with lichen. The sky above us was palest blue, empty of cloud. A curlew keened over towards the abandoned airfield, and the belt of trees stood guard around the corpse of the old house.

We approached the gatehouse. The boards had been removed from the upper windows and the crazed leading had been renewed. The windows were clean and clear of inveigling ivy, which had been clipped back neatly. Asters grew in pots along the path which led to the door. The old lean-to had been demolished. A two storey extension had taken its place. The tangled garden had been cleared; there was a hen house, a couple of raised vegetable beds, a greenhouse. I was vaguely envious, but it did no good to wish for what could not be.

We admired the garden for a while and then Kenneth took out a key and unlocked a brand new door. He opened it and ushered me inside. The new addition housed a small but well-fitted kitchen. There were herbs in pots on the window; scoured saucepans hung from hooks in the ceiling. The living room had been cleaned and painted; it was fresh and bright. The Weeks' old furniture remained, polished to a high shine. Blue Willow crockery stood upon the dresser. There were flowers in a vase on the window ledge, new curtains. The old chairs had been reupholstered and set before the fire. The fire was laid with kindling and coal; matches stood ready to light it. The ghosts I had felt on the night Kenneth had found Awan seemed banished; I could feel no presence except our own - Kenneth's and mine. All that had been between us from our childhood and since, and whatever was burgeoning now that at last I understood, filled the space to overflowing. It was wholesome and benign and yet strangely stirring - more than sufficient for that small room.

'Look upstairs,' Kenneth said. 'See what you think.'

In the upper room the divan was made up with fresh sheets, the floor sanded, the walls papered. The westerly sun streamed in through the open window bringing the scents of the moor and the sound of birdsong.

It was perfect, just perfect, I thought, and envied the woman who would live there.

But then other details caught my eye. The paintings John had made of me after the death of Cameron Bentley had been framed and put up. My own belongings began to make themselves evident; my clothes hung on a rail in one corner, my quilt was folded at the foot of the bed. Those were my books on the shelf. I stepped into the newly formed room above the kitchen, a tiny bathroom where my toiletries had been placed, and a bale of new towels.

All the while Kenneth waited in the middle of the downstairs room. As wondrous as the gatehouse in its new colours was to me, it was he who formed the focus of my thoughts. Each delightful new discovery simply increased the intensity of my sense of the man waiting, patiently waiting, in the room downstairs. I had a vivid recollection of those times - years before - when John had stood where I now paused, and tried to see what was before him but found his mind inexorably drawn to a figure in the room below.

Slowly, I descended the stair. Kenneth remained still and implacable on the new rug, and said nothing, and, in doing so, as he always did, said everything there was to be said.

'This,' I said wonderingly, 'is not for Mrs Beverage's sister, is it?'

'No,' he said. 'It is for you. It is yours.'

I frowned and shook my head a little. 'How..?'

Kenneth gave a sly grin. 'Colonel Beverage has no sister in law, deranged or otherwise. He acted for me. Ratton wouldn't have sold the place to me.'

I looked at him lost for words. He wore his working trousers and old boots. His shirt cuffs were turned back, his hands hung loosely by his side. His hair flopped, as it always had done, over his forehead. He returned my gaze, steadily. He was not, I realised, shy at all. He was not awkward or tongue-tied or taciturn. He was just contained, at peace with himself. He was sure of things and he didn't need words to explain or justify them to anyone.

Of the two of us it was me, in fact, who struggled to speak. 'And what…' I began. 'I mean, how…?'

'Just as you like,' he replied, easily. 'You will live here, and work at the shop. You will be free, and safe and independent.'

'And you…?' I ventured.

He put his head on one side. 'I will not be far away,' he said.

'And if I…?'

'Yes,' he said, and took the step or two which closed the gap between us, such a small gap, in the end, it proved to be. 'Yes. If you want, we will.'

He put his arms out and held them there until I stepped into them. Then he cradled my head onto his shoulder. It felt comfortable and familiar and entirely natural to stand thus, saying nothing, saying everything; a whole volume in the quietness.

Down in the crater, Tall Chimneys would be in gloom and shadow, the trees blocking out the last rays of September sun. But at the gatehouse, it was light, still. The old stones of the building were warm and mellow and birds still busied in the trees. The soft wind came across the moor and made the ivy quiver with pleasure.

Epilogue - 2010

Sometimes, when Grandma Wyman had drunk too many Martinis, she got to talking about the old house. She'd lived in the new ranch-house for thirty years, and in the old one for twenty years before that, but, to her, the house in Yorkshire where she'd spent her childhood was 'home'. Grandpapa Wyman was a Texan to his bone, with a big hat and a Texan swagger and a well-head of oil spouting from his acres of Texan prairie. But Grandma called herself a Yorkshire-woman until the day she died. She said Yorkshire was 'God's own County', something that never sat easy with Texans, who think God, like them, has no interest in anything beyond the pan-handle.[20]

I was the only one of her grandchildren who would stay behind to listen to her talk - the other boys would likely be off at the stables or down at the swimming hole - but I was always different from them. I liked the way she talked; her voice thin and clipped, the words bitten neatly off one by one, instead of chewed, like tobacco. To my childish mind she was a mix of the British Queen and Mary Poppins; all-knowing, poised, kind in a cool, detached kind of way, but at the same time pretty frightening. She was at all times beautifully and classically dressed, like Audrey Hepburn or Bette Davis, her hair and make-up immaculate always. She'd sit in the shaded parlour of the house, the air conditioning keeping her as cool as a corpse, the shades pulled down to keep the sun off her English-rose skin. Her chair was hard and upright - she abhorred the fashion for low, slouching lounge furniture. She'd drink tea from a translucent china cup at three in the afternoon and at five a Martini. She would mix it herself from a tray on a side-table. She did these things habitually - almost ritualistically, as though they constituted cornerstones of a civilisation which would crumble away if they were ever neglected. Sometimes she would have a second Martini, and then, when the glass was empty and she had offered me the olive, she'd begin.

She'd speak of the old house, hidden in a dip in a broad-stretched moor. It was surrounded by trees, with towering chimneys reaching above and damp, scary cellars below. It was built in 1600, before the Mayflower set sail, before Jamestown was even thought of. In my imagination the house was like a sunken ship, its chimneys like masts, its cellars like rotten timbers. The woodlands around it were the frondulant depths of a deep-sea crevasse, the moor above the green, endless sea. And Grandma, in the cool shadows of the room, the pearl-white sheen of her afternoon dress

---

[20] The northerly boundary of Texas, which is shaped (roughly) like the handle of a saucepan.

and her nails painted pink like sea-shells, seemed to me like an ancient sea-goddess. I sailed away on her words, and lost myself in their mystery.

She spoke of our great-aunt, Evelyn, a crazed and reclusive individual who haunted the derelict rooms of the old house and bemoaned her incarceration. 'She's like the man in that song your father likes so much,' she once told me, 'she can check out any time she likes, but she can never leave.'

'Is she a ghost?' I'd ask, in awe.

'She may as well be,' Grandma said, 'and she may as well be dead, for all I know, but she wouldn't realise it either way. As long as the house stands, she'll stay in it.'

Grandma died in 1993, when I was 17. I wanted to go to Art College but the family asserted itself and I followed my father into Grandpapa's oil business after I graduated MIT, and married Tammy, also at the family's behest, in 2006. We began raising a family. My daddy died last year, 2009. It hit me hard; we were close. I've run the company in his stead since then but it has been a struggle. With Daddy gone I have felt as though I don't belong, as though I have been wearing clothes made for someone else. My marriage to Tammy isn't happy, and my children seem like strangers to me. If I wasn't an oil man, a big shot in the county and a Wyman, I might confess to having depression, but Texan oil men don't allow themselves to be afflicted that way.

In April I had a heart-scare and my doctor said I should take a trip, to rest and recover. I knew straight off where I'd go - the old country, the old house. Driving back from the doctor's clinic in downtown Dallas the idea lifted me like a buoy so that by the time I got to the ranch I was fizzing with it.

'A trip,' I enthused to Tammy, 'to find my roots. To find out about - you know...'

But Tammy looked at me - a cold, flat stare. 'I don't care to go to England,' she said. The look in her eyes told me she didn't care, period.

So here I am, groggy from the red-eye, in a rental car, driving north.

It is May, and this is England and, in contradiction of all I have been told, the sun is out.

It takes me a while to find the village. It has been by-passed by a new road and I skim past the turning in cruise control before I know it. It's a few miles before I can double back but the scenery is good; rolling hills either side of the road, intensely green like the prairies at home are only seldom, after heavy rain, and a stretch of moor in the distance. The moor is exactly what Grandma described and, in spite of my tired eyes, I know I am close. I run my hand over my face, feeling the stubble of my unshaven chin, picking the sleep from my eyes. I bought coffee at a rest stop a few miles back. It is cold, now, but I drink it anyway. I know I am close.

The village street is deserted, narrow, as all British streets are, buildings on one side and the moor on the other. I park the car on the street and walk past an old grey church with an overgrown churchyard, then a single-storey building with a clock tower. I gather from the engraved founding stone it used to be a school but it's been made into a dwelling, now, and a dog in the yard tells me to stay away. There's a row of cottages with tiny yards out front, and a place which used to be a farm but where the barn and stables and what I suppose must have been a milking shed have all been converted into vacation rentals. I wander round the cobbled yard, hoping somebody will show up so I can make enquiries, but there's no sign of anyone. A tiny shop and a pub are both firmly closed. They look as though they have seen better days - the by-pass must have taken away all the passing traffic. At the end of the village is a shack of a place with a corrugated iron roof and a rotten door. A notice board displays the minutes of the latest parish council meeting and a poster for a thrift sale from two months back. At the side of this building - I take it to be a community meeting room of some description - is an open lot where a solitary woman walks an ancient sheep dog. I wade through the knee-high grass towards her.

'Good afternoon, ma'am,' I say, in my best Texan English, 'I'm looking for Tall Chimneys.'

Whatever she says back to me is unintelligible in terms of the words she speaks, but she gesticulates back down the village street and then indicates a turning to the left.

'Opposite the church?' I clarify.

She nods.

The turning I find is little more than a track, hardly wide enough for a vehicle, pitted with pot-holes and surfaced with dusty grey gravel. The moor sweeps out on both sides of it; iridescent green and sage-grey with boggy pockets as black as liquorish and pools of water. They reflect the sky like mirrors. The heather is not in flower but the spent seed-heads rattle and whisper around craggy boulders as though they are excited to see me, and somewhere there is running water, but I can't see where. The textures intrigue me; soft mosses and spiky grass, spongey-crumbly peat and a shimmering haze of insects and pollen and I don't know what else hovering above like a shimmering veil, and I grope in my knap-sack for a sketchbook and pencil.

For a while I am lost in my drawing. I hear the water and bees and above my head some bird singing like its heart will burst and for some reason I can't fathom it all has to come out on the paper before I can move another step.

Then I walk along the track in a kind of a dream, like someone walking into their own history.

Ahead of me there is a belt of woodland, and a red-stone house, hexagonal, with self-important stone-work above and windows crazed with leading and a wisp of smoke rising from a stubby chimney and they wind me in like I am a fish on a line. This is what Grandma called the gatehouse. I am amazed it is still standing, still more that it is inhabited.

To the left of the house is a pair of gates, once-imposing but now rusted and derelict and infested with creeper. The stone post securing one of them has collapsed altogether, allowing the gate on that side to teeter inwards, prevented from falling only by the stout chain anchoring it to its brother. He is also badly askew, having parted company from his hinge. It will be easy to get through them. Beyond, there is a tunnel of dimness, green and frondulant, and I am reminded of my childish image of Grandma, the sea-queen.

At the other side of the house is a yard - a garden, it is called here - small and fairly neat; it stretches back a-ways into the plantation like an inlet at the shore. There are some vegetable beds and many terracotta pots with fading tulips and other flowers I can't name, and a line looped between two trees where a flowered apron and a dish-towel and a gingham table cloth are drying in the breeze. To the rear of the house is a two storey addition, where a door stands open. I lean on the stone wall and take all this in - the solid presence of the house, the eeriness of the moor, the over-arching sky, the domestic detail of laundry and fading flowers - and have such a strong sense of destiny and serendipity that when Grandma says 'Is that you, John?' I am not at all surprised.

She is sitting on a wooden bench I hadn't noticed, hard against the warm stone of the house, where the jut of one of the hexagonal faces of the façade shields her from the little breeze skimming across the moor. She is nothing at all like the cool, elegant woman I remember and yet she is indisputably the same. She is shrunken, bowed down by age, her face much lined and her hair silver which, in the past, was always golden brown, but her eyes are the same intelligent points of light and her brows have the same arch. Her voice is the same - English, musical - but carked, croaky with age. She is shabbily dressed, as she never was in the past, in clothes so faded it is impossible to say their original colour or pattern. Her dress is gathered in at the waist with a knotted cord, her stockings sag around her ankles, her buttoned sweater slips from her narrow shoulders and her shoes are somewhat broken and shabby. Yet even in this sorry state she still has elegance and poise. She is somebody, and she knows it. She has half-risen from her seat, one thin arm is stretched out towards me. The skin of its hand is freckled by age-spots and trembles a little, perhaps with a kind of palsy, perhaps with excitement.

'John?' she says again, half wonderingly, and with an undertow of deep emotion which really moves me - I had not expected her to be so pleased to see me even though I have always known I was her favourite grandchild.

Then, in a flurry, I know of course this cannot be Grandma. She has been dead for fifteen years or more and I saw her buried in the family plot on the hill behind the house. As impossible as it is, this must be Evelyn, her sister, my crazy great-aunt, and she has mistaken me for someone else.

'I'm John Wyman Jr,' I say, removing my hat and smiling. The wind ruffles my dark hair. In hindsight, I wish I had had cut before my trip. I run my hand through it in an attempt to tame it and then hold it out for a hand-shake. 'I'm...' I am about to tell her I am Amelia's grandson but some alteration in her face, a shadow of what I make out as disappointment, tells me she has already seen her mistake.

'You're Amelia's boy,' she says, quietly.

'My daddy was her son,' I clarify. I am still smiling. I still have my hand extended over the low copestones of her garden wall. She, though, has dropped the hand she had held out to me.

She nods several times, and I see the loose skin of her throat working, as though she is swallowing a bitter pill. 'He must have been born in - what? July? August 1945?'

'Yes ma'am,' I say, 'July 20th. He passed away, I'm sorry to tell you, last year.'

She sits back down on the bench behind her. 'She was expecting him, when she left, then,' she says, almost to herself. She clasps her hands on her lap, a gesture I have seen Grandma make a thousand times, and lets out a heavy sigh. She isn't telling me anything I don't know. It is no secret my father had no Wyman blood in his veins; he was born before Grandma and Grandpapa got married. But Grandpapa raised him as his own and gave him the family name. If my father had wondered about his paternity, he had never done so aloud.

I wonder about it, though. It is one of the things on my bucket-list, a question I feel I need to have answered. 'Do you know who my grandfather was, ma'am?' I ask. I put my hand on the latch of the wonky little wooden gate to access the yard. 'Can I come in? And will you tell me about him?'

'Yes, yes,' she says. 'You had better come in.'

She leads me inside the little house. It is dark, after the brightness of the day, and it takes my eyes a while to adjust, but she goes to the fire and pulls a blackened kettle over the glowing coals and reaches cups from an old dresser as though using some ancient sixth sense born of long habitude and familiarity. When my eyes get used to the gloom, I make out a gaggle of other furniture, pots of herbs, surfaces crowded with nick-nacks and ornaments. A skein of knitting spills out of a bag besides a threadbare chair on a balding hearth rug. A faded quilt is draped over the back of the chair and I guess some nights she sleeps in the chair by the fire instead of going upstairs. On the dresser there are packets of seeds, a ball of knitting wool, a vase filled with silverware and an old brass oil lamp. In the corner is a perilous-looking staircase leading aloft but the treads are occupied by many stacks of books and other paraphernalia. Many more books are crammed along the window ledges and there is a tower of newspapers on the floor by the hearth reaching to the height of my waist. Garden hand-tools hang from nails near the door along with a faded print dress on a wire hanger. There are saucepans on the hearth and a basket under the table containing vegetables and also a pair of shoes. On the mantel a large clock ticks, but it shows the wrong time. To me it all looks like something in the Williamsburg Living History Museum - a collection of old fashioned artefacts gathered together to show what life was like long ago, but I know this is the real deal. This is how she really lives; her whole life is here. The room tells me of a life shrunken down to this small cell of existence. I can see no sign of modern living; no television, no refrigerator, no microwave, certainly no computer or tablet. I can't even see a telephone. We passed through a kind of kitchen on our way to this room but I saw nothing in it that would not have been there fifty years ago and I feel outrage on her behalf. Where is her family? Why has she been left to moulder here? The place is a mess. Perhaps she just hasn't gotten round to cleaning, or maybe she is too old to do it. Either way, it doesn't seem right to me.

'You live here alone?' I ask.

'I do now. I have done for...' she cocks her head to one side, considering, 'thirty years.'

'How do you manage? I mean, forgive me, ma'am, but do you have help?' I try to estimate her age. I recollect she is Grandma's younger sister, but she can't be much less than a hundred years old. Surely, she ought to be in a care home?

'I don't need help,' she says, quite sharply, 'and don't call me 'ma'am'. I'm Evelyn.'

'Sure, Evelyn,' I reply, quickly, feeling reprimanded.

'I can make coffee, if you like,' she says, in a softer tone. 'An American man showed me how to do it.'

'I like English tea,' I tell her. 'Grandma used to make it for me.'

She busies herself with the tea things, moving slowly but deliberately. Considering her age, I think she is doing pretty well.

'So, you're John's grandson,' she says, presently. 'Tell me, do you paint?'

A spark ignites inside me, a quickened flame. Art is what lights me up. 'Yes, Evelyn, I surely do.'

We sit in the cramped, grimy little room and drink our tea, and she tells me about my grandfather. An artist! How could he not have been? I get out my 'phone to Google him, but she waves at it impatiently.

'It won't work here,' she says.

She is right, there is no signal, and I feel again as though I have stepped over some invisible boundary into the past.

We spend the afternoon here, Evelyn and I, locked into a time long passed and yet, to us both, there, in that little bower of memory, vividly present. She takes up her knitting as she speaks, and the click of her needles punctuates her story, and the spool of yarn gets smaller and smaller as the garment - whatever it is, an afghan, perhaps - grows on the bony platform of her lap. At some point she makes more tea, and smears butter on bread, and we eat it without tasting it, and the light outside, filtered already by the smeary windows and the lattice of leading, fades into afternoon and then evening.

When I eventually leave the gatehouse low cloud has drawn itself like a shroud over the moor, and rain is beginning to darken her washing. She gathers it in and holds it to her body.

'You used to be able to stay at the Plough, in the village,' she tells me, 'but not these days.'

'I'll find somewhere,' I say. I must sleep. My eyes are gritty and I am starving, the tea and bread and butter going nowhere towards satisfying my appetite. Yet I do not want to leave her. I am gripped by the silly idea that if I go away I won't be able to find the place again, or it will be a shell, a pile of rubble, and my aunt Evelyn long dead and buried in the churchyard, and all of this day will have been some enchantment I cannot get back.

'I don't want to go,' I blurt out. 'I feel, at long last, from what you've told me, I know who I am, and if I drive away, I might lose myself again.'

She nods, undisturbed by my outburst. 'Don't worry,' she says, and it is with more resignation than reassurance, 'I'll be here.' She cocks her head backwards, to indicate, down in the glen behind her, through the woods, somewhere in a hidden hollow of history, the old house. 'It won't let me go,' she adds, cryptically.

'I want to know all about it.' I tell her. 'I want to see it. Can I? Tomorrow?'

'Yes,' she says. 'You can go down there, and see what's left of it. And I'll tell you what I remember. I wrote everything down, years ago - let me see, in 1955, it would have been.'

'I'd love to read what you wrote.'

'You will do,' she nods.

She looks up at me, the affection in her eyes tempered by a sad longing. 'You look so like him,' she murmurs. 'When I saw you there, I thought, *at last.*'

'You're waiting - for him?' I venture. My voice, like hers, is quiet. The buffeting of the wind across the moor and in the branches of the trees behind the gatehouse is louder. The spatter of the rain on the flagstone path is louder. My sense of her history, of her suffering, of her fortitude is louder than our low voices as we speak solemn truths.

She sighs and I detect such weariness in her. 'For *one* of them,' she says, almost to herself. 'Surely *one* of them will come back for me?'

 **I FIND A** motel on the outskirts of the nearby town and dial in pizza before taking a long hot shower. I Skype Tammy but she doesn't pick up. She must be out - I have no idea of what time it is at home - or, more likely, she chooses not to answer. I text the kids because I promised I would even though they didn't seem to care either way, and then I sleep, dreamlessly and deeply, until morning.

I shower again and check my cell - no reply to my text messages. Well, what did I expect?

The motel offers no breakfast but I am directed by the clerk to a café in town which serves 'A Full English.' Afterwards I buy rolls from a bakery and flowers and fruit from a fresh produce store, and cheese from a deli, fumbling with the unfamiliar coinage. I get back in my car and retrace my route to the gatehouse, parking at the end of the track and almost running until I can be sure it is intact, and my aunt Evelyn is there.

It looks as though she has been looking forward to my visit; the table has been cleared of some of its clutter, the saucepans have gone from the hearth and the shoes from the vegetable box. Evelyn wears the same clothes as yesterday, though and I can see no sign that she has prepared or eaten food in my absence.

I present the things I have bought.

'What are these for?' she asks. 'Haven't you had breakfast?'

I make an evasive reply. 'Have *you*?'

She waves her hand in a gesture, telling me food is of no importance to her. I place my hand on the teapot - it is only just warm. 'Why don't we have a fresh pot,' I suggest, 'and some bread and cheese.'

She gives me a shrewd look. My scheme has not fooled her for a moment. 'If you like,' she says. 'In any case, I can make you a flask and some sandwiches to have later. You're going to need them, I think.'

On the table are a number of sketch books and propped on chairs ranged against the wall are three small oil paintings, studies of a woman painted from oblique angles. 'Those are for you,' Evelyn says. 'They were to have been...' she breaks off, '...but she has no need of them.'

I approach the paintings. 'Are they...?' I begin, 'I mean...' I indicate the woman in the pictures. 'Is this you?'

'Ah!' she replies, 'well, that's a question, isn't it?'

Her remark makes me shy of examining the paintings in detail and I turn instead to leaf through one of the sketch books. There are many pictures of a baby done in soft pencil; the creases at the wrist, the downy hair, a cherubic mouth all tenderly rendered. I recognise the style as well as the fascination; I have similar sketches at home of my own children as infants. Who was this baby, I wonder, and did she, like mine, grow into a stranger?

I flick the pages. The rest of the book is filled with studies of a building I presume to be Tall Chimneys, especially the chimneys themselves - decorative brickwork, fretted stone, a black bird poised for flight from the topmost pinnacle. I see details of mullions, a cornerstone mapped with intricate tracings of lichen, thickly leaded windows reflecting scudding clouds and crowding trees. Other sketches show the whole house - majestic with a gothic, darkly romantic dignity, rendered in grey and sepia tones, standing against a tangled forest of ancient trees. They make my heart sing - they show exactly what I have imagined; impressive age, rich antiquity, tradition, romance - a treasure-trove of history we Americans envy to our hearts' core.

I look up from the sketches and my heart is too full to speak. Evelyn is looking at me over the rim of her teacup. 'You see it,' she says, quietly. 'And when you see the house, you'll feel it, too.'

A second sketch book seems to me to contain later works. The style is less precise; colour is used to more dramatic effect. There are a dozen watercolour studies of the moor, done when the heather was in bloom; sweeps of violet muting to lilac and brightening to pink, spikes of green, a brooding lavender-grey of cloud overhead melding with the heathered horizon so seamlessly it is impossible to tell where one ends and the other begins. One catching my attention in particular shows a dark circle of black bog fringed by spiny foliage, the sky above reflected in oily, iridescent water. It seems like my grandfather's skies are often heavy with cloud during this period of his work, the cloud laden and low over the moor. I recognise the bleakness, the discontent, the frustration which has no specific source and yet is palpable and real. I have felt it in myself since Daddy died.

The edges of each picture are smudged and indistinct, as though there was something else my grandfather had wanted to capture but couldn't quite. Or because things have no finite end or beginning; life is not framed and separate, it is joined, it is whole, all a piece with the past and the future in the same way that the east is connected to the west and the sea to the sky to the land. I look up at my aunt as this thought comes to me and she meets my eye. As I am connected to her, I think to myself, and always have been, across the ocean and the continents, along all the years, not only through my grandma but also through a man who has been utterly outside the picture and yet there, an indelible part of it, all the same.

After our bread and cheese she sends me through the knock-kneed gates and down the drive. 'You won't come with me?' I ask her. She remains outside the rusted, creeper-choked metal-work, standing in a patch of sunshine, while I, already, have been swallowed by the gloom of the tree-lined tunnel. She seems small and impossibly frail, her hair blowing in wisps, revealing the pink of her scalp, the hem of her dress flapping against her thin legs.

Her voice, when she speaks, is like the murmur of the wind through branches, the whisper of seed heads. 'I don't need to,' she says, and lifts her hand to a place between her breast and her neck. 'It's here.' I cannot tell, from her gesture, if she means it is in her heart or at her throat. I turn from her, once again fighting the hunch that when I return she will be gone, a figment of a fevered dream. But the forest is real, the path before my feet is solid if badly pitted and, at its end, Tall Chimneys waits.

The day above is bright with sun and a brisk breeze blows, but here, beneath the trees, a preternatural dimness and stillness prevails. Trees crowd to left and right, brambles have sent arching canes like barbed wire across the path; they catch at my clothes and my backpack with spiteful thorns. Nettles have invaded what must once have been a broad, smooth carriageway and I have to walk through them with my hands above my head to keep from being stung. I am glad, now, that Evelyn isn't with me - I'm not sure she could have managed this hike. At times it is hard to see the way at all. Boulders and screes of clay have slid down from above and there are crevasses where runnels of water have gouged their way into the path. Branches and whole fallen trees often block the route. The forest is reclaiming the drive.

The way switchbacks left and right down the slope of the valley, falling sheer from its crumbling sides into a drop thick with vegetation and sharp rock. What might have caused this crater, I wonder. Is it a prehistoric quarry, hewn by iron-age men eons ago? Or older still, the landing point of a meteor? And why on earth would anyone build down here? I pick my way carefully, scrambling over roots, pushing through rampant scrub, stopping often to listen. The wood creaks like arthritic joints, branches above slash and crash. I hear birds - but they seem distant - and water, and the gentle, inexorable creep of undergrowth. The light becomes greener and more murky the further I descend. Images of lost worlds and prehistoric creatures flicker across my thoughts - who do I think I am? Indiana Jones? And yet something - a hum, a resonance - comes to me from deep within the basin. It is in tune with my own acute anticipation and what even I - ornery oil-man that I am - recognise as destiny. It is what has brought me to England, after all, a search for the place of my grandmother's birth, a search for my own roots. I have come to 'find myself' as the modern parlance has it, although, until very recently, I had not known I was lost. Some of the things Evelyn has said to me in our brief acquaintance have resonated with me, too. 'You see it,' she said, 'and when you see the house, you'll feel it too.' And I think I do feel it, a sense of natural belonging, like a pearl in an oyster, a baby in a womb. In spite of the wild, jungle-like setting and the weird, other-worldly sounds of the woodland I have a profound sense of being home.

Then, the path levels out, the forest falls back and I am there.

The place where I am standing is where he - my grandfather - must have stood to make his pictures. I have seen the angle, the light and shadow, the perspective of what lies before me already today, in his sketch book. But it is as though some hooligan hand has vandalised his vision. The house has been decimated, it is a ruined shadow of its former self and I cry out as the horror of it hits me, as my romantic dream shatters.

Home? What had I been thinking?

The house is all-but roofless, its walls weathered and compromised; here leaning perilously inwards, there bulging out. The topmost stones are blackened and crumbling, the bottom ones crusted with yellow lichen or eroded by frost. At some points it seems only the strangle-hold of ivy keeps the structure intact. Mullioned windows stare out blindly, their glass long gone. Creepers snake over their sills and into the desolate rooms. A single chimney remains, balancing precariously atop a teetering chimney stack attached to the end gable of the house. It is a lone spire pointing to the sky, its bricks frost-damaged and corroded, impossibly tall - frankly, a rather ridiculous addendum. A spindly shrub sprouts from the flashing where the chimney meets the pot and as I stare up at it, a large black bird alights, then disappears into the chimney; I can hear it cawing from within. I am conscious of a piercing arrow of sadness in my heart. Whatever hope, whatever bubble of expectation has been enlarging and buoying me in the run-up to this moment bursts instantly and my utter deflation is so strong I want to collapse under the weight of it. I feel the trickle of tears down my cheeks and because there is no one there to see, I let them flow unchecked.

Presently, with a heart so heavy just putting one foot in front of the other seems like a terrible effort, I push through the undergrowth of what must at one time have been a stately drive, towards the front door. I feel gravel beneath my feet but it is infested with every kind of weed, matted and tufted by years of unchecked growth and decay, woven through by thorny vines. A few shallow steps lead me to the entrance; they are slimy and green. To one side, half buried by undergrowth and some pieces of a broken urn lies an official sign. 'Warning,' it says. 'Unstable masonry. Unsafe structure. No admittance.'

The door is weighty, hundreds of years old, I guess, its ancient wood pitted by centuries of lashing rains and UV light. It isn't locked, and opens at my push.

Within, the place has been ransacked, raped of every valuable fixture. It isn't even possible to wander through the rooms. Floorboards have been torn up revealing the damp hollow of the original foundations hazardous with unstable rubble and broken glass. The fire surrounds are gone, hauled away for sale on eBay, I suppose, likewise the panelling which must once have adorned the walls of the hall and stairway. The stairs have also gone, and I can only look up into the void of what must once have been an elegant landing, imagine the chandeliers and the formal artworks and speculate about the design of the Jacobean balustrade and spindles. The plaster has disintegrated, revealing the bare stone of the house's construction; mould, lichen, moss and weeds proliferate. Above me I can hear birds amongst the charred rafters, the eerie moan of the breeze through some lofty aperture. The smell is a cocktail of dampness, animals, mould spores and something else I can't identify - just age, I guess.

I place a tentative hand on the oozing wall, and close my eyes, partly to support myself while I try to get a foothold and partly in the vain hope I can kindle some connection. What am I expecting to hear, to feel? Some tremor of a long-dead forebear's ghost, a whisper from beyond the grave? Or something even less tangible? I wait for something; a reciprocal throb, the house answering back the hammer of my heart, some telepathic communication of flesh and ancestral stone. And what I feel is an overwhelming sense of sadness, of neglect and abandonment, and it does reflect so uncannily my own mental state it brings an odd kind of comfort and, almost, of empathy. Perhaps, I think now, this is what my aunt Evelyn had meant when she said I would feel it too - this is the kindred state she meant. This is how I feel when my kids walk past me without saying hello. This is how I felt last night, when Tammy didn't answer my call, and how I feel every time she turns away from me in bed. This is how I feel when I sit in my boardroom and look at my empty desk while others carry on the business of producing and processing and selling oil; I am not needed, I am utterly superfluous, but I must - I *must* - persevere with it because it is what my grandma and grandpa started and what my daddy carried on and for their sakes it must continue. This is what Evelyn feels - left behind by a trajectory of destiny which has veered wildly off course and left her marooned and yet bound - compelled - to soldier on. I understand, now what she meant when she said the house would not let her go.

Unconsciously, I raise my hand to my collarbone. I feel it there - where Evelyn felt it - forlornness like a little hollow over my heart encased by a shell of responsibility and, yes, a feeling of being indelibly connected I have not felt with Tammy ever or, recently, with the children either. I feel more in tune here than in the expensive downtown Dallas penthouse apartment I inhabit during the week or in the ranch-house where the family gathers at weekends. I am myself, as I am not in the office or shouting over the din of the drilling rig but the 'me' I only ever find rising up from that inner place when I have a pencil or a paintbrush in my hand.

Outside, across what must have at one time been a manicured lawn but is now a rank meadow, I find the stone bowl of a defunct fountain. It is choked with decomposed leaves, weeds and moss, but it is a sunny spot and I instinctively know there will be a seat nearby. I find it, all-but buried in foliage, and sit. The sun is warm, the wind funnels down to me through the trees and smells fresh, of sap, of spring, and in fact I can see, from here, bursts of exuberant blossom on fruit trees behind the house and herbaceous plants struggling through the thickets of invading weeds which will soon be in glorious flower.

I reach for my backpack, thinking I will open the Thermos Evelyn made for me, and get out my sketchbook. But what I find in the bag makes me forget both those things.

It is a book, thick, with a scarred leather cover, its pages laboriously hand-written. Evelyn's book, I realise, the one she told me about.

I open it, and begin to read.

 **IT TAKES ME** about a week to read Evelyn's memoir. In between I visit with her every day, but we agree not to discuss what's in the book until I've gotten to the end. While I am with her I do my best to fix the place up, but discreetly - she is proud and independent. I stand on a stool and wash the windows for her and fix the shelves in her kitchen so the saucepans and dishes can be put away. I saw logs in the yard and arrange for a new hen coop to be delivered. She is ridiculously pleased by this, declaring it 'as good as Kenneth ever built,' which I take to be praise indeed. Her pleasure pleases me, and I get a sense of satisfaction from the little improvements out of all proportion to the effort or the cost. My new best buddy is the man at the quaint little hardware store in town, who supplies me with tools and timber and delivers the hencoop.

Every time I visit Evelyn I take food with me, which we share while we talk. I tell myself that, with the additional meals and the stimulation of someone's company, she is improved in health; she seems brighter to me, anyway.

Sometimes we sit outside on her garden seat, and occasionally we tour her yard while she tells me the names of the plants and how they crop or fruit. Mostly we sit indoors; the weather is changeable - rain one minute, sun the next. I become familiar with the place and I feel comfortable there. I feel comfortable with Evelyn and find myself telling her my troubles; she is a good listener.

Most afternoons Evelyn takes a nap, and that's when I walk down to Tall Chimneys, getting used to the obstacles and taking a scythe to the nettles and some secateurs to the brambles.

Often it is there, on the stone seat near the fountain, where I read her story, and when I look up from the pages it is not the derelict shell I see but the house as it used to be - whole and sound. I can imagine the ministry men strolling on the terrace, my mind's eye pictures the children building snowmen on the lawn and, beyond the refracted glass of the window, I think I glimpse the shade of Evelyn herself, watching them play.

Of course I explore the house, defying the warning signs and breaking down barricades to find the kitchen where she spent so much of her time. In a tiny room off a narrow corridor is the place they used as Awan's nursery, and some of John Cressing's artwork is still visible amongst the patches of mould and broken plaster. The colours, even today, are vivid - lush and exuberant. I take some shots with my cell phone and then trace his brush strokes with my hand, standing where he must have stood. Having my feet in his footprints and my hand on his art makes me feel complete in a way I haven't done since Daddy passed, and when I move on to the room where John died, I am overwhelmed by grief. I couldn't cry at Daddy's funeral but I cry now, sinking down onto the filthy floor and letting it take me. I cry for my daddy and for John Cressing and also for myself; I am so miserable in my marriage, in my home and my work. I wish I could ask their advice, but I guess they'd each give me different counsel.

At night, in my dreams, I return to the house. It is restored - the roof is fixed, the chimneys tower - or perhaps I have gone back in time to when the house was in its prime. Either way, it is mine - I am in sole possession of it and wander at will from room to beautiful room, my hands stroking the rich window fabrics and the smooth patina of the Jacobean panelling. I sink amongst the deep cushions of antique sofas and my grandpapa's paintings smile down on me from the walls. Outside, the trees in the orchard are in glorious blossom, the petals showering like confetti at a wedding, I brush them from my face in my sleep. Once I am up on a narrow walkway that skirts the steeply sloping roof and gives access to the ornate brickwork of the chimneys. From here I can see the whole bowl of my domain, the neatly laid-out gardens, the industrious working areas behind, the slope of the lush plantation which protects me from the world at large. Waking from that splendour into the blandness of my motel room is a daily bereavement. I can't wait to get showered and dressed and grab some groceries before heading back out there.

As the days progress something quite dangerous begins to happen. I am looking at the house in two different directions: backwards, and forwards. As much as I am picturing Evelyn's history amongst the fallen stones and creeper-infested gardens, I am also projecting into the future; what *could* it be like? How *might* it work? My business-head hypothesises possible commercial uses for the buildings - a health retreat, a rehabilitation centre, a conference venue - but my selfish head wants it all for me. *This* room could be my study, *that* space would make a great gym. I know it's a pipe-dream, but it's one I can't shake.

One night I stay up to Skype Tammy with the idea that I might broach the subject with her. It is 8pm her time, the time she usually retreats to the sofa to catch up on the day's soap operas, glass of wine in hand. Even as she listens to me, I can see her eyes sliding from her iPad to the television screen. I labour on with my story - the house, Evelyn, my grandfather, his painting. It is like force-feeding a child with greens; she has no interest, no taste for what I am offering.

At last I hear the theme tune for the closing credits, and she leans forward to switch off the TV with the remote. 'How much longer are you going stay out there?'

'A couple more weeks,' I reply. 'Haven't you heard what I've been telling you?'

'Well,' she tucks a tendril of hair behind her ear and turns her head slightly to inspect a blemish. She is looking at her own image in the thumbnail, I realise, not at me.

'Tammy?' I say, 'pay attention, will you? It's 2.45am here. I waited up to talk to you.'

She looks taken aback. 'Did you? You didn't need to.'

'I wanted to talk to you. To tell you all about it. I hoped - I hoped you'd be interested.'

'Well,' she says again. 'So you've found the old house and an old aunt. Did you take pictures?'

'Oh Tammy,' I rub my eyes with the heel of my hand. 'This isn't a tourist trip.'

'It isn't?'

'No, that's what I've been trying to tell you. This is - I know it's corny - it feels sort of like fate.'

I have her attention now. She looks really spooked. 'You're crazy!'

'I know it sounds crazy...'

'No, it doesn't sound crazy, John, it *is* crazy. For Christ's sake! You go on a trip down memory lane to look up a few places your grandma used to talk about and now you think that some kind of providence has been guiding you? Like this is your destiny? Get real, John! You're being like Martha was when we took her to Disneyland and she thought she could move in with Princess Aurora! Wake up! Grow up! You have responsibilities here, you have family, here!'

'Chas is copying me in on all the emails. Work is doing just fine without me.' My cousin Chas is Vice-President of the company. It comes natural to him. He's a tough negotiator and people respect him. He's good with the riggers too - at home amongst the rednecks like I never was. It was only an accident of age that handed me the President's desk. He wanted it more than I did, and that's the truth. 'And as for the family,' I conclude, bitterly, 'well I wouldn't know about that. I haven't heard a word from any of you since I left. Not one word.'

Tammy passes over that. 'I had lunch with Chas today,' she tells me. 'We both think you need therapy.' She looks directly at me for the first time. 'You're sick, aren't you?'

'My heart...' I begin.

But she cuts me off. 'Not in your heart,' she says, 'in your head. You're having some kind of breakdown. When you get home, I'm going to book you in somewhere, a rehab facility. Chas says he knows of one near Austin.'

'You've been discussing this with Chas?'

'Who else do I have?'

We finish the call and I turn out the light. I know Tammy is right. I'm chasing rainbows here. Crazy rainbows.

The next day I don't go to Tall Chimneys at all but back to London where I visit the Portland Gallery, the place where John's works are exhibited and sold.[21] At the gallery I drink in the pictures' style, their execution, their variety. I recognise some of them from the sketch books - particularly the dark studies of the moor. They replicate views which are so familiar to me now I can almost hear the wind through the scrub, the flap of Evelyn's laundry on the line. Eventually the concierge approaches me and asks if she can help.

'I'm John Cressing's grandson,' I tell her.

She gives me a quizzical look, 'Really?'

I nod, and turn back to the canvas. I don't want to explain it to her. 'Yes, really.'

Behind me, I hear muted conversation. An older colleague makes an entirely unnecessary visit to a neighbouring work to remove an invisible dust mote. As he does so, he gives me a frank appraisal.

When I approach the desk, a brochure is open to a page with a photograph of my grandfather. I point at it and then at my face. 'See?' I say.

They both make obsequious gestures, and these increase when I tell them in a loud voice that I wish to make a substantial purchase.

On the return train, I finish Evelyn's book, and close the cover gently, almost reverently, because it is precious and personal. I like how she

---

21 Throughout this book I have been inspired by the work of John Piper, a contemporary of the imaginary John Cressing. Piper's varied and evocative paintings have informed my descriptions of Cressing's work, and they can be seen at the Portland Gallery, London.

separates herself at last from the house; it was dragging her down. It was the right thing to do and it took guts.

And I wonder if I'll have the guts to do the same.

 **WHEN I GET** to the gatehouse the following day, Evelyn is not there. There's a small automobile parked on the grass outside the gatehouse and a woman doing something practical at the sink. At first I mistake her for a housemaid or a care-giver - at last, I think, someone has come to supervise Evelyn's well-being. At the same time I am mad - I had wanted to talk to Evelyn about her story, I want the loose ends tied up, and now I won't be able to do it.

I give a little cough to announce myself, and the woman turns and steps out of the gloom of the kitchen into the sun. She has blonde, curly hair and I know immediately that this is Awan's daughter. She is perhaps two or three years older than me - which puts her in her mid- to late-thirties - and she is a fine looking woman. Her jeans and a sweat-top are casual, but they look good on her. She gives me a warm, genuine smile revealing white teeth and a cute dimple, and reaches for a towel to dry her hands.

'Cousin John,' she says, shaking my hand warmly. 'I'm Emma. Granny sent a letter. I've been summoned to look you over.'

'Oh my,' I make a grimace. 'I hope I pass inspection!'

'I say cousins,' she makes an impatient 'over it' type of gesture, 'but many times removed. Let's not be so boring as to work out the exact genealogy.'

'Kissing cousins?' I suggest, and then wish I hadn't.

'What does it matter?' she brushes over my gaffe. 'We're related and, apart from Granny, I have nobody else in the whole world.' That tells me that Awan is dead. I am sorry for it - I would have liked to have met her. In fact I am eager to meet all the participants in Evelyn's story. Their stories, their epilogues are, really, what I have come for, today. It is time to tie up all the loose ends, and go home.

Emma's hand is still in mine, small but strong. I glance at the other hand, which still clutches the dish towel. No wedding ring.

She follows my glance. 'Divorced,' she says, airily, 'no kids. You?'

I can't keep my true feelings from showing on my face, 'Married,' I tell her, 'two kids.'

'Oh.' She is nonplussed by my tone, and I can't blame her. What should be a matter of pride and happiness is clearly, to me, neither. 'Where have you come from?' I ask, to change the subject.

'From York - not far. You've heard of York?'

I know York was a place Evelyn distrusted - where she wouldn't go to the movies. But I must remember that the world which has occupied my waking thoughts for the past week - as well as my dreams - isn't the here and now; it isn't real. I rack my brains and recall a leaflet in the diner. 'There's a Minster? And walls?' I hazard.

'That's the place.' Emma eases her hand from mine. 'I run a small hotel there. It isn't mine! I'm only the manager, but it suits me, and it isn't too far from Granny. She's gone to the chiropodist, by the way,' she says. 'I am tasked with looking after you until she returns.'

'You're busy,' I say, indicating the dishes I can see on the drainer. I take the towel from her hand. 'Let me help.'

'Alright.' Emma plunges her hands back into the sink. 'You're reading Granny's great tome?'

'Tome?'

'Her book - her memoir.'

'Oh, yes. I just finished it last night. Now, of course, I want to know what happened next!'

'I can help you with some of that. Let's finish this, and I'll make us some coffee.'

We take our coffee to the garden seat. The hens roam around us without concern. 'I let them out,' Emma says. 'Granny will scold me - she says they dig up her seedlings and make a mess, but I can't bear to see them shut in. I like the new henhouse though - a vast improvement on the old one.'

Emma tells me about Kenneth and Rose's boys. She does it neatly, one strand at a time, satisfying my need to know how each story-thread pans out, right to its end. 'Bobby wanted to marry my mother, but she wouldn't have him,' Emma says. 'He proposed every time she came home on vacation from university and on the rare occasions she came back, afterwards. I think they did have a fling, later in life. He turned up, soon after my parents split up and,' she makes speech marks with her fingers, '"slept on the sofa." He was already married to someone else by then. I haven't told Granny that, by the way.'

'Neither will I,' I assure her. 'Did his marriage last?'

'Oh yes. They lived here in the village. He took over the business from Kenneth. He and his wife retired before the millennium and moved to Scarborough. He died there a few years ago.'

'Kenneth and his wife?'

Emma laughs. 'No, Bobby and his wife. I'm not going to tell you about Kenneth. That's Granny's story to tell. So that's Bobby. Who's next?'

'Brian?'

'Brian emigrated to New Zealand where he married another ex-pat girl and bought a farm. They brought up four girls but none of them has ever come home. I offered to take Granny to New Zealand but I might as well have suggested a trip to Mars.'

'Some things don't change,' I remark, 'she never was one for travel.'

Emma frowns. I prefer her smile; it is full of sunshine and honesty. 'I don't think that's true,' she says. 'She would have done, if she hadn't had that old-fashioned idea that she would be a pariah. You've read her story. Don't you think that she's an amazing, strong, resourceful woman?'

'Incredibly strong,' I say, 'Oh, don't get me wrong. I think she's a wonderful woman.'

'Such a pity that she was held back by some misguided idea of sin and judgement.'

'Is that what held her back? I thought it was Tall Chimneys.'

'Oh it was that too, of course. She felt they belonged together.'

'I know that feeling,' I nod. 'I've been down there every day. It's ridiculous, the pull it has on me.'

Emma's smile returns. That's better. 'I love it too,' she says, enthusiastically. 'When I was a child, and here for the holidays, I played down there all the time. I imagined living there - a forgotten princess in an enchanted castle. Imagine if it hadn't burned down? Imagine if you could restore it?'

'I've thought of nothing else,' I admit.

She gives me a straight look, then. '*Have* you?'

I laugh off her scrutiny. 'It's a pipe-dream.'

'Hmm,' she narrows an eye for a moment. 'So, where were we?'

'Anthony, I guess.'

'Yes. Uncle Tony was gay. My grandfather was locked up for being gay, you remember?'

I nod. 'Wasn't he chemically castrated?'

'No, he did his time in prison but it broke his health. Mum did visit him before he died, which he did before they legalised homosexuality - that was in '67. Don't you think that's a terrible shame? In a way, that law would have released Giles Percy like walking away from Tall Chimneys released Granny. Anyway, Uncle Tony came out in the 70s - not that it was a surprise! Granny puts it down to him losing his mother at such a young age. She thinks that being gay is a bit like eczema or depression - something that circumstances in life can cause you to have. But - whatever - Uncle Tony had a happy, gay life. He and his partner took over the shop when Granny retired. They were pillars of the community - running the village hall committee and organising the annual fete. Everybody loved them!'

'You're speaking in the past tense, though.'

'Oh,' her face falls, 'yes. Uncle Tony was diagnosed with dementia. He died three years ago.'

'So there's nobody here, in the village, now? For Evelyn, I mean? Don't you worry about her here, on her own, at her age?'

'About Granny?' Emma turns an incredulous face towards me. 'You must be joking! She's as tough as old boots.'

'But,' I indicate the house behind me, 'is this place even fit for human habitation? There isn't any heat. There isn't a refrigerator. There isn't a telephone. What would she do in an emergency?'

'She had a fridge,' Emma replies, a little defensively, 'but it broke and she wouldn't replace it. She eats mainly fruit and vegetables and they don't need refrigerating. As for heat, she has the fire and the fire has a back-boiler which makes hot water. I come over whenever I can. I do on-line grocery shops for her. She won't have a telephone. She'd be glad of an emergency and she has told me specifically that the last thing she'd want would be to be 'saved' or resuscitated if she was taken ill. She's ready to die.'

I am gripped with sadness. 'She is?'

Emma nods. 'She's old. She's tired. She's a hundred years old, you know! But something is holding her back.'

I sipped my coffee. 'It's the house,' I say, in a low voice. 'She says it won't let her go. I thought she'd gotten free of it.'

Emma swivels on the seat to face me. She looks me in the eye - I like it, her frankness, and that we both have Evelyn's welfare at heart. 'She had,' she says, 'But Ratton...'

'That guy!' I burst out, 'he's a low-life!'

'I know,' Emma says. 'He left the house to her when he died - it was his last act of callous vindictiveness, to shackle her to it again.'

'She owns it? And she hasn't ever..?'

'Oh God no.'

I like it that Emma follows my train of thought.

'Much too expensive, and these days everyone would want to stick their oar in: English heritage, the planning officers, the listed buildings people. You can't move in Britain these days for red tape, and, usually, the tape has the EU written all over it.'

'The EU?'

The European Union. We've been roped in by stealth. Don't get me started.'

'Okay, okay,' I hold up a hand in surrender, 'I won't. But, if she sold it to someone, do you think she'd feel released?'

Emma shrugs. 'She might do.' Her face begins to crumple, 'but then - it's selfish of me, I know - but I can't imagine life without her.'

I put my hand on her arm, 'I'm sorry,' I say, 'I know how it feels, to lose someone.'

Emma sniffs, and draws a Kleenex from her jeans pocket. 'Don't take any notice of me,' she says, with a thin smile.

Presently she goes on, 'Yes, she might feel released if some-one bought it. But who'd do that? You've seen the state of the place! Only a multi-millionaire or a fool would contemplate such a thing.'

Her words sound like a call to arms. Or a prophecy.

That afternoon I get the conclusion to Evelyn's story. While she and I talk, Emma busies herself discreetly about the place. She brings in a bale of clean laundry I gather she took away with her last time, and spirits away some soiled stuff for washing. At one point she places a bowl of hot soup in front of Evelyn, then I hear her upstairs, changing the bed and cleaning the little bathroom. But often she is in the room, interjecting, reminding Evelyn of dates and details, and I find my eyes drawn to her, where ever she is.

Evelyn tells me her version of the history of Kenneth and Rose's children. I listen patiently although I already know much of what she tells me.

Then, as the afternoon draws to a close I say, 'Now, no more delay-tactics. Tell me about you, and Kenneth, and Awan.'

Evelyn sits on her chair by the hearth. She seems engulfed by it, incredibly small and frail, a wisp of a woman, and very tired. Perhaps her outing today has been too much for her. But her eyes are as sharp as gimlets. The papery skin around them folds now, as she smiles. 'Oh, well,' she says, with a coy twinkle, 'yes, as Charlotte Bronte once wrote, 'reader, I married him.'"

'I'm so glad,' I burst out. 'I wanted you to have married him - or that you'd be together at least. Oh! But on the other hand, I wanted you to be free, too. I wanted you to choose, to be able to do anything you wanted, like other women. It seemed to me, Evelyn, reading your memoir, that you hadn't had any choices in your life. Things just happened to you and you handled them.'

'She handled them alright,' Emma comments from across the room.

'I did choose,' Evelyn assures me, 'I didn't marry Kenneth because he was the only man left! I married him because I realised that's what I really wanted to do - more than anything. And Kenneth was patient. He waited - well, I suppose he waited for me to fall in love with him. He made me do all the running. Talk about playing hard to get! By the end I was absolutely *desperate* for him!'

'Ew! Granny! Too much information!' Emma groans.

Evelyn ignores her. 'He let me come to him and when I did he folded me into his arms and it felt *wonderful.*' She heaves a heavy sigh, remembering it. 'We married in '53, the same week as the Coronation. The bunting was still up in the village! We had two street-parties in one week!'

'It sounds very romantic. But you told your friend Patricia that love wasn't all about reckless romance and dancing,' I remind her.

Evelyn considers. 'It isn't *all* about that. We were friends. That's what counts. He was a good, good man. I was lucky. He was so... solid. But,' she adds with a mischievous glint, 'I did teach Kenneth to dance.'

'Ah!' I breathe. I wonder if I can settle for 'solid' from Tammy, if I can compromise with friendship. It feels like a bleak prospect, without even the occasional dance.

'We were very happy,' Evelyn says. 'We had twenty seven years. I ran the shop and he had his business. His mother suffered a stroke and I nursed her until she died. I looked after his boys until they flew the nest. He was a tower of strength, my hero in every way. But,' she falters, and looks down at the knitting in her lap, 'I didn't forget my John, or that poor American boy. I loved them all, you know.' She looks up at me then, and her eyes are glassy with tears. 'It is possible, you know, to love more than one person at once. Our hearts are big enough for it.'

Emma leans over to kiss her. I find the puckering of her full lips very distracting. 'Of course they are, Granny,' she says.

'I'm thinking of John,' Evelyn says. 'He loved me *and* Amelia, I think. It needn't detract from either one of us.'

'No ma'am,' I say, thinking that my grandma would have seen it the same way - reasonably, pragmatically.

We sit in silence for a while. Evelyn's knitting needles rest in her hands. Of course, I want to know the end of Kenneth's story, but it seems indelicate to ask, and Evelyn's eyelids are drooping - her head rests back onto the wing of her chair.

'He died in 1980,' Emma murmurs, as though sensing my thought. 'He was eighty - he aged with the year, you know. He never knew a day's illness and then one morning - he just didn't wake up.'

'He died in his bed,' Evelyn murmurs, wistfully, 'better than your poor mother, Emma, who managed to make a spectacle of herself even in death.'

'Tell me about your mom, Emma,' I speak quietly, so as not to disturb Evelyn, and because I am sensing a kind of valediction. The picture is almost complete, my questions all answered, and then there will be nothing to keep me here.

By now Emma is sitting on the floor in front of the fire, which we have lit, the late afternoon having turned chilly. It casts the only light into the room and sets her hair aflame, like so many filaments of gold in a halo round her head. 'Mum was a wild child,' she says. 'She went from school to university where she studied politics and graduated just in time to throw herself into the mass hysteria of the 1960s. A proper beatnik, if you know what that is?'

'Erm, flower power? Anti-war?'

'That was part of it, certainly. Anyway, she travelled - she hitchhiked round America and she spent several years bumming round the Greek islands.'

'Emma!' Evelyn murmurs, scolding, but gently. Her eyes remain closed.

'Sorry, Granny. She *worked her way* around the islands. She partied and did music festivals. Let's say she sampled everything that life had to offer.'

'Drugs?' I venture.

'Oh yes, lots of those.'

Evelyn lifts her hand in a gesture which tells us she has something to add, but is too tired.

'Granny says Mum was a free spirit with a thirst for life. That's right, isn't it Granny?'

Evelyn's head nods assent but Emma throws me a look which tells me that Evelyn does not know the half of what Awan got up to in her youth. 'Moving on, she came back to the UK in '68 fresh from the Paris riots - although she had no reason on earth to have got embroiled in those. She was over thirty by then - her student days were long passed. She hooked up - sorry, Granny - got involved with my father. He was a music producer, he managed various pop groups. He was very successful for a while and Mum changed from wild-haired hippie to sophisticated socialite overnight, attending launch parties and awards ceremonies, rubbing shoulders with the likes of Tony Blackburn and Debbie Harry, Marc Bolam, the Sweet.'

I look suitably impressed, though I haven't a notion who any of these people are.

Emma laughs. I don't fool her for a moment. 'Google them,' she says. 'It was a very glamorous decade, you know, the 70s, celebrity culture was just taking off, but it was a tawdry kind of glamour and lots of things have come to light since that show it was an era of abuse and shame. Outside the charmed circle of fame life was very hard; there was a miner's strike, power cuts and the working week was reduced to three days. Not that I remember any of this, you understand, but,' she cocks a head at Evelyn, 'I have been told.'

I nod. I am child of the seventies myself. 'Anyway,' Emma goes on, 'the tinsel-seventies gave way to the new-romantic eighties and left Mum behind. She turned her back on celebrity and qualified as a teacher. She didn't become any more conformist, though. She drank wine and smoked cigarettes and supported left wing politics. She 'wore purple' as the saying goes.'

'Purple?'

'It's a poem about disreputable old age.[22] You should read it.'

'I will. Your mother and father didn't stay together?'

'Sadly not. He was a man who went from one hare-brained scheme to another. He thought he'd like to buy Tall Chimneys, at one point. He wanted to knock the house down and build something monstrous in pre-fabricated concrete and plate glass, didn't he Granny?'

Evelyn gives a slight frown. She is not asleep, but she is in that state where the body sleeps while the mind remains active.

'Appalling idea. It had Granny quite worried for a while. But, like so many of Dad's enthusiasms, it waned.'

---

[22] A poem by Jenny Joseph.

'Ratton had died by then?'

Evelyn shakes her head. Emma answers for her. 'Not until after Kenneth. I forget the exact year.'

'But he didn't bother Evelyn any further?'

'No. She never saw him again. He sold his businesses and moved to Spain. The Costa del Crime. He had a yacht and a swanky villa, I believe. And also skin cancer, which is what did for him in the end.'

'A thoroughly unpleasant man,' I say, 'but still, cancer is horrible.' I am thinking of my mom, who died of it too.

'Mum died when she was seventy, three years ago,' Emma says. 'She retired from teaching and took up horticulture. By which I mean that she grew cannabis on an allotment.'

Evelyn, in her doze, gives a little chuckle.

'She had terrible arthritis - she said it helped with the pain. Anyway, she was up there, in the poly-tunnel, when she had a heart attack. It was a swift end, but nobody knew where she was. She got her three days of fame and once she was found she had her front page splash: "Missing woman discovered dead on cannabis-farm".'

'Oh, don't,' Evelyn mutters.

So there it is: the end. I ought to get up and shake their hands and leave. I have got what I came for, and more. There is no point in remaining.

And yet I do remain. I am rooted to my chair; the gatehouse around me feels as comfortable as a womb, Evelyn and Emma my oldest friends.

Presently Emma helps Evelyn up the creaking stairs and I hear the soft music of her voice as she helps the old lady to undress and wash, and then the slight creak of the bed, the sound of clean sheets and warm blankets being drawn up, the squeak of the window being opened to the night scents of the benign moor.

When Emma comes downstairs she makes straight for the dresser, rummaging in the back of one of the cupboards before coming out with two glasses and a bottle of scotch. 'Granny's guilty pleasure,' she smiles, pouring us both a couple of fingers. 'She thinks I don't know, but then how she thinks the bottle gets replaced when it's empty, is a mystery!' She speaks quietly, and as the evening progresses we both keep our voices low, intensely conscious of the woman upstairs.

Emma takes her grandmother's seat by the fire. I lean forward and throw on another couple of logs. We have not lit any lamps and the shutters are open. The amber-blue glow of the fire is met by a strange gloaming light which comes in through the windows, softest mauve, greenish grey. The palette of Yorkshire is difficult to define and almost impossible to capture. I see, in my mind's eye, John Cressing's enormous canvas of the moor, dramatic, brooding, in some way tortured and yet viscerally appealing, vibrant with colour and texture. From Evelyn's memoir I know - as she did not, at the time - what was on his mind when he painted it. By 1942 he must have been deeply embroiled in his under-cover work and involved with my grandmother both professionally and emotionally. His sense of being torn in two, his warring responsibilities, must have been almost crippling. Well, I know how that feels. That painting is being shipped back to Texas for me but even that vivid evocation will not, I fear, replace the real thing for me when I am home on that flat, featureless, loofah-coloured prairie.

'I should go,' I say, into the flames, as much to myself as to Emma. Of course I should go; my work here is done. I should walk away and consign it to memory, perhaps talk about it in my turn, when I am old, to my indifferent grandchildren. Emma offers no reply. I wonder what is on her mind. 'Will you be here tomorrow?' I don't have her number, her email address. I don't know if she's on Facebook. Sure, I am attracted to her but there is something else; I feel aligned with her, through Evelyn and through Tall Chimneys. I don't like the idea that I may not see her again.

'Yes,' she says, addressing some place on the rug. 'I'll be here.'

I drag my eyes away from the fire. I try to make my tone light, conversational. 'You'll stay the night here?'

She nods, and sips her scotch. 'All day,' she says, 'I've been answering your questions about our family. But you haven't told me anything about yourself.' She looks at me then, a straight look, which I return as steadily as I can.

She's right. But what can I tell her? That my wife doesn't understand me? That my kids are strangers? That I wish I'd made different choices in my life? She's been so honest with me, holding nothing back. I want to give her something honest in return, something essential and authentic about myself. She's looking at me still. I feel that she's watching me work out the dilemma she's given me. I don't want to duck out of it so I give her the biggest and boldest and most dangerous thing I have. It's the thing that has been eating me up and buoying me up and tantalising me and tormenting me since I got here.

I lean forward in my chair, resting my elbows on my knees, so that there is as little space as possible between us. I don't want what I am going to tell her to get diluted by the firelight or the purple evening air. 'Here's the biggest thing about me I can tell you right now,' I say. 'I don't want to go home to Texas. I want to stay right here. I want to buy Tall Chimneys off Evelyn and I want to rebuild it. There.' I lean back to watch the effect of my words on her. To my surprise, she isn't as shocked - or as pleased - as I expected.

She raises a quizzical eyebrow and says, 'I see. And, you could afford that, could you?'

I drain my glass. 'Sure.'

'I only ask because I couldn't let Granny sell it to you cheap. It wouldn't be right, just because it's you, as opposed to some big-shot American stranger with a pocket full of dollars and no taste.'

'I understand that. I guess it's your inheritance. You'd want top buck.'

She smiles. 'I don't need the money, particularly. Your grandfather left my mother all his work, which sells pretty well, even now. I suppose by rights it should have been yours.'

I wave my hand to dismiss her suggestion. John Cressing gave me more than a collection of canvasses and sketchbooks. I have his genes. 'I'll pay whatever Evelyn wants.'

'Whatever?'

I shrug. 'Sure,' I say again.

'So, you're wealthy then?'

I smile. 'Like JR, the one who was shot in *Dallas*.'

'Wasn't that Kennedy?' But her mouth twitches, and I know she is teasing me.

'We're not quite as rich as the Kennedys,' I laugh.

Above our heads there's a shift, a little tremor in the wide oak planks; Evelyn must be turning over in bed, but it feels eerily like she's sitting up there, listening. From now on I speak as though she can hear every word I say, as though she is in the room, part of our conversation, as she was earlier - listening, reacting, but not contributing.

'Do you think she'd agree?'

Emma pours us more scotch - another two fingers for her, just one for me. It's a displacement activity - she is thinking things over.

'Do you think she'd trust me?' I add, 'to restore Tall Chimneys respectfully?'

Emma ignores my question. 'You know it's more than just a house, don't you? You'd be taking on the mantle.'

'The mantle?'

'The responsibility, the bond. And it might... do to you what it did to her.'

'Shackle me? Restrain me?'

She nods. 'Yes, it might do. There might be no turning back, once you'd begun.'

I consider it, very carefully. 'I wouldn't want to,' I say, lifting my head and speaking in a voice which is designed to carry. It is a kind of declaration, almost a vow. It would feel appropriate to have my hand on a bible, but the only book to hand is Evelyn's where it sits on the low table at my side. Deliberately, I lift my hand and place it on the cover.

Emma raises her glass in a silent toast, and we both drink. 'How will the people at home feel about this?' she asks.

'Oh,' I sigh, 'they'll be mad as hell!'

Later, I rise to go, and Emma sees me to the gate. A pale moon has risen. The moor stretches out before us, its humps and tussocks silhouetted against a pewter sky, mere shadows and charcoal textures to counterpoint the silver dim. The road to where my car is parked is an ashy line, its dust almost luminescent, a fairy trail. Behind the house, the trees of the plantation shiver with a sudden wind, a swift rush of noise and air which seems sucked from the bowl itself. It is surprisingly warm, smelling of forest and damp stone and wood smoke and something primordial - ancient earth. A ripple of leaves and twigs escalates in an instant to a storm of clashing branches, setting the canopy into a thrashing whorl of wild agitation. It catches Emma's hair, sending a turmoil of curls around her head and across her face and I want, more than anything, to put my hands in it, but instead of walking into the embrace I am so ready to offer, Emma puts out a formal hand for me to shake and it is such a stiff and British thing to do in the midst of this cataclysm of wind and noise that I want to laugh. Above us, Evelyn's bedroom window is wrenched off its catch and smashes back against the façade of the building.

Then, as soon as it arose, it is gone, sucked up, it seems, into the vortex of the heavens. A blanket of stillness and sudden silence descends. I take Emma's hand in mine, and pull her towards me.

'Kissing cousins, remember,' I whisper.

Above our heads, through the wide-open window, as clear and distinct as the call of a nightingale in the tranquillity of a midnight forest, we hear Evelyn speak. Her voice is not the parched voice of a centenarian, it is younger, sweeter, full of life. 'Oh, there you are,' she says, 'I hoped it would be you.'

Thankyou

Thank you for reading this book. I really hope you enjoyed it. As a self-published author I don't have the support of an agent or a huge marketing department behind me. I rely on my readers to spread the word about my books. Please would you consider returning to Amazon and leaving a short review? Just a few words to accompany your star rating would mean so much to me.

You could connect with me via Facebook or visit my website at www.allie-cresswell.com where you will find details of my other books. If you don't live too far away from me I would be happy to visit your reading club, WI or creative writing group to give a short talk or a reading.

Bibliography

An English Country Girl: Memoirs of Nellie Self 1899 - 1997 Ed. Liz Griffin

The Mitfords: Letters between Six Sisters Ed. Charlotte Mosley. Harper Press

Requisitioned! The British House in the Second World War by John Martin Robinson. Aurum Press Limited

Our Vanishing Heritage by Marcus Binney. Arlington Books

Diamonds At Dinner - My Life as a Lady's Maid by Hilda Newman with Tim Tate. John Blake Publishing.

About the Author

Allie Cresswell was born in Stockport, UK and began writing fiction as soon as she could hold a pencil.

She did a BA in English Literature at Birmingham University and an MA at Queen Mary College, London.

She has been a print-buyer, a pub landlady, a book-keeper, run a B & B and a group of boutique holiday cottages. Nowadays Allie writes full time having retired from teaching literature to lifelong learners.

She has two grown-up children, one granddaughter and two grandsons, is married to Tim and lives in Cumbria, NW England.

Tall Chimneys is the sixth of her novels to be published.

You can contact her via her website at www.allie-cresswell.com or find her on Facebook

Also by Allie Cresswell

Relative Strangers

The McKay family gathers for a week-long holiday at a rambling old house to celebrate the fiftieth wedding anniversary of Robert and Mary. In recent years only funerals and sudden, severe illnesses have been able to draw them together and as they gather in the splendid rooms of Hunting Manor, their differences are soon uncomfortably apparent.

For all their history, their traditions, the connective strands of DNA, they are relative strangers.

There are truths unspoken, but the question emerges: how much truth can a family really stand?

The old, the young, the disaffected and the dispossessed, relatives both estranged and deranged struggle to find a hand-hold amongst the branches of the family tree.

What, they ask themselves, does it really *mean* to be 'family'?

Readers' Reviews of Relative Strangers

'... unexpected twists to this story about a disjointed family. Thoroughly enjoyable and highly recommended.'

'Beautifully written and observed.'

'...A really powerful and beautiful novel.'

'...a very fine observance of character .... as though she is watching developments from a hidden corner.'

'.....keeps you guessing right up until the end.'

' A lovely book heavy on character development. Fans of this sort of story will not be disappointed.'

'....the complex politics, desires and heartache of family relationships are at the heart of this book.'

'Brilliant and compelling reading.'

'...quite a writer, a unique voice; it is strange that someone who writes so beautifully is toiling alone in the Indie world, but there it is.'

The Hoarder's Widow

Suddenly-widowed Maisie sets out to clear her late husband's collection; wonky furniture and balding rugs, bolts of material for upholstery projects he never got round to, other people's junk brought home from car boot sales and rescued from the tip. The hoard is endless, stacked into every room in the house, teetering in piles along the landing and forming a scree up the stairs. It is all part of Clifford's waste-not way of thinking in which everything, no matter how broken or obscure, can be re-cycled or re-purposed into something useful or, if kept long enough, will one day be valuable. He had believed in his vision as ardently as any mystic in his holy revelation but now, without the clear projection of his vision to light them up for her as what they *would be*, they appear to Maisie more grimly than ever as what they *are*: junk.

As Maisie disassembles his stash she is forced to confront the issues which drove her husband to squirrel away other people's trash; after all, she knows virtually nothing about his life before they met. Finally, in the last bastion of his accumulation, she discovers the key to his hoarding and understands – much too late – the man she married.

Then, with empty rooms in a house which is too big for her, she must ask herself: what next?

Readers' Reviews of The Hoarder's Widow

'I recommend this book to anyone who enjoys superbly written, character-driven fiction. There is nothing flashy in this simple tale, but it is a rich and filling feast of real and complex characters muddling through life's challenges and finding their way forward together. I would write more, but I need to go find out what else Ms. Cresswell has written, and settle in with a cup of tea and another of her stories.'

'...a lot of dry English wit, [but] it's certainly not a funny story. Allie Cresswell does a remarkable job of telling of a seemingly ordinary life in a way that you can't put it down.'

'There are twists and turns aplenty, and her lyrically descriptive language paints a compelling picture of the house Maisie lives in.'

'It strikes just the right balance for me; approachable, allowing me to relax as I read, and elegant, fortifying her scenes and enhancing them with flavours and sensory experiences.'

Lost Boys

Kenny is AWOL on a protracted binge. Michael is a wanderer on the road to wild and unfrequented places. Teenager Matt is sucked into the murky underworld of a lawless estate. John is a recluse, Skinner is missing, Guy is hiding, Ryan doesn't call.

Then there is little Mikey, swept away by a river in spate.

These are the lost boys and this is their story, told through the lives of the women they leave behind. Mikey's fall into the river sucks them all into the maelstrom of his fate; the waiting women, the boys lost beyond saving and the ones who find their way home.

Lost Boys uses some disturbing, contemporary phenomena; an unprecedented drought, a catastrophic flash-flood, a riot, as well as the much more enduring context of a mother's love for her son, to explore the ripples – and tsunamis – which one person's crisis can send into another's.

Readers' Reviews of Lost Boys

'A clever interweaving of fate and consequences.'

'….draws upon emotional experiences at many different levels.'

'The joy of the novel is to discover how the characters all have overlapping and intertwining stories.'

'I was utterly wrapped up in the story.'

'Allie Cresswell has the ability to flesh-out all her characters into a reality that kept me totally engrossed right to the last page.'

'…linguistic banquets of colour, texture, and imagery.'

'Lost Boys is a treasure.'

Tiger in a Cage

Who knows what secrets are trapped, like caged tigers, behind our neighbours' doors?

When Molly and Stan move into a new housing development, Molly becomes a one-woman social committee, throwing herself into a frantic round of communal do-gooding and pot-luck suppers.

She is blinded to what goes on behind those respectable façades by her desire to make the neighbourhood, and the neighbours, into all she has dreamed, all she needs them to be.

Twenty years later, Molly looks back on the ruin of the Combe Close years, at the waste and destruction wrought by the escaping tigers: adultery, betrayal, tragedy, desertion, death. But now Molly has her own guilty secret, her own pet tiger, and it is all she can do to keep it in its cage.

Peer Reviews of Tiger in a Cage

Erudite, character-driven drama at its best. Allie Cresswell is a literary assassin. Just when you think you're safe, the atmosphere and tension in her novels slips home like an undetected, whetted blade between the ribs. What truly makes this novel stand out is the masterful way in which the plot strands are woven together in the final quarter of the book; the explosive events, the straining to release what has been bottled up for decades, the Tiger in a Cage. The climax is satisfying and worthwhile. Highly recommended work from a fine novelist.

Marc Secchia, author of the **Shapeshifter series**.

Cresswell crafts her novels lovingly, taking time to polish them to perfection. She plays with words, linking them together in unique ways, creating stories rich in detail and lavish in language. Her plotlines are subtle and weaving, the characters and their lives all overlapping and inter-connecting in unexpected ways. She is a wordsmith in the true sense of the word.

Ali Isaac, blogger and author of the **Conor Kelly novels**

Cresswell writes about commitment, fidelity, and the gap between public and private lives, as she lays out what we risk when our desires, behaviours, and values are shaped by social convention.

Beth Camp, author of **Standing Stones**

All of the Combe Close characters are so true-to-life that I am extremely relieved not to be one of Ms. Cresswell's neighbours. I would be terrified of ending up skewered to the page in the next episode...

Deng Zichao, author of **People Like Us**

Game Show

It is November 1992 and in the suburbs of a Bosnian town a small family cowers in the basement of their shattered home. Over the next 48 hours Gustav, a 10 year old Bosnian Muslim boy, will watch his neighbours herded like animals through the streets, witness a brutal attack on his sister and be caught up in a bloody massacre perpetrated by soldiers who act with absolute impunity; their actions will have no come-back. The only way he can rationalize events is as 'a game without rules. No-one was in control.'

Meanwhile in a nondescript British town preparations are being made for a cutting-edge TV game show. It promises contestants dangerous excitement and radical self-discovery in a closed environment where action and consequence bear no relation to each other; the game has no rules, no structure and no-one is in control. 'Game Show' explores issues of personal identity, choices and individual accountability against a backdrop of a war that becomes a game and a game that becomes a war.

Readers' Reviews of Game Show

'A powerful, disturbing book.'

'...Gripping.' 'Compelling.' 'A real page-turner!'

'Love this idea and the way the author handles it.'

'The tension builds up beautifully.'

'All the strands are pulled tighter and tighter together then tied into a very satisfying knot, complete with bow, at the end.'